Raised in Yarrow, British Columbia, Jan Lars Jensen attended the University of Victoria and graduated with honours from its Writing programme. His award-winning short fiction has appeared in magazines in Britain, Canada and the United States. He currently lives in Halifax, Nova Scotia, with his wife.

'Jensen's sly and colourful tale is told with intelligence, vigour and wit'
Washington Post

'Projecting exotic, multifaceted India into the far future, Jensen whirls readers off on a colourfully surreal series of peculiar adventures'
Publishers Weekly

'Jensen's imagination never flags in its vivid surrealism, as the most amazing gods and events leap from the virtual-reality factory of his brain'
Kirkus Reviews

JAN LARS JENSEN

SHIVA 3000

PAN BOOKS

*The author respects all religions and does not intend,
in his story, to cast any in a negative light.*

First published in Great Britain 2000 by Macmillan
This edition published 2001 by Pan Books
an imprint of Macmillan Publishers Ltd
25 Eccleston Place, London SW1W 9NF
Basingstoke and Oxford
Associated companies throughout the world
www.macmillan.com

ISBN 0 330 39237 9

3 5 7 9 8 6 4 2

A CIP catalogue record for this book
is available from the British Library.

Phototypeset by Intype London Ltd
Printed and bound in Great Britain by
Mackays of Chatham plc, Chatham, Kent

For Michelle,
who renews
my spirit daily

THE TALE OF
THE BABOON WARRIOR

⟞⟐⟝

THE BUDDHIST SAT watching the tide. Daybreak, but the red of the ocean was not simply dawn. Bodies rolled with the breakers, bodies and more bodies, carried from a calamity at sea. The Buddhist watched, wishing he could take credit for the capsizing. He wished he could point at the snout of that vessel, the last part of it sliding into deepness, and say, *It goes down because of me.*

But it went down because of someone else.

There had been twelve Buddhists, to start. Twelve travelers who made the mistake of disembarking in Mangalore. They never expected to be welcomed, but, arriving in the port, they walked up from its dilapidated wharf into a particularly hostile reception. *Look at this! Worthless bastards! Don't pollute our city, you sons of whores!* Coming from prostitutes, the epithet seemed severe. Unfair, for twelve monks, celibates in saffron robes who turned their heads away at the remark's immodesty.

An old man wanted to throw stones at the Buddhists. He wanted to, but he was feeble, and so paid a boy a rupee to collect a bag of rocks and throw on his behalf. The old man hobbled alongside the monks during their pelting. 'I'm devout,' he explained, as they shielded their faces. 'Mangalore is impure enough without further distractions from the faith.' He lectured them on being a good Hindu until the boy's arm was sore.

Other Hindus chased them from spots where they attempted to settle, drunks and other stumblers pulling traceries of smoke from bhang parlors, running out to shout, *You can't sit there, that section of road I have reserved!* The manager of the market advised the Buddhists to leave Mangalore. Immediately.

'And keep from sight until you are gone.'

Their leader agreed this was a sound idea. 'But we wish to rent a spot instead,' he said. 'We brought money.'

He revealed their satchel, and the man scratched his potbelly as he gave the group a second look. 'No. The other renters would revolt if I allowed Buddhists to compete with them.'

'But we're not selling anything,' said the leader. 'We want only a place to practice our faith.'

The manager looked reluctant, but the bulge of the satchel won him over, and he led the group to the only spot he could offer. On a septic field used past capacity. Patches of sod were damp and fetid. The next plot was occupied by a dung brick manufacturer, and the process of refining guaranteed more odors. Opposite rose a bicycle graveyard, where any hour, day or night, could be violated by the clatter of another busted bike thrown on the heap. Better spots in the market were vacant, but this, the manager repeated, was the only one available to them.

'We accept,' said the leader.

'One hundred rupees per day.'

Anil protested, but his leader raised a hand and paid the exorbitant rent.

The Buddhists wanted a public place where they could be seen practicing their meditation, their philosophy, and they hoped to draw others to the Eightfold Path. They would not force it on anybody, so they sought converts simply by providing themselves as an example.

The following days saw them ridiculed by shoppers and vendors alike. The Buddhists did not bridle at the taunts. They offered sincere answers to sarcastic questions. They withheld comment on the vice they witnessed, the thievery, the fights, the dung bricks debased with dirt. When not practicing their way, the monks toiled at the septic field, correcting its shortcomings; for the locals, such filthy labor proved the men were untouchables who had assumed a different faith only to disguise this fact, and for the manager of the market it provided an excuse to raise the rent.

'The earlier price was discounted, because of the smell.'

'We're wasting our time here,' the monk Anil complained. 'And our money.'

The leader chided him for seeing the situation materialistically. Their effort would be fruitful, he said, just as their labor had improved the lot. Anil saw only the stains on his robe and the sneers on passing faces.

The Buddhists would not force their beliefs on others. They demonstrated restraint, even when teenaged Hindus tipped them over during meditations. To passersby the monks offered liberation from caste, but even those who suffered it the worst scoffed at such an idea. *There is a middle path*, the Buddhists suggested whenever the day slid toward night. *You can follow it to a true release from suffering.* But always the residents chose temporary releases, and purged any new ideas with bhang lassis or soma-laced drinks, or a contest of transvestites, which saw men dress as women and parade through town as no real Hindu woman would ever feel permitted.

And very late, after revelry faded, the monks heard the rattle of something deep in the bicycle graveyard. A demon or a god? They were vulnerable to both when they spoke against caste, and wondered which rummaged in the forest of corroded spokes and frames.

The Buddhists depended on their savings. Mangalore depleted their satchel, yet failed to yield a single convert. Anil put this observation to the leader, who, after watching a transvestite sit in another man's lap and suck his beer bottle, made the decision.

The monks gave up on the port city.

Their departure, ten days after arriving, attracted little attention. They were no longer a novelty. 'Good riddance,' a sailor growled as they walked humbly down the wharf. Their dhow they found vandalized, green stripes and purple dots splashed over the hull. Unfurling the sail, they discovered a further vulgarity: ASSHOLES. The word was dyed into the fabric, and they set out with it flying like a flag.

It was morning, and the Buddhists were pleased to be leaving. They were missionaries of a minority faith, and so traveling was often the best part of life. They would sail north, try another city. They allowed themselves a mantra almost songlike in rhythm. They studied their map and speculated about brothers they would surely find in cities with names like Talguppa, Honavar, Kuval.

But they never reached these places.

They were careful to stay within a few kilometers of the shoreline, and seeing a chariot approach their boat was not immediate cause for alarm. First, only an upright wedge appeared, cutting crests like a dull, dark knife, but that wedge rose into a water craft, huge, whose tapered form suggested a predatory sea creature when it had fully surfaced. Some outer cladding had fallen away to reveal an understructure of ribs, smooth as glazed ceramic, with flexible joints between like black muscle. The chariot was big enough to carry a town on its back, and this appeared to be the case – huts and shacks clung where possible, and these scrappy dwellings were clearly manmade additions.

Worry curled into Anil's stomach. Gods built chariots to transport themselves across India, and when these crafts no longer served their purpose, they were abandoned, left to common Hindus, who often made temples of them or used them in some other second-hand capacity.

This chariot carried no god. It was populated by men, operated by men – but for what purpose?

The monks tacked to avoid its path. Now that the craft was closer, they could see persons aboard, moving about, working to effect some change in the undulating motion that carried the great vehicle forward. Then boom, with a minor explosion the crew caused it to swish one powerful stroke and shoot toward the dhow.

Alarm spread through the monks. Each grabbed an oar. They paddled, hard, alarm increasing when they glanced back at the behemoth, water splitting violently at its prow, more figures emerging from within, lines in the craft complaining as men, common men, worked to direct it further. Hooting, yips. Anil saw men on the deck throwing hooks, hooks that splashed beside the dhow, thumped in the stern. Caught the rigging.

The dhow was snared. The monks struggled to unhook it while more ropes were tossed. The chariot powered past the dhow, which rolled on the wake but was pulled along by the tethers now linking the two.

A smaller craft was launched.

Brutes, men too rough to live among sailors and stevedores. Each of them came onto the dhow with one blunt weapon and one edged weapon hanging from his belt. The captain had a dented face, so he seemed to look in two directions at once, and maybe that accounted for his bumping the monks as he walked among them, appraising them with a crooked stare, up and down. He jerked a thumb.

'Too ugly.'

His cohorts grabbed the monk and bound his wrists and ankles. The others watched horrified as their brother was lowered into the water, thrashing in his bonds but unable to stay afloat, and eventually, terribly, coming to rest. The captain walked among them, eyeing them unevenly.

'We've done nothing to you!' the leader of the Buddhists exclaimed.

'You called us a foul name,' said the captain.

'Foul name? Never!'

The captain gestured to their sail and the word dyed across it.

'But that – '

'And you snuck into Mangalore without paying the proper entrance fee. So twice you offend us.'

'If it's money you want —'

The leader pushed the bag of cash into the captain's hands, and the captain weighed it before tossing it to another wretch. 'We always kill the leader as a lesson,' he said. 'You are the leader?'

The monk shrank. Another said, 'You just drowned our leader.'

'Then you will serve as his replacement.'

And he too was brought to bubbling, kicking, jerking calm.

'Remember how he looked,' the captain advised, 'at the start of each day of your life with us.'

The monks were shackled before being lifted, like cargo, onto the chariot.

Aboard, their existence was a catalogue of insults, physical and mental. The wretches knew that rupees were quickly spent, but labor kept giving, and so they made slaves of the Buddhists. Two more monks died within days of being taken aboard, and Anil envied them. Could dying be worse than the depravities he suffered? What could be more degrading than acting as a handservant to criminals? They prevented him from meditating, and he could not transcend his pain. His only hope was that his next life would be less cruel . . .

There was no chance of rescue: whatever passed for law enforcement in this state would feel no urgency to rescue Buddhists — even if people on land knew of their predicament, they wouldn't care. Nobody would save Anil. He was doomed, and a few days after realizing it, he decided to abbreviate his misery.

His brother monks no longer seemed aware of him,

or of their surroundings. They made no reply to his suggestion that they, too, take their own lives. No comment when he walked away from their allotted crates of hay. Anil stole to the deck and without further hesitation threw himself over the side.

He fell with a smash. Dazed, he looked around. Through bleary pain, he recognized the green-and-purple vandalism of the dhow. The criminals had left it tied to the chariot.

Realizing what had happened, where he found himself, Anil unhooked the craft and silently pushed off. He didn't bother with the sail. Instead he let waves separate him from the chariot, as he lay, holding a broken elbow, watching the night reveal itself in pinpricks of cold stars. Uncaring stars.

Waves returned him to Mangalore.

He pulled himself out of the dhow and lay on the wharf for a while, splayed like a starfish.

People recognized him when he walked into the city. His arrival drew attention, and the crowd, for once, did not jeer him. Shock creased their faces. How bad did he look? Not as bad as he felt, anyway.

The manager of the market said, 'Port Authoritarians did that to you?'

'You did this to me,' said Anil.

'Me? *Me?*'

'All of you.'

'Not us. We have nothing to do with – '

'You killed my brothers. You tortured my friends. All of you.'

You got what you deserved! someone volunteered. But the others standing on the street kept silent, appalled by the monk's condition and troubled by his accusation.

They let him continue limping and said nothing more. Nobody claimed the spot where he stopped. He slumped against a tree trunk, clutching his elbow, staring at them with contemptuous eyes.

The residents of Mangalore were less vocal than usual. If Anil had been alert as hours deepened into night, he might have noted that the city did not celebrate with its usual abandon, the locals going home sober, lights glowing in upper stories, discussions passing window to window, none of it slurred by vice.

He didn't care. There was nothing for him here. India offered no solace to a Buddhist, no mercy, no kindness. He stared down the wharf, past moored craft rocking with tidal rhythm, past a river of moonlight on the ocean, to the chariot, still moving, tracking across a black horizon, venting steam. Anil fell asleep to this symbol of his plight.

Early next morning, he awoke and saw someone climb up onto the wharf. A man – or so Anil thought. Sopping wet.

But when the man shook his great head, he flung from side to side a mane of hair, and as he moved, his eyes reflected animal colors. A flash of canines, a snout. It was the face of a monkey. A baboon.

The figure held a long knife in one hand, and despite rising from the ocean his chest and forearms were stained, scratched, slick with something other than water. He walked into Mangalore, and Anil might have followed him, if not for a more dramatic sight.

The chariot – former chariot of a god – was belly up and sinking steadily. Smoke rose in place of steam, and Anil saw that the ocean was red not simply with dawn but with blood, blood spread on waves.

He got to his feet quickly.

That stranger with the form of a man and the head of a baboon – clearly he had done this service, and Anil limped down the wharf, clambered into his dhow, switched between sides as he rowed with one arm, into aftermath, against bodies, amid pirates with faces of fear and wounds like bloody smiles drawn across their necks. Was this the work of a fierce savior? Could there be a Hindu god righteous enough to have done this vengeance – could that strange figure have saved Anil's Buddhist brothers?

The baboon was no god. Anil knew it when he spotted the first of his brothers, floating, a wound pulled across his neck, too. Anil retrieved as many of their bodies as he could. All dead, their faces expressing that same, sincere shock. Who did this thing? Who was the warrior with a monkey's head?

When Anil returned to Mangalore and demanded answers, the locals claimed no knowledge and dismissed the notion that any one person could have rid them of the Port Authoritarians – they denied it even as the tide made vivid testimony to his prowess. Word of his act spread from state to state, with legs of its own. The story changed over the years, acquiring extraneous details, local flavors, but the core remained intact, the questions, and the curious figure with the head of a baboon became famous, as more tales of his might were devoured by everyone in India, especially me.

JAGANNATH

I found the Brahmin on a spindly tower that supported in Vs of tied bamboo the symbol for prosperity. He sat on a platform several levels below the glittering woodcut, which was braced with four views of Sholapur. The Brahmin had his back to me and did not turn when I climbed up, despite the creaking of bamboo joints. He repeated a mantra, the mantra I'd heard several times, and either he felt no threat from my presence or my presence did not penetrate the attention he gave to each syllable rising from his belly, flowing over his lips, drifting into heat-waved cityscape.

. . . *sim wi ta sicc'm, ep fel sim* . . .

I listened carefully.

Once, I heard a drone lute whose warble struck me so keenly that I dropped on the street and could not rise again until the musician had passed. A few times I had heard gandharvas, when gods wished to mark a day of special holiness and filled the sky with a weather of music to make laughter or tears break from one's face. Many years ago, I was a baby lying in a cradle, and my father whispered my name into my ear; he gave my name to me with the delicate instrument of breath and lips, and from its music I knew who I was. And much, much time ago, the syllable *om* interrupted a great emptiness, one syllable whose resonance created atoms that are the substance of me, this tower, Sholapur, India. All this to say that sound has a power that must not be underestimated.

The Brahmin and others of his sect had come to Sholapur knowing the power of sounds. At first the men were discreet, meeting in private places and sharing with one another sounds that some of them had known since childhood, syllables, meaningless of themselves but when combined correctly – *sim wi ta sicc'm, ep fel sim* – mantra. After agreeing on the mantra, the Brahmins began to recite it together. Somehow they could speak in unison even when located at opposite ends of the city. I could not explain this feat, but imagined them synchronizing their voices at daybreak and walking off with a perfect sense of time.

Sim wi ta sicc'm, ep fel sim.

I heard the mantra beneath my feet, a Brahmin down in the plumbing using ducts to distribute his voice. Another Brahmin had inserted himself in a statue of a god other than the one he worshiped, hiding in a fold of plaster flesh. Today I heard the mantra hovering over me like a kite, and I climbed the tower to find the person who spoke it.

He stopped to eat. From other places, the voice of his sect continued speaking through the chatter and bustle of Sholapur. *Sim wi ta sicc'm, ep fel sim, sim wi ta sicc'm, ep fel sim* . . . The Brahmin took a mango from his pocket and split it with his thumbs, holding out half the torn fruit. Offering me half. I had been noticed.

'No, thank you,' I said.

The Brahmin turned with a smile, putting the pulp in his mouth. He had a smear of yellow across his forehead — sandalwood paste — and I took the rough shape to represent a flame. He licked juice from his fingertips and, still smiling, nodded to Sholapur.

'You hear it?' he said proudly.

Sim wi ta sicc'm, ep fel sim, sim wi ta sicc'm, ep fel sim . . .

I nodded.

Not just mantra.

But from the horizon, a reply.

Sholapur quaked. South, its streets were cemented with people attempting to get out of the city, and I saw whole families roped together so they wouldn't be separated in the exodus. The rope of such a clan rubbed my waist. Another man carried a bundle of furniture on his head, balanced there until the binding snapped, which set lamps and chairs adrift on the crowd, each item taking time to find a route to the ground. I also kept seeing a black bale of human hair, something a wigmaker had deemed worthy of slowing him down in his flight; perhaps it would cost him his life.

Against the exodus, I walked. Clenched faces confronted me, and I felt the desperation to leave in communal heaves against my body. I held my arms before me and leaned, summoning the resolve not to be swept back by other people's panic. A man of Kshatriya caste was visible in the crush, and I don't know how in this frozen flood of brown limbs and bright saris he saw me, but his eyes found mine. *Where are you going?* his glare demanded. *Why are you going the wrong way?!* He had been attempting to direct the crowd, rescuing and prodding people with a staff – a losing effort – and I thought he might try to hook me with his questions. But the crowd was voluminous, sheer force of numbers rendering him inert, and another surge of desperation carried him away like flotsam.

Vehicles too were locked in the jam of escapees – lorries puttering on dung drive, rickshaws and tongas, a trailer pulled by eight bicycles welded into a single motive unit. The eight cyclists stood on their seats shouting for people to move. *Move, move!* I squatted and crawled under their elaborate gears and chain, coming out at the far end to thinner crowds, where I could proceed with only the occasional jostle of someone bumping me, one more person hurrying in the opposite direction.

Another tremor. I climbed a hill for a better view, and felt tempted to return to hands and knees.

The mantra was no longer discernible. It had been overcome by the reply, and I wished to record this sound in memory, too, this landbound thunder risen from the horizon, with suggestions of axles, valved modulations of ancient engines, occasional deafening roars of heat vented from some deep wooden well. The roar shook Sholapur. North lay a cloak of dust, over the source, over structures toppled or slouching.

A few untouchables lingered near the hill, but farther north, only those people remained who worshiped the Jagannath. There had been many conversions during its approach. A line of converts strode toward the dust, toward the uproar, following one of those Brahmins with a sandalwood flame on his forehead. I moved around the hill, hoping to keep them in sight, thinking

I might glimpse the god as it received them, but a temple screened the procession from view. Climbing the hill, I saw something else, however, something floating in the air.

A straggler.

A balloon craft. It floated over the spire of a temple, bumped an adjacent tower. Earlier in the day, the sky had been clotted with silken vehicles hurrying to leave Sholapur, people clinging to the sides, paying to cling and get out of the Jagannath's path. So why did one aircraft stay behind? The purple of its balloon was a shade reserved for government craft, and maybe that was the explanation.

Maybe it wasn't a straggler. Maybe, like me, the craft had come here deliberately. Getting close to the god was unwise, but the balloon craft showed no fear, sailing toward that roiling segment of Sholapur's skyline. I had seen it and wondered. Now I couldn't leave.

A pack of dogs ran the other way, terrified. When they had cleared the street, I met no more living things. The area was vacated. Loose oranges rolled along the ground. Dust pushed forward, unstoppable motes. Engine noise shook my bones, buildings vibrated, empty crates buzzed on the sidewalk. I moved faster, looking up as I jogged. I ran beneath the balloon craft, then ahead of it. I turned inside a building.

It must have been used for some high-caste labor, because I climbed seven flights of stairs before reaching the top floor. It shook flamboyantly; my teeth chattered in sympathy. I could feel the rumble, the source very near. Windows faced the street, and I leaned out for a better look at the balloon.

Wicker enclosed the carriage, and its size prohibited

more than three or four passengers, but as it got nearer, my heart beat with a wild idea. What if it was *him?* This was why the sight of a straggler had stopped me from leaving Sholapur — that and the rumors. They had circulated as the Jagannath approached, rumors that the Baboon Warrior would come save the city, and for now I was possessed with the chance they might be true. Was he drifting toward me? The hero of India?

One passenger.

The carriage came within a meter of my window, and inside — my heart sank — the face was human.

Rigging, I noticed, was absent from the craft, giving the passenger no means to guide its flight. It had not flown up this street deliberately, then. It was out of control, here by accident . . .

I turned back into the room, fast. My curiosity had put me in danger. Danger hummed through my marrow. The building shuddered, I heard something buckle, crash.

'You're a lucky man!'

I looked back. The passenger was pressed to the wall of his gondola, face waffled by wicker. He stuck a finger out to point at me, and shouted:

'You are the man who will rescue me!'

'How is that lucky for me?'

'I've been abducted!'

'I don't see my benefit.'

'Never mind just now — you can reach me! Hurry!'

'You're not the one I expected,' I told him.

'Not the one — ?! Listen! I need assistance! Do you understand? I'm trapped!'

The balloon was close. It would have been simple to lean out and pull it over.

But I turned and walked back across the shaking floor. Behind me he was shouting, 'What are you doing? Where are you going? I demand – ' and then the god consumed his voice. I slumped against a column. Sunlight dropped inside like a curse, falling through the walls, a ragged seam splitting wood and mud brick, peppering me with debris, and I watched the stairway swing back on the opposite side of a widening gulf. Part of the roof followed this downward sweep, and the building pitched to acknowledge the breach. I swung forward too but pulled back, not wanting to tumble down after the falling planks and fragments. I had only glimpsed it briefly, but I assumed the dark wooden hammer that fell before me was the fist of the god Jagannath.

I steadied myself. Outside, through the rent and rolling debris, I saw what appeared to be another building. The shape wasn't rectangular; it curved, tapering downward, a marvel of a million wooden staves creating what I slowly registered as the chest of the god. It rotated – whole torso pivoting – and I heard a cable whine as a hand rose into view, great fingers, clamping on to this floor, grabbing it like a flap of bark. I swayed as the hand yanked, yanked, other floors complaining, screeching, beams cracking above and below, crashing. I edged away from the broken margin as the floor slipped into the divide. The staircase stood across the rift, bathed in sunshine and dust. Then it dropped away.

I returned to the window.

Below, road. A drop of several stories. I might survive a jump from this height, or maybe I could climb down. But my eyes returned to the balloon, which had drifted farther, the passenger or prisoner, or whoever he was, still pressed against the wicker. He shouted protests lost to the uproar and continuing disintegration.

I swung my legs over the sill, balancing. Narrow ledge: a difficult place to run, to build speed. But with little steps I moved quickly, and heard something the passenger hollered – 'What are you doing!?' – as I leaped, before the craft drifted on, I leaped, I would die on pavement, with smashed flesh, surely, but these thoughts stopped when I felt wicker against my fingers. I clutched the gondola; it pitched with my weight.

'What are you – '

My impact made the balloon swing in a new direction. I climbed the exterior, improving my hold.

Moments later, the passenger dropped to his knees in his wicker cage. He had seen what I saw now, the Jagannath, a closer view than I had any reason to hope to survive.

We hovered, a flea against sheer breadth. The god towered over the institute of commerce it presently demolished. Its torso rose uninterrupted from a long chariot, perhaps a hundred meters below. Both torso and chariot were a shade of blackness I had not seen elsewhere, and I didn't know whether this was the coloring of the wood that was its primary component or some patina the god had acquired during its long life of divine actions. Its head was the size of a small temple, the same dark hue. Staves of its face rearranged themselves to convey mood, a righteous determination, as the god plunged hands through whole floors of architecture. Behind the god was a swath cut through Sholapur, where other structures had fallen.

I looked to the window from where I had jumped

in time to see the building go down, collapsing inward, the facade standing a moment longer before it toppled under the Jagannath's advance, the god rolling into the downfall and spearing with its wheels broken materials, turning them inside the chariot.

The head of the Jagannath lifted. Its face flowed, a thousand wooden staves re-forming with deepened brow, narrowed eyes.

The god had seen us. We stared back at its broad face.

The man in the gondola halted his prayers to rock wildly, changing our location in the air but not enough, and making it harder for me to climb. I pulled out my knife, stabbed the balloon. Gas gushed out, warm, and the dung burners worked against depressurization, but my hole was more efficient, and the balloon crumpled in its net of ropes. The god rolled closer, raising an arm. Our craft descended, turning. We sank past the hand as it was rising, and I ducked and heard hinges of fingers closing on empty space above. We continued down, down, that wooden wall of chest expanding until the balloon collided against it, I saw the pattern of offset planks, and we sank again and bounced a few times over the flat of the chariot before dragging to a halt. I threw off deflated silk, stumbled to my feet.

The god roared.

I leaned back to see its head high above, mouth open, a bellow so loud it was visible, dust swirling aside in the sky. The balloon could have sailed into that open maw.

I ran to the edge of the chariot, looking for a place to jump.

Why stop? I should dive over the side, run, get away —

But I returned to the balloon craft.

'Come,' I told the terrified passenger.

'It's locked!'

The door. I broke it open. The man stumbled out, legs weak, uncertain. The Jagannath reached, and giant fingers raked the surface of the chariot as we jumped clear, tumbled over the side. I hauled the tall stranger to his feet.

'Follow me.'

I pulled him over rubble. Without looking, I knew when the god turned behind us: the sense of a great weight moving was telegraphed through the ground. Another roar made the man stumble. I dragged him by the collar until we reached a street not yet crushed.

The Jagannath followed. I glanced over my shoulder and saw the tumult of its spiked wheels, turning. The street was narrow, but this was no impediment to an unstoppable god, and it simply ran over the smaller structures.

Earth and pavement flew up beneath its wheels.

I knew the mandala on which Sholapur was built and where we needed to go.

We came to a sunken cavity in the road. My hole was covered by bags of garbage, local merchants having used it for trash. I threw the bags aside, clearing the way, and found the mirror. After wiping off the dust, I put it back in place and climbed down. The man in the suit paused; I grabbed his pant leg, pulled him in.

We descended.

In the days before the Jagannath's arrival, I had known I would want a safe retreat and spent hours exploring beneath the city, climbing past small skeletons of children, setting up mirrors so sunlight could guide my explorations. The man warily followed. Except for reflected light, the underground was all gloom and claustrophobia. Our earthy enclosures shuddered as the god passed overhead.

'This is deep enough,' I said finally.

'What is this place?'

'Underground. Old Sholapur.'

'*Sholapur!*'

He seemed stunned, and sat. He put his face in his hands, leaned forward. Obviously he had not expected to encounter the god Jagannath, or run across its chariot, or flee from its wheels. It was understandable that he should be jangled. I tried to think how he must feel and gave him time to recuperate.

'My name is Rakesh,' I said.

He straightened, still breathing hard.

'What is your name?' I asked.

'No business of yours.'

'You won't tell me?'

'I think' – he wiped his face with his sleeve – 'I am wise to remain anonymous.'

'But we're alone.'

'Until I find myself in a more stable . . . environment.'

I lit a candle and moved it toward him. His face bore the plumpness of regularly scheduled meals. His eyebrows were thin and angular as pencil lines. Several days' growth of beard covered his cheeks, but I assumed this was from his imprisonment in the balloon, because his haircut was formal and crisp. I gathered he was high caste. A light complexion. Straight teeth.

'You're from Delhi,' I said.

He brushed dust from his trousers, as if I hadn't spoken.

'Are you a criminal? Is that why you were locked in the balloon?'

'Help me return to the capital, and I may furnish a reward for your efforts. But no questions.'

'I don't care about money,' I said.

'That is your problem.'

Our vault trembled, dust trickled down my collar. My tin cup rattled, and the beam of light blinked off. Now only the candle separated us from darkness.

'What happened?' said the bureaucrat.

'I think our route down here has collapsed.'

In unsteady candlelight I saw his fear expanding. I lit another candle, illuminated my stockpile: cooked rice, jugs of water, water for drinking and for purification. But seeing these supplies, the man only looked angry.

'Did you get us trapped down here deliberately?'

'It's safer,' I said.

'I would have been better off in the balloon!'

Perhaps.

Or perhaps we were meant to meet.

The series of crevasses and drops were no longer accessible, blocked by a pile of broken concrete run through with corroded orange bars. As I picked up individual pieces and stacked them, the bureaucrat watched, perhaps not wanting to be left alone.

'Usually it casts more light,' I said.

'What?'

'My lamp.'

'Of course,' he said. 'The air down here is limited. Don't you find it difficult to breathe?'

When I cleared enough rubble to make a difference, the rubble was replenished with a clatter and cloud of dust. I waited for it to settle. Frequently our enclosure shuddered with movements of the god, accompanied by movements of the earth itself, and I imagined great veins of rock settling overhead, filling any gaps in the way back to the surface. 'Futile,' said the bureaucrat. Rubble fell several more times before I stepped back. I picked up the lamp, walked away, and the man followed me through connected corridors.

'You know another way out?'

'No.'

I dropped through a crack. His face appeared above me.

'We'll go deeper,' I said.

'We're too deep already!' He looked over his shoulder. 'Don't you know about these places?'

But when he saw I wasn't dissuaded, he grunted, followed.

We moved through earthen rooms compacted with time. Our vision was limited to the glow of the lamp, but often the rooms felt bigger than what was illuminated, our footsteps echoing past the perimeter of light. Occasionally we passed an image from long ago, the giant paper face of a woman, with words from some forgotten language. Strange what persisted and what succumbed. The carapace of a vehicle now like a crust of earth. A fungal corridor with dead lights still studded along the ceiling. Thoughts shrank, and old Sholapur closed in a ball around us.

'Your lamp is out,' said the bureaucrat. 'Didn't you notice?'

'We'll feel our way forward.'

'With all these pits and cracks? I don't intend to break my neck.'

'Then we'll have to go back.'

As we retraced our way through the crumbling maze, I said, 'Do you believe those stories, about people continuing to live in old cities, after new ones were built overtop?'

'I don't care to discuss it,' replied the bureaucrat. 'Other people are the last thing I am worrying about, down here.'

'We could talk about something else.'

He was silent.

'You do work for the Palace,' I said. 'Tell me that, at least.'

But he would not indulge me.

'I only wondered if you attended that ceremony where the Baboon Warrior was awarded a medal.'

'The Medal of Valor? Everyone in the Palace attended. It was mandatory.'

'Was it really the scandal I've heard described?'

'I think any event that ends with public sex must be considered scandalous.'

'So you've seen the Baboon Warrior.'

'I stood within arm's length of that princess when he sprang on her.'

'Did you attempt to separate them?'

'The Palace goondas were there. It wasn't my place.'

I thought: he might have touched him. Might have reached to feel the arm of a celebrity, or that famous

mane of baboon hair. My body tingled. Energy pulsed
from my chakras, filling me from head to foot. I had
to concentrate to speak slowly, understandably. 'Tell me
your story,' I said, 'and I'll share my own.'

'I'm not interested in you. I don't care.'

When we returned to the vault, he dropped to the
floor. I was still tingling with energy and would have
gladly resumed exploration after refueling the lamp
and better equipping myself. But he slouched over,
breathing hard. He needed rest, sustenance. I offered
him a ball of rice from my stockpile, but he sniffed it
and tossed it aside. 'Polluted,' he said. I took one for
myself and watched him wipe the sweat from his face
with his jacket. He put his hands together and prayed
for a safe return to Delhi.

I'm not sure how much time passed.

Most Indian lives are decided by caste, reinforced
with dharma. But my dharma was unique. It led toward
a specific goal, and the goal sometimes involved people
and places whose significance I might not understand
at first. I watched the bureaucrat make a pillow of his
jacket and lie on the floor, closing his eyes.

When he awoke, I was outfitted: candles, more fuel
for the lamp, food, water. He blinked at me, and I
returned to the corridor. 'Wait! Wait!' He hurried,
flustered. 'As a subject of Delhi you should consider
yourself obliged not to leave me in the dark.'

I handed him the lamp.

This time I proceeded with strategy. I outlined in
my head the hallways we explored, a mental string
unwinding with my steps. The bureaucrat bumped
along, frowning whenever I glimpsed his face in lamp-

light. We passed decrepit vehicles, and these seemed to intrigue him: he would pause and stare, as if he'd seen movement, as if they mesmerized him slightly. Then he would shake himself and continue, perhaps lamenting how much time we had already spent underground. Once, we reached a dead end. Possibilities for further travel seemed exhausted, but the floor was like sod beneath our feet, and with some digging I made a hole big enough to squeeze down to another level.

'I'll have to burn this suit,' I heard him mutter.

Surfaces became hard, stony. We descended into a mineral age. Water glistened across the ceilings. Stalagmites interrupted the rooms, erupting like a crop. I was uncertain if these caverns were rooms, if they belonged to old Sholapur. No longer could I hear the thunder of the god above, and I wondered if the Jagannath had come to rest, or if we'd put enough solid material between us to absorb its roar.

'People thought you'd protect Sholapur from the Jagannath,' I said.

'*Me?*'

'The government.'

'Delhi doesn't interfere with gods.'

'So the Sovereign never considered sending the Baboon Warrior?'

The bureaucrat laughed.

His laughter seemed to repeat. Ahead, something jabbered, and we came upon an underground stream. Water moving through Sholapur. It would have improved the self-esteem of the citizens to know that water ran through the city, however far beneath their feet.

Water dark as ink. The bureaucrat removed his shirt

and set himself by the edge to wash ritually. I drank and recited a prayer to Shiva. Among my supplies was a straight razor, and after wetting my scalp, I shaved, the bureaucrat watching with disapproval.

'You'll cut yourself,' he said.

I closed my eyes and continued shaving. When I was done, I showed him the blade: clean.

'Why shave your head?'

'Hair distracts me.'

'You mean keeping it clean and styled?'

'It makes me feel things. The wind, grime, distractions.'

He raised his thin eyebrows.

'I must keep my senses clear,' I explained. 'So I can fully attend to my dharma.'

'You're mad.'

'Listen.'

'You probably hear voices, too.'

'Yes.'

The babbling was not only water. Someone else was down in these caverns.

I waded into the stream, walking against the current, passing under an irregular arch. The bureaucrat cursed and rolled up his pants before splashing after me. 'What if it's . . .?' He didn't add a word for what it might be. 'It is your responsibility to keep me from harm,' he said quietly as we approached another light.

We walked up a narrow bank. Light and sounds leaked from a rough opening. Intimate conversation. We approached the breach surreptitiously, peering into the next room.

Two women, one man. They huddled, arms over shoulder around waist. The women wore tight-fitting

garb similar to the man's, not saris but gauzy outfits
with winding lines of small buttons. One woman kissed
the man's shoulders, pulling his shirt open wider as her
lips covered an increasing area of flesh. He passed his
hand over her back, to the other woman's breast. The
three were a knot. Behind them floated a balloon craft
built for subterranean forays, a barge with swollen sacs
of gas and an ornamental peacock head rising from the
bow. A globe built into the frame cast light, and as
they touched one another, the vehicle bumped about,
changing their knotted shadow against the wall.

I moved to climb through the opening, but the
bureaucrat grabbed my shoulder. 'What are you
doing?!'

'They can show us out, maybe.'

'Do you realize what those people are?'

'Kama Sutrans are strange,' I said, 'but famous, too,
for exploring unknown places. If we approach them
with care, with respect, they might show us out of
here.'

'*I cannot let those people find me,*' he said.

'Why not?'

'I . . . have a history with their sect.'

'Nonetheless.'

I returned to the opening, and again he pulled me
back. But he must have known he could not physically
restrain me, and in fact there was only one way he
could delay me.

The bureaucrat glared. 'My name is Vasant Alamvala,' he said tersely.

'Should that mean something to me?'

'I am Chief Engineer for the Royals of Delhi.'

And he made a gesture for us to walk downstream, away from this aperture and the unseemly trio in the next chamber, so he might reveal his story without unwanted attention.

THE PALACE
KAMA SUTRANS

◆═══◆

WHAT IS THE *worst way a man could betray India?*

Beside us the stream babbled; Vasant was silent for a moment, looking down at his hands, his suit, as if he knew the answer to this question but needed to summon the courage to speak it aloud.

And as Vasant Alamvala told me of recent events in Delhi, I realized I *had* heard his name before. Outside those affairs relating to the Baboon Warrior, little about government interested me, but it was impossible not to have heard of the airship under construction in the Royal Hangar – the Royal Extravagance, as critics had dubbed it – and I realized that this dignified gentleman trapped underground with me was its principal architect, the famous engineer who kept promising it would fly. The man who insisted it would fly; I recalled an arrogance associated with his person. The airship he wanted to build reinforced his reputation, and had caused great consternation, because the craft would be grander than any other vehicle assembled without divine participation. Many believed the project was sheer palatial hubris and doomed. Vasant enjoyed such criticism, I soon gathered. He savored reminders that nine hundred million taxpayers had a stake in his project. He liked to feel relevant.

He was on his way to tour a group of southern dignitaries in the hangar when from the rafters sounded: 'Vasant Alamvala, Vasant Alamvala.' It was a royal summons, announced by a series of men in yellow brocade jackets, and it had traveled here at the speed of a shout from some royal quarter. He frowned and climbed staircases into an arm of the Palace, striding with a gait appropriate to his annoyance. Lesser bureaucrats stepped aside, tongas swerving around him. A bicycle jitney circled, the page standing on the pedals and craning his neck.

'I'm right here.'

The boy fell into his seat. 'Your attendance is required in the court of Prince Hapi,' he said.

'Hapi!'

Vasant waved him off and turned back to the stairs.

The page caught up, ringing the bell on his handlebars. 'Please, sir. Please?'

'Too busy.'

'Prince Hapi . . . he *demanded* you come to his court.'

Vasant halted. The boy applied brakes.

'And what is your name?'

'Me . . .? Manik, sir.'

'I will mention you, Manik, when the Sovereign asks why his airship isn't ready for Holi.' Vasant stepped into the jitney and slammed its flimsy door. 'Now pedal. Or I'll also tell him how slow you were to perform your task.'

The jitney zipped down the street corridor. The Palace was an aggregate of buildings arranged in four bent arms, according to an ancient symbol: a svastika whose mammoth geometry defined the metropolis of Delhi. The Palace's private roads delineated the roofs and ran through component buildings, with traffic flows unrelated to the surrounding city. Bridges connected the arms; the jitney traveled over one such link of bamboo trusses and bamboo deck, crossing south to west, and Vasant could look down into the royal forest below. Sometimes one was lucky – giant lotuses were known to blossom among the trees here, revealing Vishnu in divine repose when their petals opened. Today Vasant could see no gods, but the sight of treetops and their ambient scent leavened his mood, as did the humming overhead. Golden orbs floated, broadcasting the syllable *om*. It repeated *om, om, om,* sounding from several points. An air transport also hovered, descending in stages, and Vasant enjoyed the sight of it dwindling above and re-forming on the roof.

He returned his attention to the page, poking him in the back with his foot.

'Your name isn't Manik.'

'Sir?'

'I know Manik; he is a colleague of yours.'

The jitney slowed as the boy stiffened.

'Don't fret,' Vasant told him. 'You did what was necessary, facing the wrath of an important Delhi personage. That is survival, and I don't fault you for it. Next time, I suggest you fabricate a name rather than borrowing someone else's.'

The boy nodded, and they resumed. They crossed into the Palace, and on floors of interlocking teak the noise of the jitney's wheels changed. The road inside was wide, allowing freighters to roll through the Palace on six sets of wheels. The jitney passed under one such freighter, whose driver sat in a mesh carriage slung under the bed, watching, bored, as faster craft wove between its wheels. Much traffic busied the indoor road, vehicular and pedestrian, and Vasant overrode courtesies the page attempted to show gurus, swamis, cricket stars, all of whom occluded the route with various airs of self-importance. A performer who looked like a puppet wearing baggy scarlet pajamas ran down the corridor, pursued by royal children, and the page swerved through this meteoric storm of brats. He also veered to avoid a trough; troughs were gilded, and were moved periodically to provide a pleasant surprise to the cows who wandered the Palace. Frequently they surprised jitney drivers, too, and caused some terrific accidents.

The jitney soared into Hapi's court. Vasant smelled musk, something derived from bull's gall. The court was round and rose to a dome ceiling, like an amphitheater, with heavy vermilion curtains hung throughout. Curtains drew shut behind the bicycle, making the space smaller, and then narrower, as they closed across the perpendicular. The court was filled with beds. How many beds did one adolescent need? Prince Hapi apparently collected them, and the jitney slowed considerably to pick its way through the various interpretations of mattress and frame. Vasant had heard that Prince Hapi sometimes spent days not touching the floor, preferring to step from bed to bed. Prince Hapi was nineteen years old.

The jitney arrived at a long divan, where the Prince awaited in languorous recline. He wore only his dhoti, exposing his smooth dark chest and one leg he'd pulled

up. Some adolescents adored Hapi like a mortal
Krishna, able to draw young girls with the exertion of
nothing more than his beauty. The only feature Vasant
found remarkable in the Prince was his self-absorption.
Hapi did not greet them, acknowledging their arrival
with nothing more than a bored glance. He said,
'You're to inspect a gift.'

'A gift?' said Vasant. 'That's why you called me here?
Because you got a *gift*?'

A second figure stood in the court. Lithe and peculiar, it stepped forward; Vasant couldn't tell if this was
a man or a woman. One breast was like a woman's, the
other not. One hip curved, but the other didn't. The
face? It looked malleable, like something formed of soft
brown clay, and the features were hurried afterthoughts
– or compromises. The two sexes ran through this body
like twined ribbons, but the face was really neither, no
remarkable jawline, the lips full but not unequivocally
feminine. The person moved as if lubricated, and raised
pressed-together hands to Vasant, but this was a greeting
he chose not to return.

'Thanks for coming so quickly!'

The voice, flutey, did nothing to settle the matter of
gender.

'What a privilege to meet Vasant Alamvala,' the man-
woman continued. 'Maybe someday you'll take me for
a ride in your special vessel? I've heard so much about
it, I've followed news of your progress – oh, it sounds
fantastic . . .'

Vasant blinked. He turned to Hapi. 'I don't have
time to spare for you or your unusual guest. I ask
that you not postpone work on the Royal Airship any
further.' He told the page to return him to the hangar.

'Boy,' said Hapi. 'The Engineer doesn't have permission to leave this court. Neither do you.'

The page gave Vasant a meek look. What, Vasant
wondered, would be the price for striking a Royal
whom the Sovereign disliked? Not worth finding out:
even token punishments could be gruesome.

The page turned the jitney so that Vasant faced the
pair. But Vasant refused to get out.

'All right,' he sighed. 'A gift?'

'You must make sure it's not a trap,' said Hapi. 'No
risk to my body. You must inspect it for me.'

A sculpture sat on the divan, and Vasant presumed
this was the gift. It had a brass base filigreed with lotus
designs, and from that rose a short, upright pole, with
a lump of copper mounted to it. The lump was a
depiction of two lovers, who made an explicit and
unlikely tangle of their bodies around the shaft.
Unlikely for proper Hindus, at least . . . Vasant turned
to reconsider the she-male.

'You're a Kama Sutran,' he said.

The figure steepled hands in acknowledgment.

Vasant turned back to Hapi. 'Nineteen,' he said.

'What about nineteen?'

'The age of someone who doesn't know better. The
age where boys allow their private regions to do their
thinking. The age, Hapi, where bad judgment is king.'

'Don't act as if Symantaka is the first of his kind in
Delhi. Only a few years ago the Treasury was run by
a Kama Sutran!'

'And his coins continue to degrade India. That is
part of the reason why Kama Sutrans are forbidden.
You do realize you're breaking the law by allowing this
person in your court?'

'If you think I'm the only person to break that law – '

But here the Kama Sutran interrupted. 'You don't know what my gift is?' he or she said to the Engineer, pleasantly.

'I see two people fornicating.'

'We call it a capacitor. A precious instrument.'

'It looks like the kind of fetish you people make by the thousands.'

'Very special, this. Rare! Kama himself assisted in the manufacture. The capacitor doesn't simply inspire erotic impulses, you see; it absorbs them.'

'It what?'

'It stores sexual urges.'

Vasant laughed.

'Is a demonstration in order?' the Kama Sutran asked.

'Yes,' said Hapi, 'a demonstration would be very good.'

Music started from somewhere beyond the draperies, a sitar and flute playing sultry raga, and red fabric ruffled to produce another Kama Sutran. She entered to music, with no ambiguity: she might have served as the model for the female half of the sculpture, her hips, her breasts, her long hair – these came in a supply that Kama Sutrans believed appropriate to the female form. The music's tempo quickened and seemed to change her body, its rhythm finding her steps. She was formal-ized, she was defined. She lifted her arms, and Vasant realized this was a dance. He felt a surge of sympathy as he watched her move her hands and feet through stylized gestures, the various weights of her body revealed through these motions, and he found himself anticipating further illustrations the music might supply.

Hapi swayed. The page, too, was agape, and this was what returned Vasant to his senses.

'Turn around,' he ordered.

'Sir . . .?'

'You're too young to be corrupted. Turn!'

'If I may redirect your attention,' the she-male said, pointing at the capacitor.

The sculpture moved: the figures seemed to pursue each other around the pole, copper bodies swimming together, their rotations carrying them up the shaft. They rose about ten centimeters and continued to climb. Vasant studied this capacitor.

The music – not to mention the continuing circuits of the dancer – made concentration difficult, but he looked hard, and the device seemed to peel apart, becoming a schematic of itself, revealing structure. He didn't recognize certain blue striations in what was revealed – Kama's input, if the stranger was telling the truth – but the fundamental mechanism was nothing more complicated than a nut twirling on a bolt. He didn't know what compelled the sculpted lovers to spin up the pole, but he saw in it no threat to the Prince.

'Enough,' said Vasant.

The music stopped. The woman sidled over to the other Kama Sutran.

'The dance aroused you,' observed the ambiguity.

Vasant crossed his arms.

'Your feelings, your urges – they now sit in the capacitor. Collected.'

'A fanciful idea.' Vasant turned to Hapi. 'And you'd be a fool to believe it. A capacitor? Ludicrous. What the Kama Sutrans want is influence over you. They don't even have the decency to bribe you! You should be insulted: they've given you a whirligig.'

The Prince was staring at the dancer, running a finger over his lip. 'But it won't . . .' he said. 'It can't hurt me?'

'It is a toy, Hapi. With a naughty subject.' He added: 'The sort of thing that might amuse a mental defective.'

The face of the teen darkened. He was subject to mood swings, Vasant remembered.

'Out! I've had enough of you! Out!'

'I'm not sure why they bothered with the sculpture,' Vasant went on, considering the Kama Sutrans. '*She* was obviously enough to capture your imagination.'

'I said you must leave! Before I have you beaten!'

Vasant gave them an elaborate farewell gesture, and the dancer made a mock kiss. As the jitney pulled through the court and its hundred beds, the sitar resumed playing, notes twanging, returning to where the raga had been stopped. 'That didn't take long,' Vasant muttered.

The page tried to look back over his shoulder at what was happening.

'We are purer,' Vasant said. 'Because we can resist.'

The page turned and cycled with obvious reluctance.

Kama Sutran influence. It would seep into the Palace. Vasant made a mental note to watch this court in coming months.

In the coming months, however, he forgot Hapi. Gladly. Other issues pressed on him, such as the battle among his subordinates and how to keep it going. Lately it centered on a silver-plated compass and who had stolen it from an engineer named Mena. It was a family gift Mena was angry to lose, and she expressed her anger by filing complaints with Vasant, insisting the others were slovenly in drafting and uncharitable in their sharing of common resources. Adding friction was Mena's romantic involvement with another engineer that ran contrary to marital arrangements. Vasant knew of their indiscretions, just as he knew the compass would soon turn up in the possession of Samarat. Or maybe Anshul. He hadn't decided yet.

A measure of turmoil could be healthy. When subordinates fought, they seemed less inclined to question him or envy him his position. It was sensible. And the fights wouldn't hinder progress on the airship.

Its critics couldn't understand what made Vasant so confident of its flightworthiness. When he led groups through the quarter kilometer of vaulted royal hangar and web of silk spun by hundreds of weavers stationed throughout the bare but ambitious skeleton, he looked at this same scene but saw more. He concentrated, and watched the future balloon inflate like a blue lung, struts growing in frets and crossbeams to add geometry and mandalas, engines evolving through the core, woodwork blistering into cabins appropriate to a royal clientele, all of it materializing in his mind, a private vision that blazed in a climax of fine furniture and silver portholes and mooring hitches of lapis lazuli.

He could see what others could not. His gift.

As a boy he realized he could see into mechanisms, and as he grew older, this strange talent expanded. When he focused on a mechanical device – something as simple as a padlock, or as complicated as a dung-driven engine – layers stripped away, allowing him glimpses into the inner workings, as deep as he wished.

Mechanical relations revealed themselves. If nothing was in front of him and he let himself imagine, as with the airship and other royal projects, something new materialized, complete with innovations of power supply or control, things that to his knowledge had never before been constructed by mortals. All he need do was transfer these visions to paper, and build. Or command others to build. He was of Kshatriya caste, and from early childhood it was clear he was meant to use his talent and become a leader among engineers. Were others so gifted? Did they too experience private, schematic visions? After making carefully worded queries, he decided not, so he kept his talent mostly secret, and gave it a secret name: assemblage. Assemblage had allowed him to see into the Kama Sutran device, and assemblage would guarantee his relevance to the Palace for a long career spiced with privilege and influence. The airship would be completed. It would fly. As it neared completion, he faced again the only question that ever challenged him. What next?

So, after a particularly violent meeting with his ungifted junior engineers (it had ended with a chair fight), he returned to his dwelling in the Palace and sat at a desk, letting assemblage spin out ideas as he twirled Mena's heirloom.

Someone knocked.

'Please go away.'

The knocking continued, and he opened the door to find yet another page.

She said meekly, 'Message is from the Sovereign.'

'Oh? What does he say?'

'You're to come to the Royal Abode. He needs your help.'

'With what?'

'Lights are out.'

'The what?'

'Lights are out.'

Vasant was long opposed to female pages. 'You want a work crew,' he advised, and moved to close the door.

'I was told to bring you. Please. These are my instructions. You frighten me, but not like the Sovereign.'

She did look nervous. Vasant sighed, put on slippers. The lights are out! 'Amazing to think this man is our leader,' he said. The small insurrection made her smile.

From the height of the svastika, four leaves of stone rose to form a tapered bud; this was the highest point in the Palace, the highest point in Delhi. The Royal Abode was situated in a long reflecting pool but at this hour and with no lights, only scattered black ripples suggested the liquid surroundings. It was so dark, Vasant had a hard time seeing the stone path along which the jitney traveled; it must have looked as if they cycled across the pool's surface. Vasant stepped off when they reached the front entrance, and although the doors swung open, no guards stood outside, or within. His first warning.

The night followed him inside without interruption. Why had nobody lit dung lamps? Or candles? Why hadn't he thought to bring something?

At least he knew his way inside. This was not the first time Vasant had been summoned here, alone. *They're plotting to overthrow me*, the leader of India would gravely announce. *My advisers want to see me gone, and they've hatched a scheme to replace me. You're the only one I trust, Vasant*. The Engineer liked being invited to such meetings, however paranoid: they confirmed his importance to the highest level of government. He stopped – had someone moved, ahead? Probably a servant. 'Where was the Sovereign when you spoke to him?' Vasant asked the page.

But she must have stayed by the doors.

'Sovereign?'

He walked through remembered rooms. Somehow it seemed darker here. At least outside there had been city lights and the smudged glow of pyres along the Yamuna. Where was the staff? The Brahmins? The crones? Vasant bumped a table and heard something crystalline rock back and forth. He paused, continued. Prior meetings had always occurred in private chambers, and Vasant dutifully made his way, finding the door open enough to slip through, without even the sound of a latch disengaging. Inside, he stopped. Listened to someone breathing.

'Sovereign? You wanted to see me?'

Lights came on, blinding.

Squinting at him from the bed was the First Wife, her hand on a lamp's long cord. She shaded her eyes, and purple blotches sailed across his vision.

'The lights – ' he said. 'They . . . work?'

'Vasant?'

'First Wife!'

'This is a surprise.'

'Apologies, apologies. Yes, it is I. A victim of a prank! A terrible prank, for which I beg forgiveness. A page gave me an "order" from the Sovereign that I inspect your lights.'

'He's in Rajasthan,' she said.

'Oh yes. Yes. How stupid of me to forget!' He

felt hot, conspicuously ignorant. 'And the lights do work . . .'

In his distraction he was unsure if it was more respectful or less to look directly at the First Wife. The pointed face, the narrow nose. Her marriage to the Sovereign had sparked a brief but fiery conflict with a jealous nobleman, now anonymous and dead. She looked like a character from tales of gods; indeed many artists admitted to inserting her face in their religious scenes, suggesting that her beauty could only have divine explanation. Hair twisted across pillows in a swirl of dark braids. Her skin was the color of coffee heavily creamed. He couldn't help but note where her collar-bones met the fabric of her night garment. But Vasant stopped himself before considering any more of the royal form.

'A thousand apologies. I should never enter your home without full understanding.'

'No harm,' she said.

'My blundering is inexcusable.'

'The Sovereign won't be back for days.'

'When I find that page!'

'Is that the best way for you to spend your night? Tracking down some prankster?'

'Of course not.'

'Then leave her. She was probably bored.'

'Hardly an excuse.'

'Maybe she was bored and lonely and looking for something to do.'

'Maybe . . .' he said.

The First Wife met his gaze: she had uncommon jade eyes, and nothing in them suggested he should be looking at the floor or the ceiling. They held him in place.

'The Sovereign won't be back for some time,' she said.

He nodded, felt himself weakening. But to what?

'There's a question I've always meant to ask you, Vasant. The moment never seemed right.'

'Oh?'

She seemed comfortable, despite the situation, and Vasant attributed this to the extraordinary self-control of the highest members of society. She said, 'Maybe an unusual circumstance is a suitable time for an unusual question?'

'You will please ask me anything you wish to know.'

'Why are you not married?'

'Why . . .' he said. 'Me?'

'You.'

'Well.' He flushed. The First Wife never inquired about personal affairs, and it was the first time in years anyone had probed this particular issue. 'The pressures of my position . . .' But he stopped himself. Didn't the situation call for honesty? Frankness? He tried to think what honesty and frankness required. 'It's partly due to leaving home at an early age. Before my parents could make arrangements.'

'You could be making such arrangements on your own.'

'I spend much time working on the airship. It's impossible I should – '

'Let me ask you this: you're not unmarried because you find women . . . unappealing?'

He tilted his head. What did she mean? Certainly he knew women were appealing. But he chastised himself.

Such conversation, it wasn't becoming. Not appropriate given their relative castes, and if the First Wife didn't realize this, he would have to behave properly for both of them.

'I've bothered you enormously,' he said. 'I will go.'

She kept staring at him.

'I leave you now. With additional apologies for my indiscretion.'

'Perhaps I should apologize to you.' She indicated her pajamas. 'Seeing me like this. Such disarray.'

'Oh,' he said, 'please.'

And then, before he spoke the ruinous words, he saw it.

The capacitor sat in the bedroom of the Sovereign, beneath a night-stand. *How did that piece of pornography get here from Hapi's court?* But he didn't think through to an answer. He talked like a fool and kept talking, glancing at the device, because he couldn't summon the will to stop what he was saying, and as he spoke, he realized that weeks ago, he hadn't seen the demonstration to completion. He said:

'If only I could see you in such disarray more often.'

And he observed that his choice of words affected the sculpture; the pair of bonded lovers turned with them, one revolution, two, and on the third, it reached the summit of the pole.

He looked at the First Wife with new understanding.

Grabbed her sheet, yanked it aside.

Her eyes widened.

What he felt was lightning without a flash, interior lightning, cracking as jagged as the nerves throughout his body. He arched his back and shook his head trying to expel it, be rid of it. But the energy only found its center – below his belly, thrumming. The capacitor must have affected her, too, because she pulled a string meant for the Sovereign's convenience, and her garment fell open, revealing more pale royal skin than Vasant had ever been so indiscreet to imagine. He was naked – he realized this as he clambered across the bed and pressed against her – he must have stripped off his clothes, because he could feel his flesh meeting hers as they rocked back into pillows.

While they rutted, Vasant glanced at the capacitor and knew it was to blame for their behavior. The sculpture spun down its pole, a blur, transmitting sensations stored within, the energies that had been expended in simple flirtations, double entendres, surreptitious glances at somebody's curves. Who had supplied these passions? He didn't know – no faces were attached to what he received, and it didn't matter. What those strangers had given up became his, and hers, and more than he could suppress. He buried himself, to the root. Curiously, the capacitor seemed also to infuse them with knowledge of erotic methodology; he and the Royal Wife swiveled from position to position without pause, without deliberation, it only made sense for them to come together in disparate styles as surprising and diverse as illuminations from the Kama Sutra itself.

He felt his whole body climax. Once, and again, he felt it echo deep within the Wife. But the urge didn't abate. He checked through the door and looked down the corridors to a distant square of light. What if someone saw them? The Sovereign? What if palace goondas came and found them? *They would rip him apart, and rightly so.* But he wasn't concerned.

Not until the capacitor stopped.

The sculpture twirled down to its base.

His energy faded. Passion evaporated as quickly as a cinder landing on water. Fear displaced lust, spreading in him like cold poison.

He withdrew.

What, what had he done?

Her face answered his fear. He sputtered confusion. She said, 'Vasant, I – '

She pulled sheets over her glistening body. Vasant fell off the bed. Did he hear footsteps? He stumbled upright. Grabbed his clothing and pointed to the exit. The First Wife tried to say something, but he stumbled into his pants and turned and hopped away.

He managed to avoid seeing people during his flight back to his quarters. There he bathed, shuddering. What had he done? Afterward he sat on his bed, wet, knees drawn to his chest, and stared at the door. He expected it to be broken down at any moment.

What had he done?

Committed the ultimate act of treason. Kama Sutran gimmickry didn't change that.

What had he done?

Through the night he stayed awake on a chair, his legs pulled up from the floor. The next morning, he went to beg her forgiveness, but before reaching the front doors he was turned away by crones who informed him that the First Wife would entertain no visitors today. He disliked the choice of words. Throughout the day he listened for news from her, expecting the men in yellow jackets to sound a summons. None came.

What would she say to her husband?

Would she tell him?

'Shiva help me . . .'

The Sovereign wasn't due back from Rajasthan for several days. Vasant sought to regain control, forcing his nervous energy into regular routines, and his colleagues stared when he gave fumbling replies to simple questions or barked without provocation. He was sure they noticed his change of mood. How could they not? And did they hear rumors, too? Did they know? He walked with hunched shoulders and bumped into so many people.

Days wore on. He slept little, spent time staring at his reflection. His haggard face. 'Sovereign, I have bad news,' he said. 'Your wife has been unfaithful.' He shook his head. 'Sovereign. There is a plot against you. I was compelled to mount your wife.'

Unhelpful.

Maybe she would keep quiet, he thought, and he proceeded to remember her nipples. And hated himself! He did hate himself. But if only she had exercised self-control. Wasn't she chaste enough to remain faithful to her husband when he went away for a few days?

Vasant attempted to speak to her, and was consistently rebuffed.

Finally, five evenings after the indiscretion, he looked out a window and saw lights like a string of loose pearls tracing the mandala of Delhi: a sight so majestic, he couldn't help but vomit. The royal entourage making its grand return against nightfall. Watching the approach, he knew he'd waited too long. He couldn't leave his fate to the First Wife. He searched deep in his cabinets for a knife, a rope. He looked to his statue of Shiva and said a quick prayer for strength. Then he snuck from his room and took a discreet route to the courts of Royalty.

Hapi would confess. That was the only solution. Vasant would force the teen prince to reveal what he'd done to the Sovereign's two closest allies. The ultimate betrayal! That was Hapi's dishonor, not Vasant's. He puffed himself up and marched.

The Palace was sepulchral for his last night within its walls. He stepped through long rectangles of moonlight formed by a balustrade, the shadows in between like prison bars. This entire wing seemed to have put its head down to sleep. It was cleared of people: he sensed that people had left deliberately. His footsteps resounded without dwindling, ahead and behind him.

He looked back.

First he felt it, a dromedary disturbance of shadows, and he looked back a second time to be sure, as moon-glow drew it into being, fading again as it crossed to darkness, appearing, fading. An elephant, following him. Many elephants inhabited the Palace; they were used for labor, they served in ceremonies, they were dear acquaintances to some residents. But they were not allowed to lumber down corridors without a mahout. As the animal strobed in and out of sight behind him, Vasant knew it must have business with him.

He quickened his pace.

So did the elephant, and Vasant realized he hadn't yet *heard it*. It was getting closer, but still no huffing, no snuffling trunk sounds, no drumbeat of feet hitting the floor. A word never used to describe elephants was 'stealthy,' but this beast moved as silently as some black-painted military balloon sliding through the night. It got closer, a muted bulk.

Vasant made a sudden turn. He hastened his steps, waited. He looked back, and for a moment believed the elephant had continued on its way, ignorant of him. I'm not being pursued, he told himself. I am not being pursued. Then it was coming, fast, hurtling, turning down the corridor, and here he stood paused, telling himself a lie.

He bolted. The elephant bridged the distance, silent, strange. Not moving with animal locomotion. Vasant glanced over his shoulder to see it toss its head but not trumpet. Its body was a lump of bodies: a composition. When it opened its mouth, he glimpsed a pair of legs in black stockings.

The Engineer ran. The elephant, or whatever it was, blocked every return to his quarters. Maybe he could cross to the south arm and climb down into the hangar – surely an elephant could not follow him through rafters and beams. Or maybe this one could.

Closer, he could see it was no animal but a group of people dressed in dark gray and clumped together cleverly. This was human sculpture, with false tusks and ears completing the illusion.

Vasant remembered his knife.

His pursuers abandoned the charade; one masked man dropped from the body of the elephant and hit the ground running, then a second, a third, so the beast didn't slow but rather broke apart. The head dropped away, the torso; tusks clattered on the floor, and the charging elephant was replaced by six or seven people, running, coming fast, spreading in a line.

Vasant was no sprinter. He was breathing hard, con-

fused, terrified, and he knocked against one of the
gilded troughs. He turned, staggered, and was jumped.
One person, then two, they dragged him to the ground
as more jumped aboard, four, five, they heaped on him;
he succumbed. They said nothing, but he could feel
their willingness to smother him, they enjoyed making
this weight of themselves, these people who preferred
the guise of an elephant. He was pinned, and counted
the black pressure of each additional slam until it
became impossible to see, and difficult to breathe, and
hard to hear anything but their suppressed grunts, as
he made his last conscious effort, turning the blade up
into the pile of attackers.

CEILINGS OF
EARTH

⟵⟹◦⟸⟶

'I LOST CONSCIOUSNESS under their weight,' said
Vasant. 'And awoke in the sky. They put me in that
balloon without any means of control. I went wherever
the wind carried me, no sign of Delhi, just nameless
reaches of India scrolling below. Do you know how it
feels when the only people who can hear your pleas
for help are too far away to do anything but look up
and wave? For three days, this was my situation.'

'Until Sholapur.'

Vasant nodded. He drank from the stream, after
having spoken for so long, and then we sat in lamp
glow, listening to water over stone.

'They will know a way to the surface,' I said.

'Those degenerates' – he glanced downstream –
'abducted me! I can't fall into their number again.'

'We won't tell them who you are.'

'No. I can't risk it. I refuse!'

'If we follow them, quietly – '

'Can you not understand? I was ousted by members
of the Kama Sutran sect. If they find me again, they
will surely kill me.' He glared like a superior repri-
manding his subordinate. 'You may not have realized it

until now, but you are charged with a grave responsibility: keeping me safe, helping me avoid those disgusting people. This is your duty.'

'I have my own duty.'

He made a dismissive noise. 'This is of national consequence.'

'So is my dharma.'

He frowned. 'What caste are you? Which varna?'

'Vaisya.'

'Ah! I am Kshatriya.' He smiled and opened his hands. 'You see? By caste, too, you are bound to my service.'

I nodded. 'There is one way we might get out, safely,' I said.

'How?'

'Stand up.'

'Why?'

'Stand, please.'

He got to his feet.

'Look at that rock formation.'

'Which? The stalactite?'

When he turned, I struck him, with a wallop that rose from the pit of my belly and connected to his chin. The Chief Engineer of the Royal Family dropped like a sack of flour. I made sure he was unconscious before wading upstream.

Nothing was more important than my dharma.

I walked to the irregular hole, checking to see that the three Kama Sutrans were still in the next chamber. Now they made a triangle on the ground, each attending to the feet or hair of the one nearest. Presumably they had come down here looking for precious artifacts – nobody descended without good reason –

but Kama Sutrans always allowed time for the body, and I noticed they had brought pillows along to make more comfortable their present activity. What they did to one another was unhurried and tame, and I only vaguely recognized it as sex.

'Help!' I shouted. 'Please, come help!'

They broke, startled.

I stepped back and sank, waiting underwater as they came to the opening, their curiosity aroused. They pulled along their balloon barge; I surfaced, took a breath, and turned up one ear.

I heard their surprise upon finding Vasant. There was discussion. I remained in the dark, so silent that my heartbeat seemed stopped, and my lungs. Minutes later, the light returned, and I heard them negotiating the barge through the hole, careful of its load. I checked to make sure. Yes. The bureaucrat lay in a hump on their vehicle. They guided it forward, one woman questioning the wisdom of this action, asking if the other two even knew how to tie a person with rope. *What was he doing down here?* she wondered aloud. *Why would anyone wearing such a fancy suit come down here?*

I waited for their voices to recede, then their light.

My own lamp I left behind. I removed my sandals and tied them around my neck, because my bare feet could better feel vibrations through the stone. I touched the walls, trying to find the condensation of human breaths. And I listened for voices, guessing what path the echoes took from them to me so I could follow in the dark these bouncing, muted sounds and not become lost.

How long did I follow them like this? Worms have no concept of time: without demarcations of light and

dark, there were only occasional pangs of hunger to
suggest the passage of time. A day? Deep down below,
was there still such a thing as a day? I didn't know, or
care. I would do whatever was necessary to get back
to the surface and return to my task.

The interjection of a louder voice jolted me. Vasant
must have woken. Or perhaps he'd been awake for
some time but now felt ready to speak. His voice was
easy to follow, and soon, he gave away the secret of
me.

'Where is he?' he demanded. 'Where's the thug who
turned me over to you?!' The Kama Sutrans said they
hadn't seen anybody else. They responded as if he were
ranting about a ghost.

'He's probably nearby,' the Engineer insisted. 'Following us.' I backstepped, and lambent light followed
me, illuminating contours and cracks. I pressed myself
into a niche until it retreated.

Maybe they felt haunted. Once, they stopped to rest,
and I crouched in the dark as footsteps approached –
one of the women. I heard fabric sliding over skin, and
her knees crack as she squatted. We must have been
only a few meters apart, because her urine was still
warm when it trickled between my toes.

I heard from their book, too.

When my uncle came for my wedding, he brought
a copy of the *Kama Sutra*. We shared my room, and
each night he announced that he would read from the
illicit text so I would not find marriage an unpleasant
surprise. But he never got further than a few paragraphs
into the prologue before nodding off, the book splayed
over his chest as he fell into grinning sleep. I remembered that image. I listened to the Kama Sutrans recite

memorized passages, and I recalled lovers from a cover illustration, the cover so worn that their act blurred into the colorless grain of paper.

When the Kama Sutran woman informed her partners it was time again to experience the physical, when the sounds of dropping clothes reached my ears, of flesh on flesh amid fragments of poetry, and moans belonging to both, I stayed immobile as a statue. What did chaste Vasant do during these episodes? Who knew? For me, the ghost, it was a time when dharma relaxed enough that I could remember my fatigue, shutting my eyes, allowing drift.

I was sleeping when they were killed.

As always, I dreamt of the Baboon Warrior.

I have seen gods like cities on wheels, clashing on lonely plains. I have seen Varuna in his chariot full of seawater as it rolled through Varanasi, him riding his sea serpent inside the watery bowl. I saw the King of Vultures plucking passengers from an airship as it spiraled down toward a river. I had never seen the Baboon Warrior, but I knew he was unlike these others. He was not a god. However mysterious, he was a mortal being who acted – with the exception of a few ravished princesses and bystanders who got in his way – on behalf of the populace. This was his appeal. He was the only mortal creature of India who made as much impact as the gods themselves.

I dreamt of his battle with Varaha, the Lord Boar. In life, the fight lasted one hundred days and was glorious. In my dream, however, the pair waltzed along the ridge of a mountain, the god Varaha clutching in four arms the famous Baboon, hugging him, squeezing him. The Baboon's face opened in pink gums and canine studs. I heard him shrieking. This was not how the fight actually went; the Baboon Warrior never cried in surprise or pain. But in my dream, both welled from him in a terrible howl . . .

I woke in the same grotto. All was tranquil. Usually I saw my dreams through to the end. The unpleasant twist of this one left me jangled. My skin crawled. If I had hair on my head, it would have been standing.

What?

I lay back and placed my bare feet against the wall. There were no vibrations. The Kama Sutrans and Vasant were gone.

I hurried in the direction they had probably taken. This was not easy; we'd been moving upward for the last several hours, and the tunnel bifurcated, branched. I pressed a palm to the walls, for any hint of them. The underground remained silent. In my anxiousness to find them again, I launched into stone walls, hitting my head, my elbows.

What happened to them?

I persevered, blundering through what seemed a long closed loop of stone corridor. But I got . . . somewhere. Walking became difficult; rocks, porous and shell-like, rattled whenever I slipped and sent them spilling across one another.

Slowly I entered light, and saw that its source was the balloon barge, floating in place ahead of me. I saw, too, that what I stood on was skulls and hoops of ribs. Bones were abundant, full human skeletons lying twisted out of shape or compounded.

I considered calling out. Somebody was here. I crept

over the rubble of bone. With little ballast, the craft floated high, and dark liquid dripped from one side. The tow rope was broken, a frayed end hanging.

I gazed at the chamber in which I found myself, and imagined the long, sinuous body that must have shaped this place . . . I heard a hiss and whirled, almost falling.

He sat in a small recess, his legs pulled to his chest. 'I knew it,' he said. 'I told them you were following us.'

'Where are they?'

'Kama Sutran dogs . . . got what they deserved . . .'

'You look – What happened here?'

He lowered his head.

'Did you come upon a Naga?'

He didn't answer.

I moved ahead quietly. The tunnel was blocked by flesh. Hissing breaths came from the next chamber, timed with the expansion and contraction of this wall. Scales rippled. I measured the bulk against the opening, then stepped back on tiptoe.

Vasant had retreated even more.

'It killed all three of them?'

'What do I care?'

'We must go now.'

'Where?'

'Past the Naga. While it sleeps.'

'She's blocking the tunnel!'

'There is room.'

'You're mad. You're not a real person. You're unstable.'

'You'll die here, when the Naga feels it's time.'

He said nothing.

'You will come with me,' I told him. 'If necessary, by force.'

He glared at me, anger drawing him from shock. He thumped his chest. 'I am a member of Palace society!'

'The more reason for you to survive.'

But his legs continued to resist; his knees were so weak that he fell repeatedly back to his corner. I pulled the barge over so he could use it for support, holding the frame as we walked toward that pulsing wall. Vasant's feet slid noisily over bone, but the respiration in that next chamber did not change. Ssssss. Sssss. I removed the last ballast as Vasant stared at the breadth of scales drawing and redrawing their pattern. I tied my rope to the chassis, handed him the remainder.

'Three tugs, and you reel it back,' I said.

He nodded, still staring.

I climbed on the barge and drew up my legs. It rose as Vasant let out slack. When I reached the ceiling, I extended my hands and feet, found finger holds, pulled forward. A gap of about a meter separated the height of flesh and the top of the opening. I could squeeze through. On the other side, I rose in a much larger chamber.

The chamber was not only filled by the Naga but perforated to suit serpentine body mechanics, designed with holes and subchambers to support her interminable length. Below me, she lay in a long spiral of uncolored flesh, graphed by a pattern of scales. Scales rippled down her body, a mesmerizing sight if studied too long. At the far end, the lines continued to extend and intersect, furthering the pattern even where flesh had not yet filled in the body; in other places, the flesh was worn down to the pattern, making for segments like mesh tube. The vaguely human aspect of this demoness extended from the front end of her coil-body, a face with slit eyes, slit mouth, a wedge nose, but the sum was too simple and angular to be described as a human face. It was an oval supplied with organs she needed. Inset in the crown was a light source, emitting a ruddy glow, a gem worth thousands of rupees in Bombay bazaars to anyone unwise enough to attempt an extraction. The light was modulated by the Naga's hissing breaths.

Her head rested on the male Kama Sutran, who lay squeezed between two segments of her. One of his legs appeared thoughtfully damaged – twisted out of socket – so he could not squirm away. As I floated overhead, his eyes opened. Really he was a dead man, a casualty, but whether or not he realized it yet . . . He made no sound.

Part of her curved around the upper surface of the chamber. I steered away from this. Holes led to holes. I selected the smallest, the one that looked like she would have the most trouble squeezing through. I disembarked and tugged the rope three times.

The barge drifted back. It scraped the ceiling, and rock crumbled and sprinkled the pale flesh below. I saw her shudder, the shudder appearing and reappearing in different areas.

Vasant came in jerks and bounces. Making noise. The craft struck rock several times.

Another shudder.

'Rakesh?' Vasant whispered. 'Where are you? I need help!' He thrust against the ceiling, zigzagging.

I said nothing. A reply would hurt his chances.

Below, her breaths became shorter, shallower. Vasant knocked against a stalactite, and the light brightened.

Everything seemed tinged by the blood-red glow of her jewel. With a slithering noise her tail awoke, sliding over other coils, closer, a thing of only limited consciousness. Vasant was still a good distance away from me. I waved my arms.

The Naga raised her head. Her eyes stayed shut, but the jewel shone bright and her tongue seemed to pour forth, a prehensile wire the color of muscle, and it too demonstrated a limited consciousness as it dabbed the air, tasting for us.

The Kama Sutran lifted his hand. The Naga's tongue found it, wrapped tight, pulled his hand and arm into her mouth. The simple slit became a smile, and she put her head down again, apparently content.

I grabbed the barge and pulled it home. Vasant unloaded without grace. One last glance down at the Kama Sutran who had made possible our exit, then we proceeded.

'I wouldn't have abandoned you,' I said.

Vasant's eyes flickered my way. He rubbed his jaw. In all the time we'd been walking, this was the first acknowledgment he'd made of my action.

'Unconscious, you could provide no information,' I said. 'I planned to retrieve you.'

'You delivered me to them, at the first opportunity.'

'Without their involvement, we were lost.'

'Do you know what I had to endure in their company? Do you know what I *saw*?'

'I have an idea.'

'You are a country simpleton, and the ramifications of my situation are beyond you.'

'I have my own agenda,' I admitted.

He wasn't interested.

We had towed the barge for its supply of light, but this became unnecessary when we reached the upper levels of the depths. We crossed cavernous space, threading our way through columns that might have been buildings once, now roots to the crumbly roof of earth. Over antediluvian roadways fractured like seashells we plodded, past husks of vehicles and machinery that seemed imploded with corrosion. These objects sometimes gave Vasant pause; he would stare with a slack expression I assumed related to his talent. Occasionally we heard serpentine movements but were careful to stay away from any place whose dimensions were reminiscent of a snake. The Naga had left this region sterile and uninhabited.

'My dharma guided my actions,' I said.

Vasant exhaled. 'If that's how you wish to view it.'

I almost told him my other realization – why I had bothered to help him get out of here – but decided it would upset him to hear the reason now.

'I will make them sorry,' he said.

'How much sorrier could they be?'

'I mean *all* Kama Sutrans. The entire sect.'

'I heard you talking to those three. You sounded comfortable.'

'I did more listening than talking.'

'Oh?'

'Now I can better warn the Sovereign of their plot.'

'They told you about a plot?'

'Not exactly.'

'What did they say?'

He smiled and shook his head. He wouldn't elaborate. I supposed he couldn't trust me.

After a time I said, 'The Baboon Warrior defeated several Nagas.'

'So?'

'He was trapped in one of their kingdoms, very deep. He defeated several.'

'Why are you telling me this?'

I recounted the Baboon's experience. His dialogue with the serpents, his survival after being swallowed. Vasant said, 'Yes, yes, I know the story. Why are you going on about it?' I kept talking. It pleased me to share my knowledge of the Baboon, to hear other people's stories of him, but Vasant kept requesting me please to shut up. When I finished, he gave me a sidelong, appraising glance. 'You certainly talk a lot about the Baboon Warrior,' he said. 'You must be his biggest fan.'

I smiled, and about the same time, we crossed into sunshine falling through earth.

MUSIC I WILL
NOT HEAR

⁂

THIS WAS NOT Sholapur.

I knew we hadn't surfaced elsewhere, because the ruin was interrupted by ditches that Kshatriya men had blasted open, attempting to defend the city. But as we climbed up, I could not match what surrounded us to what I remembered of Sholapur. Hills had been flattened. We were without demarcations or landmarks; columns of crooked smoke stood throughout panoramic rubble and not much else.

The Jagannath was gone. Tracks pointed southwest, but to the horizon there was no other sign of the god.

Restoring moral order was the Jagannath's objective, and recent behavior suggested there was a great imbalance that needed to be corrected. But the chariot and the massive form it transported made the deity inexorable, unpredictable, crushing, and when devotees summoned it to a place like Sholapur, they did so knowing that much would fall to its massive wheels, and the end result could be as severe as anything wrought by a destroyer like Shiva. This was part of the cycle, and procreative gods no doubt already rolled this way; they would come and shape the rubble into a mandala, a diagram on the ground intimating what should rise in Sholapur's place. A god with a hundred arms, perhaps, would aid in construction. People would return, and a new city would be built that better matched divine will. For a moment I stood trying to remember all that had been here, so I could appreciate the might of the god that had brought it down, and what this meant for me.

A gunshot broke my reverie.

The crack of a rifle over level plain.

Another shot.

We ran, dove behind an upturned stall, and peered through the slats.

It was an old man with a white beard and simple gown. Easy to spot: he was the only thing moving as far as we could see. When the wind picked up, his gown lifted and exposed knobby brown legs and genitalia. He raised his rifle and popped off another shot. He wasn't shooting at us. Little remained of Sholapur to stop the bullets. Belts of dull gray ammunition were looped over his skinny chest, and we saw he knew how to reload. He stumbled toward us.

'Is he blind?' said Vasant. 'Are you blind?!'

The old man took another shot.

'Maybe blind and deaf.'

'He's a veteran,' I said. 'There was a home in Sholapur for veterans of the Astrological War.'

'Why are you shooting at us?' Vasant yelled. 'Your war was over a long time ago!'

The veteran looked back and fired the opposite way.

'Those veterans don't see well by daylight,' I said, remembering. 'When the Pleiades are in the sky, the veterans can see more than you or I. But common daylight doesn't suit them.'

'I wonder how many people he accidentally killed by daylight.'

I wondered about how desperate Sholapur must have been to hand out weapons in a military asylum.

We dared emerge from our cover but often tripped, watching where he pointed that gun rather than the broken ground. Then we realized how greatly noises distracted him. He seemed to confuse sounds for sights, and a good shout could make him look in another direction, aim at some invisible target.

'Ha! Ha! Ha!'

Shouting, we made him walk an agitated circle, stopping only to reload, while we trudged over tangled bicycles and collapsed balconies on our way to the edge of the former city. We came to a crumpled lorry.

'Help me get it upright,' said the Engineer.

'It's crushed.'

'It will work.'

After we righted the vehicle, Vasant climbed underneath to make adjustments. Meanwhile I watched the veteran, who was walking in a manner that must have seemed stealthy to him. When he tripped over the arm of a corpse, he put a hand to his ear, trying to understand what happened. He worked the bolt of his rifle. 'Ha!' I shouted. He fell on his rear.

The engine fired, and I turned to see Vasant in the driver's chair. I climbed up the damaged side and sat in the lopsided seat beside him. He frowned.

'I'm coming,' I said.

'To Delhi?'

'Wherever you're going.'

'What about your "priorities"?'

'You will help me with them.'

He looked at me, dumbfounded.

'I meant to tell you earlier,' I said.

'You're a deluded young man.'

The veteran fired another shot.

'Please,' I said to Vasant, 'go where you wish. Do what you must. You don't have to believe my dharma is correct, just let me accompany you for the time being.'

'I suppose you could feed the engine.'

'Gladly.'

'And you will obey my instructions? Not raise a hand, or compromise my safety?'

'Whatever is in your best interests.'

'Cause me grief, and I'll deal with you in Delhi.'

'I consider myself warned.'

'I can be harsh.'

With that he engaged the clutch; the lorry lurched forward, rocking as he drove it off a bank of broken concrete to a grassier section, looking for a road. I indicated parallel grooves on the opposite side of the pits, and he eyed me before turning the lorry toward an earthen bridge. 'Help you,' he muttered.

We drove past the old man, and Vasant leaned over to ask him, 'Did you fight in the Astrological War?' The veteran ejected a shell from his gun and fumbled to put another in the breech.

'He's witless,' Vasant said.

After we pulled past, the old man walked. Turning one way, turning back. For a time I checked over my shoulder to monitor his progress, and almost an hour went by before we lost sight of him. Vasant only wanted distance.

'That must have been upsetting for you,' he said, 'to see your home ruined.'

'Sholapur wasn't my home,' I replied.

'Then what were you doing there?'

'I heard the Jagannath was coming.'

'And you wanted to get in its path?'

'I need it.'

He snorted. 'You think a god is also going to help you?'

'Yes.'

'I suppose I shouldn't be surprised by your heresy. And what kind of delusion would make a Vaisya boy like yourself expect help from me and the god Jagannath? What are you compelled to do? Save India?'

'Kill the Baboon Warrior.'

The smirk remained on his face for a moment.

'It's my dharma,' I said.

'You are some kind of anarchist.'

'No.'

'Then don't make such comments in my presence! I could have you arrested. How outrageous! What would your parents think, to hear you say such a thing?' He returned his attention to the road, shaking his head.

'But it's true.'

'I'm warning you, I can make only so much allowance for mental defects – '

'It is my duty to kill the Baboon Warrior. My holy duty.'

He made a noise of exasperation. 'I'm forced to report this.'

'Do whatever your dharma demands,' I told him. 'Like me.'

'Listen to you! You're little more than a boy. A Vaisya boy. Do you think your life has any bearing on that of a famous and celebrated warrior? A national hero?'

'I am his end.'

'Let me give you some advice, Rakesh: don't indulge this delusion. Someone may mistake you for a threat.'

But I was a threat.

I might have told Vasant I felt as certain of my dharma as he did about his caste and calling. There was no doubt I would kill the hero of India. That I would be his assassin. My strategy was not yet determined, but such details arose with time, like knots from a length of wood. Vasant himself was an example of a detail emerging from the grain. Seeing him on the Jagannath's chariot, I knew he would assist me in yoking it to my task.

But let him drive, for now. Let him think he was heading back to the capital and his former life.

'Kill the Baboon Warrior,' he muttered with disbelief.

I remembered the night, years ago, when I realized it.

I had been sitting near the shore, facing the repetition of breakers. It was night. Very late. I should have been somewhere else. Home, maybe. I had a string of flowers wrapped around one hand, my bow in the other, and I was shooting arrows at the black susurrus of the sea, one after another. I wasted dozens. But who was counting? Nobody. In my mood, this seemed anything but wasteful. The arrows disappeared with a whine the instant I let go, so I built a fire. When it was going strong, I nocked another arrow and held the tip to the flames, until the shaft took fire. I stretched back and placed my feet against the bow so I could pull with both arms.

The burning arrow sang over the ocean. I sat up to watch its flame recede, and resolved to keep watching until it disappeared. Time passed, and to my confusion I could still see the speck of light and its reflection. My bonfire petered out, yet the arrow remained visible. My flesh crawled. Something changed around me.

'Rakesh.'

I started.

Before me the ocean retreated, and she rose on hands and knees, the waves having created her body from the black sand. I might have mistaken her for a sculpture, had her eyes not popped open, and a red tongue appeared at her mouth.

'Kali!' I stumbled backward.

'Do not fear me, Rakesh.'

She changed position.

'I am not here to harm you.'

'Wh – wha – ?'

'I am not here to consume you,' she said with a terrible smile. 'I am not here to drink your blood.'

'What have I done?'

'I am not here to break your bones. I am not here to eat your flesh.'

'What do you – ?'

'I came to ask a question.'

'Anything!' I lay down, forehead to sand. 'Kali, anything!'

'Why are you on this beach, so late at night?'

'Because of my life,' I said, lifting my head. 'My ruined life.'

'Ruined?'

'Today, I was supposed to become a man.'

'What does that mean, become a man?'

I couldn't bring myself to say it. I held the string of flowers for Kali to see.

'Today you were supposed to be married.'

I nodded.

'But today you are not married.'

'I thought my life would change today.'

She smiled. 'It has.'

'But – '

'Do you know why you were not married?'

'Why?'

'Your life has changed in a way you did not expect.'

'What do you mean?'

'You are not married because you are meant to do something else.'

'Do what?'

'You are special to the gods, Rakesh.'

Kali ran her red tongue across her lips. Kali the destroyer.

'What am I to do?'

'Rakesh,' she said. 'You know why you are not married today.'

'I know who is responsible.'

And when I said this, she lowered to the beachhead, and I saw my arrow over the darkness of the ocean, my dot of light refusing to die. What was I meant to do? Waves rushed in, and with each gush Kali lost definition, substance washing away, features dissolving, until she was no more than a lump in the beach. What had been eyes were only white clamshells, and her bright red tongue was the single arm of a starfish sticking out of sand. The destroyer was gone. But beyond, my point of light remained. A little fire I had put in the sky, it hovered until morning brought bigger fire, the rising sun, and I knew.

I knew what must be done.

My life *had* changed. I had a duty, and the arrow would burn until it was fulfilled.

Like Kali, I was a destroyer.

I woke.

Still traveling, still moving, but Vasant not driving. He held the steering wheel, but the lorry more or less drove itself, the ruts of the road having grown so deep that they now decided our course. Vasant shifted in his seat and sputtered. He was snoring.

I looked back but could no longer see the columns of smoke marking Sholapur. Yet something familiar plodded behind us, and I had to look again to be sure.

Him.

I saw the gown first. The veteran showed no obvious intention to trail after us, but there he was. His haphazard and seemingly random turns meant that to keep up with us, he must have walked several extra kilometers, but he showed no signs of fatigue. I watched until a knoll erased him from view.

Vasant's stomach growled. I couldn't remember eating since my rice ball in the dark. There were villages in the distance, so I closed my eyes, pretending sleep, and kicked Vasant in the ankle.

'. . . hm . . . what?'

I felt him sit upright.

'Rakesh. Rakesh!'

'Are we in Delhi?' I asked, rubbing my eyes.

'We're closer.'

He made a show of steering, even though the ruts continued to dictate our progress. I resisted a temptation to ask where we were. Cinnamon trees gathered, the aroma of their heated bark as thick as dusk. The lorry continued making *pukka-pukka-pukka* progress, but behind our seats the fuel cabinets revealed a much dwindled supply of dung brick. We had been traveling for quite some time, and it was apparent we could not reach Delhi without refueling.

I said, 'The Kama Sutrans fed you?'

'Of course I refused their offerings. But I suppose you're hungry.'

'It's of no concern.'

'For a fast meal there may be time.'

I protested.

'You need not apologize for your hunger,' he said. 'But please try to stay awake. I can't be expected to eat for you.'

We passed through several towns, until Vasant saw one he thought suitable, and our lorry turned under the extended leg of a dusty Shiva with a corresponding statue of Parvati forming the other half of an entrance. We passed a goshalla, a home for aged cows, but only the cows themselves were visible, one sticking its head out of a second-story window to see who came puttering down the street. The other thing that struck me was the fact that no street lamps had been lit. Ours was the lone vehicle moving in the street, and I saw only one person. At the doors to a Shaivite temple, a man stood on one leg. He waved and hopped over.

'We're looking for something to eat,' I said. 'Is there a place we could buy a meal?'

'Everybody's gone. You can probably take something from a kitchen and leave a few rupees. Nobody would mind. Probably nobody would notice.'

'We wouldn't want to trespass.'

'Well, maybe someone is still around.'

He hopped forward, and we got off the lorry to follow.

'How long have you been standing like that?' I asked.

'Over three years,' he said proudly.

'You're wasting your time,' Vasant said sharply. 'If you think Shiva or another member of the million will be impressed just because you are standing on one leg for so many years, you should reconsider. Gods don't respond to that kind of penance.'

'Sir, you misunderstand,' he said. 'This is not a tribute to a god: it's an apology to the man who lost his leg due to my carelessness. A factory accident.'

'Oh.'

He smiled at us and continued hopping, and I noticed how the leg he used was well developed, whereas the other, his left, had withered so much, it could probably no longer support any weight. It flopped, dead meat. He checked over his shoulder that we were following, as we passed groves of lemon trees with much fruit surrendered to the ground. The area was dotted yellow, baskets and oxcarts sat abandoned, and I wondered about the absent farmers. Lemon spoilage sweetened the air.

'Where is everyone?'

'At the filmee. As usual.'

'Filmee? You have filmees here?'

'Oh yes. They're the only thing people seem to talk about anymore. Through those hills. I've never been, myself; it wouldn't be right for me to indulge in such leisure.'

'How can a lemon-growing town afford a filmee projector?' Vasant asked.

'Kind gentlemen gave it to us. No cost! They came with equipment and labor and filmees. Kind gentlemen, wishing to enrich our lives.'

Vasant eyed the hills. 'Can you show us the way?'

'Yes, of course.' He hopped ahead. 'But what about dinner?'

'I want to see your theater first.'

'Though it pleases me to help strangers, I must refrain from entering the valley theater. It wouldn't be right.'

As we walked, he talked about the comrade who lost a leg due to his carelessness, describing with great reverence a man who sounded quite boring. We didn't listen. Vasant focused on the glow ahead, and I thought of the Baboon Warrior. A lucky thing we had a guide, because the dying of daylight made for a dark trek. Eventually he stopped talking, and only the sound of one foot hitting the ground interrupted the silence. Then, a murmur. A sitar. The passage narrowed. Blue light played over facing cliffs; foliage blinked on and off. It was as if we walked toward a rent in the fabric of existence. Our guide hopped aside and leaned against rock. He smiled at us.

We proceeded through the breech and stood among giant figures, blue nudity splashed high and long across a wall of escarpment. We stumbled at the knees of a woman receiving attention from one man behind her and another at her mouth. Blue light washed us, the color of the filmee becoming our own, and three sitars played mad raga, over and over, a description of flesh pistoning flesh.

Opposite this display sat the audience, quaint fruit farmers who complained like stevedores, shouting at us to sit the fuck down. And worse! *Get out of the way, you two who fuck your mothers! You two who fuck each other!* And behind the hundred villagers a single bright eye blinked, rapidly, hypnotically, light almost blinding, so bright I felt my pupils contracting to the point where they might not return. Vasant met the cyclopean gaze, his face dreamy and furious, like someone from a political poster betrayed by an entire population.

I sat eating lemons as Vasant slept. His was a bad sleep, apparently: he rolled and twitched, and I could not tell if it was sweat or tears streaking his cheeks. He mumbled the same word over and over.

A name.

'Kavita . . . Kavita . . .'

Chevrons furrowed his brow. He arched his back, struck the ground. Difficult to watch, but I suspected he suffered not exactly from pain.

When he woke, he didn't seem to know what had made his face wet and his breath ragged. He blinked at the niche in the rocks where we were camped, and at me, fire-lit, with my seventh lemon. He stared at me as if I should fade with waking.

'I dreamt the Kama Sutrans came to the farmlands.'

I nodded to the east, where blue light made the hills shift and flicker. 'No dream,' I said. 'But why have they bothered?'

'Because they want to corrupt all Indians! And these yokels have no defense.'

He shuddered, and anger carried him to silence. He pulled his knees to his chest and stared at the flames. The fire crackled, and I poked a lemon that I'd put at the edge. Its skin had browned to a color not unlike my own.

'What is the name of the First Wife?' I said.

'Hm?'

'We always call her First Wife, news messengers call her First Wife. But she must have a name. I don't believe I've ever heard it.'

'Don't ask me stupid questions.'

I nodded. So, he hadn't told me everything about him and the First Wife.

About him and Kavita.

But I didn't want him to feel scrutinized. I thought of my flaming arrow flying over the ocean and wondered if a story more pathetic than his might relax him.

My story about a young man in Varanasi.

A boy, really.

The boy had noticed his parents working on a secret project. Trips across town. Consultations with grandmother and aunts. Visits to the bank where his father's savings were enshrined. When the boy asked what was happening, he was politely rebuffed. The activities continued, and he might have been able to put them out of his mind as his parents suggested he should, had he not suspected that they directly concerned his future.

One afternoon, alone, the boy explored his parents' bedroom and his father's desk, and discovered a picture.

A painting, and looking at the eyes of the subject, the boy realized he was going to be married.

Weddings were not simply a concern of the two people whose lives they joined: a Varanasi wedding was a contract between two families, two trees of relationships brought together in a careful process. His parents obviously didn't want him to be disappointed if early discussions failed. The girl's rituals might clash with those of the family. Astrology might recommend against the two mothers' becoming friends. And of course there was the issue of dowry . . . Many factors might jeopardize the arrangement of this girl's life with his own.

But, too late. The picture married him to her. She had a cleft lip, an imperfection that seemed to heighten the perfection of her face. The delicate brown egg of her face. The small teeth. He wanted to be with this girl for life. He wanted soon the anointment of their bodies with wedding oils and aromatics, then he wanted those scents to mingle in a first clutch. And right now, he wanted to make the portrait real.

So he followed his aunt across town as she made one of these discreet trips, visiting a home roughly the size of their own. That must be the house of the girl's family, he decided. Thereafter he made clandestine trips to this address, and vigilance paid off when he finally saw her returning from school. Younger than he. She carried a piece of artwork, gingerly, something she must have made at school, and she looked down as she walked, as if the ground could not be altogether trusted. The one time she raised her eyes, they found his. He ran, terrified and excited. She ran in a different direction.

Her name was Shanti Mookerjee, and a month later they were formally introduced. Families spread behind both of them. She would be his wife. The boy touched her once, his hand grazing hers lightly. It happened under a table, when nobody was looking. Her skin felt softer than the neck of a calf, the petals of a lotus, the braid of his mother's hair.

The boy continued making secret trips while wedding plans progressed. It would be a celebration worthy of both families. The boy's little sister was making paper flowers, and after a few weeks paper blossoms overran her floor. But the boy's mother did not participate so much. She left many tasks to her sisters, and spent an increasing amount of time in bed. She coughed, and sometimes her hand came away spattered red. The boy spent many hours at her side, but his thoughts drifted back to Shanti, and, to his shame, he hoped his mother's illness would not impede the wedding.

Shanti, Shanti, Shanti. One afternoon, his mother sleeping, he snuck into the bedroom for yet another look. He took Shanti's picture and sat on the floor, quietly yearning to run a finger over the faint scar across her lip.

The bed groaned behind him. His mother sat up, awake.

The boy tried to sit on the picture, and he braced for his mother's censure. But she surprised him. All she said was 'Love is easier if you work for it.'

His embarrassment increased. But later he thought about what she said and realized that his parents had wanted him to find the picture. Shanti, too. They wanted love in the arrangement, emotion of his own making. He had been meant to discover her.

He saw Shanti once more.

He climbed the wall of her house and looked in through her window. At this point they had still not spoken much without their parents nearby, so he was unsure what to say.

'Can you read?'

She shook her head.

'Oh . . .'

'What do you have there?' she asked.

'I wrote a list for you, of all the words I could think of that I enjoy.'

She took the paper and placed it under her pillow. 'I will find someone who knows reading.' Then she looked around the room and opened a small jewelry box. She selected a nacreous pebble streaked with purple and pink.

'A pearl?'

'I found it in a clam!'

Could anything be happier? He felt her fingers again when she passed it to him. Like the sound of her name, the pearl became another fetish to help him survive the interminable hours apart. Shanti, Shanti, Shanti. He gripped it so tight, it dented his palm.

Their wedding day approached, but he was unable to steal away to see her again. The house was transformed with guests and preparations. An uncle from Bangalore took up residence in the boy's room, and brought along a copy of the *Kama Sutra*, each night promising to enlighten the boy regarding certain mysteries of women, but each night falling asleep a few paragraphs into the prologue. The book lay splayed like a lover on his uncle's chest. The boy stared at the cover, trying to decipher the faded illustration.

The day before the wedding, he heard his aunt mewling. Disaster, he sensed.

Meekly, the boy stepped into the room where his aunt sat brushing away tears. Shanti's father was present and appeared uncomfortable, shifting from foot to foot. He avoided looking at the boy. The boy felt his heart becoming unhitched in his chest, sliding. The conversation died. They had been talking about a god.

No. Not quite a god. A celebrity.

The Baboon Warrior. He had recently quashed a rebellion of thousands, the Soma Uprising, and saved face for the government, leaving hardened soldiers to pity their enemies. Flower petals showered the Baboon whenever he appeared on city streets now, and musicians would lean out of windows and strike up impromptu ragas. India had many gods but only one hero, and this added to his glamour.

The hero had visited Varanasi the night before. Late, very late, when few people remained awake. But some woke after midnight when they heard a whooping. They learned later that it had been the Baboon. He had climbed a bridge, and those who looked out their windows glimpsed a silhouette standing against the moon. The boy recalled hearing something but hadn't connected it with the Baboon. As to most people, the call meant nothing to him.

'We heard her get up,' Shanti's father said. 'I didn't think much of it. But in the morning . . .' He looked meekly at the boy. In the morning . . . He raised empty hands.

Shanti was gone.

Gone, where?

Gone to the Baboon.

He might as well have said gone to her next life. She might as well have been dead.

Anyone could understand her compulsion. The boy recalled pictures of the Baboon tacked to the walls in her bedroom. Great would be the attraction; nobody underestimated how strongly she must have felt the celebrity's appeal. But it was ruinous. The marriage had already begun. Only ceremony remained. Only chickpeas and special yogurts and curried vegetables prepared in advance. All the tables decorated with hibiscus, which the boy walked among, stunned after hearing the news. All his relatives from afar, staring at him, speechless. All the paper flowers stuck to his sister's fingers.

The boy pushed through a gauntlet of sympathy. He went outside, and stood. He looked back at the house, heard his father's voice, and Mr. Mookerjee's, getting louder: an argument. Upstairs, the wet coughs of his mother. Someone would have to tell her the bad news.

Not the boy. He couldn't do it. He wasn't brave enough.

He walked to the bridge, and after climbing up it found a lump of hardened dung glued to a beam, the only indication the Baboon Warrior had been there. The boy climbed back down and continued walking.

Shanti was gone. She had deserted him. Gone to a man with the head of a monkey, like so many clamoring virgins before her. Gone to a hero, a celebrity.

He did not expect to see her again.

Now was my turn for quiet. My throat was sore.

Vasant, who had looked bored at first, stared at me. 'So?'

'So what?'

'Did the boy find Shanti? What happened after that?'

I shook my head.

'After that I wandered,' I said. 'Until I found myself shooting arrows at the sea.'

THE BITE OF
THE BOAR

+=◦=+

AS THE MAN on one leg had predicted, nobody noticed
the next morning when we crept back into town to
appropriate food and dung brick. Men and women
slept off the night's filmee, and whatever degradation
it had spurred, they slept curled together, they slept
among trees, surrounded by dropped fruit. Children
frolicked without supervision, running and shrilling,
and Vasant used a stick to separate two boys engaged
in mock copulation. A grandmother swore at us from
a window as we pushed a wheelbarrow heaped with
dung bricks to our lorry, but her old-fashioned curses
were the sum of the resistance. For the sake of karma,
Vasant fixed a pump in the local irrigation system, but
didn't compensate the town beyond that (in fact, he
spat on the ground before we pulled away). He'd
attempted to find a representative of the Royals, but
the man on one leg said the only person associated
with Delhi had been run out of town weeks ago. The
Engineer wasn't surprised. He surveyed the ill-behaved
children and suffering old cows and slumbering
farmers, and told the man, 'I pity you. You should hop
to some holier location.'

But the man on one leg liked it here. He smiled and waved goodbye as our lorry pulled away.

I asked Vasant how long it would take to get to Delhi, but he stared ahead, gripping the steering wheel, his face tight. He seemed bothered by what he'd witnessed, just barely suppressing some tirade, glaring at the road. Dark piles appeared before us. There was a fire, too, and Vasant slowed the lorry to maneuver around piles of dead rats stacked four feet high and smoking. His eyes narrowed, as if we were seeing bad omens.

'Irulas,' I said.

'What?'

Soon enough we saw them, a family of the rat catchers who wandered from farm to farm selling their services. Father and eldest son blew smoke into a warren, and children thrust their hands inside, yanking out the asphyxiated bodies of rodents. Vasant's eyes widened. In the background was the chittering of a vast population, and we gazed at the fields darting with frantic life.

We drove even slower to get around the fire, as an elderly woman tossed black bodies into it. I smelled flesh burning with fur. She smiled up at us.

'You boys are hungry?'

Further smoking piles. Children pursued rodents with bare feet and laughter. Another woman of the family inserted her hand in a smoked-out lair, scooping rice collected by the rats.

Vasant abandoned the steering wheel and proceeded to the rear of the vehicle, pouring water from our supply so he could wash.

'It is how they have lived for generations,' I said.

He didn't reply.

'Without Irulas, these fields would be overrun.'

'That's what's wrong with rural people like yourself,' he said. 'Anything to fill your bellies.'

I might have mentioned that I was born and raised in a city of five million, but Vasant preferred to lump me together with whatever group he criticized. He dropped back into his seat.

'As if Kama Sutran influence wasn't enough! It will take strong and systematic actions from the Sovereign to improve India's moral fiber. I will speak to him about this. I will urge severity.'

He pushed my hands from the steering wheel and retook control.

If Vasant wasn't upset enough by the Irulas, we only needed to see the rat god working in a field not twenty kilometers ahead. Its body was divided between silver bands and shags of dark fur, and with its conical snout it appeared to be digging some trench – perhaps for irrigation – much to the appreciation of the farmer riding its back. As we pulled into view, the god paused and lifted its head from the dirt. Vasant shouted, 'We have nothing to do with those monsters down the road!' The god looked at us, eyes multifaceted and bright, absorbing us in a thousand slightly different reflections. It swung its head, and the display of reflections changed, showing a figure with elongated legs, a warped face, and a multitude of arms; the rat god was looking at someone behind us.

When I turned, there he was. The veteran, still walking in a foolhardy direction. His hospital cottons had taken on shades of the earth, and his skin had become darker from the sun, as if he were part of the scenery.

'Whether he realizes it or not,' I said, 'that veteran is following us.'

We traveled for a long time without significant delay. Then, Jaipur. I stared at the approaching city shimmering into form from heat. The Engineer kept returning to the sack of water and smacking his lips loudly after he drank. He drank, then peed over the side of the vehicle: nothing would delay him. When our supply of drinking water ran out, Vasant began to drink our other water, used for purification rituals. He wiped sweat from his eyes and squinted at Jaipur, as if a lapse in concentration might allow it to vanish.

'Did your mother recover?'

'My mother?' I said.

'The story last night. You were the boy in the story, yes?'

'Oh. Yes. I was he.'

'Did she recover?'

'I suspect the news about Shanti killed her.'

'You *suspect*?'

'I didn't return home after realizing my dharma,' I said. 'Nothing else mattered afterward.'

Again he took issue with my dharma, but a figure materialized from the cityscape, and we fell silent to watch him come. Camel and rider seemed part of one package on four knobby legs thundering across the way – the rider extended from quarter pieces of cracked leather armor, sitting with a selection of rifles also bound into the unit. Both animal and man wore leather masks; the man's eyes were hidden behind a band of opaque glass, suggesting a career in harsh sunlight. He held no reins and made no discernible commands, yet nonetheless steered the camel toward us and rode alongside.

'What do you want?' Vasant said.

'Who you work for?'

'We're making a pilgrimage to holy rivers,' I said. 'Mother Ganges.'

The rider leaned to Vasant, scrutinizing his face. 'Ever been to Delhi?'

'What does that have to do with – '

'We're on a pilgrimage, a holy tour,' I said, cutting off the Engineer before he could say anything provocative. 'All we seek is liberation of the spirit.'

'And Rakesh is unstable,' Vasant put in, 'so you would be well advised not to rankle him.'

'You look like you come from Delhi,' the rider said.

The camel dropped its head over the side of our lorry and bit the water sack, causing water to gush forth. It spilled over the floorboards beneath my feet.

'Listen to me, Fancy Suit. In Jaipur, we are getting rid of outside influences. I don't mind being the one to get rid of you.'

But a trumpeting seized their attention. The camel tossed water from its chops and without instruction broke away, galloping toward the sound of that horn. They left as abruptly as they'd appeared, and I could see the man readying his guns.

The trumpet blew again.

We motored forward. Vasant looked indignant; possibly he followed the rider just because the rider had warned us away. A crowd came into view, and an aircraft above. It hovered lower than Vasant's balloon in Sholapur, a triangular craft, three fat balloons supporting a wedge of woven fuselage. The craft dipped to one side as if struggling to rise. Or to avoid a crash.

More camels moved beneath the aircraft, riders having thrown grappling hooks to it, preventing its departure. They urged their camels to walk and drag the vessel down, down, down. Others lobbed more hooks. On board, I could make out the crew frantically trying to release themselves from this bondage.

'Robbery,' said Vasant.

'What?'

'It's a robbery!'

We accelerated, and the craft turned so I could see what must have sparked the Engineer's outrage, the royal symbol emblazoned on its flank.

Our full speed was not overwhelming, but the lorry bounced forward and jackals or wild dogs scattered as it advanced. Shots were fired, between men on the ground and one of the purple-vested figures aboard the government airship. Jaipur rose nearby us, and we barged through a dusty border district, home to untouchables and other forms of outcast. A crowd had gathered around the struggle, and its unsavory components thrust arms at the craft, hooting, bursting apart when lines of fire strayed too close.

'Ungrateful louts!' Vasant shouted.

Above, the government employees jettisoned chairs and furniture as much to hit the mercenaries as provide lift, and this succeeded partially, the craft surging up and pulling two connected camels by their hindquarters. Spectators cheered. We hurtled through them, and people cleared our path or were knocked aside. The man who confronted us before had his array of weapons blazing, trying to shoot the balloons or at least a civil servant.

'You don't deserve peace and order!'

This was Vasant's battle cry as we plowed into the camel, pushing the beast so the rider was thrown, his shots straying and people dropping in the crowd. Vasant swerved, but the camel tripped, and we rolled over it with a nasty crunch and cry from below. The lorry swept through a turn too sharp and lifted its wheels. I leaped off. Dust and the underside of the vehicle, wheels spinning, camels in mad gallop. Unwashed bodies rose and fell with excitement. I stumbled, covered my face, dove into the crowd. Cheers, gun-shots, the smell of gunpowder and male sweat.

As the lorry crashed, with chopped dung making a rooster tail from its engine, I elbowed through the untouchables, trying to locate Vasant. The crowd pushed past me, and the camel riders came around; their attention shifted to the Engineer, who was bent over. Someone grabbed his shirt and hauled him upright, dragged him. The mercenaries closed in. Derelicts shook their fists and jeered.

Vasant's shout of 'How can you –' was drowned by hooting, greater anger, animal snorts. One of the mercenaries dismounted to face him, with a riding crop.

A rope dragged past me: one of the grappling ropes, still attached to the aircraft. The vehicle continued to hover overhead as the attackers held tight. I tested the rope, started climbing.

Aboard the craft, one government employee lay on the deck, leaking blood. I proceeded on hands and knees, allowing minimum target area. Below, Vasant shielded his head as the man with the riding crop smacked him repeatedly. Others held him so he couldn't avoid these lashes.

The airship lurched when I got my footing; the mercenaries kept shooting. I scurried into the cabin.

Inside, a second government agent huddled in the corner with hands over his head. He looked at me, terrified, and turned to the wall as if expecting his death blow. In the cabin was a counting machine that operated by hand crank, and several rows of wooden chests. I grabbed one and pulled it from its bracket, rattan cracking and splintering, and the cowering tax collector glanced over his shoulder as I wrenched it free.

I dragged the container to the deck as holes popped across the floor. I pushed it over the edge, and – smash. On the ground it had become broken sticks glinting with money.

The sound brought change: the sound not of mantra or holy syllables but of money. People emerged from their slapped-together domiciles at the clink of coins; the destitute swarmed the broken vault and drowned it from view. Good fortune made them unpredictable. They flowed forward, pushing and shoving, unintentionally getting in the way of Vasant and his attacker. By the time I split open a second container, the ground seethed, desperate bodies grabbing for the rain of coins, figures leaping onto the backs of others to clutch at fluttering paper money.

The tax agent, finding his nerve, tried to put himself between me and the chests, but when he glimpsed the scene below, he threw up his hands.

I punched through another rattan vault, tore open

flooring, and rocked the aircraft so money fell through, showering the masses. Below, a simple beating had become a delirious riot. The camel riders joined the party, and in the maelstrom only one figure remained motionless, and if there wasn't such a ruckus I'm sure I could have heard his whimpers.

I could imagine what Vasant felt upon waking. His body stings, resists reconciliation with its senses. Wounds stripe his face and arms, and shifting in his chair makes him wince. He recalls the blur of an arm bringing down a riding crop. Figures fade in, fade out. People watch him, await his recovery. He rubs his eyes and makes another attempt at consciousness. He remembers. How he got *here* is a mystery . . . but the figure sitting across from him is familiar. Vasant recognizes immediately the leather implement the man twirls in his fingers.

'Whip me like a dog?!'

I intercepted Vasant as he lunged at Madhav, and Madhav stepped back quickly and knocked over his chair. There was laughter. Vasant snatched at the riding crop, but I wrestled him into submission. Still he struggled. Madhav, unfazed, simply picked up his chair and tucked his weapon in his belt.

'What are you doing?' the Engineer snarled. 'Do you know what he did to me?'

'Vasant,' I said, 'look around. Look where we are.'

We were in a constabulary. Dirty plates and cups littered the desks. Cells could be seen down a hall, but the iron doors were open and the cots looked slept in. There were no prisoners. More cots were set up in the large office where we stood. Through a window, camels

could be seen awaiting assignments. Vasant blinked up
at a painting of the god Rama in police uniform,
subduing a criminal with a nightstick. Then he looked
at the men we'd assumed were mercenaries, some of
whom wore dented badges on their uniforms.

'Police . . .?'

'In a way.'

'You tried to kill me!'

Madhav, the man with the crop, said, 'There have
been circumstances.'

'What circumstances could justify robbing a tax
collection vehicle?'

'The government in Delhi has been overturned.'

'What?!'

'Yes. Several days ago now.'

'The Sovereign . . .?'

'Dead.'

'By whom?'

'Beetles. A parade of them, as he slept. They filled
his lungs. Or so we have been told.'

'But his guards – '

'Yes, the guards should have heard the march of so
many thousands of tiny legs. Or the First Wife. She
should have noticed . . .'

Vasant looked pale, but I could tell this news was an
extension of his worst fears, not a surprise.

'What is Hapi's involvement?'

'Prince Hapi?' Madhav consulted the other constables. 'None, that I know of.'

'Who controls the Palace?'

'The First Wife,' said Madhav.

And a grumble rose from his cohorts.

Jaipur was divided on the legitimacy of the First

Wife's sudden power. If the Sovereign had died of natural causes or by assassination, then it was right she should assume power. But if she'd had any role in his death, she should be executed. When the Palace rishis requested the Sovereign's body for examination, the First Wife refused, claiming it would serve no purpose. Brahmin priests repeated this demand, and her crones turned over bags and bags of dead beetles but no body. Yesterday, the First Wife announced that the Sovereign had been cremated, at night, in a private ceremony on the ghats of the river Ganges. Casting the situation in even worse light was the fact that the Palace had recently been subject to a string of mysterious deaths, and disappearances of high-ranking officials.

Madhav dryly explained that in Jaipur, as in other large cities, resistance to the government had grown. The constables had refused to act on Delhi's behalf, and for that disobedience they had been summarily fired. In spite of this, they continued to enforce order in the eastern half of the city. West, those loyal to the First Wife held sway. The constables and their supporters believed not a single rupee should go to royal coffers until the issue of legitimacy was settled, so Madhav and his associates had conspired to seize the government airship.

'Of course we assumed the worst when you charged us with your lorry,' he said, smiling. 'But Rakesh reached us. He told us you were Palace Engineer Vasant Alamvala – one of the famous missing persons! And that you were fiercely devoted to the Sovereign.'

Vasant shifted and glanced at me. I had not mentioned his unique relationship with the First Wife, or that sleep routinely produced her name from his lips. He seemed to struggle for a moment. Then he stood.

'Gentlemen, disgraced constables, others. Let me tell you who is responsible for the turbulence in Delhi. Kama Sutrans. Kama Sutrans brought into the Palace by Prince Hapi.'

The constables made noises of surprise.

'I was abducted in what I now recognize as a purge orchestrated by Kama Sutrans. I met a pair of them prior to my abduction, but regrettably I did not expose them. Whatever skulduggery surrounds the First Wife, I assure you that Kama Sutrans are in fact to blame.'

The constables murmured with surprise and interest.

'He doesn't know,' I said.

Eyes turned to me.

'Vasant,' I continued, 'has it occurred to you that someone other than the Kama Sutrans could have played a part in your abduction? Even in placing the capacitor where you found it?'

He flushed.

'Have you considered that it might have been placed there by the First Wife herself?'

He shut his lips tight, frowning, resisting the urge to bark at me. Then he blurted: *'Burna bridda shalla minka. Felles mensos Delhi maltisis bride mengoko. Mrisis bride shalla mengoko.'*

Madhav looked confused. 'I don't believe that language is spoken by anyone here.'

'No language,' said Vasant. 'Kama Sutran code. My proof of their plot.'

'Please explain?'

'During my absence from the Palace, I performed some surveillance against a group of Kama Sutrans' –

he eyed me – 'and they often spoke in code. I understood only one word: Delhi. The rest is unknown. But I memorized as much as I could, and with the assistance of the army code breakers I'm sure it can be deciphered. Perhaps it will reveal the Kama Sutran role in this crisis.'

'The military is very busy with the crisis,' said Madhav. 'I don't know that they'll spare you any resources.'

'You could try the Pragmatics,' suggested another constable. 'They're not far from here, and they can break any code.'

'Who?' said Vasant.

'The Pragmatics of Ranthambhore. Surely you've heard of the Pragmatics? Less than a day's ride, and they would be neutral in this dispute, as with most issues. They could give you an unbiased opinion on your code words. If you could convince them.'

The Engineer stroked his growth of beard, considering the suggestion, but shook his head. 'No. The matter is too delicate for common ears. I must go to Delhi.'

Madhav smiled. 'You won't be going anywhere today, Vasant. You have received a professional beating.' He held up his riding crop, as if the Engineer might need reminding. 'Today you would find even a brief stint in the saddle intolerable.'

'Nonsense,' Vasant said.

He rose to make a show of striding around the office, but halted soon after, putting a hand to his forehead, and I could almost see the stars descending to orbit his head.

Madhav kicked a chair over to him. Vasant scowled at the gesture but nonetheless sat. 'You will stay with us until you're fit to travel,' Madhav said. 'Then, we will provide an armed escort to the capital.'

Vasant transferred himself to one of the cots, using chairs and desks along the way to steady himself. He lay down, shading his eyes from whatever swirling vertigo he suffered. Madhav watched him and continued to nod and smile, taking what I read as professional pride in the Engineer's condition.

The day drew to a close, and from somewhere upstairs came wives and daughters bearing bowls of rice, yogurt, and a spicy lentil dish. 'Don't you have homes?' I asked a girl as she served my meal. Madhav answered for her: Yes, but they found security in numbers, and the constabulary remained a symbol of power in the city. One constable always stood at the window or door, rifle ready.

'It is important that rightful power be restored in Delhi soon,' he continued. 'For Jaipur this situation has been very terrible, and I do not mean only the attempt to strip us of authority.'

I ate with them, enduring their discussion. They spoke enthusiastically of the beating of Vasant and others necessitated by the crisis. The constables were renowned for their thrashings, I inferred, and later I would hear stories of their most celebrated attacks on suspect individuals. They showed me a newsletter they published, composed entirely of illustrations (I doubted any of these men bothered with the old art of writing) that depicted recent beatings and none-too-subtle hints that the reader should watch his step or risk finding his own case so documented.

Talk centered on the capital. Part of their anger at Delhi, I realized, stemmed from the fact that they had been expected to take orders from the First Wife. A woman. A woman who to their thinking should have spent her final day standing amid the flames of her husband's funeral pyre. The situation was an affront to both politics and Hinduism, they argued, while around them women cleared the dishes, changed the dressing on Vasant's wounds, field-stripped rifles, and performed the daily rituals. I did not point out that this constabulary could probably not function without women; saying so would make no difference. I also refrained from participating in the dour speculation about what lay ahead for India and those heretics who had steered her into chaos.

'But should we prepare for war?' one constable asked soberly. 'Will there be open conflict between her supporters and her detractors?'

Madhav shook his head. 'The Baboon Warrior won't allow war.'

I bristled.

'How could he prevent it?' someone asked. 'Even the Baboon can't be in a thousand places at once.'

I stepped back, trying to remove myself discreetly. Madhav noticed. 'Rakesh!' He tilted his cup at me. 'Don't you take an interest in politics?'

'No.'

'You must have an opinion!'

'I do not.'

'What about the Baboon Warrior? Do you think he could stop war from erupting?'

I looked at their interested faces. Some police officials, I recalled, regarded the Baboon as the ultimate enforcer of law. These men wanted to hear me say something to fit that image of him.

'He won't make any difference,' I replied.

'No? Why not?'

'Because I'm going to kill him.'

The constables burst into laughter. All of them laughed; even the women seemed to feel permitted. I sipped my chai. Guffaws were hearty, and the mirth lasted for several minutes. Then the laughter tapered off. They could see from my stony expression that I wasn't joking, and humor turned to puzzlement. Some looked away. 'Did he say *kill the Baboon Warrior . . .?*' An awkward snigger. 'The Baboon saved my son's life!'

Madhav, mercifully, changed the subject, and I received no further invitations into conversation.

Nobody complained, later, when I stepped outside, but the constable standing sentry raised his rifle to my chest.

'We avoid venturing out alone at night. Where do you wish to go? I'll have someone escort you.'

'No escorts.'

'You might be ambushed.'

'They would regret it.'

Whoever we were talking about wouldn't harm me. *Couldn't.* A feeling of invulnerability enshrouded me. My dharma provided the smugness of a cow. Camels stamped their feet as I passed by, perhaps adding their disapproval.

The constables had holed up in their former jail, but that meager luxury was unavailable to the remainder of the population. Fires burned in barrels, and I could see faces as far as the glow carried, and heard bodies farther and farther into darkness. Untouchables mostly. The faces nearest the flames looked guileless and benign. Others wore smirks that might have been the product of the flickering light. I had the distinct feeling that people watched where I was going, but when I turned, they receded in shadow. An amputee hopped down a flight of stairs.

I headed for a blue glow. Another Kama Sutran filmee played here in Jaipur, in the terminus of a blind alley: naked bodies bending in right angles over brick walls and the road. It was the same type of projector creating the display, decorated with Kama and stylized peacocks, its power supplied by a man pedaling a connected unit, as if he rode a stationary bicycle. The audience sat wherever space allowed another filthy bottom: children, grandfathers, lepers, businessmen. As I stepped through, they leaned to maintain their view of the images. I could see no one who was obviously a Kama Sutran. The man pedaling or someone from the audience could load another cylinder onto the machine's spindle whenever one filmee flickered to its end, I supposed, and load the lamps with ghee fuel. They stared, rapt.

'Who's in charge?' I asked.

'Quiet! Don't spoil it!'

'Who gives you these filmees?'

Nobody would answer, so I stood in the way until one raised an arm to point. West.

Businesses had nailed planks across windows and doors. Chinks between the planks made a slanted and narrow thing of the light within, and sometimes forms blocked the light to look at who dared walk past. People considered shooting me: I smelled that impulse, and an incense like hair and sugar. Flakes fell on the city as thousands of families burned fires of unrefined dung; I could feel ash on my bare scalp, see the flux turning through lamplight.

I passed a dozen bodies of people killed in conflicts before I came to an impromptu wrestling match that blocked the street. There was much shouting, much jostling; the combatants grunted and fidgeted across the ring of chalk, their four legs rising into a twined mass of exertion, sweat, excruciating labor. They didn't so much wrestle as slap each other and adjust their grips, and even minute adjustments sent ripples of appreciation through the crowd. The crowd was hungry. Fights were waiting to happen all around them. Here they could pour energy into a tangible contest simply by tossing a few rupees in the wager pot. I watched the larger of the two wrestlers, a man massive enough to be a professional thug, win abrupt advantage in the match; he hauled his opponent upside down and dropped to his knees, driving the man's head against pavement. A crack cut through the fervor of the crowd, and frenzied appreciation changed to cold horror. The wrestler must have known it, he must have felt it in his arms, and he released the broken body. The dead man flopped over, neck crooked, his homemade wrestling tights looking suddenly absurd. The crowd disintegrated row by row, dissolved like a heap of rats discovered by torch. Soon the wrestler stood alone, arms raised and bellowing with triumph. A train shuddered overhead, and the noise of engines and rattling grain cars seemed to issue from the killer's mouth. Faces were pressed to smudged windows of the train; silhouettes clung to the exterior and briefly flashed into people staring down. Did they look on me too and wonder how I figured in the killing?

'You want to wrestle?' the victor shouted. 'You think you can beat me?'

I pretended not to hear.

Trains ran elevated through the city, straight through buildings, stopping on second floors of apartment blocks, banks, warehouses, special tall temples of modern design. The weight of an approaching train on the tracks would open the gateways of these buildings, making temporary tunnels through them. Jaipur bore evidence of civic development – the train, the wide avenues, the walkways spanning the street so higher castes could cross without worrying about traffic – but as I continued west, I saw that one of the walkways was toppled, brought down whole. Blocks of stone sat on the road, and mortar, symptoms of a city in turmoil. The odd bicycle rickshaw drifted down the street, dusty domes bearing a shadowy iris of the operator, and they slowed to navigate archipelagoes of debris. White light sometimes cracked the street, and I realized that the rickshaws were responsible, their operators having rigged devices that converted pedaled energy into a more hostile form, zapping rival rickshaws with a bolt of something like lightning, jagged in the blackness.

I passed from an area so overcrowded as to be functionally paralyzed into a neighborhood that equaled the constable faction in organization. WE SUPPORT HER read an amateurish banner draped from a domed roof. I felt rival security. A great weight rose, a tremor, nothing in comparison to the Jagannath but something big, something walking on all fours.

An elephant.

Coming toward me, it made a *clack-clack* of component panels slapping together. It was an elephant armored in wood, or perhaps it was a wooden elephant, a divine beast built of unfathomable mechanics. I tried to see through gaps in its exterior, but inside was all black, and I could smell only pungent smoke. Even the trunk was a segmented wooden hose, extending to point at me. The architecture of the creature's torso swelled into a hump on top, forming a shack big enough to contain one midget, or someone who didn't mind crouching for hours on end. Creaking, clacking, the construction trod toward me and stopped, swaying on its stout, paneled legs. A lamp put me in a bright circle of light. I squinted.

'You don't belong here,' said a voice.

'I'm a Hindu obeying my dharma – no threat to something like you.'

'What's your opinion of the First Wife?'

'I have none.'

'Well, you can't enter this part of Jaipur without an opinion. This is not a place for strangers. Turn back. Back! Stay in the middle!'

I gambled. 'I came hoping to find Kama Sutrans.'

Silence.

'If I could find any in this city.' Was I speaking to someone inside the little dwelling on top? Or the elephant itself? 'It would please me very much to be among their number.'

'You're a Kama Sutran,' it said, and, unsure of its attitude toward the sect, I didn't correct this assumption.

The light clicked off. The elephant took a step in reverse, another, turning and *clack-clacking* down the road.

'Well?!' the voice shouted. 'Do you want Kama Sutrans or not?' I hurried.

'It would easily catch fire,' I said, following behind.

'What?'

'Your body. One flaming arrow is all it would take . . .'

'My wood has been treated,' the voice replied. 'Don't ask more questions.'

However surly my elephantine accompaniment, I was glad to have it. Teenagers sat on roofs, with pitchforks. The pitchforks had been painted in what I took to be faction colors. They eyed me, the teens. They might have gotten skilled, over the past week, at throwing those implements; they looked hopeful for an opportunity to try. Whatever their skill level, they would have made an unpleasant gauntlet, but with my sizable escort the teens limited themselves to contemptuous stares, and as we walked down the middle of the street, bulbous rickshaws drifted far to either side to get past the lumbering behemoth.

'Down there,' it said, lifting its trunk. I followed the straightened length of wood segments to see steps that led below ground. A diamond-shaped window was inset in the door, yellow light pulsing behind.

'Do I knock?'

'How should I know?' replied the elephant.

It plodded on. Dung dropped from a portal in its torso, and I was unsure whether this was waste or wasted fuel. Dung tradesmen materialized from the shadows and removed it from view. I stepped down dirt stairs. The yellow diamond was face-level, but, looking through, I saw only color.

I pushed the door open.

Inside, they slept. Three, four, five of them. A trio was curled together on bolsters in the corner. A young woman slept against a drowsy cow with a yellow champac flower behind one ear. Incense burned, insufficiently masking the odor of bhang. Quietly I shut the door behind me. The room was immersed in sticky yellow glow emanating from a globe in the center. A slow pulse in the light made everything seem to swell and recede, giving the room an underwater quality, as if maneuvering here required more effort than outside, my body rippling through some indefinable medium. For members of a persecuted sect, they were certainly lax in security. But they were lovers. Kama Sutrans had difficulty mustering resistance even when intolerance became pogroms.

Dried and shredded bhang sat in mortars labeled Northern, Southern, and Kashmiri; true aficionados were as particular as tea drinkers about the origins and curing of the plant. The bhang delivery system was a blown-glass affair half as tall as I was and shaped like a buxom woman, whose body consisted of various chambers for burning the intoxicant, and hoses that ran to handcrafted masks so participants could share smoke. I turned off the flame between her legs, hoping to reduce the odor, which was affecting my stomach, my head, my fingers. I circled the room, stepping carefully over Kama Sutrans, who seemed to increase in number the more I walked.

I found the forbidden book.

I recalled the story I had told Vasant, about my last days of boyhood. How when my wedding day approached, my uncle slept in my room and promised to read something to help prepare me for married life.

The edition of the *Kama Sutra* I found here shamed the faded softcover my uncle had fallen asleep with. This edition was big, with a mahogany cover carved with motifs of the lotus, the yoni, the lingam, and it was a pleasure, I discovered, to lift. The text was handwritten, the illustrations meticulous and explicit. The pages were interspersed with special images composed of translucent panels. One such panel depicted lovers Splitting the Bamboo, and when I shifted the page, the man leaned forward against the raised leg of his partner, and she tossed her head back. Kama Sutrans knew how to manipulate imagery. These panels were like minifilmees packed into the book. I opened randomly to a page listing the Eight Bites of Love. The Hidden Bite, the Line of Points, the Coral and the Jewel.

The Bite of the Boar is for marking the shoulder. It consists of many broad rows of points close to one another, with red intervals. These are to be impressed on breasts and shoulders, at the summit of passion.

I found my fingertip at my teeth. I'd never imagined erotic uses for them . . .

But why would I? I would never need such information, however intriguing. Sex was insignificant compared to the urge from my chakras, the need to fulfill my holy purpose. Nonetheless the book drew me in, first with the picture panels then gradually with the text. I found a recipe to make a man's ejaculate black as licorice paste. I flipped through Hair Play and the Ritualized Blows of Love, amazed by how imaginatively Kama Sutrans interpreted sex, and at some point it dawned on me that every Kama Sutran, regardless of caste, must learn to read – a skill considered virtually useless by most people. The book had many thousands of words, and its binding ingeniously allowed for additional pages to be inserted. I read a warning against performing sexual acts in certain positions that would guarantee deformed children, read what Professor Kapila of Calcutta regarded as the best method of summoning chakra energy to the lower body (a sound spanking), and flipped back and forth a picture panel to see a demonstration upon a proffered ass.

'You must be Sajvit.'

The woman on the cow had spoken. Now the cow was asleep and the woman's eyes open. She looked too relaxed to move. She blinked slowly. 'You must be Sajvit.'

'I must.'

'Don't look away,' she said. 'Your eyes are welcome to me. Come closer.'

'The door was unlocked.'

'We like it that way.'

'What about trespassers? Fanatics?'

'We've never had problems in Jaipur . . .'

'How fortunate.'

'Our time is coming.'

I nodded as if I understood.

'Closer.'

She studied me, frowned, smiled. 'You're a virgin . . .?' she guessed. 'Peculiar, for a Kama Sutran.'

'I'm more a reader,' I told her, nodding to the book.

'Of course.'

'I have questions.'

She laughed through her smile. Her torpor bordered on sleep.

'May I ask you some questions?'

She stared at me as if I were an open and explicit book.

'In Delhi,' I said, 'there was a Kama Sutran part male, part female.'

'Symantaka?' she replied. 'Gender follows the cycle of the moon, for Symantaka. You must have met during the first or last quarter.'

'She or he – '

'She *and* he.'

' – has struck bargains with certain royal personalities.'

'Symantaka has a way.'

'So he/she did make a deal?'

She laughed, louder. '*Melles bridda mon seka.*'

I was puzzled for a moment before realizing why the gibberish sounded familiar. Code. Of course. I shook my head and took a step toward the door. She knew I didn't belong here.

'Wait,' she said. 'I'll tell you what Symantaka is doing in Delhi. Come back. Please?'

I returned. The oscillating glow, the smell of bhang. My balance, wrong.

'Who are you . . .?' she said.

'Will you remember in the morning?'

'I suppose not.'

'Just an obedient Hindu,' I said. 'Nobody, really. Just someone who is doing what Kali asked him to do.'

'I'll tell you what deals have been done.'

'Yes – tell me.'

'Not so quickly, not so quickly.' She stretched, shut her eyes for a moment. 'Important to go slowly,' she said. 'Build up to it.'

'Okay.'

'You have to do something first. For me.'

'What?'

'Just one thing . . .'

'Tell me.'

She shifted, put her head to one side and shook her hair so it draped her face. She raised her shoulder, a perfect apple of brown flesh, and when I stepped closer, I could see downy hairs, I could smell her skin, and the perfume that was poured into her last bath – camphor.

'What do you want me to do?' I said, looking at the flawless skin.

'I want the Boar,' she replied. 'The Bite of the Boar.'

A BATTLE
BETWEEN SPICES

❦

CONSTABLE MADHAV LAY sprawled, looking up at me with surprise. I found myself holding his riding crop.

'Forgive me,' I said.

Presumably he'd been poking me while I slept, and I had disarmed him, put him on the ground. I wasn't certain of this, but he seemed to expect an apology. I helped him to his feet and offered the crop, which he snatched back, still eyeing me.

'Did you wake me for a reason?' I said.

It was early; not nearly warm enough to rouse junior constables and their families, who continued purring in cots nearby. The constabulary smelled as if many bodies had been sharing the space for too long. Madhav wore only his dhoti and sacred thread, which exposed his chest and what it meant to be Kshatriya: the old bullet wounds, slashes, scars of a devout fighter. He puffed himself up. I apologized again for the flinches in my sleep, blaming them on dreams of persecution.

'You returned late last night,' he said. 'You went out, against our advice.'

'I wished to experience for myself Jaipur.'

'And does the situation differ from what we described?'

'Perhaps it's worse.'

He looked around the room, scratched his chin. He stared at a nearby cot, where a boy slept.

'Almost the same age as our child,' Madhav said.

'Boy or girl?'

'A boy.'

'Very nice for you.'

He agreed. Then he leaned closer, motioning for me to do the same. 'Many of my fellow constables know already,' he said.

'Know what?'

'The secret I'm going to tell you.'

'Why tell me a secret?'

'You don't seem inclined to share your knowledge. You're . . . reserved.'

'I make no guarantees.'

'Rakesh,' he said. 'My son is adopted.'

'Oh.'

'Despite our appeals to Shiva, my wife could not produce a son. Because of her barrenness, we were forced to hire an adoption broker.'

I wondered if his wife had faked a pregnancy before they brought the baby home; it would have been important to maintain appearances, especially for a Kshatriya officer of the law. Nobody gave up sons for adoption – not willingly. And only someone desperate to see his name carried on would associate himself with the malefactors who made children available.

'We paid a very high fee,' said Madhav. 'Because they guaranteed us a boy of Kshatriya caste. What use was a child, if not our caste? It was the essence of our desire for a son.'

'I see.'

'Difficult to call him our son if he wasn't Kshatriya . . .'

I asked, 'How did you find out the truth?'

He was quiet for a moment. 'My wife suspected. She claimed she could smell the difference. We took him to a rishi in Delhi, and the rishi confirmed our worst fears. An untouchable! Can you imagine our dismay? We'd been defrauded. Polluted! We'd taken an untouchable into our family. An untouchable had lain his head at my wife's breast!' He looked at the floor.

'I suppose you could have made him . . . available for adoption.'

'Yes, we considered that. But do you know? We loved the boy. We considered him ours. Despite better judgment, we couldn't give him up.'

And the brokers had no doubt fled Jaipur with the couple's money. But this I didn't mention.

'We raise him as Kshatriya. He will not know any different. Nobody will know the truth.'

'Madhav,' I said, confused. 'Why are you telling me this?'

'Because I asked your companion about you. He said you believe it is your holy duty to kill the Baboon Warrior. To kill the beloved hero! So I want to do you this favor. I am telling you, beliefs are not set in stone. You can resist. You can choose another life.'

'This you believe?'

'I know from experience.'

'Well, you will know differently.'

He raised an eyebrow.

'One day, your son will express an interest in feet,' I predicted. 'Perhaps he'll make a pair of shoes, even though he's never seen it done before. Or maybe he'll feel compelled to clean floors.'

Madhav darkened.

'One way or another,' I continued, 'his true nature will make itself known. Nothing you do can change it. Just as nothing you say can change me. Your son was born an untouchable. He will live an untouchable life. You're a fool to convince yourself it might be any other way.'

His eyes narrowed, and he smacked the riding crop against his palm.

'What will you tell your son,' I asked him, 'when he wonders why he is compelled to service the feet? Or tend dead bodies? Or work with leather? He will suffer for your charade. As will you.'

He didn't respond.

I suspected Madhav had little interest in doing me a favor. Rather, he wanted to share his secret and hear me agree with his decision. He wanted affirmation from an outsider. I couldn't give it to him, and this made him angry and scared. He stood abruptly and stomped to the stairs, at the last minute whirling to make a prediction of his own:

'Someone who thinks he will kill the Baboon Warrior isn't long for this life.'

'Maybe so.'

And with this pronouncement, my second day in Jaipur began.

Because mine was a Vaisya caste, the constables had given me a cot away from the rest of them, near the toilets, whereas Vasant, a Kshatriya like them and a respected holder of power, had been given the fanciest of the meager beds and was located among them. I walked past the sleeping constables to where I'd seen him last night, but his cot was empty. I dressed silently and left.

Most of the city remained asleep, but some color leaked into the morning streets – cucumber green, copper, vermilion – as women in saris came outside. The older parts of the city were pink or coral, faded with sunlight but still lustrous. Hindi chatter rose, sacred mutterings occasionally overpowered by the noise of trains complaining against the tracks or lorries packed with bodies. Rat traps lay uncollected, and the rats screeched, some thrashing so violently that their cages bounced off the ground. I saw one cage go hopping down an alley, the rodent within making a valiant attempt at escape before the municipal workers came around with their slingshots. I wondered if the rat catchers were loyal to the First Wife; perhaps they would not work today.

Increasing numbers of people clogged the street, in increasing states of undress. Splashing dappled the chatter, and the street became an open-air bath. Crowds stood, waiting for turns in a pool filled with slick brown bodies. I walked along one side of the pool, thinking that if I fell, I would probably not even touch water, it was so full. Children bathed in a fountain, water burbling from a stone elephant head. I cupped my hands, rinsed my mouth, spat.

Bathers converged from all directions, some wearing opposing faction colors but ignoring one another while they stood in line. The bath was separate from the dispute.

I passed an ancient astrological machine consisting of squat granite buildings that also served as home to the astrologers. From an adjacent dung-brick manufacturer lorries departed with loads of standardized bricks, the colors varying with the fuel's grade. From there, I found the jasmine factory I'd spotted yesterday: a series of statues running through the neighborhood, several gods represented in the line of production, in different poses, their jointed arms extended to nearby build-jyings. Various stages of manufacture occurred in heads or torsos. A window in the belly of one Shiva revealed heaving shoulders of women as flower heads dropped into a vast cauldron and a pestle churned and turned to mash them. Some of the men or women glanced out at me from these figural structures, their faces masked with incense.

The final product ran from Shiva's open hands to awaiting bags, and here Vasant worshiped, sitting in the lotus position. Humped nearby was an untouchable, wiping down the massive brass feet of the statue. Vasant's eyes were closed, and I didn't want to disturb his meditations. Bruises from the beating darkened his face, but his suit was immaculate: one of the wives must have cleaned it. I placed my right hand on the statue and made silent prayer for what I always prayed for. Vasant's eyes found me, narrowed. I licked my lips.

'My strength has returned,' he said. 'Praise Shiva.'

'And the constable's wives.'

He shrugged.

'Repairing the damage done by their husbands.'

'I forgive Madhav,' he said. 'He acted on his best judgment.'

'He thinks the First Wife murdered the Sovereign to seize power.'

'An unfortunate assumption. I will prove her innocence.'

A dove flew from the assembly line, flapping incense.

'You're very loyal to the First Wife,' I said. 'I suppose she's more correctly called the First Widow, now.'

'I'm privileged to know her personally. People like you do not understand. I've had many years in the Palace to see what a fine – ' He looked at me. 'Stop doing that.'

'Stop doing what?'

'You keep licking your lips.'

'I tasted an unusual dish last night . . .' I explained. 'The flavor persists.'

'It's distracting. As I was saying: those of us who have worked in the Palace have a better appreciation of the machinations within. I assure you, the First Wife is innocent of wrongdoing.'

'You're fooling yourself.'

'I beg your pardon?'

'Last night I spoke to a Kama Sutran, and she revealed some of what has happened in Delhi: the First Wife guaranteed freedom to their sect. Royal sanction. It will soon be made a crime to persecute a Kama Sutran.'

Vasant's expression changed, reminding me of the killer wrestler. 'You make too many poisonous statements,' he said. 'They will come back to you. Karma! Every hateful word will manifest itself as a sore on your lips. And when I'm restored in Delhi, I'll arrange for your arrest. You've given me no choice!'

'You feel obliged to protect her,' I continued, 'because your commitment is not only political.'

'Bastard!'

'You didn't tell me everything about your relationship.'

He would have sprung at me had I not put my index finger on the center of his head. For all his efforts, Vasant could not rise from the ground. He struggled and shifted, he glowered up at me, but my finger remained in place and he remained sitting on the ground. The untouchable lifted his head and shuffled to another pair of Shiva's feet. I waited for Vasant to wear himself out, cool down. When he stopped swinging and cursing, I removed the finger, even tried to help him up, but he slapped away my hand.

'Do you exist to hound me?'

'I told you why I exist.'

'Then stop following me! Leave me alone! I don't want to hear your crackpot ideas about the Baboon Warrior or insinuations about me and the First Widow! I'm none of your concern, and you are none of mine! So go! Stop attaching yourself!'

'But you matter to my task . . .'

'Pah!'

I let him storm away, sensing he wanted time to himself. The street absorbed him, one more pixel of color. I circled Shiva with another request for a moment of weakness in the Baboon, then headed in a direction different from the one I'd come in.

Rat traps continued hopping and shrieking. The catchers probably wouldn't make their rounds. I entered a bazaar, the kind where women sold figurines of the Baboon Warrior made of clay or cloth; sometimes, if a figurine showed talent, I would buy the toy and attempt to eat it. I moved from stall to stall, idly.

A constable moved through the crowd, both he and his camel eyeing people suspiciously. The criminal element was capitalizing on local turmoil in government. A thief soon marked me and made fruitless attempts to dig into my pocket. A boy, ten or eleven. He made several passes, but each time he approached, I would change the rhythm of my steps, throwing off his timing. By the fourth or fifth attempt he was laughing at his inability. I stopped abruptly. He knocked against me, and I whirled. He laughed aloud; a game. He clapped a hand over his mouth and ran. I had pulled a coin from my pocket for his efforts, but the instinct to flee seized him, and he darted through pedestrians, between somebody's legs, under a stall. I would have given him no further thought had I not noticed the rope sewn to his pants.

A rope stiffened with wire. Like a tail.

Inside me, a change in temperature; I saw my fire over the ocean.

This might be better than a clay figurine.

He looked back with alarm – I was pursuing. I waved the coin, hoping to convince him to stop, but he ran faster, demonstrating lurid agility as he sprang over tables and slid between the wheels of a moving bullock cart. The tail seemed justified. His leaps didn't interrupt his strides, and if not charged with my dharma, I would have lost him. Instead it was the chase of his life. When he looked back at me, he grimaced with fear. I was grinning, and that couldn't have reassured him, as I easily cleared the bullock cart.

Coming faster.

Someone stepped on his tail, slowing him down. The crowd parted, anticipating me. We ran through the periphery of the market, with colored swaths of bystanders blurring past. The boy remained in focus. He turned down an alley impossibly dark for so early in the day: less an alley than a crack between tall brick buildings. The walls were black with grime, adding to the shadow. The boy sprang over a bank of trash. I ran through it, sending papers flying and old boxes bursting. The crack narrowed more. Overhead shone a seam of light, but the alley was a deep trough.

The boy chittered, leaped sideways. He knocked through a geometrical opening. I skidded, thrust my hand after him, groping for his tail. Inside I heard legs kicking, and he was too fast, climbing some inner shaft. I stepped back, appraised the structure.

Regained control of my breathing.

Standing between steep walls felt peculiar. In the dark, but with sunlight far overhead. It was like being among high trees, except there were no trees in the city. Ropes, swaying . . .

Something fluttered down.

My skin tingled. I may have lost the boy, but –

I walked a little farther and, craning my neck, saw them sitting on platforms, fire escapes, niches and nooks. Like the boy, they had ersatz tails attached to their posteriors. The tails of the adults hung all the way from their perches forty or fifty feet above to piles on the ground. The alley was draped in false appendages. One male hung by his tail and swung gently. All wore makeup; faces were painted black, and ruffs of brown hair were tied around heads.

'How would you like it if we chased *your* young?'

I said, 'I wasn't chasing your young.'

'Oh? Not chasing our young? Are you here, then, to pay homage?'

'You mean, to the Baboon Warrior?'

'Of course to the Baboon Warrior.'

'You're a sect?'

The one hanging upside down rappelled without using his hands. 'Much good he does for India. We are grateful. We express gratitude. We have no temple but worship in our way.'

'The Baboon Warrior is not a god,' I said.

'The Baboon Warrior is not a god,' the man repeated. 'He is more.'

'You send children to steal money. Collect donations. So you can spread the word, maybe someday build a shrine?'

'Maybe a shrine. Maybe a very big tree is good enough.'

'A big tree?'

'Nainpur big.'

Nainpur. I'd heard that place mentioned before in connection with the Baboon.

'Tell me,' I said, tingling, 'where could I find the Baboon Warrior? If I wanted to meet him for myself? Would I find him in Nainpur?'

The devotee started to answer, but shrieks from above interrupted. A figure leaped across the alley, her tail seeming to stitch the sunlight, her chatter verging on language, and she arrested her motion at a window ledge. She raised a painted-black hand to point at me.

'Don't trust him,' she said. 'I don't.'

'Mind yourself,' replied the other. He rose at the

waist and climbed his tail to her level. 'Mind your manners.'

'He makes my flesh crawl. He wants something from us. He makes me nervous. He's dangerous.'

'Mind your manners!' the other scolded. 'He's curious. He wants to know more about the Baboon. He is a fan.'

'He's dangerous.'

'Your manners!'

Male swatted female, and she sprang, grappling his torso with all four limbs. They swung back and forth and found ways to bat each other, shrieking madly, and pieces of something – fake fur? – floated to the ground. Others dove across the alley to get closer to the fray, then retreated: a chain of nonsense traced by long fabric tails. Some displayed teeth in ritualized fashion. Another fight erupted, someone biting someone else's shoulder spontaneously. Howls and hoots spread, like madness.

'Stop!' I shouted. 'Stop!'

They continued.

'She's right to be nervous! She is right!'

The pair stopped swinging, but chatter continued for another minute or so.

'I am a threat to you,' I said.

They stared at me, silent.

'I'm a threat to your monkey,' I admitted. 'I appreciate your time and honesty, and wish you luck in your efforts to honor him. Because he won't be alive much longer.'

I started to walk away but remembered my coin.

'And here! Something to get you closer to the first brick in that shrine.'

I tossed it up into the light. I turned and walked down the alley. One of them must have caught the rupee, because I didn't hear it land.

I decided to drink an entire pot of tea in order not to return to the constabulary too soon. First, however, a bath. Jaipur generated a heat different from what we'd experienced in open country, a city heat that had human dimensions, contributions of the bloodstream, irate foreheads, clasped hands, urine hitting a stone surface. The body was a vessel of the soul, I told myself. Temperature had no effect on my dharma; I tried convincing myself that the sweat rolling off me was merely a by-product of actions and efforts that took me closer to my holy murder. But walking, I found myself at the public bath, and removed my shirt and trousers. I stepped into the pool without waiting my turn, surrounded by wet, brown bodies of men, men, men, pushing, conversing, touching, scooping water and rubbing their faces. My soul became cleaner even if my body did not. I was lightened. This was the renewal of water: a bath in the depths of heat.

Afterward I drank my tea. As I sat watching the cityscape bleach under the sun, I tried to remember as many words as I could for hot. But soon I ran out of words and started to have visions. My arrow. Whenever I closed my eyes, whenever I blinked, there it was, burning above the ocean. I walked back to the constabulary.

'Where are we going?' I said.

Vasant didn't look at me.

He stood beside two camels that were being outfitted for a journey. One of the constables was checking their feet, and they submitted to his inspection with a professional calm.

'Time for Delhi?' I said.

Vasant turned. 'You're going nowhere. Not with me. I can no longer tolerate your company.'

I handed saddlebags to the constable and helped strap them into place, but this only irked Vasant more. He told the constable, 'He's not coming with us.' *Fine, fine*, said the man. He didn't care. He wore a red turban of a size one might have expected to topple a person so wiry. When the saddles were cinched, he made a motion with his fingers, and the camels stepped back from their posts; he gave Vasant a boost to the saddle before climbing his own. The man said something, and his camel started walking down the street, nudging pedestrians aside with its head. Vasant's camel followed.

'You won't be able to follow us in this heat,' Vasant informed me, looking back. 'Not even you.'

'Maybe not.'

'You are a deluded young man,' he continued. 'Dangerous to yourself and others. Don't you realize it? Don't you know how crazy you are? I can't allow you to jeopardize my restoration of the First Widow. Stay where you are! Stop following us!'

'Vasant,' I said, 'I can help you. And afterward, you'll help me to – '

A wail cut me off. I doubt the constable would have paused if the sound hadn't issued from the constabulary, but he stopped and looked over his shoulder, stroking the white tails of his mustache. The wailing repeated, protracted.

'Back,' he instructed his camel, 'back home,' but he told Vasant's mount to stay where it was. Vasant exhaled pointedly, but the man rode back to the building all the same. I followed him as other wails joined the first, the voices of women when a great tragedy befalls.

Inside, a swirl of despair, hands thrown up, people weeping, women consoling women. Some of the constables were shouting. I was pressed against the flank of a camel and struggled for a better view. From upstairs came the woman; I recognized her cry, which continued as she walked into view. Her sari was streaked with blood, and the sight triggered another gush of sound and emotion from the others. I touched the shoulder of one of the more rational constables.

'What happened?'

'There's been a murder. A child is dead.'

My throat constricted. 'Madhav's son . . .?'

His eyes flared. 'Yes,' he said, 'Madhav's son.'

I watched the woman descend into the embrace of sisters, aunts.

'How did you know?' said the constable, turning toward me.

I pretended not to hear.

'How did you know it was Madhav's son?!'

'A guess.'

'Where have you been today?' He poked my chest. 'Who have you been with?'

'You're getting the wrong idea.'

'You and the Engineer were the only strangers here,' he said, and I could see the Kshatriya in him coming to the surface as reason left proportionately. 'You and the Delhicrat.' His eyes changed size.

'I'm not responsible for what happened here,' I told him. 'Neither is Vasant.'

The tenor of the grief changed – Madhav appeared

at the top of the steps. He looked jangled, frightened. I hoped to meet his gaze, but he didn't notice me in the crowd. He held a knife in one hand. Blood inked the blade. He raised it for all to see. The handle was daubed with green, purple, orange. A roar erupted from the constables: I'd seen this same combination of colors last night, decorating pitchforks in opposing neighborhoods. The implication sent the crowd into paroxysm. The constable who'd been poking me lurched toward the armory, forgetting me instantly. The involvement of an enemy made too much sense. I was pushed aside as constables headed for the stable. Others handed weapons through the window. Parts of a gun I did not recognize, its barrel the size of a cannon yet made of wood.

I studied the figure at the top of the stairway. Madhav didn't look my way; he was looking at the knife in his hand. Then he turned without further display, retreating into the upper bedrooms.

I felt tempted to follow him, but activity quickly shifted out the doors. The crowd drained from the building and hurriedly mounted camels, who stepped into formation. Pedestrians emptied the street, seeing what was happening. A mother picked up her child and ran into a brothel. Camels brayed. They knew too.

At once they were moving, filing down the street, some of the constables holding rifles high while others assembled those cannons of bamboo. Wives joined them, getting onto a wagon now pulled from wraps by three more camels.

Bystanders thickened the troop, making it bigger, noisier; without the epithets and vows of vengeance, it might have been a festival procession. I struggled in the flow, trying to reach Vasant. His camel had noted the shift in mood and was trotting ahead to find a place in formation. The Engineer cursed the beast, kicked its ribs, but there was no dissuading it from joining the advance. I pushed and shoved through hooting pedestrians.

Ahead, wooden ramparts rumbled down the road and swung together to block the way, elephant labor driving them into place and locking them shut with the force of their steps. The opposition. An equally large and noisy group surged behind this mobile barrier, waving colors of loyalty to the First Widow. The blockade was several meters tall, and paneled coverings rattled open to reveal large fans. Their wooden blades started to rotate, slowly at first, then faster as the men supplying power pedaled madly. The fans became circular whirs. I felt the breeze.

As the constables marched into this artificial wind, their adversaries emptied sacks into the fans. A fine red dust carried quickly into our number. I smacked my lips. Threads of color became ropes, and a haze thickened around us. The street was abruptly flavored.

My eyes watered. A camel sneezed explosively. People paused to wipe their eyes. Somewhere, a child started crying.

Hot pepper succeeded in breaking the ranks; the constables complained, averted their eyes, and people and animals turned from the stinging wind, but turned in opposite directions, so nobody got anywhere. The redness accumulated, everything tainted by pepper. It hovered in a cloud at my chest, and I could see more sacks being passed to the fans, and more wind machines rising into position.

'Terrible! Terrible!' a man kept shouting, with one hand clapped over his eyes as he pushed people aside. 'Terrible! Terrible!'

The constables responded suitably. Standing on the wagon, they cranked around their bamboo cannons to fire tumbling yellow wads into the sky, which burst over the enemy in bright yellow explosions. One such gun went off nearby and sprayed me with tracery: turmeric. Not a turmeric anyone would willingly ingest but something cultivated in the spirit of wickedness, something to bombard the lining of the mouth and make me wish I'd been born without a tongue. The constables launched these volleys over the ramparts, and buds of yellow became grotesque flowers as shrieks issued from the other side. Someone operating a fan tried in vain to expel the turmeric but only dispersed it, then I lost sight of what was happening as spice suffused the area, with more pops from one side and more red bags emptied on the other, the haze insufferable.

Red silt screened my vision, and people collided with me in their effort to get away. My lungs burned; I spat repeatedly. Others gagged, retched. A camel sneezed, and I felt gluey phlegm on my neck. Then the first gunshot split the disorder.

Which side fired, I do not know, but the reaction spread like a crack through glass. Guns went up and shots rang out and the camels wheeled wildly. In the colored haze, the constables were as likely to shoot one another as their enemy. Still it thickened.

I wiped my eyes and caught a glimpse of faction troops emerging from the ramparts, wearing goggles and handcrafted masks connected to some sputtering machine they wheeled between them. On their shoulders they rested pitchforks with special grips.

I struggled through the coughing, the blind shoving. Someone slumped against me following a gunshot. I reached Vasant's camel. He sat atop and, although he looked down, I don't think he saw me, red tears running over his cheeks – as if he were crying blood – and the camel batted its long lashes laden with pepper. I grabbed the ring in its nostril and yanked. The animal was willing to turn away from the irritant.

People shrieked. I heard wet sounds I could only guess were pitchfork tines thrust in and out of meat. Gunshots battered my ears, and the elephants trumpeted with distress. The flavor was unbearable, and when I tried to deaden my tongue, my eyes seemed to compensate. I saw people with gummy red mucus hanging from their nostrils, red streams running from their eyes.

'Where are you going?' Vasant demanded. 'Where are you taking me?' Presumably he spoke to the camel. I was almost as blind as he, my eyes heavily spiced, so I let my dharma guide me, silent through the uproar, and led his camel out of the savory riot of Jaipur.

THE BUDDHA REMOVED
FROM HIS LOTUS THRONE

◆━●══●━◆

VASANT AND I walked through barren hills, I laden
with saddlebags from the camel's back and he stopping
often to wipe his eyes. We'd attempted to ride the
camel but found it increasingly uncooperative; it would
constantly look back at Jaipur with a snort, stamp a
hoof, and despite repeated corrections wheel around
and trot toward the city's dusty outskirts. When finally
we dismounted and released the animal, it loped to
Jaipur as if heeding a biological imperative. 'Say what
you will about the constables,' I said. 'But they know
how to train a camel.'

Vasant did not respond to this. Occasionally he
stopped walking. He sat on the ground, lay flat, and
pointed at our flask (we had not spoken since Jaipur,
even though his vision had cleared sufficiently for him
to see I was leading the camel, and now guiding us
through trails). I uncapped the flask and doused his eyes.
He stared up at me through the water, his expression
neutral. He raised a hand when he'd had enough. Was
he planning never to speak to me again? I replaced the
stopper. He remained where he lay, his face wet.

'I told you not to follow me,' he finally said.

'True.'

'It was an order. A demand!'

'You'd still be in Jaipur. Maybe you'd be dead.'

He sighed. 'We're not moving north, are we?'

'No.'

'Why not?'

'Ranthambhore is closer. We can reach these Pragmatics much sooner than Delhi. Jaipur was too unstable, I think you'll agree, and the problem will be worse closer to the capital.'

'Are you suggesting I trust a group of amateurs with my information?'

'Think of it in this way: these people in Ranthambhore have no political power, no influence, should your code phrases reveal anything . . . sensitive.'

He sat up and stared at me with red eyes, trying, maybe, to tell whether I was a fraud or a fool. Probably he would have been relieved to learn that I had some secret motive. But I raised empty hands. No secret, no scam. What I did, I did for only one reason.

A few decrepit villages existed through the hills, but as the terrain became more difficult, they dwindled, and we found ourselves alone. We made camp early, our experience in Jaipur having worn down Vasant, who still suffered from his beating, with purple and brown bruises making him much less the noble creature. The taste of pepper stayed with me, its only recommendation that it overpowered the lingering taste of the Bite of the Boar.

During the night we spoke little, surrounded by animal sounds. We could hear noises from many miles away, so when the footsteps approached, we had ample time to squint, watching for who or what was coming.

When he entered the flickering perimeter of firelight, I relaxed and sheathed my knife.

'Are you still following us?' snapped Vasant.

The veteran didn't reply as he lurched from the bushes. He continued to wear ammunition and carry the rifle, but he'd worn through his shoes; only ragged fringes of material enclosed his feet. He marched past us, and must have felt heat from our fire, because he paused and cocked his ear, as if someone had whispered his name. Dirt covered him head to foot; it suited him; perhaps it was some addled idea of camouflage. He launched back into the dark as quickly as he'd come, the night no impediment to one linked with the stars. Gone.

'Surprising we actually won that war,' Vasant muttered. 'Now what are you doing?'

I examined the veteran's footprints and tried to step from one to the next, stretching. 'Did he seem taller than before?' I asked.

'Why don't I get my measuring tape and track him down?'

I preferred the Engineer's silence over such comments. We had stopped near a wayside shrine where he made an offering to Shiva with some of our food. Then he removed a bandage to rinse a laceration, and he made disapproving clucks as he looked at the wound.

'Overpopulation is Jaipur's problem,' he announced.

'Hm?'

'They blame government, but none of that trouble would have arisen had the city kept within its recommended population. Too many people make a city crazy. And poor. But can we tell people like you? No.

You're too fond of big families, too anxious to spawn a hundred sons.'

'My parents had only me and my sister.'

'You can't help yourselves,' Vasant continued, as if he hadn't heard. 'You can't resist the urge to breed.'

He lay back against his bedroll. 'If only India could be more chaste . . .'

He fell asleep and was quiet for about an hour before he resumed talking. In sleep, the subject was no longer chastity. He tossed from side to side. *Kavita, Kavita.* Night creatures fell silent, he called for her so loudly. These were two different people, Vasant and the sleeping Vasant. He called for her to stop whatever she did to him in dreams. Then asked her to resume. *Please, Kavita, please.* I felt that if I closed my eyes, I might find her summoned to my own subconscious.

In deference to the sun, we started walking very early the next morning. The landscape changed from barren hills to bushland, and the trail degenerated with splendor. Vegetation had toppled stone pavilions, green tendrils of ageless patience lifting slabs from place and pushing out of square the vision of long-gone architects. Old bones lay jumbled throughout. Why didn't people live here anymore? It had been a long time since we'd seen even one of the nomadic blacksmiths who wandered Rajasthan, yet the area was fertile, it supported abundant wildlife, as was evinced by a heron that startled us, flapping up from nowhere and noisily away.

Ahead, I noticed a disruption of tall grass. Or perhaps I smelled the danger first: bad breath, animal musk. Vasant put a hand on my arm, halting, and the disruption became a mass of stripes. Orange and black, orange and black. The bush parted as the tiger stepped into view.

Its face opened to a maw of teeth and a roar that shook me. I felt it. The murderous, remorseless snarl explained how a lush wilderness could go uninhabited. It snarled again, regarded us with malice. Vasant was paralyzed, and I doubted that any movement could save us. But I also knew I hadn't come so close to Ranthambhore only to be mauled. The tiger advanced. Vasant made a wilting noise. It pushed between us.

We felt its musculature briefly as it brushed against our legs. The feline proceeded down the path, its interests lying elsewhere, and it disappeared in another anomaly of stripes and high grass.

Vasant and I stood speechless. We resumed walking. The natural order of things did not demand, for now, that we fill a carnivore's belly, but to speak of our amnesty seemed unwise, as if it might be vulnerable to spoken words, so we only exchanged a look and hurried on.

Ranthambhore, as anticipated from our conversations with citizens of Jaipur, opened to lakes and rivers set among steep crags. Several times Vasant and I paused to gaze at water ablaze with sunshine, but, still shaken by our encounter, we did not remark on the beauty of these vistas. We kept trekking along the path, past more toppled buildings, and I wondered if we would know the home of the Pragmatics when we saw it.

We did.

The top of one mountainous crag had been sculpted: the peak was a fortress, carved directly from rock. It had high, crenellated walls, the same color as nearby crags, and a turret extended from each corner. Below, a path circumambulated the base and wound to a single gated entrance. We hurried over and started up, energized by the knowledge we'd found the Pragmatics.

The climb was long, half in direct sunlight. We passed a lotus hewn from stone, tall as me, which I recognized as the throne of Vishnu, although here Vishnu was conspicuously absent.

Sweat rolled off us as we rounded the last bend and the first turret came into sight. We were near the fortress, but our view was limited, since the path hugged the wall. I had given up craning my neck to find signs of life in the squared rock.

A brief whistle, a *thwap*, and I stumbled. I could not lift my right foot. I pulled, but my shoe seemed glued to the ground.

'What's the problem?'

I was about to suggest a theory when I heard another whistle, equally succinct, another *thwap*, and my other foot was fixed in place. I would have fallen forward had I not been so expertly nailed. Vasant bent to look at the bolts pinning me in place.

'Arrows,' I said.

'Through your feet?'

Not quite. On each foot, an arrow had struck the indentation between my big toe and the next. I felt the shaft, but it was my sandals nailed to the ground, not my flesh. How the marksman could have successfully landed such a shot – *twice* – I couldn't fathom. We were a considerable distance from the turret where he presumably stood; such aim was supernatural. I could see in Vasant's face that he was arriving at the same conclusion. He stepped back slowly, then turned, scrambled, and drew three further punctures of the air, three further *thwaps*. He stumbled, fell, hitched to the ground by three strikes through a trouser leg. The Engineer looked at his predicament and yelped. Then he began madly untying his pants.

'Stop,' I told him.

'Take off your shoes! We can escape!'

'If we disrobe, we give them only our bodies for targets.'

He paused, the drawstring of his pants limp in his hands. He squinted back at the turret.

'What then?'

'Wait,' I said.

'Give them more opportunity to strike us down!'

Maybe. I removed my saddlebags and put them aside. I called hello. I announced who we were, where we came from, and what service we hoped they could provide. My voice echoed against the dull rock, but a reply was not returned. No movement on the turret, no more missiles. Shadows crossed the face of the crag as the day wore on. Vasant complained that he needed to relieve himself. That these people were treating us in a discourteous and prosecutable manner. That he was too tired for this. The day faded. He fell asleep in position. I thought of the empty stone lotus.

'Vasant. Vasant!'

'Wha – ?'

'They're coming.'

They approached, a group of ten or twelve, filing through the gate and silently walking down the path. Thin and limber, they all wore saffron robes, and when they got closer, I saw that their hair was cropped short.

Vasant said it first. 'Buddhists,' he breathed. 'The Pragmatics of Ranthambhore are *Buddhists*.'

I was equally surprised. Buddhists figured in stories but in daily life were less common than benevolent tigers. Strange that the constables of Jaipur hadn't mentioned this detail; surely it would have affected their opinion of the Pragmatics, as it undoubtedly did Vasant's, who grumbled with disbelief. But when the delegation came closer, I suspected that the whole story of this order could not be summarized by the simple observation that they belonged to one of the most minor of Indian minorities.

Because some of these monks were women. And two of the women were pregnant.

'Pala will speak to you,' said a monk.

'We can come up?'

'Yes.'

They surrounded us but staggered themselves to leave avenues of opportunity for the archer on the turret; I had little doubt he could hit us, even in the diminished light. I tugged at my feet, popping them off the arrows. Vasant ripped his trousers.

'Nobody told us you were Buddhists,' he said.

'For good reason,' said a tall, slender monk. He gestured for us to walk. Someone collected our saddle-bags, and the group accompanied us in two loose cordons, nobody speaking a word. Walking beside me was one of the pregnant women, who showed no fatigue for the steep climb.

Inside, the marvel of the fortress doubled. We walked along a colonnaded corridor that ran around the peri-meter. Torches were lit, and I could see higher tiers which looked into the open middle area. Groups were scattered throughout, chatting, laughing, playing chess or sitting in lotus position, meditating. Staircases led to upper levels, and two long bridges spanned the width of the plaza – all this cut directly from the mountain. Apart from natural cracks, the fort was seamless, emphasizing the fact that we were passing not through a building but through a sculpture. We climbed one of the freestanding staircases, and from the second level I could make out figures on the turrets, silhouetted with the arcs of bows against the first stars of evening. Humans, then. I'd held on to the possibility that these Pragmatics might harbor a god who loosed arrows in their defense. But what god would defend *them*?

The walls were austere: they had brackets for lamps and boxes for flowers but little in the way of ornamentation. The only motif interrupting the gentle dimpling of chisel marks was the lotus, inscribed every meter or so along the corridor. Cells were carved into the walls, allowing tiny but comfortable homes lit by candle. The Pragmatics appeared to be excellent gardeners, as ledges spilled with nasturtium and marigold. We passed over a water reservoir, then a large garden – almost a meadow – all contained in stone, and I realized the monks must have brought up countless loads of soil to make possible the corn, potatoes, and other crops growing within. I smelled bread, and we were shown into the home of Pala.

He bent before an oven, illuminated by the glow of coals, and didn't stop looking at whatever held his attention while we filed inside. Bread – the smell of its baking was powerful. Throughout his abode candles were lit, and books lay abundant and half read. We were

invited by one of the other monks to sit while our
saddlebags were emptied and their contents scrutinized.

Pala turned with a smile. 'Vasant?' he said, pointing
at the Engineer, and 'Rakesh?' pointing at me. 'My
name is Pala. I serve as spokesman of the Pragmatics.'

He was a slight man, and the fairest-skinned Indian
I had ever seen. His complexion verged on beige, and
combined with the fineness of his features this gave
him an effeminate face. He had blue eyes — another
rarity — and long, delicate fingers. Regarding us, he
frowned, leaned forward, and took a sniff. 'You two
smell . . . spicy.'

'That's Jaipur,' I said.

'You've walked a long way. Let us eat before we
decide what to do with you.'

A rice dish was brought in, and masala dosa, an
airy crepe stuffed with onion and potato. This was
accompanied by cups of wine, and Pala remarked on
the excellent flavor. I ate but didn't really taste the
food or drink because of the ongoing numbness of my
tongue. Vasant would not eat, his scowling face propped
on one arm. Pala noticed, and asked if Vasant didn't
have an appetite after such a long journey.

'I've lost it.'

'What a shame! I hope my humble offering isn't to
blame.'

The Engineer spoke with clenched teeth. 'I assumed
you were Hindus. How can I share a meal with people
like you? My soul blackens from the sight of you.'

I opened my mouth to downplay this comment, but
Pala appeared unfazed. 'What an ordeal for you. Think
of the effort you'll need to make when you next visit

one of your holy rivers! I'll ask you not to bathe in our reservoir, however, as we have sanitation concerns.'

'Bastard!'

Pala smiled prettily.

'What arrogance,' Vasant said. 'It is incredible to me that you people reject Hinduism – even after the gods have denounced your faith! How can you ignore such condemnation?'

'How can I not?'

Vasant's disdain grew plainer.

'To us,' Pala explained, 'your gods are like lightning, or monsoons. Such things are powerful, and may sometimes hold sway over our lives, but that doesn't mean we must fall down and worship them. In fact, to a Pragmatic, doing so seems the epitome of folly.'

Vasant crossed his arms and might have left the cell had five or six Pragmatics not blocked the door.

Pala tilted his head, as if hearing a cue we could not. 'Ah!' he said. 'Time for dessert!' He opened his oven and removed a loaf of bread, which he transferred to another plate and set before me, beaming, waiting for my reaction. The bread was in the shape of a lotus blossom.

'Very clever.'

'Is there any miracle greater than a loaf of bread?' he said. 'If I were a Hindu, I might give this loaf a place of honor in my home!' With his ladylike fingers he tore off a piece, and indicated I should do the same. He called to his brother and sister monks in the room, and they shuffled over to take pieces. 'Vasant. Please.' He held a hunk to the Engineer, who only glowered in return.

We ate.

I complimented Pala on his baking skills, and he agreed that they were unparalleled.

'More wine!' he said, and filled my cup. 'Tell me, Rakesh, are you here to have phrases decoded, too?'

'I'm here because Vasant wanted to come here.'

'Ah! Are you and he – ?' Pala pointed at the two of us, implying some unmentionable connection.

'I am a Hindu,' I said, 'following a unique dharma. By helping Vasant achieve his goals, I hope to further my own.'

'And your dharma? It demands you do what, exactly?'

I remembered how shocked the constables were by my revelation. But I could not be vague when I described my task.

'I'm going to kill the Baboon Warrior.'

This brought the room to a pause. Pala stopped chewing, and I sensed the monks behind me also freezing. This time there was no laughter.

Pala said, 'The Baboon Warrior . . .?'

'Will die.'

'Well. You have come to a very interesting place, indeed.'

'We are not Buddhists,' Pala said. 'We haven't been since my father came to Ranthambhore, a failed missionary.'

'Failed missionary . . .' I said.

'You know the story?'

'If I'm thinking of the right one.'

'The first sighting of the Baboon Warrior. That was my father. Anil. He was the sole survivor.'

'You're the son of the traveler?' I straightened. 'I must speak to him. Hear his account firsthand – '

'He died years ago, regrettably.'

'Oh.'

'Presumably you haven't given him much thought?'

'Him, no. But the events. What happened.'

'It transformed his life,' said Pala. 'Made our order what it is.'

'How so?'

'My father was appalled by the sight of those bodies rolling with the tide. It exposed a chink in his belief system; as a Buddhist, he should have regarded the fate of his comrades simply as proof of life's suffering. He should have seen their demise in terms of karma, but he could not imagine any previous actions that should demand his brothers meet so terrible an end. He could not accept it, and he came to blame their deaths on the passivity of Buddhism. This caused him great discord. Buddhist teachings were all he knew, and, for the most part, he continued to cherish them. But he would no longer tolerate suffering.'

'What did he do?'

'He wandered. He traveled by foot, without itinerary or goals. Instead of waiting for donations of food, he occasionally worked for it, or stole it. He continued his meditations, searching for insight into his dilemma. At last, he came to a decision. He would reshape the aspects of Buddhism he valued to concerns of the physical world. He sought lucidity as before, and wisdom, but now he did so with a mind to how they could yield material benefits. Nirvana was no longer a final goal, only a means. He trained himself to think critically, to achieve deeper perception.'

'I think I understand.'

'As my father wandered, he met others who appreciated his new outlook. He wasn't seeking like-minded people, but they seemed to find one another whenever he spoke his opinions. To his surprise, he was a missionary again. Only this time he was drawing converts without trying – merely by talking sense. Their number grew. Twenty-three people, exchanging ideas, developing powers of perception. Eventually they realized their need for a base of operations, as they still suffered at the hands of Hindus like you and Vasant, and no Buddhist monastery would have them. So they climbed this crag with tools and insight.

'They drew no plans: they verbalized the fortress as they set to work, sculpting the building they described. They began with the roof and worked down to the top of the path you climbed. I can't imagine their ordeal, huddled on this rock, fully exposed to the elements! But they continued sharing thoughts of the home they wanted, with such clarity that they could work as a unit, linking their labors with straight lines and perfect right angles.'

Vasant sniffed doubtfully, and Pala graced him with a smile.

'That was the beginning,' he went on. 'It was how we came to be Pragmatics. My father and the other original Pragmatics abandoned the Buddha; his teachings and those of subsequent schools can be informative – some. But they are best seen as blueprints for deeper consciousness, and stepping stones to our current explorations. We apply such learning to the greatest vehicle – thought – and the tangible rewards it can provide. We've discarded the Buddha as a figure of independent merit, just as we have abandoned the idea of worshiping any deity.'

'I saw the statue beside the path,' I said, 'and thought it represented the lotus throne of Vishnu. But the Buddha, I recall, is also depicted on such a seat.'

'There may have been a time when Hindus considered the Buddha an incarnation of Vishnu.' Pala shrugged. 'That time is gone, and here, we have always considered the lotus to be the vital element.'

'I'm keen to see more of the fortress, more of what you've achieved.'

'Tomorrow maybe. Another part of our heritage we've discarded is the need to meditate all day. Evenings we reserve for pleasure. Music, bread, wine.' He clapped his hands, stood, bowed. 'Enough for one night. We'll show you to rooms, and see what morning reveals. For now, I have a massage waiting.'

We were escorted to other cells, cool because of the stone, with handmade bedding piled over rock-cut beds. There was a book on the night-stand – more books! Did every persecuted minority consist of book readers? *The Advantages of Pragmatism.* Maybe they hoped we'd convert, or maybe Pala was just leaving a door open for the possibility. I flipped through handwritten pages but couldn't concentrate, certainly couldn't sleep; I was charged with what he'd told me. *The Baboon.* Whenever I trusted my dharma, I found myself closer to him. But just how close was I now?

I left the room to find out.

'Sir,' said a voice, 'excuse me, sir.'

They had posted one of the pregnant monks – or nuns, I suppose – outside our doors. She rose fluidly and positioned herself behind me. She was perhaps a few years older than me and shorter. She stood erect, as did all the Pragmatics, her belly making no difference to her posture. Her eyes were green as hills of tea.

'We would like for you not to wander,' she said. 'You might get lost and not be able to find your way back.'

'He bested Varaha in unarmed combat.'

'Sir?'

'Varaha, the Lord Boar,' I said, 'robbed a royal entourage. Among the items he stole was a bracelet very dear to the Royals, a prized piece of jewelry meant to circle the wrist of Princess Asha. The Baboon Warrior went to the Boar's mountain lair and demanded its return.'

'Oh,' she said. 'The Baboon Warrior. That's what you're babbling about.'

'On the hundredth day of their battle, the Baboon defeated Varaha, throwing him from the height of a cliff. Afterward, he bit off the Boar's hand so his monkey servants could pry the bracelet free, and – '

I looked at her.

'Am I babbling?'

'The subject of the Baboon seems to excite you.'

'Were you aware I am to be his assassin?'

'I was in the room,' she said. 'I can't understand your enthusiasm about killing another living being.'

'No?'

'You sound surprised.'

'It's just nobody has ever said that, after learning of my goal. The common response is disbelief. People don't think anyone is capable of harming the Baboon Warrior. The second most common reaction is disapproval: for example, Couldn't you have chosen someone *unpopular* to assassinate? So many demons, they complain, so many criminals, so many Kama Sutrans. Why not devote your life to ending *their* existence?'

'And how do you respond?'

'The decision was not mine to make. My dharma guides me.'

She raised her brow slightly.

'Do you have a comment on my dharma?'

But she only said, 'Let me recommend again that you retire to your room.'

I looked at her, at the way her belly lifted her saffron robe, and I asked, 'Do you marry, as well?'

'Sir?'

'When I thought you were Buddhists, I was surprised to see you and one of your sisters with child. Are you married to the man responsible for your condition?'

'Oh,' she said, 'that.' She looked down at her belly as if she hadn't thought of it in months. 'I have no husband. Pragmatics live individual lives. Apart from the group, we recognize no bonds or divisions.'

'I see.'

'Can you read?'

'Yes.'

'Then I recommend our book: *The Advantages of Pragmatism*. If you return to your room, you might find a copy, with answers to many of your questions.'

But instead I walked down the corridor, around the courtyard, my pregnant guard taking up pursuit. Maybe thirty or forty monks milled below, and if not for the simple orange robes and cropped hair this might have been the reunion of some extended family, devoid of rivalries. I noted that a few wore loose saffron outfits tailored to resemble pants or shirts, but the attempt at fashion was weak. There was laughter and backslapping among the monks. The difference in mood between here and Jaipur was profound – no pitchforks or debilitating spices. I could understand how a life encapsulated in rock might appeal to someone. But like Vasant, I was disturbed by the fact that these people rejected our religion. How could anyone *not* believe? Pala's explanation had struck me as flimsy.

Walking, I also saw it was untrue what he'd said about evenings being reserved for pleasure. I peered into rooms where monks worked late. What they were doing beguiled me. In one long stone room they sat on stools, leaning over a corpse. They worked with long knives and forceps, and an elaborate spray of strings held the chest open, layers of skin and viscera hoisted from a cavity of the corpse. This did not appear to be leisure activity. A monk with paintbrush recorded images of organs.

Behind me the pregnant woman continued to follow.

Another room I might have mistaken for a Hindu shrine, because inside was a clay Ganesha, and a circle of brass flames around Shiva-nataraja, and a papier-mâché depiction of Parasurama. But the room contained too many images of deities, and was too crowded for proper worship.

And there were more books.

I waited for my guard to catch up.

'In my life I've seen few Hindu texts,' I said.

'Is that so?'

'It is strange that I should see so many here, among people who have no interest in our faith.'

'We store them,' she said.

'Why store objects of somebody else's religion?'

'We deal with Jaipur and other cities. Trade and barter sometimes leave us with things we don't have use for.'

'So you keep them? For things you have no use for, it seems a well-organized collection.' I peered inside. 'Some of it even appears catalogued.'

'Remember,' she said, 'you are slightly less than a guest here. You have no right to snoop around our home and question what you see.'

'I apologize again. My dharma. Once I get curious . . .' I made a babbling gesture with my fingers.

'Of course,' she said, with a smile of pure courtesy. 'You can hardly help yourself.'

The sound of an arrow splitting an arrow repeated every few seconds. The interval between was as long as it took the archer to nock another in his bow. Pala and I stood on one of the rock bridges spanning the courtyard, watching the demonstration below. The archer, at one end of the courtyard, so consistently struck the target at the opposite end – a circle painted on a wooden background – that there was nothing for him to do but split the shaft of his last shot.

'Have you ever seen such skill?' said Pala.

'I knew we were in the company of an outstanding marksman yesterday, when he pinned us to the ground.'

This comment seemed to please him.

'Once,' I said, 'I shot an arrow that struck nothing.'

He brightened. 'Oh! I like that. It could make a good koan.'

'A koan?'

'Like the tree that falls in a forest when nobody is

present to hear it. Does it make a sound? That is a koan. A simple paradox that serves as an aid to meditation.'

'Like a mantra?'

'Koans help empty the mind and make way for clear thought. They expel interference, so we can concentrate fully, on philosophical problems or more tangible concerns. Such as hitting a target.'

'That archer has been practicing for years.'

'At meditation, yes. At clear thought, yes. But archery? It's a skill he appropriates with the other two. You don't believe me? Here, see for yourself. Any well-trained Pragmatic is also a marksman.' He leaned over the bridge. 'Yamuna! Take a bow!'

The pregnant woman who had stood outside my door last night rose and took bow and arrow from a rack. I would indeed be impressed if she could hit the mark as reliably as her male counterpart. But he didn't leave his position, and Yamuna strode to the opposite end of the courtyard to place herself in front of the target, facing him. Both nocked an arrow. Yamuna compensated for the bulge of her stomach as they both drew, pointing their weapons at each other.

'The child . . .' I protested.

Pala chuckled. 'Yamuna! Our Hindu visitor is concerned for your safety!'

A double twang and crack, and an instant splintering. They had let arrows fly, and both Yamuna and the bowman remained standing. What had been arrows were now broken sticks lying in a pile between them. Each had hit the other's arrow.

I envied their accuracy, and wondered if I too might achieve so deep a level of concentration. 'If I could block my ears, cover my eyes, my nose – '

'Your problems would remain.' He tapped my fore-head. 'Sounds, smells, sights – they're a fraction of the interference in here. And here.' He touched my back, at the spine. 'What you call dharma is another problem.'

'It gives my life structure and meaning.'

'But could you ignore it, if you wanted to?'

'Dharma is the path one must follow.'

'Not an answer to my question, yet revealing.'

'But what good is all this?' I said. 'You're excellent archers, yes. You probably excel at many activities. But living up here, walled in stone, you can only impress one another. That's self-indulgence.'

'We do not simply indulge the self. Far more important in Ranthambhore is the group. Brother-and sisterhood. As a group focused on a task, we can accomplish much more than the total of our separate talents.'

He called for assembly, and in unison the men and women rose from the lotus position. They took bows and arranged themselves, those in front crouching, the next rows kneeling, the back rows standing, all facing the target. As one, they nocked arrows. As one, they let fly. I felt the fabric of air split in a hundred places, coupled with a dry, shrill explosion, and the wooden target spun off its feet and burst open at the center. I glimpsed the tumult of arrows drilling its painted heart all in a fraction of a second, then only raw and unpretty wood was left, sundered pieces lying across stone. Someone exchanged his bow for a broom and cleared away the remnants.

'I believe that's enough demonstration,' Pala said. 'If your friend still wants our services . . .'

But I wasn't listening.

Interference. I remembered my lone arrow streaking over the ocean. But this time I saw it differently: my point of view approached the missile, and I could see it wasn't really alone; the arrow was in fact a composite, several hundred united in a sheath of flame.

'Rakesh? Rakesh?' He waved a hand in front of my eyes. 'What's the matter?' he asked.

'My dharma . . .' I said. 'A new revelation.'

'Are you going to keep me in suspense?'

'You and the Pragmatics.'

'Yes?'

'You're part of it.'

'Part of what?'

'You're to assist me . . .'

'Assist you? In what?' He clapped his forehead, smiling. 'The Baboon's death?'

'Yes.'

Pala threw back his head as if to laugh, but no sound issued from his mouth. 'Delightful!' he said. 'Your imagination is delightful.' He shook his head, still smiling, and went on. 'But we value time in Ranthambhore. A saying: Time is the only commodity both abundant and rare. That's from *The Advantages of Pragmatism*. So. Does the Engineer engage our services? Or does he feel that association with us too greatly jeopardizes his future lives?'

I wasn't sure.

Earlier I had confronted Vasant. He lay on his bed, dressed. Sunlight found an angle over the fortress walls, landed in his eyes. I'd asked him essentially the same thing Pala wanted to know. Would he take advantage of the monks' skill as code breakers? The toll of the journey compounded his beating from Madhav. We had come a long way, and much depended on Vasant's understanding of the Kama Sutran dialogue he'd over-heard beneath Sholapur. His allegiance to the First Widow depended on it, and I sensed in him a reluc-tance to put that relationship at risk, a devotion that ran deeper than logic and was spoken only in depths of sleep. *Kavita*. That single word weighed on him like the yoke of a bull.

They're not even Buddhists! he had complained to me.

I reminded him that the Pragmatics knew none of the circumstances surrounding the phrases we wanted decoded, not who had spoken them, not any of the ramifications. He could listen to their interpretation and decide about their legitimacy afterward. But lying here in the room and brooding, he couldn't pretend to be helping India. Or himself. Or Kavita.

He lay in silence.

'I'll try him again,' I told Pala.

But as I turned, a figure appeared at the bridge.

Vasant walked with aggressive self-confidence, with the swagger of a high bureaucrat, and although his bruises were plain in the morning light, I somehow felt obliged to ignore them.

'May we begin?' he said to Pala. 'You're not the first man to put a value on time.'

'One small matter,' said Pala. 'No Pragmatic services are free.'

'There was money in the saddlebags you confiscated last night,' I protested. 'Several hundred rupees! That's all we brought for payment, and you people took it.'

'We are not thieves, just cautious businessmen. Now that you've asked us to accept that money, there's no

reason for delay. Let us begin.' He pointed at Vasant.
'Uncivil engineer, come with me.'

I stayed on the rock bridge. The monks below
arranged themselves so their orange figures crisscrossed
the courtyard, and they kneeled as one. Vasant received
instructions from Pala, who then took the last position
in the grid. Silence settled over the fortress. A crow
cawed somewhere in the valley, then its cry faded. The
Pragmatics stared ahead. Regulated their breathing.
This went on for a few moments, a common respiration, then Vasant stepped over to Pala as instructed
and spoke into his ear. '*Fringa topi kappa.*'

Pala repeated the string of nonsense: '*Fringa topi
kappa.*' The person sitting beside him repeated it too,
and the person behind him – or so I thought at first,
but in each case the phrase was altered slightly. Each
monk took up the phrase, playing with a syllable, while
the persons adjacent and behind altered in their own
way the phrase they heard. It reminded me of traditional weavers who still make rugs without the use
of devices. In their workshops, a leader calls knots and
threads to the weavers around him, a rapid litany,
and fingers fly according to his instructions, which
sound to any outsider like babble. But the babble is
precise.

Quickly it became impossible to track the alterations
to the original, the reiteration of syllables becoming
indistinguishable to me and certainly nothing like
language. The noise rose as the phrase found its way
across the assembly: a mechanical chorus, monotonous
extensions of some very brief and literal thought procedure. The voices swelled until I felt them in my
chest, in my sternum, a vibration. Babble rose up the

rock walls and frothed in the open center. So insistent was the drumming of syllables, I started to make noise myself, cords in my throat quivering in sympathy with the mass manipulation of sound. I placed both hands on my chest.

When I thought the noise could get no more complicated, I saw Pala gesture for the next phrase. '*Mosi renum aki.*' This soon entered the shuttle and loom, and sound again was woven through the courtyard. I steadied myself against the ledge. Vasant looked pained. We had both experienced intense mantras, but this noise was an evolving, calculated drone, difficult to bear as patterns teased the mind yet remained outside our powers of articulation. Vasant persevered, feeding phrases, adding to a racket that had an underlying foundation as solid as mathematics.

The noise subsided, falling in the same pattern in which it had risen: Pala stopped first, then those sitting around him, and their silence rolled in a graduated wave toward the edges.

Only one monk still spoke. Pala gestured for me to come down.

We threaded a path to the corner where a young monk sat and stared ahead, no particular sight in his gaze. He spoke in a monotone as uninflected as the iterations that had preceded it. With him, however, there were no more alterations to be made – we heard decoded language – and again I thought of those weavers in the north, how something that seemed like babble produced a carpet with crisp patterns, straight lines, stripes, colors, design.

I looked at Vasant's face as he listened.

Sometimes from separate threads comes a picture.

SECRET WOUNDS AND
OPEN WEAPONS

⤙●⤚

THE MONK WAS saying:

> . . . to the surface before noon we can join the
> group in Delhi by end of week
> so dank down here my clothes
> and our loudmouthed baggage
> Symantaka will know what to do with him
> Symantaka has his-her own concerns
> \<untranslatable\> time in Delhi
> how does Symantaka like the First Wife
> Kavita
> any closer we would have to make wedding
> arrangements
> she is a great asset . . .

The picture was clear. I was not surprised by the uninflected words issuing from the young monk, but Vasant appeared physically reduced. He turned and looked north. Toward Delhi? His bruises flushed; he slouched. Before now I had not seen in his bearing anything less than rigorous pride. His reduction

continued as the monk went on describing the First
Wife with great familiarity and from a Kama Sutran
point of view.

Pala said, 'You two are from the capital?'

'Not me, but . . .'

Vasant walked away from us.

'Why did you come here?' asked Pala.

'Jaipur and Delhi, they are unstable at the moment.
Dangerous.'

'Why?'

'You haven't heard? The Sovereign is dead. Murdered by the First Wife, some say. We don't know if
that's true, but it appears she made bargains with certain
disreputable elements of Hindu society. With Kama
Sutrans. All of India suffers for the situation.'

'Such intrigues! I'm thankful once again we live
apart from you and your ways.'

I shrugged and left to follow Vasant.

I intended to speak to him. But at the top of the
staircase I felt a tingling in my spine, through my whole
body.

Nobody was watching. The assembly of monks had
separated into labor, tending the garden, sweeping
floors, mending robes, sharpening blades, cutting hair.
They threw themselves into menial duties with the
same single-mindedness they exhibited in archery and
the decoding. Pala himself was washing the floor – I
was shocked at first, then realized the caste system
did not delegate tasks here. Whatever the chore, the
Pragmatics accepted it, and let it absorb them fully.
Which gave me an opportunity. I turned in the
opposite direction and stole from one column to

the next, knowing they were too engrossed to notice a trespass.

The room in which I'd seen the dissection last night was again busy, so there was little chance of my slipping inside. But this was not where my dharma most wanted me to go. I proceeded to the smaller, more puzzling room. I didn't even bother trying the door; I jumped through the small horseshoe-shaped window, landing cleanly inside.

The collection.

The statues that had first drawn my attention were familiar and would not have surprised me outside of Ranthambhore. Many of these gods I had seen myself, live: Durga, Chinnamasta, the carriage of Ganesha, a rat with wheels. Far rarer were the books. Several were in languages I could not recognize, and I wondered if the Pragmatics could unlock these as they could a code. What intrigued me even more were the titles I could read and recognize: works holy to Hindus, like the Vedas, the Mahabharata. I had seen books like this in the collections of Brahmins, but it always struck me as strange that anyone recorded their contents on paper. Why bother? Entire castes knew them by heart.

And why would the Pragmatics possess such material?

Perhaps it was no mystery. The monks studied teachings of the Buddha even though they didn't consider themselves Buddhists; maybe they took the same attitude toward Hindu texts. Maybe they could make use of the philosophies within, even if the monks didn't subscribe to our faith.

But looking at the spines, I saw not all the books were old – some seemed new, and handmade. Nearby was a stack of pages, with thread and needle to sew them together. My skin crawled. Were the Pragmatics also *making* books? Books about Hindus? I was about to pull out a volume entitled *Reincarnation Debated*, when another struck me. *Further Tales*.

Further tales of what?

The illustration on the cover startled me: a very monkeylike soldier standing on the chest of a defeated combatant. Energy rippled from the center of my body. My fingers trembled as I ran them across the cover. I turned to the window for better light. He looked strange in the picture, more animal than human, but bore too many similarities to be anyone else. The binding crackled when I opened to the first page.

'You don't have permission.'

I jumped.

A pregnant silhouette interrupted the light.

'You're still guarding me?' I asked. 'I didn't hear you enter.'

'Please hand over the book,' Yamuna said.

I looked at her swollen torso. 'If I refuse,' I said, 'will you use force?'

'Yes.'

'But you're outnumbered.'

'How does that figure?'

I nodded to the visages of gods.

She said, 'I'm not sure you could depend on clay figures, in a fight with me.'

'Last night you explained why you might collect such information. But not why you would *record* it. Not why you would make books.'

Silence.

'You live in isolation. You hold Hinduism in disdain.

So why write down your ideas? Why write down anything?'

She said carefully, 'It's important to understand those who surround you. Even if you don't want to be like them. Even if you disagree on fundamental issues. Understanding is useful.'

She put out her hand.

The book wasn't mine to keep. But I did not surrender it. I squeezed it, as if to absorb the contents. I wanted it badly, physically. At the very least, I had to get something in return.

'Your pregnancy,' I said.

She stared at me.

'The father is not one of your fellow monks,' I said.

After a moment she said quietly, 'You have intuition. The father was not a fellow monk.'

I nodded. 'This will cause pain,' I said, and handed her the book.

I yelped, clutched my stomach. It felt as if someone had driven a spike through my navel.

I dropped.

'Rakesh? What's the matter?' She leaned over. 'Are you hurt?'

'I . . .' My chest felt wrapped in barbed wire. 'My duty. My dharma.'

'What about it?'

'This will pass . . .'

She moved back a little, allowing my spasms. It would pass. I'm not sure how long I remained on my knees, my forehead against the stone floor. The pain rippled out from my chakras, intense. I retched once, twice. I was dizzy when the pain subsided, shrinking back into me.

Yamuna helped me to my feet. 'Was that because of the book?' she asked.

'It's over. You can throw me out of your book room, now.'

'I didn't come here just to throw you out.'

'No?'

'I came to ask why you didn't leave with your friend.'

'Vasant! Vasant!'

I should have spoken to him first. Apparently he had gone to his room, grabbed our depleted saddlebags, and left without a word. There was no reason for the archers on the turret to stop people from leaving, and the rest of the monks were concentrating on morning chores and meditations. I jogged down the path, forgoing goodbyes.

Barefoot, I hiked the trail we'd used to come to the fortress, and the series of crags and the stone-cut structure subsided behind a scrim of trees. Kilometers grew between me and the home of the Pragmatics. My feet bled – my sandals were in one of the bags Vasant had taken. The blood on my soles picked up pebbles. 'Vasant!' I cried. 'Vasant!' For an hour or more, the only response was explosions of surprised birds. My throat became sore from calling his name. I hoped that no tigers had come between us. It didn't occur to me at first that Vasant might hear and simply not answer.

I spent most of the day looking for him. Could he keep ahead of me, during high heat? No. When I didn't find him north of the fortress, as expected, I headed east. There were many ways to leave Ranthambhore, but I chose to search the routes pointing toward Delhi.

After several hours, I sat in the shade of a tree and

wondered if this was punishment for returning the
book about the Baboon. Losing Vasant would be a
setback. I knew he factored into my goal, and I felt
physical discomfort at the thought of having to confront
the Hero of India without Vasant's assistance. But how
could I find the Engineer in the many stretches of
wilderness and city separating Ranthambhore from
Delhi?

Then, wiping sweat from my brow, I realized I wasn't
thinking like Vasant. I remembered how often, on the
way here, he'd required rest.

He wasn't walking right now. Not in this heat. I
doubted he was even out in the sun.

Directly before me I could see through the vegetation to one of the ruins. A roof slanted, suspended
in a reticulum of brown vines, twisted out of position.

'Vasant?'

The entrance was askew, forcing me to squeeze
inside. After the sun, the dark seemed absolute. But
someone sat, and as my eyes adjusted, I saw he was
looking at me.

'Va – '

I held the name in my mouth. The veteran squatted
in shadow, staring right at me, although how much he
saw remained unclear. His eyes were bright in the
darkness, yet he was immobile as stone. What was he
doing here? Why did he always appear? His gaze
unnerved me, and I stepped back, retreated.

Outside, I felt strangely chastened. I no longer cared
how hot it was, or how long it had been since my last
drink.

I trekked almost all the way back to the fortress
before I found Vasant sitting against the wall of another

dilapidated structure. His arms rested on his knees, and he looked straight ahead, not turning to me when I approached.

'Was this a temple?' I asked.

'It's shade.'

'I begin to think you don't want my company.'

He exhaled.

'Are you going to sit here forever?' I stepped closer.

'There's nowhere to go.'

'What do you mean?'

'The First Widow has allied herself with Kama Sutrans. No role for me exists in a government that gives their sect legitimacy, or worse, some kind of backroom power. I'm not returning to Delhi.'

'Then come with me,' I said simply.

He laughed without humor.

'That's why we found each other in Sholapur,' I said. 'You are meant to accompany me.'

He rubbed his brow, looking simultaneously amused and pained.

'My dharma,' I said. 'I've known all along you figure into it.'

'You have too much gall.'

'We were brought together. Now you are severed from the Palace. We are meant to travel together.'

'Stop saying that! Have you never taken a critical look at your goal? Has it never occurred to you that your fixation on the Baboon might come from the undoing of your wedding?'

I said nothing.

'Think! You deluded yourself into this twisted idea of dharma because you're like so many others, a crea- ture of stupidity, jealousy, and sexual frustration. You're obsessed with your former bride-to-be! You want to kill the Baboon as a way of taking revenge against *her*! You've deluded yourself into thinking this is a holy duty, but to me, to any thinking person, your goal sounds much less noble and is in fact plainly pathetic.'

'Kali said – '

You imagined meeting Kali! You were drunk on self-pity; you hallucinated.'

'No. And I know what I feel inside.'

'You know nothing. You're a boy. A boy who knows nothing.'

In a sober voice, he continued: 'Life doesn't arrange itself around you; it's caste and politics and money, systems bigger than any man can comprehend. It doesn't provide individuals with purpose. Lives are not decided in grand revelations.'

The following silence seemed intensified by the heat.

It was difficult for me to respond. A long time ago, I might have felt hurt. Vasant thought I was foolish? A foolish *boy*? It might have angered me to have someone who'd spent time in my company come to that con-clusion. But not now. Convinced of the futility of his own existence, he wanted to convince me of mine. But neither of us was worthless in the grand order, and I would prove to Vasant that India did provide purposes. A significant man like this, and with his peculiar talent? Of course his life had meaning. But his stare kept me silent, and I could shape none of this into words.

A roar. Our tiger.

I stepped away from the old temple. The tiger roared again, and I looked up, squinting.

'Vasant,' I said, pointing.

A blue ellipse hovered against the clouds, and since

it was some distance away, I knew it must be enormous. Without seeing the Engineer's reaction, I sensed what I was witnessing. The monster of the sky. The largest man-made aircraft. The luxury airship drifting over the forests of Ranthambhore.

'Your grand purpose.'

Vasant bumped past me and hurried down the trail so he could keep the vessel in sight. He followed as if connected by a long tether.

'It's not as I imagined,' I said. 'Is that a figurehead at the bow?'

Also, a ring of supplemental sacs floated at the stern, keeping the vessel aligned. Or perhaps they were purely decorative. I couldn't imagine Vasant designing friv-olous flourishes into his craft, and yet this thing in the sky had a definite — flamboyancy. He stared up, agape. 'What in the — ?!' He continued staring as he walked, not looking where he was going. We traced our way through the trails.

Back toward the fortress.

The airship sailed over the chiseled mountaintop, and I heard volleys of arrows. The craft, longer than the fortress, cast a long shadow over it as doors opened in lower cabins and figures dropped with folded arms. We were running. Getting closer, we could better see the shimmering blue vessel, and the figurehead or perhaps rudder at front, made to resemble the neck and head of a bird, a peacock. Vasant cried out. The peacock was a symbol of Kama.

High above, I could hear muted sounds of a clash, more arrows, shouts. We sprinted. A scream grew, and I looked up to see a person pitched against blue sky. He or she tumbled in midair, trying to find grace during the descent; then, with an enfilade of breaking bones, the monk fell splayed on a boulder. The body flinched, the head spat blood, and the rock seemed to flower purple.

This time, no arrows warned us from the fortress gate. It was shut, but I found handholds and footholds in the rough surface of the wall. Vasant tried following me but slid to the ground with each attempt. Inside, shouts overlapped, and something pounded against rock. More screams, a patter of feet, and dry ratcheting sounds, like wooden balls in wooden sockets. I climbed to the turret and opened the gate so Vasant could follow me inside.

Pragmatics clustered through the fortress, battling figures that had dropped from the aircraft above – goondas, a number of them, each wielding six arms. One waltzed blindly with arrows rooted in his eyes, but the rest were not dealt with so easily. As the archers let fly, the goondas swept their arms through elaborate pinwheels of motion, accumulating in each of six hands arrows snatched from trajectory. The scene pulsed with arrows; the goondas tossed aside hundreds of broken shafts. And this tossing pulled them forward, pell-mell, their bodies systems of movement in which each step was a calculation influenced by the angles of those multiple arms. The goondas were quick, lithe, and mathematical in their attacks. Their advance came in six prongs of unexpected vectors, with mincing little steps backward, forward, side-to-side, and clattering volleys of Pragmatic arrows attempting to predict them. I tied my knife to its string and ran into the fray.

One goonda lifted a woman over his head and shook her like rags. With his other arms he swatted away the lunges of her fellow monks, their shovels, brooms, rakes, making a staccato racket as these weapons knocked against his false limbs.

Goondas were flesh and blood living within mechanisms of wood clamped to their chests. Their own arms fit into two sleeves; the remaining four were wooden analogs run with cables. As the monks battled these six arms, I swung my blade in a tight circle.

I approached from behind and let the weapon fly, aiming for his head. It struck where I wanted but rang too sharply: part of his head was also wooden. But the blow got his attention, and with little steps he wheeled about to face me, then flung the monk at me. We bounced across stone, and she pinned me to the floor, inert.

The goonda tilted his head, flexed his six limbs, advanced.

I lifted the dead weight of the woman, but he was coming too fast.

A monk saved me: dashed forward with a straight razor and slashed the back of the goonda's knee. That stopped the goonda; he howled. While he was distracted, a spear was plunged into his ankle, hitting a spot behind the tendon. He flailed and forgot himself. Arrows blurred. I lifted an arm to shield my face in case one strayed or deflected off his body. When I looked again, the tall figure had become a pincushion, cloaked in bolts. He dropped to his knees. I pulled the woman aside before he fell forward, snapping and crackling against the stone.

I passed the woman to her comrades. Already the monks had arranged first aid. The goondas had dainty power and surplus limbs, but the Pragmatics were

organized; they didn't scatter or flee, didn't show the
confusion or fear they must have felt, but instead
formed groups and applied themselves in concert to
each remaining interloper. Rope was wound around
one warrior's legs. Another succumbed to the sheer
number of monks throwing themselves on him; two or
three wrestled each of his arms, and more monks
sprang, until he buckled under the mass of saffron-
robed bodies, and more jumped aboard, so his head
disappeared, and the rest of him, and still they kept
coming.

The greatest violence centered around the dull
clanging noise on the second floor.

Running up the steps, I saw a goonda hammering
at the book-room door, *crack, crack,* chipping into it
with four armored fists. With his other two arms he
battled the Pragmatics behind him, who were ham-
pered by the narrow corridor. Then, with a crash he
pushed through the rent he'd created, fighting backward
as he minced into the library. Inside, more racket, the
smashing of plaster statues, crashes that must have been
overturned bookshelves. A monk with a spear ran
inside but almost immediately came sailing out the
window, over the railing, landing in the courtyard to
the ministrations of his fellows. Another attempt
yielded similar results, a shriek, a body airborne;
goondas could not be defeated one-on-one.

I ran toward the room.

What did he want in there?

A monk grabbed my shirt, hauled me back before I
got any closer. '*Further Tales!*' I protested, and kept
pushing forward, but the monk insisted, using some
trick with his weight to pull me off balance, and I

tripped down the steps. The Pragmatics worked on the next floor above; they rolled a barrel along the corridor over the library, and stopped at the signal of one of their brothers. A sledge appeared, two sledges, and the monks took turns driving a spike into the rock. Directly below them, documents shot out the library window, whole books, pages, the goonda inside awhirl with vandalism.

The Pragmatics banged away until a thin shaft of light shot down into the library. They opened the barrel and poured, and every Pragmatic in the vicinity shielded his face and averted his eyes. I smelled kerosene. They retreated, someone pulling me along, and I looked back to see a candle tossed, and, *whumpff*, a fireball.

The goonda did not shriek; I saw him for a moment, his many-armed silhouette like a tree blossomed with flames, and the flames rolled out in a turbulent sphere of chemistry as I covered my head. When the explosion abated, I heard the crackle of fire, topped with a slow clatter, wood and metal parts dropping to stone, and something landed right in front of me, smoking.

Part of a blackened wood hand.

LEAVING
AT NIGHT

WALKING THROUGH THE courtyard, I saw smears of blood marking where the Pragmatics had dragged away their wounded. Red footprints crossed the grounds, and there were red stains in gutters designed for the monsoon. Cinder still floated, and blackened scraps of paper lay scattered amid arrows and remnants of arrows. I cut my foot on one before retrieving my sandals. Putting them on, I watched a fire continue to make problems in the library, and another on the level above, ignited by the barrel. The goondas were the only corpses that remained. Their arms had all folded in an identical manner, interleaved upon their chests, and I paused at one of the bodies to look at the expression on his face. No lingering anger, only pleasant satisfaction.

The monks' faces and body language suggested stoicism, but when I studied them long enough, I came to recognize a series of lip movements as a mantra for calm. They were shaken. I didn't see Yamuna, and wondered if she numbered among the casualties. She was no longer guarding me, whatever the case.

I found Pala sitting with arms crossed over his chest, one hand on his mouth. It was time.

I said, 'What would your father think?'

He blinked at me.

'This is the kind of devastation he wanted to insulate you from, correct?'

'Are you saying I'm somehow at fault?'

'No.'

'Well – what are you saying? Why are you still here, Rakesh?'

'You study Hinduism to defend yourselves against Hindus,' I said. 'That's my guess.'

Pala was silent.

'But you haven't studied hard enough.'

'There are limits . . .'

'I told you of changes in the capital. It's difficult to guess what is happening, but that was a Palace vehicle that delivered the goondas. Somebody with power wanted something from you.'

Pala shook his head. 'Why are you still here?'

'My dharma.'

'Oh, yes, of course.'

'You are part of it.'

'What?'

'You're going to come with me.'

'Why would I even consider doing that?'

'Because you're defenseless against the unknown. And I can help you understand. I'll provide an opportunity for you to increase your knowledge in a way available to nobody, ever before.'

He raised his brow.

'Come see a god,' I said.

His face went blank. Or not blank. He didn't say anything for a minute, surveying the smoky ruin of the fortress. He looked across the courtyard, and I followed his gaze to Vasant, who sat opening and closing his hands.

'What about your friend?'

During the melee I had glimpsed Vasant; during the explosion. The aircraft had repositioned itself so the peacock head appeared over the wall and seemed to be peering at the chaos within. Those balloons tethered to the stern had an eye painted on each; they looked like tail feathers and thus completed from end to end a tribute to the peacock. Vasant had stood facing this brilliant bird craft; I had seen him, radiant for a fraction of a second, awash in reflected blue, bent in the act of launching a spear at his brainchild, which had become a symbol of Kama.

'He's coming, too.'

We left the fortress that night, and must have looked like a leper army. Pala had addressed the Pragmatics and outlined my proposition. He suggested that if the brothers and sisters believed an 'expedition' such as I described was worthwhile, they should send a team. But when he asked if anyone might be interested, hands rose from the wounded, from the women, then all hands went up; everyone wanted to go. Perhaps they had been captive too long to their fortress, or perhaps the missionary element in their blood had seized them. Or perhaps what happened here had spurred them to take action – any action. Unable to read their tranquil faces, I couldn't presume to understand their motives.

To my surprise, there was a stable carved into a lower niche of the crag, where well-rested and well-groomed horses waited to be hitched to wagon carts. These were outfitted for transporting the infirm and supplies, which the monks had in abundance. They seemed prepared for a trip, and I recalled hearing that they did make journeys to Jaipur and elsewhere. Weaponry might be a problem, I thought, given the number of arrows broken and scattered throughout the fortress, but here too the Pragmatics surprised me, showing me into an armory where neat bundles of arrows were stacked to the ceiling; they must have spent many idle hours whittling sticks into bolts, and they had accumulated enough to supply a small war.

Yamuna I found loading dry goods onto a wagon.

'You're coming.'

She didn't stop working. 'Why wouldn't I?'

'I thought the journey might be hard on you, in your condition.'

'Don't make assumptions.'

'I'm glad so many Pragmatics are willing to come,' I said. 'It amazes me, in fact. Are you anxious to get away?'

'I can't speak for the others. But I want to see one of your gods, as you promise.'

Only five or six Pragmatics stayed behind to maintain the fortress – scant defense should it be challenged a second time. Someone climbed to the turret to see our long column out, rolling the gate shut behind us without a goodbye. We must have been a sight. If someone had seen the crag from a distance and could make out our exodus by starlight, it must have appeared as if some saffron fluid had been tapped from the peak, slowly wending to ground level.

It made sense to go at night; the Pragmatics were confident of their sense of direction and unafraid of forest dark. At night we wouldn't suffer the heat and we could cover more distance. The monks carried lamps on the end of poles. The lights swung with our steps, clunked like dull bells. I mentioned the possibility of tigers, and Pala told me someone saw a tiger during the raid, captured, aboard the airship.

I found myself at the front of the group, my body tingling. For a long time I'd known my dharma – years had passed since I shot my arrow over the ocean – but never before had it taken shape so dramatically. Now the Pragmatics marched behind me, and Vasant, who only hours before was trying to puncture my ambitions, seemed to take a proprietary interest in the position beside me. Although he'd put no intentions into words, I sensed that his eyes still contained the faux-blue flash of the peacock airship, and that he realized my plan could make that sight disappear.

Like this we walked, a procession pulling light through the forest.

A young Pragmatic stepped up to me and tried several times to initiate conversation. 'Beautiful night, yes? I admire the moon.' His name was Azis, and he had the look of a northern birth. Kashmiri. He kept offering to carry my bags; I had none. When he ran out of things to say, he whistled a melancholy tune while his brethren remained silent. Eventually the notes petered out. He approached again. 'Can I get you a drink of water, Rakesh?'

'I don't need a servant.'

'Sorry, sir. Sorry.'

Azis looked smaller for my comment, so I tried to rekindle some of his enthusiasm. 'Were you anxious to get away from the fortress?' I asked.

'Yes. Well, no. Not anxious.'

'You just wanted to travel.'

'Oh, I've *traveled*.'

'You're from Kashmir.'

'I've traveled more than that. I've been south. Bombay.'

'What were you doing there?'

'Looking for my sisters.'

'Pragmatic sisters?'

'Family sisters. We lived very poor in Kashmir. My parents went to work in the mountains, trying to make payments on our family debt. My sisters and I, we almost starved.'

'What does that have to do with Bombay?'

'One day, men came to our village in a fancy lorry. They had fancy clothes and pretty wives. 'You're so beautiful,' my sister said to them. 'How do you afford such saris and cosmetics?' We work in Bombay, the women told them. Come to the city, and you too can afford fine clothes and jewelry. We need smart girls in our carpet factory. We will give you good jobs in Bombay.'

'Oh,' I said. 'You needn't tell me any more.'

'Come to Bombay, make lots of money,' Azis continued. 'Lots of money in the carpet factory. That's what they told my sisters. In the afternoon, a man visits our home. He asks me, How much must I pay to take your sisters to Bombay? One thousand rupees each, I tell him. I didn't want to send my sisters away, but we had the family debt, and there was no food. So he gives me two thousand rupees. Everybody is pleased.'

'And later, you went looking for them . . .'

'In Bombay I found carpet factories but not my sisters. And then someone told me, 'You have been tricked.' My sisters were tricked. Men don't go north looking for carpet workers. They go to buy whores.'

And now Azis must have felt I knew enough, because he stopped talking. I didn't ask if he'd searched the brothels of Bombay. He might not have recognized his sisters if he saw them, and even if he had, he couldn't have extricated them from their new roles. Azis had unwittingly sold his sisters into prostitution. Probably they continued to function in that capacity. Probably they were working now; it was the right hour of night. He dropped back in the procession.

His whistling resumed.

After we walked for about three hours, a wheel came off, and the whole line stopped while monks repaired the wagon. That's when we saw him.

He was ahead, in a clearing west of us. Vasant saw him too and groaned with disbelief.

The veteran's beard seemed to collect starlight. He was shouting at a tree, and used his rifle to threaten it physically. He circled, jabbing the trunk with the barrel. He seemed bleached by the moon. 'Liar! Damn liar!' He aimed the gun and squeezed off a shot. Bark splintered. He shook a fist. His legs looked longer than before, and the dirt covering his body was ashen.

'You know him?' said Pala.

'He's been following us. A veteran.'

'A tree fighter?'

'This is an improvement.' I turned my head to the sky and squinted at constellations. 'The Pleiades must be coming out.'

During the halt for the wagon's repair, the wounded and elderly were consulted to see how traveling had affected them so far and if anything could be done for their comfort. Biscuits and ladles of water circulated. The Pragmatics took turns watching the veteran's antics, but nobody attempted to speak to him.

The monks urinated, standing in long rows with their robes hiked, and it was a sight to see them lined up, pissing in one direction. Why did they all have to pee at once? When I saw the women pulling up their garments, I wandered away, out of respect for them and for myself. Returning, I saw Yamuna supporting a sage old monk. His close-cropped hair was white as a Himalayan slope, and he walked with a stoop. When they saw me, he exposed big crooked teeth.

'Rakesh,' said Yamuna. 'I'd like you to meet Firdaus.'
'Very pleased.'

Firdaus put his hands together in the Hindu manner.
'One of the founders of the sect.'

He shook his head and said, 'Long, long time I have been a Pragmatic.'

'Firdaus spent much of his time in recent years working in the library. I told him about your . . . goal. About the Baboon Warrior. He is interested, you see, because he was a major contributor to *Further Tales*.'

My eyes must have widened, because the old monk's smile increased. 'Yes,' he said, and placed a soft but firm hand on my wrist. 'You must hear a further tale.'

A FURTHER TALE OF THE
BABOON WARRIOR

⊷═◉═⊶

'BEGIN WITH THE disappearance of a train,' Firdaus
said.

Between Tamil Nadu and Kerala, several tons of
rolling stock and mineral cargo vanished, never arriving
at their destination. The last known sighting was by an
untouchable, who claimed to have seen the train
rumble into a mountain pass, the sound dying in the
mountain like an inward groan.

Investigators were dispatched, and they too disappeared. They walked the tracks looking for evidence
of robbery or derailment, and when they entered that
tunnel, it was the last of them. After more trains vanished at the same point, the entire route was shut down,
so it was no longer just the loss of trains, it was the
crippling of two economies that depended on their
operation. Nothing that went into the tunnel came out
the other side. The Prosperous Rail Company of Delhi
sent a party of officials who brought a strong lamp,
which they positioned at the entrance, expecting its
beam to reveal a jumble of cars and bodies.

They saw the head of a boar with long glinting
tusks.

'Keep the trains coming,' the head advised.

The officials retreated, praying, stumbling, making placatory gestures.

There had been rumors the tunnel was occupied by a demon. But this was worse.

An open railcar moved toward the infamous tunnel, carrying near-naked men with long matted hair and stripes of ash across their foreheads. They were sadhus, four yogis who had achieved a level of purity that made them ideal intermediaries between men and gods. When not toiling on the pedal engine of the railcar, they sat on its platform, enduring the penance of the sun with nothing more than holy syllables to soothe them. *Om. Om.* The railcar clacked down the line at a very slow speed: the sadhus could have reached their destination quickly by airship or some dung-driven vehicle, but as ascetics they couldn't approve of travel unless it sufficiently taxed their bodies. The railcar was designed with this in mind, its inefficiencies guaranteeing that the men would expend more energy to go where they wished than walking would have required. The sadhus had been traveling for several days out of Delhi. When they passed through centers of population, they slowed, rattling their damaru drums so the locals would know to bring them food and water.

'*Om, om.*'

The junior of the group, a forty-year-old named Samtani, was pedaling when he interrupted the group meditation.

'Someone is blocking the way.'

The sadhus opened their eyes.

A man sat on the tracks. Samtani stopped pumping

his legs, and the railcar coasted toward the figure, whose chest was ablaze with little reflections of the sun – medals. The sadhus pressed their palms together when they realized who it was, the Baboon Warrior in full military uniform. The famed soldier extended a hand and with a single finger brought the railcar to a halt.

'Good soldier! Beloved hero!'

'Enough,' said the Baboon. 'No time for courtesies.'

He regarded them with his small animal eyes. 'I know where you're going,' he said. His simian face did not lend itself to speech, and the words he spoke were guttural, part growl.

'The Palace informed you?'

'I learn things when necessary.'

'May we hope to benefit from your prayers in this effort?' asked the eldest sadhu.

'If you continue, you won't come back.'

The sadhus looked at one another. 'We're not afraid of death, of course.'

'You should be.'

A heretical reply, given their faith in reincarnation and spiritual liberation, but the sadhus knew how much the Baboon had accomplished on behalf of the government and good people of India, and so were not inclined to correct him. Diplomatically the elder said, 'Do you know something we don't?'

'You're going to try to reason with a god whose capacity for reason has badly decayed.'

'The Lord Boar will answer prayers from the holy.'

'He has lost his mind and will consume you.'

'That I doubt. But we'll learn what he plans for us, no matter what his condition.'

'Go back.'

'We will pray to him. We will make offerings. If he doesn't reply to our requests, then we will appeal to Shiva to intervene.'

'I would save your lives,' said the Baboon. 'Shiva will not help you in this matter.'

'Your concern is touching,' said the old man, again putting his hands together, 'but I think we are at least as wise as you in matters of holiness and communion with gods.'

The Baboon stepped off the track. The elder gestured to Samtani, and Samtani resumed toiling at the weighted pedals. The railcar pulled past the warrior, slowly gaining momentum. The sadhus closed their eyes and returned to *om*, expelling from their minds the impure (and disconcerting) words of the Baboon. Only Samtani glanced back at the famous enigma.

Vegetation closed upon them as their car climbed toward the tunnel. The big lamp stood, abandoned. For many kilometers around, this region was deserted, locals having heard that an unpredictable and voracious god had entrenched himself in the mountain. The railcar drifted to a stop. Samtani stared at the mountain face and the gaping mouth of the tunnel; he'd had time to consider the warning of the Baboon.

'I can't,' he said.

The other sadhus regarded him.

'He was right,' he continued. 'How can we expect to reason with Varaha?'

'The Lord Boar will listen,' said the elder, 'because we are holy.'

'I don't know that my soul is as pure as when we left Delhi.'

'Very well, Samtani. Get off the railcar, will you,

please? I thank you for your admission, but we can't risk imperfect faith while approaching Varaha.'

The other sadhus murmured agreement.

Samtani dismounted and stepped off the car. 'My apologies,' he said.

'You always were prone to pollution,' someone muttered.

Although no longer aboard the railcar, Samtani walked behind it at a distance, watching his former comrades position themselves at the entrance. They knelt on the platform and repeated long mantras and hymns celebrating the life of Varaha.

They prayed: 'O Varaha, Lord Boar, master of this pass and half the state of Kerala, please hear our request. We are humble Hindus who ask for nothing more than the peaceable return of a section of railroad line . . .'

So it went, each sadhu picking up where the last left off, repeating the petition that the god again allow traffic to move through the mountain, between two devout and impoverished areas.

Samtani watched the tunnel. So dark! It curved, no light reaching from the opposite end. No response was forthcoming, and the uninterrupted shadow seemed a refutation of their efforts. But the prayers continued, and after a time − a squealing.

The wheels of the railcar turned.

The sadhus didn't stop praying as it rolled forward. Some of them looked around, but their praise didn't falter. The railcar inched toward the tunnel. What pulled it? The answer was both plain and mysterious.

'. . . and we ask that if you would only reconsider . . . reconsider . . . please, reconsider . . .'

The railcar passed into the dark aperture.

Samtani stepped onto the tracks, trying to keep it in sight. The words receded, fading with their backs. 'Get off!' he shouted. 'Get off!'

No reply.

He waited a few minutes, listening for any clue as to what might be happening within, when a great clatter sent the railcar back out as if shot by a cannon, knocking Samtani aside before he could jump clear. The sadhus were no longer aboard. It glided a few meters on momentum, then rolled to a stop.

As Samtani lay stunned, he watched a lone figure arise from a distance. The Baboon came walking up the track and stopped to sniff the empty vehicle. Moving toward the tunnel, he paused near Samtani but didn't look down at him when he spoke.

'Did you see Varaha?'

'No . . .'

He lifted the sadhu and carried him to a grassy, shaded area. 'I'll wait for you to recover enough to walk away.'

'Will the Lord Boar listen to you?'

The Baboon Warrior was quiet. 'You must leave this place,' he said.

Samtani nodded, struggled to his feet, and limped away. But curiosity got the better of him, the desire to see what had happened to the sadhus – the fate he'd avoided. Instead of leaving, he crept back and waited for the Baboon to cross into the tunnel, then positioned himself at the entrance and fired the big lamp. The tunnel was illuminated. He took a few steps inside and –

Not what he expected.

The tunnel opened into a cavern. The tracks were

twisted out of shape, rising through the middle of what appeared to be a structure built of bone. When he absorbed its entire form, he could see it suggested a vast boar. Yet this was not Varaha . . . In fact, looking further, looking through the people who shuffled about, he saw the real Lord Boar lying humped in a corner. His body was blue, and he had four arms which had accomplished many tremendous feats in his day. But now those arms lay still, and seams and cracks split open the faded hide. Varaha was puny in comparison to the magnificent skeleton, through whose ribcage a train could easily pass.

Parts of missing trains lay throughout the cavern. The trains appeared to have been overturned, disassembled, cannibalized for this new boar, this colossal figure with points of a crown rising directly from its tapered bare skull. Former passengers – even the sadhus – carried parts and labored like slaves to advance its construction. Samtani reeled. Beneath his feet the ground was spongy and bluish, with long black shoots that he realized were bristles. Why did bristles grow on the ground? Unless this was the new hide, meant to cover the imposing framework . . .

'Who are you?'

The question issued from somewhere near the smaller body. Varaha's boar head lay detached, cables from it snaking throughout the great room.

The Baboon Warrior told the head, 'I'm here to end your life.'

Workers scuttled to the head and lifted it to look at the Baboon. Its lips pulled back: 'You're . . . who?'

'You know who I am.'

'My life never ends!'

'Peacefully or violently? This is your only choice.'

'Do not speak to the Lord Boar without respect.' Another worker picked up a golden crown and positioned himself near the others.

The Baboon withdrew a long gleaming instrument from his coat and held it for Varaha to see: a serrated blade.

The head snorted. The workers carried it toward the Baboon, who seemed unfazed by the approach of the god's famous tusks. The workers charged with these curved weapons forward, but the attack was flawed: the boar head stalled whenever it got near the Baboon. Its bearers halted, and the head froze. When the group retreated, it twitched, grunted, resumed movement. But with every run at him, it again ceased to function.

'Who are you?!' Varaha roared in frustration.

'Somewhere, deep inside,' said the Baboon, walking toward the body, 'you know.'

The workers made several more attempts but never succeeded in bringing the tusked head against the Baboon. He picked up a cable and sawed as Varaha rumbled. The body shuddered, and the whole cavern resounded with protest. The Baboon worked calmly. As he sawed through cables, the torso bucked, and the speech of the boar grew less intelligible, slurring until it was like a voice forced through several chambers of bubbling water. The laborers, too, became spastic, until they lacked enough control to carry the head. They dropped it unceremoniously, shaking and knocking together as it rolled on the ground. When the Baboon finished cutting the cables, he set to work on the god's worn body. He severed its multiple limbs and cut its hide down the middle. It took a long time, but he was in no hurry and worked around its thrashings. When he was finished, he climbed the second, incomplete boar, the vast skeleton rising to the height of the cavern – the next Varaha – and began severing its glossy bones, from the top down. Parts fell, and Samtani watched in shock. When the Baboon had cut through enough of the structure, the skeleton collapsed, in stages, and he rode it down, still cutting, not stopping, not for five and a half days. The sadhu left to eat or sleep, but when he came back, the Baboon was still dismembering, still cutting . . .

'Wait, wait.'

Firdaus stopped talking.

'I know the story,' I said, 'but you've got it all wrong.'

'Oh?' said Firdaus.

'He fought the Lord Boar in unarmed combat,' I said. 'Unarmed combat that lasted one hundred days, not five and a half. You missed the fight altogether.'

'What else?'

'This idea that Varaha was not attached to his head, and that a much larger skeleton of him existed . . .' It was such a queer deviation that I could only shake my head and smile.

'And how do you know this tale?' said the old monk.

'Everyone knows it! Everyone with the slightest interest in the Baboon.'

'But you heard it from, ah, whom?'

I shrugged. 'I probably heard it as a child. People always are telling it.'

The monk nodded sympathetically, and Yamuna said, 'Firdaus spoke to Samtani himself.'

'The sadhu?'

'The witness. Years ago Firdaus traveled to Madurai to get the story from its source.'

'The sadhu must have been an old man by then,' I said. 'Hardly reliable . . .'

'Less reliable than people repeating what they heard from other people who had no connection to the event?'

I frowned.

'In Ranthambhore we write things down,' said Firdaus, 'because, Rakesh, we find that even sharp minds tend to alter details when retelling stories. And when stories pass from person to person, well, the alteration is, may I say, terrible.'

'It took a hundred days,' I insisted. 'And the conflict wasn't over a railway line but a precious bracelet meant for a princess.'

'More romantic than restoring a trade route, admittedly. And a hundred days sounds better than five and a half. Such embellishments appeal to lazy minds. The discrepancies between your version of the story and mine are evidence of people who have revised the tale to suit their tastes.'

The line started moving again, and Yamuna helped Firdaus into a nearby wagon. The old man leaned out to say, 'You look troubled.'

'I've put considerable effort into learning the Baboon's history,' I said. 'It's maddening to think my knowledge might be tainted by storytellers.' I mulled it over. 'And your book is gone! You must tell me more, Firdaus, while we travel. Everything you know.'

'Absolutely not,' said Yamuna. 'He must rest.'

I felt a twinge of aggravation. 'Of course. My thanks for the story. I hope to hear more.'

The old monk smiled. 'I didn't share this with you, Rakesh, simply to demonstrate that stories are corrupted. I wanted to point out something peculiar about the Baboon Warrior.'

'What?'

'He killed one of your gods,' said Firdaus. 'And this made him more popular with Hindus, not less.'

Storming
the God

$\rightarrow\!\!\equiv\!\!\circ\!\!\in\!\!\leftarrow$

OUR JOURNEY ENDED near Bundi, at a pair of hills
that stood staring over a plain like columns joined at
the hip. We hiked the long way around, then plodded
up the saddle between, to a meadowed incline. It was
the end of the day by the time the monks hauled up
their wagons with a web of block and tackle, and
camp was made. Three days had passed since we left
Ranthambhore. The situation of these hills, looking
south over flatter landscape, was ideal. Our march was
over.

This was the place.

The monks ate, washed, and tried to relax. I heard
occasional jags of laughter that sounded nervous, and
although it was difficult to read their emotions, I
noticed that some of the Pragmatics moved between
jobs too quickly, with too much energy. One by one
they settled down, however, mantras for calm circula-
ting through the crowd. They sat on the grassy incline,
facing south.

The trip had been hard on them not for its physical
demands but because of the mood of the cities along
the way. The trouble in the capital had spread in various

forms as people argued over the legitimacy of the First Widow's reign, fought with one another, and neglected responsibilities of caste and occupation. Rodent populations had exploded, in some places tipping the balance of power to rats. We saw a tower with windows blackened by rats, and a woman told me there was no hope, for if you burned down such buildings, where would the rats go then? In the same city, a trio of corpses dangled outside a government office; dogs stood on hind legs, gnawing at the dead local bureaucrats. Tensions were high, tolerance low. Perhaps I shouldn't have been surprised at the reaction to the parade of saffron made by a few hundred monks.

Who are you people? What are you doing here?!

We tried to be discreet, but so much color was bound to draw children, the curious, the bored, the aggressive. *Who do you think you are?!* The monks didn't reply; they received the provocations like medicine. Insults, stones, occasional hard shoves. My fellow Hindus shamed me when I saw the Pragmatics walk through such gauntlets, as if blind to the people surrounding them, deaf to the hollerings, numb to the hurled fruit. But in Pala I saw stress, discomfort – to face such bald hostility after so many years of seclusion! We decided to skirt large centers of population, no matter how much distance it added to our journey. The monks waited patiently on the periphery whenever I made necessary forays into a town for information.

Rumors, hearsay, and conversations with Brahmins had slowly guided us here.

Up on the meadow, night answered the wildflowers with stars. It would have made a pleasant scene if I could have separated it from what we were about to

do. Firelight guided me through the seated monks.
Chatter dwindled. Their faces were alert and receptive
as they looked out at the southern sky, their discipline
having smoothed away any sign of nervousness.

I picked out Yamuna's silhouette. She hadn't yet sat
among her brothers and sisters.

'Where's Firdaus?' I asked.

'You don't want to bother him now, do you?
Remember, he is a very old man. This has been taxing.'

'I wish to hear another story.'

'This isn't the time.'

She hurried away and sat on the far side. No, of
course this wasn't the time. When I looked over the
field, I realized that they were in place, that I was
the only person still standing. Pala caught my gaze. I
nodded back to him. A few beats later, their voices
rose:

Sim wi ta sicc'm, ep fel sim —

Pragmatics, too, knew the power of sound. They
had been quick to learn the mantra I heard in Sholapur,
and slowly they applied their talent, as a group capable
of subtle and controlled variation. I heard slight modulations as they worked toward an ideal pronunciation
and rhythm.

The mantra rose in volume. I marveled how so many
individual mouths could make such unified sound:
same pitch, same breath. Mantra flowed down the slope
like snowmelt from some frosted peak. They spoke in
rounds to give their voices a break, but I never heard
a lapse.

Vasant sat apart. He was behind me, brow wrinkled
with disapproval. No doubt he felt forced to counten-
ance this abuse of a mantra to achieve his own goals.

They turned my airship into a tribute to Kama's perversions was one of the few things he'd said to me on the last leg of the journey. His desire for revenge must have been powerful to make him willing to sit among infidels, stare at the southern night, and watch, hoping, fearing the one thing that might change his fortunes.

Sim wi ta sicc'm, ep fel sim –

I tingled.

The mantra flowed to the horizon. *The signal*, as Pala called it. I could almost see syllables push forward, rippling through the blue-black fabric of night.

And somewhere, they were received.

The Pragmatics made mantra for an hour before my knees shook. My body. A portent from many miles away, as the Jagannath, somewhere in the darkness, turned toward us. I could feel the great chariot turning. Then, a bass note inserted itself in the mantra. Vasant recognized it, too: when I next looked at him, his eyes were wide, his mouth open.

The bass note grew. Thunder, ongoing thunder. The tremor deepened. Far, far away, lights blinked on. Patterns of villages winking on – people waking up, I realized. They woke and wondered, What? What is happening? What could make such noise? What is coming?

Rising over the horizon, a red glow sketched the ferocious head, then the vast torso. At this distance the eye could be fooled: for a moment the figure seemed the size of a man – then I heard a distant crumpling, and my eye was drawn to the village disappearing beneath its wheels, darkening under the Jagannath's advance, and scale was restored. The

Pragmatics continued repeating the mantra but gave one another sidelong glances as the deity rolled on.

Coming to us.

It was not as destructive or as deafening as in Sholapur. The god restrained itself during travel, which allowed faster movement. But sheer size made some destruction inevitable. You could believe the earth would cave under such weight.

The weight approached, and I saw the massive arms that had swung at me in Sholapur. I could see its eyes changing, scanning the landscape.

The voice of the Pragmatics quavered a little when the Jagannath got within a kilometer of our location. Pala went so far as to raise his hand, reminding the monks to stay focused. The Jagannath swung its head, looking for the source of the mantra, looking for whoever had summoned it. I walked down the meadow, closer, without leaving the security of the mountain bowl.

I motioned for the Pragmatics to stop. The mantra ceased.

The Jagannath rolled to a halt.

I heard the drone of ancient engines inside the god. I could see the pattern of wooden staves that was its hull. Two walkways crossed its chest, and there were streaks and dots, the scars from cannonshot and other projectile weapons. Wood creaked against wood as the Jagannath moved its head, looking for those people who were so devoted that they had repeated the mantra that would bring its might upon them.

Pala rose. The other monks did likewise. I glanced at Yamuna, who was staring at the god and looking very serious. All took up bows and slung packs of arrows across their backs. Enough arrows to supply a war. There would be a war, but nobody knew what to expect from it.

The Pragmatics formed a long column. The plan was to descend to the field and split into three groups. The targets for the archers would be key joints of the Jagannath's arms. In calculations earlier that afternoon, Pala had determined the monks could unleash ten thousand arrows. I'd drawn a sketch of the god, and we had decided where the shafts should fall. Hopefully, we could effect a temporary paralysis.

We started walking down the path, and I wondered if Vasant would join us. But he remained sitting on his rock, looking . . . dreamy. I'd seen that gaze before.

He came out of it, and his eyes locked on mine.

'Wait,' he said. 'Wait!'

The column stopped.

'There's a better way.'

'You can enter through a wheel,' he said.

He squatted and drew a quick, confident sketch of the hub of the Jagannath's locomotive system, where the wheel was positioned in the chariot. In Sholapur I had seen the wheel's spikes carry fragments of the city into such apertures. According to Vasant's drawing, we could penetrate the god by the same route.

'What if it notices us?' I asked.

'Then you'll be dead. Or you can try your plan. Arrows in elbows.'

'I'll go,' I said.

Pala protested. 'It should be a Pragmatic that approaches the god. You have too much at stake for an experimental approach.'

'Who, then?'

'Not I,' said Pala. 'I'm too important to the structure of the organization, for now. But I'm sure any of the others would volunteer . . .'

Azis had moved to eavesdrop on our conversation. 'Let it be me,' he said. 'I would like to try.'

I looked at him. The day before, I had mentioned Azis to Yamuna. Did their sect harbor many stories as pitiful as his? She had said, *What story?* When I told her what Azis told me, she shook her head. *Azis sold his sisters into prostitution*, she said. *That much is true. But he knew full well what he was doing. Everyone in Kashmir knows about young girls and Bombay carpet factories. Everyone. His parents brought him to Ranthambhore afterward. They wanted us to give him some sense. Azis's story is a sad one, yes, but not the way he told you.*

Yet he'd seemed so earnest. Looking at his face, I wondered if he had consciously lied, or if he'd convinced himself of the blameless version he'd told me.

'I would like to try,' he repeated.

'Very well,' said Pala. 'Come look at this drawing.'

Vasant detailed his illustration in the dirt. The young Pragmatic studied without comment.

'Try climbing inside the way the Engineer describes,' Pala told him. 'Take a good look. Then get out quickly, come back, and tell us what you've found.'

Before embarking, Azis put on cotton slippers from his pack, to help silence his footsteps up to the god. He looked at the leviathan once more before heading down the slope, carrying no lantern.

It was a long walk to the Jagannath from where we were situated. The Pragmatics had brought along optical equipment, a telescope and binoculars, and under starlight we could just make out the ghostly figure of Azis approaching those giant wheels.

'Do you hear that?' said Pala.

'Yes.'

Azis was whistling.

But the Jagannath didn't notice the puny notes floating across the plain. With the cessation of the mantra, it had come to rest, thrumming to itself. Its wooden eyelids had slid shut, and its head tilted forward. It looked as if the god was sleeping.

We watched Azis, who was carrying only his small pack, shrink against the vast backdrop of the Jagannath. I put my eye to the telescope and saw him walking with the same ease he had displayed walking beside me. He might have been walking to town for milk. No hesitation whatsoever as he came to the spikes radiating from the left front wheel. Only once did I see him bend backward to appreciate the magnitude of the god before him. Then he grabbed one of the spikes, hoisted himself, looked for the next. He had to jump to reach it, and swung for a moment before pulling himself up. There was no indication the Jagannath was aware of Azis; its eyes remained closed.

Azis climbed. With leaps he progressed up the curve of the wheel. When he had almost disappeared into the chariot, he looked back toward the hills where we were gathered, and waved. Nobody waved back. It was unlikely he could see us.

Then he ascended into darkness.

We waited.

Nothing happened.

The tune he'd whistled replayed in my head.

The god opened its eyes.

Just for a moment – they were wide open – as if it had felt a flea crawl across its neck, or a gurgle in its belly. It seemed to stare straight at us. Then, as suddenly and as terribly, the eyes shut again. It dropped its head, back to sleep. As if this minor disturbance had been identified, or silenced, or squashed.

Azis did not reemerge.

We waited. We stared through our optical instruments, looking for clues to his fate. Nothing. The Jagannath remained in stasis.

'He's dead,' Vasant proposed.

I walked down the incline. 'I can't wait any longer,' I said.

'You can't go,' Pala protested. 'That makes no sense!'

'I don't live to watch others do my work.'

'Then let's try the assault . . .'

'Vasant's idea is better. I want to see where Azis went wrong.'

'Well, don't simply imitate him; try to look at the situation pragmatically. Try something different.' He moved between several of the wagons until he found what he wanted, turning to me with rope. 'Try this.'

In the second attempt to penetrate the deity, we walked in a group of five: I accompanied by four Pragmatics. One end of the rope was tied around my waist and the other held by the monks. I led them across the field, like a fancy dog leading a family of aristocrats. The Jagannath towered before me. Unlike the Pragmatics, I had a Hindu background, and it made the sight more dizzying, fearsome. It was risky to come this close to even the most benevolent of the million. I not only came but intended to trespass upon a god whose sheer enormity made it hazardous to

devotees. The Jagannath was a mountain. I could smell
the fires of its engines and the dark exhaust implied
by the slow obliteration of stars overhead. I could smell
the wood of its hull. I could see, as we got very near,
scratches and stains on the wheel, clawed, perhaps, by
someone from Sholapur as he or she was carried inside.
I stopped directly before this surface and its multitude
of spikes.

I jumped to the first, having seen how Azis did it,
and I was more agile. I jumped to the next spike up,
landing cleanly. The rope pulled after me, the monks
feeding slack. If I fell, I would hang suspended. Which
was fine so long as the Jagannath remained stationary
– if it moved, I'd be instantly tangled. The four below
watched me with Pragmatic intensity. Grit fell away
beneath my feet. I was almost at the point where Azis
had disappeared. I looked back at the twin hills, but
from here they were only lumps. Staring long enough,
I might have picked out individual figures, maybe even
identified swollen Yamuna. But why bother? I proceeded over the upper curve of the wheel.

I had to jump another few spikes in the dark, following the pattern. I was glad for the sound of rope
slithering behind me. Inside the chassis, when I reached
the top, there was light. I crept forward, hiding behind
spikes as I moved. Who might be watching, I didn't
know. As far as I could see, I was alone.

The spikes meshed with others above a ramp angled
to a conveyor belt. There were globes of spitting, crackling light posted throughout. The conveyor belt was
wide as a street, a braided canvas material treated with
some waxy substance. Ahead, I recognized an aperture
from Vasant's sketch: a triangular opening formed of

heavy mills, where incoming fragments of material would be crushed. I jumped to the belt, careful to clear the opposing spikes. The belt was still for now, and it didn't flex beneath my landing.

I walked forward, pulling the rope. More lights shone on the other side of the mills, and a variable red glow that I suspected came from the engines. I looked around, then squeezed through.

On the other side, the conveyor belt continued. There was a dull roar in the chamber, the ever-present sound of engines now closer, and a display of light on a wall changed as some unseen aperture opened and closed. And there were people. I hadn't noticed them right away, because they wore outfits that seemed part of their surroundings, gowns of the same heavy, treated fabric as the belt beneath my feet, flowing into similar helmets with transparent eyepieces.

They didn't notice me. Or, rather, they did, but didn't care. I stood directly before them. A dozen on one side, a dozen on the other. They were attending the mouths of big tubes, each wielding a pike. Possibly their job was to pick out interesting items from the rubble passing into the god. To pick out the materials appropriate to their tube and drop them down. They could sort objects that way, things that could be reused.

They ignored me as I walked down the belt, tentatively at first, then with full strides. When I was satisfied that they wouldn't strike me with their pikes or try to deposit me in one of those tubes, I jumped off.

I whirled, surprised by the rope following me. I traced it back to the aperture. It seemed safe.

Orange-red light continued expanding and contracting across the wall. It grew hotter in the chamber when the light was brighter. At the far end, two narrow tunnels led upward. At their bottom sat piles of rice, green peppers, tomatoes – refuse? Liquid dripped from the lips of these chutes. I looked for another exit, but there was none. So I climbed into the cleanest tunnel.

It was a tight squeeze. I moved like a snake, propelling myself upward. The tunnel was ribbed, which helped, but there were no holds for hands or feet. It was dark throughout the brief ascent – no lights in here – but soon I'd climbed to another level. A narrow corridor stretched before me. It wound tightly around several vertical columns. I moved along slowly, carefully. Gaining confidence. What had been my concern, earlier? The only thing to keep in mind was that the corridor dropped off sharply on one side, to a narrow gully, where black, viscous liquid sloshed back and forth. A bad idea, falling into that oil.

Ahead of me, a black person. In reflex, I took the weighted blade from my pocket and let it fly. I pulled, and the weight sailed around his neck, the string wrapping tight. With a yank I brought him to his knees.

He fell without resistance. Blinking, breathing, not doing much else. No anger showed on the man's face.

But I wasn't sure why I had done this. I licked a finger and ran it across his forehead; color came away. Underneath the soot, he was brown like me. He lay breathing on the floor as my spittle traced his brow. I removed my foot from his chest and helped him to his feet. He had things to do.

He bumped past me without a word, the string around his neck, my blade dangling like a pendant. I let it go.

There were places to go, things to do.

Ahead, one of the columns had its cowling removed, revealing a single great piston. A group of the blackened laborers stood around the opening and didn't look at me.

I passed Azis. He carried black tubing with a bend in the middle. I kept walking. Beneath me the floor shook. Sections of floor hopped up and down with the violence of the engines. Water ran down my face. Tears, because the air was bad.

Ahead, they were waiting for me.

Another tower stood with a section of cowling removed. Maybe ten meters high. Visible inside were cogs, and the laborers toiled at one gone foul. The thing was useless, several teeth broken to stubs. When the opposing cog turned, it only batted its partner forward or back. We couldn't leave it like that.

All the cogs stopped turning. The whole shaft. Now enough of us were present. I squatted in front. Another laborer climbed my shoulders. I rose, putting him level to the problem. Someone else arrived with a special saw. I passed it up.

It was difficult to saw through steel. The floor kept shaking. I steadied myself against the open frame to stabilize the man on my shoulders. His blade had dug only a few centimeters. Frustrating! He worked. When he stopped, I pivoted so the blade could continue sawing, and he resumed. Filings trickled down. Fumes rose from below. Tears kept running down my face, but that wasn't a problem.

We would get this done. The cog had to be replaced. I looked at the new cog one of the other laborers had delivered. Its arrival made me even more anxious to complete the task. I looked back up. Pivoting my hips whenever my partner paused.

We had to replace the cog.

And then I found myself among orange robes, under a night sky.

The woman put a hand to my forehead. She said softly, 'Are you finished?'

I didn't know how to answer.

She looked over her shoulder. 'He has stopped jabbering.'

I closed my mouth. Was I jabbering? I didn't think so, but I found myself desperate to talk about a certain transmission tower on the lower left deck, column 56. Words came to my lips, and I had to resist them. I felt the individual firings of nerves in my face, flaring like match heads. The words wanted to come. Wasn't she interested to hear how incremental inefficiencies jeopardized entire columns of power? She must be interested. But when I looked into her face, there was sternness: a signal I interpreted deep inside. *Shut up*, said her face. Yamuna's face.

So I shut up. I concentrated on the stars. I tried to see them shifting into pictures, astrology.

Other faces came into view. Pala, Vasant.

'Try sitting up,' said Pala.

They helped me into position, holding my arms.

'Breathe in through your nose,' advised the monk, 'out through your mouth.'

I followed his instructions. Fresh air was welcome.

A rope, I noticed, was tied around my waist. I couldn't have been more surprised. Then I remembered

Pala tying the loop, earlier. I remembered the plan was to pull me out.

Maybe that explained my soreness: I felt thoroughly bruised. If I'd been inside the Jagannath when the four Pragmatics reeled in my rope, that would have made for a rough ride back . . . But trying to picture the interior of the god made my head spin, made me see more than I wanted to see, brought back the compulsion to get inside and work —

'How many fingers?' Pala said. He raised his hand but no fingers.

'A trick question,' I said. 'Or perhaps a koan?'

At this he smiled. 'Good,' he said. 'We feared your condition might be irreversible.'

'Condition?'

'You were talking about a cog,' said Vasant. 'Nonstop.'

'Do you remember a cog?' Pala asked.

I put up my hand. That word I found particularly difficult to bear. It threatened to spiral into relations with a hundred other words, descriptions of machinery, a thousand other pieces, components growing around it.

I rubbed my temples and said to Vasant, 'I think this might be like assemblage.'

'What do you mean?'

'I'm afflicted by a vision. Mechanics. The Jagannath. One particular part. Everything around it. The universe turns around it.' I shook my head, inhaled and exhaled as Pala had instructed.

Yamuna asked, 'Did you see Azis?'

'He was in there,' I told them. 'Working.'

They looked confused.

'Similarly afflicted,' I said. 'But he couldn't extricate himself. He had no rope.'

'Did you speak to him?'

'I was indifferent.'

'Strange . . .'

All the Pragmatics were gathered. They sat in concentric circles, I at the center. They appeared concerned for my well-being. Or so I thought until I saw that some were taking notes.

'Tell me what you saw,' Vasant said. 'I'll correlate it with my vision. We can build a blueprint.'

'I don't dare.'

Pala said, 'The Jagannath has a unique method of servicing itself, it seems. A knowledge it forces on anyone inside it. You, Rakesh. Despite your single-mindedness, you fell under its sway in less than five minutes. A powerful defense.'

'So we go back to the original idea.'

'I don't think so. When we put together that plan, I was naive. You told me about the god, but I didn't fully appreciate its . . . scope. I don't think arrows will suffice.'

'What, then?'

'A Pragmatic invasion,' he said. 'If all the Pragmatics storm the body, we can keep watch on one another. We can resist its mental coercion.'

'I doubt it.'

'Rakesh, you are a Hindu. A subject of the gods of Hinduism, such as the Jagannath. We are neutral. Perhaps immune.'

'Azis wasn't immune.'

'He is a novice, with shortcomings. Less discipline. And he went alone – we work best as a group. We can focus together, help one another, and rescue anyone at risk.'

I looked at Vasant.

'What do I care?' said the Engineer. 'If they think they can raid a god, let them try.'

As much an endorsement as could be expected from him.

'Go,' I said.

And they went. Like a prison march, they proceeded in a long file, each placing one hand on the shoulder of the person in front. Pragmatics were still leaving the meadow when the front of the line reached the field below. Silently, the line inched across the distance between our hillside and the god. The god's head remained tilted down, its eyes closed. As the Pragmatics got closer, I had the terrible sensation that it was not resting at all but, rather, playing dead, allowing hapless infidels to believe they were mounting an invasion when in fact they were being collected for labor. But it was too late to recall them. The front of the line was at the wheel now, and one after another the monks climbed inside. I could hear a phrase repeated down the line, some word game: probably an aid to concentration. I watched them insert themselves until about half their number was gone, then I turned, walked over the trampled grass of the incline.

Vasant was using the telescope, aiming at different points of the Jagannath. I paced. I would have taken the opportunity to approach Firdaus, but even he had gone to meet the god. Only two or three Pragmatics remained here on the meadow, those too badly injured to climb the wheel. I felt restless, guilty that I wasn't taking an active role. My body tingled; I itched to do something.

The last Pragmatic disappeared. No longer did their voices issue across the way; I heard the thrum of engines idling, the furnaces that fed the rumble. I walked back and forth, looking for something to divert my thoughts.

And came upon the wagons.

I had assumed the Pragmatics brought only essentials for a trip: food, clean robes, and so on. But inside one wagon I spotted something that stood like a big wooden crab, on six legs. I glanced around. None of the debilitated monks were nearby. Vasant was squinting into his telescope, and wouldn't care what I did anyway.

Quietly I climbed into the wagon.

After my eyes adjusted, the crab revealed itself as one of the sets of limbs worn by the goondas. Somebody had gone to the trouble of removing it from a corpse.

I ran a hand over a smooth hardwood arm, admiring the craftsmanship. At the elbows and shoulders, where the arms flexed, cables were visible, running to the wooden vest. When I pushed, the whole assembly swayed, corrected itself.

Would the arms work on another person?

With effort I overturned the set, lay down in the vest, and inserted my arms in the connected wooden sleeves. They were difficult to bend, and my attempt produced only a weak sympathetic curl in the four additional limbs. The device was big, designed for the tall, willowy bodies of goondas, and the fact that I hadn't buckled the garment made the poor fit worse. So I pushed my hands to the vest – using my fingers was difficult, too, since my hands were sealed in jointed gauntlets – and swung both sections over my chest.

The first thing I noticed after clamping them shut was a gentle buzz. When I next tried moving my arms, there was no resistance. The four additional limbs mirrored my action, swishing against the floor of the cabin. I tried to rise, but the assembly was too heavy. I pulled myself up, and the limbs all helped, knocking noisily against the floor, simple hands all around me grabbing at nothing. I turned my palms up. So too came the others, each hand spaced neatly apart, three per side.

I stood and swayed, unused to the weight . . . and toppled. When I put my hands out to break my fall, the others shot out and with too much force: I punched holes in three places. I was stuck in the floor. When I extracted myself, the hands came away noisily, clutching hunks of cart. I had made a ruckus; the Pragmatics must have heard me. Waiting for their reaction, however, I heard another, greater noise.

Wheels turning, ground rending. The engines of the Jagannath flaring.

I struggled to get out of the wagon, scuttling forward like a blundering crustacean. I lurched against the side of the vehicle and fell over. Frustrated, I slammed a fist against the floor, and two more such blows followed, breaking through. Some fundamental beam busted, and the cart buckled, sandwiching me.

I gave up trying to extricate myself by conventional methods. The cart was ruined, so I ruined it further. I struck through the floor. The cart creaked, complained, split toward the ground. I ripped and tore. The limbs worked around me with a will of their own. Boards came up in sections, flying up against the ceiling. Soon I'd dug through to the ground. I got on my feet, and was careful to balance the weight of the mechanism. Then I tore at the remnants about me, and the whole wreckage lifted, turned in my multiple grasps, subjected to six limbs, shrinking as it turned, its pieces picked away, the night breaking around me, and then I broke into night, throwing the remainder of the vehicle aside.

Vasant and the remaining Pragmatics stared at me. Then they turned back to the Jagannath.

It was moving, rolling forward, back, and to the sides. Its eyes had opened, its head lolled. The ground below was hashed as it lurched, and the hills shook.

A battle had begun.

I couldn't let it happen without me. I couldn't just watch. But the vest remained sealed. My fingers in the wooden gloves could not unlock the latch.

I looked at the injured monks. 'How do you undo this?' I asked.

They didn't know.

The Jagannath continued its fits. I started down the trail, extending my six arms for balance.

'Where are you going?' Vasant shouted.

'To help.'

Difficult running with the additional weight, but I was learning how to carry it. The Jagannath veered away – retreated in a sweep of whole kilometers, it seemed – then rolled forward again, and I had to dodge the tumult of spikes. The god reared. I wouldn't be able to get inside the same way.

I held back, waiting for the Jagannath to make another pass. When it came, I ran beside it, watching the flank of the chariot. Could I climb that surface? The question became unnecessary as the god surged closer; I leaped to stay alive, lifting the weight of my appliance with me, and when I struck the wall, I scrabbled for a hold. The Jagannath was of much more durable stuff than the cart: it wouldn't yield to my surrogate fingers, but they could dig in. They kept me clamped to the surface as I kicked my legs. I brought my feet to the wall, pushing off my sandals so I could find helpful cracks. Then, when I felt as confident as I could with my hold, I lifted an arm and grabbed higher. My three right hands rained down on the surface of the Jagannath. Each set of carved fingers gripped available boards.

I could do it.

I climbed the Jagannath. It continued rushing back and forth, jostling me with momentum, but one of my hands always remained affixed, so I hung in place and found purchase once again. I climbed the chariot, then sprinted to the god's torso and began climbing its back, hoping to avoid its arms, which flailed unpredictably. The ascent was almost vertical, with nodules like vertebrae occasionally protruding from the surface. But I climbed. I had a working understanding of how to control the goonda limbs, and I progressed steadily. The earth receded below me, scarred by accelerations of the god. Spiderlike, I finished the climb.

Reaching the shoulder, I could crouch, six hands spread for support. The Jagannath noticed me. Its head turned, and I saw life behind those eyes. I saw silhouettes. The god threw back its head and roared. A hand came to make a grab. I shot forward and dove into roaring mouth.

Teeth tried to clamp on me. I divided my arms between upper and lower components of the mouth and braced myself. The pressure was enormous; my surrogate limbs squealed; they wouldn't hold. Deeper into the great maw was a diaphragm. All at once I released my arms and propelled myself through.

I got to my feet. The room where I found myself was oddly proportioned, twenty feet high, three feet deep. Before me were three tiny doors. But I didn't want to go down. I turned, knocking my arms against the walls. Opposite were rungs built into the wall, leading into a chute. I climbed.

This led into the head. Those silhouettes behind the eyes were people: Brahmins of the Jagannath sect – including someone I recognized from Sholapur. They all seemed subdued, like the laborers I'd encountered earlier. They sat in a strange forest of polished levers, some levers as big as they, which extended from the surrounding walls, floor, even the ceiling. Here, I sensed, was the resistance to our invasion.

One Brahmin stood with stiff, clumsy aggression. He came at me, awkward, telegraphing his attack. I meant to swat away his outstretched arms but did this and more with my six hands, the first batting his arm away, the second striking his neck, the third his face, the fourth his ribs, the fifth – I lost track of my own assault, all accomplished with more flair and power than intended. I heard bones crack as he staggered under my blows and fell.

The remaining Brahmins stayed seated. Some stared at me in silence, continuing to manipulate large levers. I heard glass shifting and realized that the bulbs of the Jagannath's eyes were rolling open.

In came a giant finger. The god's finger thrust through the eyehole and stabbed me in the back. If not for the vest, I would have been injured, but instead I flopped to the opposite wall, diluting the impact with my array of hands. I turned. The finger thrust again, stabbing. It dented the wall, but I managed to dodge the finger and avoid being run through. Then it caught me with its tip and curled. I was rolled and yanked forward. I resisted with my team of arms but couldn't break free. The finger tightened; I felt my chest compress. One of the Brahmins watched, using both hands to adjust his lever.

I reached over, grabbed his hair, pulled him from his seat. I kicked him in the chest, in the head, pushed him down with my foot. The finger remained wrapped around me. Then I kicked at the big lever he'd been manipulating, and the finger relaxed suddenly, withdrew noisily. One of the other Brahmins reached for the same control, but I broke his hand, driving it down through the console. He didn't scream, didn't flinch, just looked at where his extremity had been driven into wood and tugged at it.

Tubes extended from the console, and the Brahmins leaned forward to apply their mouths. Something hissed. I gagged on a noxious odor. Yellow gas piled over the floor.

The Brahmins were unaffected: receiving air through their tubes, I guessed. The bilious gas climbed, swirling around my knees. I went from Brahmin to Brahmin, pulling them off their tubes. They didn't care. The gas kept coming, and they choked too but didn't turn it off.

I ripped off part of a Brahmin's garment and got down on hands and knees. Feeling the wall, I found several small holes and plugged each with fabric. This seemed to work.

They tried to bring the Jagannath's hand around again and dispose of me with another finger, and I realized there would be no compromises with these loyal servants.

So I picked them up, one by one, and tossed them through the open eyes of their god. They went without complaint. They didn't kick their legs or flail, just sailed through the air and bounced against the chest once or twice before disappearing far below.

Pala and I stood in the head-compartment.

We could find no markings of use to our comprehension. The levers were bulbous and overlong, and sometimes we had to step out of each other's way to properly maneuver one. But after some experimentation, we coaxed the Jagannath forward.

We approached the pair of hills. The Jagannath's eyes were two round portals, and through them I could see the meadowed incline. Closer, we saw figures watching us, and closer still I could pick out which were injured Pragmatics and which was the Engineer. He stood with his hands on his hips, watching intently, a posture suggesting uncertainty about how to react to the god's advance. The same was true for the monks. A pair of them, each with one bandaged arm, knelt side by side and managed to take up a bow between them. They nocked an arrow and aimed it unsteadily at the head of the god. Of course they couldn't see us, and there was no way we could shout over the roar of the engines.

We stopped, wondering how to send them a signal. In the end, we manipulated the same big levers used against me, and in a surprisingly fluid gesture extended the right arm of the god to the meadow.

The monks scattered from the landing hand. They stared at the fingers smacked against the ground. Then Vasant walked forward, climbing the hand and crossing the bridge we had made of this giant limb, his palms pressed together out of respect to the god.

INTERIOR SPACE
NUMBER 43

‹—═◉═—›

WHO ARE YOU? *Who are you?*

I heard this frequently, but never answered any question or corrected the speculations inspired by my arrival. When I walked into town, my goonda limbs clacked with my steps, and people wanted to know if I was an avatar of some particular god, or a sentinel dispatched from the capital. Curiosity was good, because it meant townspeople would follow me, and as the crowd grew, I listened to them project their personal concerns onto the mystery of me. *My daughter has a speech impediment; can you help my daughter? I'm not handing over taxes to Delhi! Will you do something finally about the rats?*

Sometimes I flourished the arms, fanning them to a collective gasp, or maneuvering them through a set of angular poses. Mostly I put the arms to use knocking on doors, rapping walls, banging windows, my wooden knuckles making the summons as loud as a hail of stones. The inhabitants stuck their heads out and, seeing the gathering, emerged to follow me. I led them through town until their number became difficult to manage. At that point I found some dais or stack of boxes where I could climb and make my announcement.

Faces looking up at me. Usually some children messing around in back. When everyone was silent, I told them, 'This town will be gone within four hours.'

They murmured.

'The Jagannath is coming, and it cannot be stopped. Nobody in its path will survive, and the end the god makes to this life is unpleasant. I urge you to leave.'

Tones of hostility often erupted here; I spoke over them.

'Listen to that rumble. It gets louder. In three hours, the god will arrive. So whatever your decision, make it quickly. If you are wise enough to evacuate, assistance is available.'

I indicated the Pragmatics on horseback, trotting into view.

And when I stepped down from the platform, I was grateful for my supplemental limbs, because the townspeople crushed on me with questions and threats. *What about my daughter? You promised to cure her speech impediment!* Employing six arms, I pushed people back in six directions, and occasionally lifted someone to remove him or her from my way.

As I picked up one old woman, she yelped.

The Jagannath appeared on the horizon.

Changing the horizon.

It's too early, I thought.

It moved at the fore of a great wave of dust, trees becoming indistinct in the haze, man-made structures vanishing in the storm of its advance. So much for Pragmatic attempts to slow it down.

Shrieks spread, people running. The Pragmatics rode

about, counseling calm, but the townies were frantic,
unreceptive to the strangers in saffron. Trying to mini-
mize the death toll, the monks helped the people pull
out grandmothers or unwieldy pieces of furniture or
whatever other house-bound articles they seemed to
value.

I walked toward the oncoming colossus. Passing a
blue statue of Shiva, I touched it with one of my right
hands. I waited beyond fields of corn, until the monks
had done as much as they could and came riding joy-
lessly out of town. One veered over and hoisted me
onto his horse.

Coaxing horses to ride at the Jagannath was like
trying to ride into a burning stable, so we made a wide
circle and approached from behind, galloping over what
the god had done to the earth, getting close to the
back of the chariot, where a ramp lowered. The Pragmatics would sometimes cover their horses' eyes as
they urged them up the ramp to an entrance they
had discovered in the god's torso. Here I dismounted,
preferring to practice with the limbs.

I was skilled enough that I could climb to the Jagannath's head before it reached the town – Shamsabad
was the name of the place with the blue statue of Shiva.
Up here, the perspective was different. Scrubby trees
disappeared one after another, then we erased the corn-
fields, then roofs succumbed beneath us, the sounds of
their going down lost in the roar. The statue of Shiva
I'd touched was only a bluish figure obscured by the
haze of our advent, then it too was gone.

And the people. The striking azure sari of a woman
who'd spoken to me was now just one more dash of
color in the scramble below. *What about my daughter's*

speech impediment? It will not be a problem much longer,
I might have said.

I watched until I could no longer see the destruction
our passing had done.

Shamsabad, gone.

I climbed the face of the Jagannath and pulled myself
through its right eye.

Three monks sat where I'd removed the Brahmins
that first night, and two more stood offering suggestions
as levers were wrangled. Another sketched the head-
compartment, with all its stalks of lacquered hardwood
of unknown purpose. On a notched wheel rising from
the floor stood another monk, who had to use the
weight of his body to adjust the wheel's position. I
watched these test maneuvers a few minutes before
feeling the urge to descend a few levels and scrape
grime from some internal chimney – I twitched,
wanting badly to do the Jagannath this service, but
quickly I thought of the diagram instead, the diagram
Pala had shown me.

Whenever I sensed the god coaxing me, steering my
thoughts to a labor appropriate to my caste, I visualized
this image: a cube that appeared possible on paper but
was physically impossible, an optical illusion that, like
koans, could clear the mind of interference. Yesterday,
one of the novices lost expression, his voice dropping
out of a mantra as he turned and bumped out of the
room. His brothers and sisters acted quickly, recap-
turing him with their own mental tricks. This was the
first time I'd actually witnessed the change come over
another person, and afterward I was careful to keep
Pala's diagram near the surface of my thoughts.

I opened one of three hatches beneath the head and

looked down a long wall that sloped into a rounded room. No stairway or ladder was available, no obvious hitches where someone could attach a rope and rappel. So I hauled myself over the edge and let go, whizzing down the smooth wooden bank, then applying my limbs to slow myself, turning and spinning before finally coming to a halt at the bottom. I looked up and saw the portal fifteen meters overhead. Its hatch swung shut. The thing about getting around in the Jagannath was that rarely could you return the same way you'd come. Sometimes, if you wanted to climb a level higher, you first had to descend several levels and find the appropriate route up. Places also existed without an entrance or exit – even though we could hear laborers bumping inside. There were places we would never see, no matter how much we explored.

I stood in a long, curvilinear room tapering toward the far end. The monks had dubbed this Interior Space Number 6, unable to think of a name that suggested its shape. I walked, my footsteps sharp against the flooring. Most surfaces were black glossy wood, but a series of globes shone above, making Interior Space Number 6 simultaneously dark and blinding. It went on for twenty meters or so before swooping toward another portal. The surface was smooth, and I was glad to have additional hands to scrabble up. I squeezed through the small portal, then down a black tube that widened to become Left Shoulder Area.

A group of monks knelt before the notched ball of the shoulder. The ball was perhaps two meters in diameter and harnessed in wires strung from pulleys and gantries. These connected to more cables running up through the ceiling and down through the floor. When

the Jagannath moved its left arm, the whole arrangement reconfigured, cables webbing across the room
anew, rotating the ball in notches and so contributing
to whatever maneuver the arm performed. The monks
sat before this strange loom, watching, transforming
their observations into a mantra.

'Ah, Rakesh!' Pala rose from the group and stood
before me, happiness in his delicate features. 'I see
you're still wearing the prosthesis of the goonda.'

'I'm getting comfortable,' I said, 'with the mechanism.' I extended one arm to tap his shoulder. At
first, making such a gesture had required pronounced
movements from the rest of my body, but I'd quickly
become attuned to the device and, flexing the right
muscle groups, could manipulate each limb individu-
ally, precisely.

Pala smiled as I retracted the arm. 'We'll want it
back, of course.'

'Don't you have enough to study?'

'More than we'll absorb in our lifetimes. Never-
theless.'

'I wanted to take it off days ago, but none of you
had time to help me understand the clasp. Now I don't
know if I can go back to two meager arms.'

'Maybe Vasant could help?'

'Possibly. But this isn't what I came to discuss.'

Pala retrieved a map. We unrolled it on the floor,
and I placed a wooden finger on our approximate
location.

'The Jagannath is farther off course.'

'True.'

'We won't ever reach Nainpur if the deviation continues. Who knows where the Jagannath wants to take us.'

'You believe it has an agenda?' Pala asked, amused, as if somehow I was being naive.

'The god does what it does,' I said. 'But I need to guide it to Nainpur, and I can't afford the time it is taking you to influence its course.'

Pala replied indirectly. 'I remember that sketch Vasant drew before we entered the god: it corresponded with astounding accuracy to what we found.'

'That's his gift.'

'We've been working day and night trying to comprehend the mechanisms here. I can only imagine how much easier it would be with the benefit of such a gift . . .'

'I understand what you're saying, but the problem with that idea – '

'He despises us! You needn't find a delicate phrasing; we know. But you might improve his attitude. You could convince him to put aside prejudice and work with us. To you, he would listen.'

'You don't know Vasant.'

'It's in your interest to change his attitude. We investigate the phenomena of Hinduism, and we do with the Jagannath what we can. But getting it to Nainpur? That will require a level of comprehension we can't quickly provide. Not without help. Vasant's help.'

Pala could be almost as compelling as the god. I felt myself tingle with the urge to do this.

'Talk to him, Rakesh. We're not the Kama Sutrans he hates – he may find we even share some values!'

I wouldn't mention that in my appeal. But I agreed to speak to the Engineer, and we changed the topic to our route and possible corrections, when a monk shouted with surprise.

One of the besmirched inhabitants of the Jagannath had crawled through a shaft to enter Left Shoulder Area. Like the others, this laborer was black as kohl. He dragged along a broken metal pole and raised it in both hands, holding it like a sword, with a semblance of hostility. He lurched and made a few desultory thrusts at the monks, missing them mostly but occasionally connecting with a very lame blow. Four Pragmatics rose. By now, such attacks were handled in a perfunctory manner, the monks pulling away the weapon and subduing the man with holds. They only had to redirect his focus momentarily, whispering some Pragmatic conundrum into one ear, and very quickly thereafter the laborer was reminded of some other task, scurrying back into the tunnel to wherever his body was required. I pulled open a hatch in the floor and dropped down, obeying my own imperative.

The descent was a long loop, and I fell with the curve, smacking and slapping my system of arms. I was looking for Vasant but also trying to get a better sense of the lay of the Jagannath. Unusual proportions made it difficult to remember how to get anywhere. I shuffled into a room three stories high and two feet wide. Interior Space Number 17, black and bright. As I made my way, the walls opened to reveal a tower of cogs or an axle, then a wall of axles, all turning. Sometimes when these panels slid open, I'd be struck with the desire to fetch a tool, whose location I suddenly knew, and I summoned the image of the impossible cube, which returned me to the relative comfort of disorientation.

Throughout were blackened laborers. Except for their occasional attacks, they seemed indifferent to us and the fact that we'd stormed the god. They ignored me, and I avoided watching them too closely. But when I saw in a dark crowd a familiar flash of saffron, curiosity overtook me.

'Azis!'

A level above, he continued doing whatever he was doing. I shimmied up a tube that ran in that direction and stepped over to the platform. A few grimy inhabitants stood with him, threading a steel cable through the eye of a big spool.

'How are your investigations coming?' I said.

Azis didn't look at me.

'Why aren't you working with the other monks?'

Nothing. As if he was deaf.

'Azis? Can you hear me?'

I pulled him from his steel cable, but the instant I let go, he went back to it. I hadn't seen him since that first night, I realized. He remained under the control of the Jagannath.

Had his fellow monks abandoned him? Maybe they had tried to retrieve him and failed. Maybe he was too far gone . . .

I grabbed him by the neck and hauled him over.

The young monk regarded me without expression. Grease streaked his face, his robe. He tried in vain to bend himself out of my multiple grasps and return to his task.

'What is the sound of one hand clapping?' I asked him.

Nothing.

I pinched his arm. 'Azis!' I shouted in his ear, as I'd seen the Pragmatics do. 'Azis!'

Zero.

I slapped his face, but it swung back into position.

'We'll take the Jagannath to Bombay,' I said to him. 'What would you say to tearing through the red-light district? We can level every brothel there. It would be easy, Azis. You can come to the head of the god and watch them go down. Just give me the word.'

But he had none to give.

I let go, let him bump back to work.

'Did they just leave you?' I said. 'Your fellow monks abandoned you?'

I watched him for a while before remembering my arrow flaming across the ocean. Azis was not my concern.

I didn't find Vasant until I descended all the way to Interior Space Number 43, which was a long, wide chamber situated in the chariot of the Jagannath, the nearest to the hearth a person could go without risk of burns. The ceiling was not much higher than me, but because of the relatively even plane of the floor and the gate to the outside, the Pragmatics used this space as stable and storeroom. Wagons rolled, clacking back and forth with the movement of the Jagannath. A horse clopped in place, its hoofbeats pronounced against the wood. I folded my arms to my torso so I could more easily move around the animals.

In space 43 was a window to the hearth. The temperature crept upward; sweat formed on my neck. I glimpsed debris from Shamsabad, in flames. The window was made of some glassy, transparent material several inches thick, and everything on the other side was somewhat blurred.

A rummaging noise made me turn.

The sound came from one of the parked wagons. I threaded my way between the vehicles, peering inside one that jittered differently. Inside, a figure hunched over, riffling papers.

'Shouldn't snoop,' I said.

'Wha — !' Vasant whirled around, dropping papers. 'Don't ever sneak up on me!'

'Did you think I was a Pragmatic?'

'Don't start lecturing me about privacy. Look at you. Did you grow those wooden limbs?'

I paused. 'Find anything interesting?' I asked.

'Come.'

Interior Space Number 43 was otherwise deserted. The wagon I entered was crammed with handwritten documents in crates.

'You may not feel so friendly toward them after you see this,' said Vasant, gesturing to the documents and other articles of Hinduism. I saw the clay rendition of Ganesha, the elephant head peering out from a swaddle of cloth. 'They're studying us.'

'You and me?'

'Perhaps. But Hindus in general. The Pragmatics brought Hindu texts. Others written in longhand.'

'When I was alone at their fortress,' I said, 'I too did some investigating. They had a book room, which was sacked by the goondas. I was able to get inside beforehand.'

'What did you find?'

'Much what you've found here. The woman Yamuna told me that this is the surplus of trade with

Hindu parties and that, yes, the Pragmatics examine our faith. To understand it better. They're a defensive people, for obvious reasons, so they want to comprehend fully the Hindu majority.'

'You believe that?'

'That's why they wanted to see the Jagannath. That's why they came in here with us.'

'And did your dear friend Yamuna explain this?'

He thrust a jar before my face. It was filled with an ocher brine, in which fibrous material floated, the shape of a diamond. Looking more closely, I saw the material was porous and curled at the edges, fleshy, fringed with veins or other strands of tissue. A label on the jar read: *Removed from Hindu on fourth day of Asadha.*

A specimen? I didn't care where the thing came from, really, but the sight of an extracted human organ made me uneasy. Through the ocher solution, Vasant's face appeared enlarged with emotion, his eyes lit with disgust and sanctimony.

'Does it matter?'

'Yes! It matters that we're traveling with people who collect human flesh!'

'But – '

'From the start they've made me wary. But this . . . this is sick, don't you agree? Enough reason for me to go. I must consider my well-being, physical and spiritual. I don't like being here, with them.'

'Vasant, you can't leave.'

'Because of your dharma? Is that supposed to be my incentive to stay?'

'You need the Jagannath as much as I do. With the god's help, you might make a difference, too.'

This silenced him. Lowering the jar, he showed a

somewhat calmer face. Only his grudge against the Kama Sutrans could overpower his distrust of the monks.

I remembered Pala's request, and stifled a sigh. Even if I could convince the Engineer to stay here, getting him to *help* the Pragmatics was a bald impossibility.

Or perhaps not.

I tingled before the thought fully crystallized. 'We need to take precautions,' I said.

He raised his brow.

'If we monitor the Pragmatics closely.'

'Monitor them.'

'I spoke to Pala. He was complaining of the incomprehensibility of the Jagannath's mechanical dimensions.'

'*Incomprehensibility*,' Vasant said with a sneer.

'If you offered your skills, your talent. Assemblage, as you call it. Well, you might determine what they hope to learn, under the pretense of working with them. You could keep track of their activities.'

He was silent, thinking, and I studied his face for signs of how well such espionage appealed to him. Around us, the canvas enclosure became suddenly bright. The Jagannath must have passed over another town.

CONTROL
FROM INSIDE

❈➡⚬⬅❈

STOLEN PROPERTY IN hand, I entered space 12.

The space was ellipsoid, and the monks had dubbed it the Factory, because the Jagannath kept a supply of labor standing in its center, waiting for the summons to a ring of machinery built into the circumference. Materials culled from trampled cities were transported here, to these murmuring devices – some like sealed cauldrons, some like churns, most of them simple black boxes that did nothing but hum. A sacred sound? Not one I recognized, but whatever the role of these devices, the Jagannath could make parts for itself here, and the begrimed faithful stood ready to assist in the process or to carry away completed products. The fresh components smelled strongly of the Jagannath – an acrid scent, edged with something like kerosene.

I felt urged to assemble a mold, but after taking a step in that direction, I visualized my flaming arrow, which I'd found as effective as Pala's cube for clearing my mind of the god's directives.

Passage was difficult, because so many laborers occupied the space and wouldn't step aside except for a task. Some flinched repeatedly, some jogged in place, and a

man did push-ups on the floor. Pala had theorized
that the Jagannath exercised its laborers in their idle
moments, to build their strength for upcoming chores.
But for me their behavior was a nuisance; I had to
shield the jar from sudden lurches. Yamuna was here
somewhere, and I meant to confront her with it. In
the jar was a specimen, another square of human tissue,
and even though these disturbed me less than they did
Vasant, I wanted to show her one. I wanted to hear
her explain.

I did a circuit around the chain of production but
couldn't see her, the laborers a shifting scrim of black
bodies. Could I have missed her? On my second loop
I still saw no saffron fabric.

'Yamuna?'

Soon I grew frustrated and put my limbs to work,
moving laborers out of my way like oversized pieces
on a chessboard. When I pulled one of them from a
job, he was almost immediately replaced by the nearest
available worker. Maybe Yamuna had finished her
observations and gone.

Then I spotted her, deep in the labor pool. Saffron
flashed through black legs when a contingent moved
to work. I pushed forward with five hands and pre-
sented the jar with my sixth.

'Tell me why Pragmatics keep parts of human
bodies,' I said.

She was sitting on the floor, staring blankly.

'Yamuna?'

I knelt before her, but she didn't notice.

'What is the sound of one hand clapping?' I
demanded, and slapped her face.

She said, 'I'm not under the god's influence.' But she was slow to meet my gaze and seemed distracted.

'What's the matter?'

'She's moving.'

'Who?'

Yamuna took my hand and put it inside her robe, so I could feel her belly. The baby moving.

Not merely kicking, or turning in sleep. It was as if the fetus walked in place, legs swinging forward until they met the wall of Yamuna's womb. Little arms, too. I could feel them working, working.

Yamuna asked, 'Do you think the Jagannath can influence an unborn baby?'

I didn't know.

'I feel her . . . She wants to do something.'

'Why are you just sitting here, Yamuna?'

'She wants to do something . . .'

I flexed all six of the goonda limbs before scooping up the pregnant monk. I shoved toward the exit with such force that the laborers fell like dominoes, and I had to step over them as I carried her out of space 12, down a long hall where we could no longer hear those whirring machines or see awaiting laborers, then down another hall, into a small spherical chamber with only one light above and no view of Jagannath mechanics.

I set her down.

When I next placed my hand against her belly, it felt calmed.

Yamuna looked at me, brought up her legs, and turned to the wall. Color returned to her face, and sweat. She put both hands on her belly, as if needing reassurance that her baby was peaceful.

'You must have seen the boy,' she said.

'What boy?'

'Some boy. Working for the god. A laborer. Maybe four years old. I saw him in a hole, a shaft half a meter wide. I suppose the Jagannath has many uses for small bodies.' She shuddered.

'Why didn't you leave space 12 when you felt the god taking control?'

'I . . . could block its imperatives as before, but . . .'

'Part of you wanted to stay.'

'Yes,' she said. 'Part of me wanted to stay. *Part of me.*'

I took a step back, allowing space for her recuperation.

After a while she asked, 'Do you think the Jagannath might be shaping her mind, in the womb?'

'I don't know.'

Yamuna straightened her robe. 'It worries me to think her mind might be vulnerable, before she is even born.'

'How do you know it's a girl?' I said.

'What?'

'Your baby. You keep referring to it as she.'

She was withholding something, I sensed. It was bothering her, and she wanted release. She wanted the mental balm of sharing a deep secret.

'Yamuna,' I told her, 'if you feel the need to discuss your circumstances . . .'

She looked up at me, eyes bright.

'I would suggest Pala or one of the other Pragmatics. It might be helpful for you. I would offer myself, but I care only about one other person, about killing him, and although I might hear what you were saying, it wouldn't mean much to me.'

She seemed frozen, staring at me.

I didn't ask about the specimen. My urge to find the Baboon had swelled suddenly, and I couldn't think about unrelated topics.

When I returned to the Factory, the jar was gone. I'd put it down, I remembered, when I lifted Yamuna off the floor. Vasant must have taken it, because I noticed him skulking around those puzzling machines, holding something in his arms.

'We're not getting anywhere,' I said.

Pala, the pilots, and six more Pragmatics stood in the head of the god. The head turned as we moved, as the god traveled through one great circle, the path in the ground heavily defined by its spiked wheels.

'There is good reason,' said Pala.

The pilots were operating the controls in the same pattern, saying a mantra that dictated their movements.

'You're circling deliberately?!'

'We've been looking for you,' Pala continued. 'To explain – '

'What is the meaning of this?'

'Look, Rakesh. Good reason.' He offered the telescope to me. 'You'll see.'

When I looked out with the benefit of the telescope, I saw that the land ahead was occupied by white humps, so plentiful toward the horizon that it seemed blanketed in white down.

'Cranes,' Pala said.

Yes. Looking more closely, adjusting a dial on the instrument, I saw that this was true. The lack of reference points made it difficult to determine their size. But they were big.

'More of your gods,' said Pala.

'Pala,' I replied, 'those are not gods.'

'No?' This seemed to give him pause.

The cranes were mostly seated, preening or puffing themselves.

'Do you think the Jagannath could survive a confrontation with so many, ah, demons?'

'Move around them,' I said.

'The Jagannath resists; we can manage no more than this circle. The detour would have to be significant, too, for us to get around the entire range.'

'How much delay?'

'Maybe a day. More.'

Unacceptable.

'We can wait until they're settled,' I said. 'They're preparing for nightfall. Maybe we can slip past them while they sleep.'

'Sneak the Jagannath through?' Pala said. 'We can't even keep it moving in a straight line.'

'That doesn't mean it's not possible.'

I felt myself trembling with energy when I left the head. I could not let the Jagannath stay here doing circles, getting no closer to Nainpur.

I returned to the head-compartment with the Engineer and said, 'Vasant will help you better understand the god.'

'As only a Hindu can,' Vasant said, with a smile at the Pragmatics.

Surprise filled Pala's face. 'Of course we would welcome any assistance you might – '

'Let's not waste time with chatter.'

When he turned to leave the compartment, Pala and the others grabbed writing implements and followed him hurriedly, looking delighted by this turn of events.

I had implied to Vasant that the monks were deliberately delaying me. I'd made it sound sinister, this circling. I'd hinted that only Vasant could foil the Pragmatic conspiracy. I would say anything to convince him to help.

I remained in the head, staring out the eyes as the pilots continued to move the god through that limited orbit like some massive timepiece marking with each revolution the minutes wasted. Occasionally I checked the telescope. Darkness fell, and the birds were reduced against it.

At last I felt the Jagannath slow, the noise of its engines tapering: Vasant and the monks were making a difference. When they returned, the Engineer watched how the pilots worked the god before stepping into the array of polished levers himself. I found it difficult to follow all the instructions he provided, and the Pragmatics must have, too, because they needed mnemonics and word games to record his advice. At his insistence one of the monks placed an arm into a slot of previously unknown function and found, as Vasant suggested, a hand control nestled deep within. In synchronization, three pilots pulled levers. The Jagannath's circle came to a halt. Pala went to the door, shouted something down to space 6. From there another shout departed.

'Adjustments are necessary throughout the god,' Vasant explained to me. 'Pala has arranged a network of Pragmatics to relay instructions.'

Night fell, and the Jagannath was coaxed forward. Slowly, quietly.

We tried watching through the telescope and other optical instruments, but there wasn't enough light. I was surprised when the first cranes began materializing in the darkness outside. Vasant had managed to reduce the Jagannath's progress to a crawl, and its silence reminded me of when Azis first climbed inside. We traveled very slowly, inching toward the cranes.

They slept with their long necks folded to their bodies. For as far as we could see into the dark, the white giants lay. The Jagannath maneuvered through them, its pilots managing to avoid contact.

Then the god reached a position where it could go no farther without touching a bird. We were forced to reverse, a tricky procedure that the monks turned into a mental exercise, reversing precisely what they had just done. We attempted another route and met the same problem, ending up in another spot where the god could not proceed without disturbing one of the winged demons. There may have been a path through them, but in the dark it was impossible to see.

'There are too many,' said Vasant. 'It can't be done.'

'Not without light,' Pala conceded. 'But if we wait until dawn, they will be waking all around us.'

The Jagannath idled, feathered bodies on either side rising and falling with one rhythm.

'Wait,' I told them.

I descended to Interior Space Number 43, where the monks kept their wagons, and searched until I found what I needed, the lamps on poles that we'd used during our walk from Ranthambhore. I gathered as many as I could carry with six arms, then went out the gate, to the chariot.

A breeze whistled up from the south. As I walked, the lamps knocked together like crude bells. I was highly conscious of the noise, seeing hundreds and hundreds of demon cranes around us. I walked the length of the chariot, watching. I heard their breathing, the ruffling of their feathers. I was safe as long as I stayed aboard the Jagannath, but we'd get nowhere while I was safe.

So I jumped down, the lamps knocking together. I watched the nearest crane for a reaction. It did not rise; its eyes remained shut. I looked back up at the god, at its eyes, where I knew the others stood watching. The expression on the god's face suggested frustration.

After some hiking among the feathered hills, I found a route to accommodate the girth of the Jagannath, and planted lanterns to mark it. I forced myself to march through the terrible smell of the birds, afraid not of death but of what disturbing the serenity of these demons might do to our progress and my goal of meeting the Baboon Warrior. As I walked, I stuck lamps in the ground as quietly as possible and lit them for Vasant and the monks to see.

The Jagannath followed the path. I could feel its advent.

Perhaps the cranes were shaken slightly by a tremor of the earth; perhaps a note of discord entered their dreams, or whatever passed for dreams when demons laid down their heads. But the silence Vasant had accomplished carried the Jagannath forward unnoticed.

Out of lamps, I walked back to where I'd started and collected the first ones. I repeated the process, seeming to cover a great distance each time I illuminated another part of the route, and my comfort increased, my confidence that this would work. Cranes still surrounded us in every direction, and I was unable to see how close or far we were to exiting their number. But I kept working at it, sweating with the effort. My

arms, I noticed, did not tire as quickly as my legs, even
though repeatedly thrusting the poles into dirt was
laborious. I took this as another benefit of the goonda
limbs, their energy supplementing my own. I became
more adept with the arms, cradling my load in four of
their crooks and with a flourish of the other two
swinging the lamps out of the bunch and down into
the ground. I had turned back to collect the lamps yet
again, when I happened to glance up at the face of the
god.

And I halted.

The expression on its face had changed from frustration to – what? There was no human comparison.
Atrocious joy? As I looked at that new configuration
of dark wooden features, my legs felt suddenly heavy.
I thought of the Pragmatics studying the mechanisms
of the god, and of Vasant effecting this present calm.
What did we know about the Jagannath? Did we
believe it could be driven like an ox, with no regard
for its character? Its will? I tried to move but felt
sluggish, doomed, regarding its huge face and knowing
that a righteous god could not be expected to move
peacefully among demons.

Its mouth opened.

The Jagannath roared, and the noise shook me.

It roared again, arms lifting and falling with exertion.
A flickering behind its eyes suggested silhouettes of
Vasant and Pala as they too were startled.

Then, around me, I felt the ending of sleep.

Bird eyes opened. Staring for a moment before heads
lifted to see what had disrupted their rest. Everything
changed – the cranes stood as one, the many mounds
of feathers rising. I was among scaly long legs, a

forest of legs, and the forest started to move. The cranes shook themselves and called, a two-toned squawk that first sounded near the god but spread, giving me a sense of just how far the flock extended.

In the Jagannath, engines flared. Dirt was flung from beneath the feet of running cranes, and I darted from side to side to avoid getting kicked. They beat their wings in time with their steps, and I was buffeted by wind and a stench of feathers and guano. In the long-legged chaos, I was battered several times, so I caged myself in my limbs, protecting my head and torso, and stumbled until I found an avenue the cranes seemed to avoid. Peeking, I could see they ran in distinct lines, diagonals of running birds that intersected but never collided.

The pattern raided the sky. They took off, line by line, the ascent spreading. One of the cranes must have snatched me in its beak, because I also took to the air, and was witness to the vast panorama, the grid of white bodies warping toward the stars. The ground receded, and I felt the repeated shudder of beating wings as the airborne lines continued to cross, flapping, squawking, always equidistant. The pattern shifted, lines moving over lines, and I sensed I was being taken farther and farther from the Jagannath, because the sound of feathered bodies thumping its hull grew fainter, the sound of its arms battling beaks, the drone of engines, its roars, dwindled, all of it dwindled, until I could see nothing but the pattern.

White bodies increased in density until they became a uniform field of white. Then the white was the feathers of a single bird, stepping back: this must have been the crane carrying me. I had been put down, and the demon bird regarded me with black eyes before stepping away. Slow beats lifted its body, slow wings carried it into a hole in a great dirt wall.

Where was I?

I sat on the rim of a vast, earthy oval.

Architecture, of some sort. But not a city. At least, not as I understood cities. Dull gray towers rose from the oval to spindly heights, and holes gaped throughout. Fires burned to provide flickering illumination, and through the holes I could see birds moving, traveling interior channels. The oval was at least ten kilometers long and several wide at the midpoint, and the whole thing sloped into a central, bowl-shaped depression. Despite the building material, which I realized was not dirt but a mixture of guano and twigs, much symmetry was evident, grooves running through everything, those towers rising according to grooves, at defined intervals. Maybe this place was best described as a nest.

I stood at the edge.

Looking out, I could see no horizon, no moon, not the ground below. It was like standing outside at night without my eyes ever adjusting. A static dark, unmarred by stars. Winds rose and fell, breezes coming in from beyond, but they provided no clue to my location.

'Pala! Vasant!'

My calls faded to nothing. I couldn't hear the Jagannath or feel it through the ground. I must have been very far away indeed.

I tried to walk along the perimeter. I *tried*, but instead turned toward the center of the nest, opposite the direction I intended.

I adjusted my angle, but the same thing happened: I

went more into the heart of the place, walking down grooved guano. I stopped, confused.

I took a tentative step. Another. No matter what direction I chose, I always went closer to the middle of the nest. Were my legs betraying me? Or was the whole nest somehow pivoting underfoot, pointing me to the center? I had moved several meters inward from the spot where I first found myself.

'What is this place?!'

No reply, no sounds except the scuttling of feathered creatures. I stopped and squatted, hugged my knees. After a few minutes in this posture, trying to work out what was happening, I made another attempt to leave, determined to do it right. But the same thing happened: I marched down into the depression as if hurrying to reach the center. I cursed and stopped, frustrated. I resolved not to move at all, to stay in place and resist whatever destination was intended for me. I spent perhaps an hour, immobile. Where was the Jagannath? Vasant and the monks? I saw and heard nothing from them, from anything. Time passed, and finally frustration won, and I started walking again.

Moving deeper into the nest.

Good Hindus had persevered in unholy places. I could, too, and I allowed myself to proceed.

No human forms were visible, but the birds sometimes moved, perched, lumbered within dusty ramparts of guano, or roosted among towers high above. Smoldering braziers had been cemented here and there to provide unsteady light. Underfoot, fissures revealed tunnels along which the birds moved, fast, appearing and disappearing with a regular frequency. Their movements followed patterns. I walked on, and found it more difficult to see my position in the nest, as contours rose on every side.

Curiosity made me rash, and I went forward to see that the entire bowl plunged down like a funnel into my apparent destination, a hole with only a dim red glow visible below. I stopped, and again tried to take a step away: it was a step closer. I now stood within a few meters of the pit.

I could only refuse to move. Sit and hold my legs, so they wouldn't betray me, wouldn't carry me down. As I sat, I became aware of a humming, and I saw a single white feather tossing above the hole. I would not go down. Absolutely not. I hugged my legs tighter, yet sensed that I couldn't wait forever, that eventually I would be driven to try to escape and, before my better judgment regained control, I would fall down the slope, down –

'I won't,' I said. 'I won't move a muscle.'

I stayed, huddled, occasionally cursing with frustration.

Time passed. I fidgeted, and even this edged me closer.

I wouldn't fidget.

But I had to squirm, didn't I? I couldn't avoid tiny movements of my body, respiration, the twitching of muscles, and these moved me imperceptibly closer – already I could see I'd got a few centimeters nearer. How could a live person keep perfectly still? I wrapped myself tighter, constricting myself within the hardwood limbs, as tight as I could, binding my body with the prosthesis. Over my arms I watched the feather dancing on warm air.

'Ah, here you are.'

I dared move my head to look.

A crane stepped around me. It moved with a queer gait, and there was something peculiar about its body. Its legs were pale but not dissimilar from the beak or feathers, as if they were made of only slightly different material. Also, the crane seemed faintly luminous; a pale light ruffled with its plumage.

'You'll do fine,' it said.

'How can you talk,' I said, 'without lips?'

'You don't need lips to talk, Rakesh.'

'Don't get any closer to me. Don't say my name!'

'You needn't be frightened.'

'You're a devil. An abomination.'

It shook its head.

'I can't stay here,' I said, resisting the temptation to move my head to watch it walk back and forth. 'I must kill the Baboon Warrior.'

'Must you?'

'Why wouldn't I?!'

It shrugged in a manner that I found appalling, given its body. 'I don't know who you're talking about, frankly.'

'Why can't I move properly? I must leave.'

'Leave? There's nowhere to go.'

'Spare me your demon talk.'

The crane rolled its eyes. 'Demon,' it said scoffingly. 'That's just a label you've given us. We are neutral, Rakesh. We are the essence of neutrality. We have no stake in people's lives; I suppose that's why you call us demons. But your prejudice, oh, it is so misplaced.'

I shook my head.

'Everything will make sense after you've accepted the count,' it said.

'The what?'

'Imagine, if you can, being part of a system, part of an enormous mind allowed to run through great questions without constraint. Imagine exploring truths of existence, and finding answers. Doesn't that sound grand?'

'I'm not moving.'

'Listen, Rakesh. The count. Doesn't it sound wonderful?'

I did hear now, in the hum . . . something. Voices, or something like voices, a chorus of numbers. Across the pit, the demon spread its wings, radiant, and the chorus became a rapid tally of all the feathers visible across its body. This must be the count.

'Everything has a number, Rakesh. Sound? My voice? It's a pattern defined numerically. A measured disruption of nothing to make something.'

Numbers wove through my thoughts, and I sensed the patterns they followed, the weight of sitting cranes against the fabric of the nest, the height of flying cranes relative to the rate of flapping wings, the amount of cranes appearing from the darkness against the amount disappearing, the sounds produced by the nest according to how many sat or flew: everything could be described by numbers, and they were all connected, and they led back here, and I could feel them, and they would not –

'Stop! Stop it!' I shook my head. 'I'm not going down there. I refuse.'

Across from me the crane squatted, and the expression on its face became stern. The glow from the pit tinged its feathers red. 'Stay where you are then, forever,' it said. 'Because, Rakesh, did I mention? The

India you remember is gone. It doesn't extend to here. You can stay huddled like a coward as long as you want, but you're not going back. Nothing of your previous existence remains. The Baboon Warrior? I don't even know who that is.'

The crane stared at me. Willing me to budge. Tremble. Anything.

I would not.

How much time passed? Hours, days. It was difficult to say because I didn't dare try to keep track, not with the numbers teasing me. How long? How many heartbeats ticked off by the pulse in my ears?

I forced myself instead to think about the crane and what it urged me to do. Enter the pit, succumb to this big zero built of twigs and guano. This was my only option, according to the demon. But demons would say anything. I tried to think past its lie: what continued to exist here, from outside?

It was obvious. It was wrapped around me.

I dug one wooden hand into the ground. I lay flat, dug in another. I used all the limbs, planting them in an array. The crane observed without comment. I grabbed the fabric of the nest and yanked myself away from the pit. My legs I could see kicking, trying to counteract this movement. I pulled myself along.

The crane said, 'That won't work.'

But it did.

The arms moved in sequence, dragging me away, away.

'You cannot escape,' it said. 'There is nowhere for you to go.'

I scuttled more quickly as I got used to moving with the arms, and while the crane watched me, I moved up the slope of the nest, and began climbing one of the guano towers. The humming subsided, but I could still see patterns around me. My handholds dissolved in weak material, but I climbed anyway, higher into the air, with more cranes coming in and out of the darkness, one, two, three —

When I reached the upper third of the tower, I could feel it bending, leaning, the pattern of its composition losing to the factor of my weight, and I wondered if it would pitch over and deposit me in the pit as the crane stepped on my head, shoving me down.

I looked out and saw birds moving on currents of air. But I was still nowhere. I had nothing with which to save myself.

Except . . . sound.

I said, *Sim wi ta sicc'm, ep fel sim.*

I had holy syllables. Faith.

Sim wi ta sicc'm, I continued, trying to control my voice, *ep fel sim*, trying to remember how the sounds were supposed to be pronounced and not let them be bent out of shape by fear, or unwanted numbers.

Sim wi ta sicc'm, ep fel sim.

A light.

As I spoke, it flared in the darkness: the Jagannath, a tiny figure glowing in the fury of its engines, very far away. Too far away, and not even looking in this direction. How would it find its way to me?

A second light appeared out there, a bundle of light, and I realized it was the pole lamps from my attempt to guide the god. Someone must have collected them, because they moved in a lump between here and the Jagannath, illuminating a small dot of the plain.

Someone must be carrying them.

Beneath me, the crane extended its wings and rose, rising in a spiral around the tower. 'You don't have anything, Rakesh. Not here. Nobody can find you here.'

'The Baboon Warrior,' I said, 'must die.'

And I saw that bundle of light moving closer, and as it did, individual lamps were left behind, one, two, three, thrust into the ground, pinned against the blackness, forming first a line, and then with two smaller lines, a symbol drawn in light.

An arrow. On the plain, pointing toward me.

My flaming arrow.

The Jagannath must have seen it, too, or someone aboard, because the god turned in the direction the arrow pointed, and accelerated, following its suggestion, arriving at the nest with its arms spread wide, in a divine gesture encompassing both glory and threat.

BETWEEN HIGHER
ORDERS OF BEING

◄══◙══►

I ITCHED, AND FOUND a feather.

I was sitting in Interior Space Number 6 with several Pragmatics who had been listening to my account. An itch below my left ankle had bothered me since the rescue, and I found a small white feather stuck into me, the quill hooked into my skin. I plucked it, disgusted. It must have got embedded during the chaos.

'Quite an experience,' Pala said, squatting.

I wiped my hand on the floor. 'The first time I've found myself between demons and a god,' I said. 'I don't recommend it.'

I remembered the sight of the Jagannath crashing into the nest. Never before had my faith rewarded me so dramatically, guano architecture breaking against the god's chest, cranes swooping forth and felled as soon as their trajectories took them within arm's reach. I'd thought I would be swept into the destruction, too, but Vasant spotted me and regained enough control over the Jagannath to extend a hand to the toppling tower, and I landed in its palm, and was quickly delivered back to the safety of the head.

'Did you fear for your life?' said Pala.

'I knew the Baboon Warrior still lived, so I would stay alive, too.'

'Hm.'

'What?'

The monk patted my knee. 'Never mind for now.'

I put my head back. A monk was making notes, putting my story on paper. A chapter for another volume?

'I have a question,' I said.

'Yes?'

'Who arranged the lanterns?'

Pala's brow creased. 'That is a mystery,' he said. 'After the Jagannath dispersed the first lot of cranes – even during – we searched for you. We hadn't seen you get swept away in the commotion, and afterward it was so very dark. As we scoured the region, that arrow of light appeared over the ground, far away, and I thought you must have done it, to signal us. I don't know who arranged those lamps, if it wasn't you. It wasn't any of us Pragmatics. And Vasant was in the head, with me and the pilots. I don't know.'

'Maybe a laborer?' suggested one of the other monks.

'Maybe,' said Pala.

But I shook my head.

'Rakesh? You have an idea who it was?'

If it wasn't a monk, then it could only have been one person.

I spent much of the next day outside, watching for him.

It must have been the veteran. Arranging the lamps was the first logical thing he'd done – and it came at a crucial moment, saving me from a lifetime of servitude. I could picture him, surprising us yet again with his appearance, this time thrusting lanterns in the dirt. He was following us. He was not crazy. He had helped.

But who was he?

Outside, I was attached to a curve of the god's head. I could use my goonda arms very effectively now, no longer needing to squeeze or relax muscle groups consciously to manipulate them; now the arms did what I wanted, as smoothly obedient as my natural pair, allowing me to clutch a vertical surface then safely forget about it. I could go to sleep hanging like this, if I wanted. But I moved from vantage to vantage, surveying the lands rolling by for an old man with the remnants of a hospital gown clinging to his frame.

I watched for him until Vasant called me from the walkway below. He told me there was something important I should see, so I climbed down and followed him into the god.

'I think the veteran is more aware than he lets on,' I said.

Vasant grunted. If something didn't interest him, he wouldn't listen. We walked down a triangular space.

'Is this about your project?' I said.

'What project?'

'I saw you in Interior Space Number 12 the other day – the Factory.'

'I was gathering materials for work of my own. No concern to you.'

'So why did you call me inside? Where are we going?'

He said simply, 'We were right to be suspicious of them.'

'Who?'

He gave me a look. Who else?

'I thought you were having success with the monks,' I said.

'I've been monitoring them successfully, if that's what you mean.'

'You don't find them easy to work with?'

'I show them parts of the god; they nod and compose a mantra to describe what they've learned. I do what is necessary – for our security. Of course I am not finding them any more . . . *palatable*.'

His tone had a note of warning that I didn't heed.

I said, 'I thought they displayed great cooperation during the encounter with the cranes. And my rescue, too, from what I understand. They worked hard to – '

Vasant halted abruptly.

We were alone, standing at the midpoint of a long black tube.

'Have I offended you?' I said.

His nostrils flared, and he expanded his chest. Then he announced: 'Rakesh, I lost everything I made of myself. Because of Kama Sutrans. Because of Hapi and Kavita. Because of that damned capacitor. But I blame myself more than them, because I am a Hindu, who knew better but was not chaste enough to control himself.'

'I don't understand what that has to do with – '

'You.' He raised a finger at me.

'What about me?'

'I have come to believe you.'

'Really?'

'Your dharma.'

He took a step closer, looking at me with intense

eyes. 'What you've said is true, isn't it? At first I could not believe you. *Killing a national hero.* It is a wild proposition and difficult to swallow. But getting into the Jagannath, influencing its behavior, rescuing you from demons – none of this could have happened without divine sanction. You are a Hindu boy, aren't you? You *are* doing what the gods want.'

'Yes.'

He seemed satisfied. He started walking again, and I followed.

Eventually I understood. Vasant needed to prove what a good Hindu he was. He needed a purpose that would lift him to a level appropriate to his caste. He needed a role beyond his desire to ground the airship.

I would let the charade of that role continue so long as it meant we had better control over the god. He led me down into space 43, where the Pragmatics had brought the head of a demon.

Vasant smiled at my surprise. 'Perverse, yes?'

We approached on tiptoe, staying behind the wagons. But the monks were probably too busy to notice us anyway.

They held saws, tongs, and measuring instruments, apparently hoping to dissect this newest specimen, but a group of laborers kept getting between them and the crane's head. The monks did their usual trick of distracting the laborers, but so many made themselves a nuisance that they effectively stalled the Pragmatics. The laborers tugged the monks, bumped against them, placed themselves in front of their tools. The monks tried to organize a barrier, but more laborers came, adding to the disruption, increasing the confusion.

I stepped into this scene.

'Where are you going?' Vasant complained.

I moved through the wagons, toward the oversized bird head with its precisely arranged feathers. Around the neck, where the monks had severed it from the body, the feathers were stained dark. I shuddered to see that plumage, remembering the pattern all too well.

'Rakesh!' said a monk named Dalvara.

'What's happening?'

'The laborers behave oddly. They won't leave us alone!'

'When did it start?'

'As soon as we brought the specimen aboard. A group of them stood waiting by the door. They got in the way, and when we pressed past them, they followed us, followed us here, and keep' – he pushed back a begrimed woman who bumped against him – 'keep frustrating our activities.'

'Peculiar.'

'Usually it's a simple matter to get rid of them, but today – hey!'

Vasant had taken a bucket from a laborer and proceeded to the crane head. He poured the bucket's odorous contents on it, splashing the liquid generously.

'Vasant, what are you doing?' I said.

'Stop,' Dalvara snapped, reaching for him, 'stop at once!'

But the Engineer continued pouring until the bucket was empty. Then he took a few steps back, as did the monks, in a hurry, pushing me, and I recognized the smell of the liquid as one of the laborers emerged with a burning piece of wood in his hands and tossed it in our direction. The head ignited with a *whumff*.

The Pragmatics raised a cry of protest and fetched

brooms and rags, beating the flames. But it was little use. Feathers changed color, white to black to gray, then fell away as cinder. The skin underneath peeled, exposing a skull like bundled black wire, which popped and hissed as it burned, coming apart, definition springing loose, and the laborers also got in the way when the monks tried to extinguish the blaze, or even to get a look at the fire's revelations. The head burned fast. Laborers came with buckets of water only after it was reduced to a bulk of char centered on a ruined, silverish core. Hisses and steam, and the monks looked at what had become of their prize, shocked, disappointed, perplexed. Before the smoke had cleared, laborers dug into the smoldering remains and broke it apart with bare hands, carrying away chunks for disposal.

Like the Pragmatics, I stared at Vasant in astonishment. 'Why did you do that?' I asked.

'The Jagannath obviously doesn't want any part of a demon inside it,' he said. He looked at the mess. 'Difficult for monks to understand, I suppose.'

THE BANYAN OF
NAINPUR

⤜●⤛

BANYANS WERE UNUSUAL, because their branches
dropped roots that grew down and planted themselves
in the ground, forming secondary trunks, so what
looked like a forest might in truth be a single tree that
over the years had spread its draping root system in
several directions. The banyan of Nainpur rose higher
than the Jagannath's chariot and covered an area almost
a quarter the size of the nearby town. I could see how
people might think of it as more than just a tree.

I stood on the right palm of the Jagannath and had
a good view as Vasant extended the arm and placed
me nearer to the banyan. In the branches below, I could
see movement. It was an inhabited place, this treetop.
The Jagannath leaned forward, positioning me over the
topmost branches, and I jumped, catching hold with
many hands, swinging down into this tree that had
been made a tribute to the hero of India.

After climbing down through tertiary branches, I
found stable footing, then paths worn into larger limbs.
I hadn't seen any inhabitants yet, but they must have
noticed the Jagannath and probably also watched my
arrival, from safe places. Hooks had been screwed into

trunks to facilitate climbing, and ropes had been hung for swinging over difficult gaps. I kept to the path and followed a set of steps winding around a trunk.

Farther down, tapestries hung in celebration of heroic moments in the Baboon's career. Scenes: he saves a child from drowning, he puts down a rebellion of soldiers, he pulls a wagon full of water into a sun-scorched town . . . I leaped and grabbed one of these tapestries, tearing it from its hitches. The ripping sound so satisfied me that I decided to pull down all of them, and I thought I heard a murmur of protest as I worked my way forward.

Overhead the sky was fractured by intervening branches, but I could see the arm of the Jagannath transferring handfuls of Pragmatics. They got their footing and climbed down after me into this place of reverence.

Baboons lived in the tree – actual monkeys. A few skittered at the perimeter, then I came across a clan posed through a network of branches, and they regarded me with hostile curiosity. Baboons were a rare breed of monkey, but there seemed no shortage here. Males paced like dogs guarding a home. The number increased as I continued on, until every branch seemed to have representation. I tossed one of the tapestries, scattering a bunch.

'Rakesh,' called a monk somewhere above me, 'I see someone.'

I saw them too, now, the human inhabitants. A few raised their heads among their simian counterparts. Just like those devotees I'd met in the Jaipur alleyway, the people here painted their faces and wore ruffs of hair – full masks, often – and if I didn't look too closely, I might believe it was the Baboon Warrior himself watching me.

More heads rose as I continued walking. Finally I came upon what seemed a shrine built in the cradle of a fat bough and several branches, a cobbled together platform with a pair of wooden statues of the Baboon Warrior in heroic poses. More tapestries hung, and fruit suspended in a net. Central was a throne, the Baboon Warrior a motif recurring along its arms and up its back. This impressive piece of furniture appeared immaculately cleaned. I paused to admire the craftsmanship before sitting down.

There was a lot of room in the seat, so I could easily arrange my many limbs. I drew up my legs and waited.

Real baboons continued to spring from branch to branch, then scurried aside as the inhabitants emerged, all of whom wore some measure of tribute to the Baboon Warrior. They looked at one another, blinking their confusion within masks or face paint.

About thirty came out to face me, some standing, some hanging by fake tails, some climbing nearby trunks. A man with a great ruff of hair moved to the forefront and raised an arm to point at me.

'That seat is reserved,' he said, 'for the Baboon Warrior.'

'Does he use it often?'

'The point is not that he uses it often. The point is that it is here for him.'

'It's comfortable,' I said, swinging my legs over an arm, getting more comfortable.

The inhabitants chattered disapproval.

'Who do you think you are?' said the man, acting as their leader.

I smiled and opened my mouth to tell them, when a voice in back said, 'I know who he is.'

A female voice.

One of the costumed figures stepped forward, and pulled open her mask by the mouth. 'He has come here for me.'

Recognizing her took me a moment, but the crease on her lip was undeniable. She'd grown since I last saw her, and hardened, too, from what I could see of her arms. Features that lent her innocence as a girl made her look scrappy and athletic now. She was less pretty. Or maybe it was I who had changed.

'I'm surprised it took you this long to find me,' Shanti said.

'I'm just surprised,' I replied.

'He's here from Varanasi,' she told her cohorts. 'Here to drag me back for a wedding.'

'Oh, no.'

'No? It's been too long, I guess. Here to humiliate me, then. Hurt me?'

'Not you in particular.'

'Then why have you come? Why do you wear those arms?'

I lifted a tapestry – the Baboon Warrior riding horseback – so everyone gathered could see. Then I blew gently and let go. It sailed to the floor.

'You want to meet the Baboon?' said the leader.

'Oh, I'll meet him. But I don't expect he's here today?'

They said nothing.

'Does he ever come here?'

'We keep things ready for him, for whenever he wants a retreat.'

I looked at them. 'I'm here to spare your lives,' I said.

The group made confused noise. 'Is that a threat?'

'I will have the Jagannath bring down this banyan,' I said. 'I hope some of you, at least one of you, will abandon it, before I do so.'

Shanti said, 'What are you talking about, Rakesh?'

'Somebody must survive to tell the Baboon Warrior about this tragedy. You'll tell him about me, and that I said I intend to visit every city he's saved, every city where he is worshiped, every city with a day in his honor, and every one of these will be leveled, by me and the god Jagannath.'

'Why would you even suggest such a thing?' the man said, horrified.

'Because I'm his assassin. I'm going to kill him. If I chase him, he can elude me forever. The only certain way to draw forward a hero is to threaten those who adore him. For people like you, he must show himself; a hero is obliged to defend his fans.'

'You're crazy.'

'It's my dharma,' I said. 'My purpose.'

'He is crazy,' said Shanti. 'He must be! Rakesh, is this your revenge against me? Do you think it will make a difference?'

'This,' I said, 'is my life. Please consider saving yours.'

The burly leader had had enough, apparently, and stomped forward, to give me a lesson. But I was defter, springing to my feet and lifting the throne behind me, transferring it among my six arms before I raised it and brought it down fast, striking him once on the head and then swinging it a second time, knocking him so hard that he staggered, tripped over the side of the platform, scrabbled to stop himself, then bounced down, out of sight.

'A third-rate monkey,' I said.

More defenders approached. I hurled the throne, knocking them down, and leaped atop, balancing, pinning the amateur brutes underneath. For the moment, the Baboon's throne was mine, and I met the gazes of his startled devotees – and happened to see monks, too, poised in the branches beyond like saffron fruit. 'Remember,' I said. 'I want at least one of you to survive and tell him about me.'

I stepped off.

They cleared away. Some hopped from branch to branch, but nobody else approached. I walked backward to smile at them as I departed, arranging my arms so the hands were steepled in three sets. Shanti appeared furious. But I hummed with pleasant energy, energy radiating from deep within. 'Watch what happens next,' I told her. 'And be sure to tell him my name.'

I began to walk back up the stairs. Their last resort was a horde of quarrelsome baboons swaggering along branches or dropping from above, crowding the path and baring fangs. The animals gave me no choice but to disperse them with kicks and blows. They snapped at me, scratched, tried to grapple my legs and trip me when I shimmied up a narrow branch. When I looked over my shoulder, several dozen followed, all waiting for turns, leaping, scrambling to get closer, and making an awful racket. But the Jagannath lowered its hand, and I grabbed a finger and was lifted from their shrill anger.

I climbed into the head-compartment, where Vasant and pilots interacted with the god. The left arm

remained extended to the tree, and the monks who
had followed me attempted to use it as a bridge back.
Baboons leaped at them, climbing onto the arm, delaying their progress with bites and howls. I put my hands
together and said a brief prayer to the Jagannath, careful
not to let it seize my thoughts, because during prayer
its mental intrusions were most acute.

Then I said to Vasant, 'Now I must honor my
threats.'

'You don't know anything about these instruments,'
he said.

'But I've been watching.' I stepped among the lacquered wooden levers, running my fingertips over their
glabrous tops. 'And you will give me advice.'

'Fine.'

He rolled the Jagannath forward, its chariot pushing
into the outermost trunks of the banyan below.

'Wait! Wait!'

Pala rushed in. 'Some of us are still over there,' he
said. 'They are getting off the arm.'

'They should hurry,' I said.

I experimented with the set of levers governing the
Jagannath's left arm and hand. It knocked forward, and
Vasant leaned the whole torso over so I could grab a
branch of the banyan in one huge fist.

'Rakesh!' Pala complained. 'Wait! Let the last monks
get off!'

'If you didn't want to put your brothers in jeopardy,
you shouldn't have sent them to spy on me.'

'Spy? It's our nature to observe, Rakesh. We weren't
spying!'

I wasn't listening.

Pala arranged for arrows with ropes to be shot over

from a walkway on the Jagannath to the tree, so his
brothers and sisters could climb back without our assistance. We started to uproot the banyan, Vasant and I,
and the Jagannath. I had realized during the episode
with the cranes that goals would be accomplished only
if we cooperated with the god. Once a few trunks had
been pulled, the process became easier, then unstoppable. The great hands no longer resisted, now eager to
wrench away more trunks and return this land to the
raw form characteristic of the Jagannath's wake. We
pressed closer, breaking thicker trunks, exposing a
scramble to leave the banyan, people falling from
branches and dangling from ropes. The baboons continued pestering the monks as they returned to the
Jagannath, following across and leaping onto their
backs.

The baboons were plentiful, darting back and forth,
throwing themselves at the god's hands. There must
have been hundreds living in the tree, and, forced from
their home, they behaved aggressively, attacking the
god's fingers. This did nothing to delay us. People
clambered to escape as we reached the central trunk
and pushed, pushed until it pitched with a groan, and
tipped, and fell with a worthy crash, bodies falling with
it. I had my arms extended to several controls around
me, telling Vasant what I next wanted to do and when,
and he would take one of my goonda hands and place
it where it needed to be to effect the right gesture. I
leaned over with the god, grabbed the banyan with
both divine hands, leaned back and lifted it up – trunk,
branches, all of it coming off the ground as I hoisted,
with the few remaining roots snapping like gunshots.
Another body dropped from the tree when I raised it

over our head. Then I threw it, as best as I could manage with my limited understanding of the god's body mechanics, and the tree turned through the air and landed with a mighty crash in the nearby town, halting traffic, caving in the roofs of several blocks of housing.

Pala stood watching over our shoulders. I hadn't noticed his return.

'They were only his admirers,' he said.

'What do you mean?'

'You've acted . . . severely.'

'If anything, I haven't been severe enough. We must consider what the Jagannath wants, too.'

Pala made a scoffing noise.

'Maybe I haven't properly explained my purpose,' I said.

'Oh, you've explained. Yes, I know what you want. But this . . .'

He stepped closer. 'Is it true you knew someone in that tree?'

'That had no influence on my actions.'

'Doesn't it bother you that you might have hurt her? You might have killed her. Doesn't that matter?'

I gazed at the fallen banyan and its smashed limbs and the ruined buildings beneath. Bodies of the wounded and the dead lay everywhere. Torn tapestries were visible, and the shrine, broken, battered, smashed.

'You Hindus claim to respect life,' Pala continued. 'Has your obsession with the Baboon Warrior made you forget this?'

I raised the arms of the god, lifting its hands into view. They appeared coated with fur – baboons. The baboons had thrown themselves at the fingers of the god and now swarmed over the surfaces, clinging for their lives, barking.

I clapped the god's hands, hard as possible. It was a thunderclap edged with a crunch. Shrieking followed.

Pala gasped.

I pulled apart the hands to reveal a red mess clotted with fur and bones. A few baboons were still alive, glued to the god's palms, thrashing and keening. Pala's jaw dropped. He and the other monks looked aghast.

I reached down to the ground and with one bloody digit of the god drew a symbol. The arrow.

'Do you think he'll know it was me?' I asked. 'Or should I sign my name to this?'

But Pala and the other monks walked out, and even Vasant withheld comment.

SIMPLE TEST

INTERIOR SPACE NUMBER 31 was dim, but Yamuna
was easy to see, glimmering in her copper garment.
Her fellow monks had made it for her, a flared tube
that clamped over her body in two parts and allowed
her to move about easily enough, although if she
bumped another object, she rang like a gong. She was
carrying a bucket, and lowered herself until the bottom
of her metal outfit cupped the floor; then she made
chittering noise to the shadows.

Shapes emerged. Seeing her, they became braver and
stepped forward to snatch away the pieces of fruit from
the bucket.

Since Nainpur, the Jagannath had been home to a
small population of baboons. They must have squeezed
through joints of the god while swarming over its
fingers. I had seen them a few times, behaving strangely.
Sometimes they loped along and made trouble, as one
would expect; other times they sat on the floor or lay
down, doing nothing, their eyes open but their bodies
in stasis, isolated groups huddling in confusion around
fallen males. I assumed we had the Jagannath to thank

for these scenes; if the god could command an unborn child, surely it could put a stop to monkeyshines.

Yamuna emptied her bucket of apple pieces and watched the monkeys stuff their faces and dip their heads into the pail when there was no more fruit on the floor. From somewhere inside her copper gown she produced a pencil and paper.

'Are you encouraging them?'

She rose, startled. Baboons hopped back.

'Sorry to intrude,' I said.

Her expression changed when she saw it was me. Darkened. 'I was just making sure they got something to eat,' she said quickly. She tossed her writing instruments into the pail and walked away, toward the exit.

'Goodwill to animals?'

'Not a concept you are familiar with,' she said without looking back.

'What do you mean? I have no quarrel with animals.'

She stopped, spun, glared at me. 'I heard what happened in Nainpur. The Jagannath's hands were so bloody, they had to be washed in a river. And you have the gall to say you have no quarrel with animals?'

'Oh,' I said. 'That.'

'A travesty.'

'It was my dharma.'

'Your dharma. Of course.'

'The necessary action at the time.'

'You think so? Is it satisfying to blame your act on dharma?'

'I think you're angry with me.'

'Not angry,' she said. 'Perplexed. Appalled.'

'I do what I must. I feel the urge grow strong, and I

know, suddenly, what action is necessary to bring me closer to the Baboon Warrior.'

'And never question why? Never?'

I smiled. It was hard for people without faith to understand. She shook her head and turned.

I tapped her new copper garment. 'Does it work?'

'The baby moves occasionally,' she said. 'But I no longer feel the Jagannath controlling her.'

'I wonder why copper should insulate her.'

Yamuna shrugged and looked away. She always became quiet when the subject was her pregnancy.

A baboon swaggered toward me, baring fangs.

'He remembers,' she said.

'I've forgotten.'

'Doesn't it disturb you that you can put such a thing behind you, so easily?'

'No.'

'Don't you wonder why you're so – cold? Why you live your life this way, obsessed?'

I looked at her. 'Do you know why?'

Pala had removed the cowling from a section of wall. He was cast in an orange glow. When we got closer, I smelled yeast and realized he must have found a way to improvise bread using some runoff of heat from the Jagannath's engines. 'You're ten minutes early,' he said.

'We're not here for bread,' Yamuna replied.

Pala turned. Seeing me, his face soured. 'Oh.'

'I was asking Yamuna about your theories,' I said.

'Were you?' He used a large wooden spatula to move his loaf around. He seemed to avoid eye contact with me, and I realized we hadn't spoken since Nainpur.

'You'll have to tell me if you're angry with me,' I said. 'I'm not good at reading emotions.'

He set down the spatula.

'We were unaware how violent your . . . goal would make you. We underestimated. And now I hear we're to ruin another city?'

'In Akot many years ago, the Baboon tracked down a rapist who had been terrorizing a Brahmin neighborhood of the city. The Baboon is considered, in Akot, as worthy as the gods. The city holds a festival in his honor every year, so I will level the city.'

'And that's your plan? To keep attacking his fans?'

'It won't take long for him to respond.'

'I don't know if we can continue participating in this, Rakesh.'

'You're seeing a Hindu god from a very rare point of view,' I said. 'As you wished.'

'We can't ignore what our involvement here is facilitating.'

'The things I do, they are demanded by my dharma. I have no more say in it than you. So why let it bother you?'

'We're not comfortable with your concept of dharma.'

'That's what Yamuna told me.'

'I think we should show him,' she said.

'Show me what?'

The Pragmatic leader replaced the cowling and clapped his hands.

'Come.'

We descended to Interior Space Number 43, where cots were suspended between wagons; a shift of monks slept while another watched over them, making sure they didn't rise in sleep to service the god. The area was hot as ever, fires rolling behind glass, and we made our way to the place the monks stored their research, a group of wagons with people coming and going. Outside one wagon, and on the ramp, and inside the door, incense burned. I didn't know the Pragmatics to be users of incense, but when I went inside and smelled the other odor, I understood. Yamuna and Pala stood on opposite sides of a table and pulled back a tarp. I turned away as the stench of decaying flesh over-powered the camphor.

'One of the Brahmins you threw out the window,' said Pala.

The corpse lay facedown, packed with poultices to slow putrefaction. His back had been cut from the base of the neck to his buttocks, and the seam was pinned together. Pala took up forceps and withdrew pins; two flaps of flesh slid apart. I cleared my head and sum-moned strength, pushing out the stench, the sight.

'He should be cremated,' I said.

'Naturally you would think so. Have you ever wondered why Hindus are so driven to burn the dead?'

Pala pulled apart the flaps, providing a clear view into the corpse. 'This is his spine,' he said, indicating with forceps the pale column of bone. 'And do you know what these are?'

He pointed out six places along the spinal column where flesh thickened into tabs, and I remembered similar veiny organs floating in solution.

'Chakras?'

'The energy centers, as they are also known. Now compare,' he said, and stepped to the other table, revealing a body even more deteriorated. The back was cut open the same way, but when I looked at the spinal column, I saw no fleshy nodes.

'You removed the chakras from this one?'

'It's the corpse of one of our fellow monks, killed by the goondas,' Pala said. 'And it had no chakras.'

'They withered away,' I suggested, 'because of your lack of faith.'

'Or maybe he never had them.'

'What's your point?'

'Our point,' said Yamuna, 'is that you have chakras and are an obedient Hindu. Neither is true of Pragmatics. We've examined many corpses and never found them, or found them to be exceedingly small.'

'What bearing does this have on me?'

'It bears entirely on you.'

'Rakesh,' said Yamuna, 'this is the crux of our investigations.'

'Into what?'

'Your faith.'

I managed an indulgent smile.

Pala forged ahead. 'Rakesh, when I was a child, I saw a boy drown. A dozen families were lounging on the beach, and they watched the boy struggle against the waves, and they commented on how terrible it was. But nobody made an attempt to rescue him. Why? Because none were Kshatriya, so acts of bravery were not part of their personality. The image of that boy thrashing in the water haunts me, along with one question: Why can't Hindus change what they are?'

'That is India.'

'But don't you wonder why? How can children know they are meant to cobble shoes for the rest of their lives? Or become a religious leader? Or kill a national hero? You Hindus must learn to count and speak, as Yamuna and I must – how is it, then, that you know your castes from birth? How is it that you feel your dharma so strongly?'

We just do, I thought.

'Possibly,' he continued, 'you are unable to ask the important questions.'

'And the chakras?'

'We don't know how they work,' he said. 'We don't understand their role. But people without them have no defined place in India. Whereas the rest of you know your places very well. You can't resist your places.'

The insinuation that our behavior as good Hindus depended on some physical component felt highly heretical, and it was fortunate that Vasant wasn't around to hear it. Yet I couldn't come up with a counterargument. I thought of the laborers and how they received direct orders from the Jagannath. I wasn't like them. I wasn't.

'Look at you,' said Yamuna. 'In that banyan tree, you found the girl you were once supposed to marry. It must have been years since you saw her last, and yet you could think of nothing more than how she might help achieve your goal – your dharma, as you call it.'

I didn't know what to say. Their comments, the stench, the sight of those open bodies, it was too much.

'If the chakras are a pervasive force in India,' I mused, 'then someone must be to blame.'

'Someone – ?'

'Who is responsible for this difference between me and you? Who gave me my chakras?'

Something flashed across Yamuna's face, but she withheld it.

'Who is responsible for my dharma?'

They didn't reply.

'You don't have an answer?'

'We don't have many answers,' Pala conceded. 'But do you understand our question?'

'My faith is unshaken,' I said.

'Good.' He threw the tarp back over the corpse. 'Then you should have no objections to a simple test.'

In the head-compartment, Vasant sat in the saddle of a very large lever, adjusting the knobs and dials near him whenever the lever changed inclination. By his feet sat an object he must have cobbled together from Jagannath scrap, and I would have asked what it was, but I had a problem. He glanced over his shoulder as I stumbled inside.

'I have a theory,' he said.

'I don't want to hear any more theories.'

'The monks are a curious bunch, with their Buddhist pedigree and their interest in Hindu gods. Maybe they want to raid Mount Meru and have come aboard the Jagannath to research their crime. No doubt they desire a better lifestyle than what they knew in that clammy fort . . .' He looked back at me. 'What's the matter with you?'

'I'm fine.'

'You look bad.'

My hands shook, my knees were weak. I was bent over.

'Are you ill?'

'I suppose.'

'You're pale.'

'It's . . . nothing.'

'Well, please keep it far from me. I have no time to get sick.'

'I want you to change course.' I said it quickly, so I could get the words out.

'What?'

'Change course –' Pain struck me, a wallop to the gut.

'To where?'

'The peacock.'

He raised his eyebrows.

'The peacock airship . . . You still want to bring it down?'

'Of course, but –'

'Go. Take us where you'll find it.'

'But can you afford the time away from your – ?'

'Yes!'

I took a deep breath before making my next statement:

'*The Baboon Warrior can wait.*'

And with this said, I dropped to my knees, put my face on the floor, and clutched my stomach.

SYRINGE

'COME,' SAID PALA. 'You've suffered enough, poor boy.'

A monk took each of my six arms. I supposed the experiment was over. If I wasn't busy retching, I would have asked what good it had done. I had lasted less than three days defying my urge to find the Baboon Warrior, and the pain had demonstrated what Pala had suggested: that I couldn't resist my dharma even if I tried.

The Pragmatics carried me along the corridors, my legs dragging. Through spaces, down levels. I was too weak to support myself, too weak to refuse their assistance. I felt the warmth increasing, and knew where we were, though I couldn't lift my head to look around.

They carried me into a wagon in the corner of Interior Space Number 43 – one where the Pragmatics conducted anatomical research – someone raising my feet as we went up the ramp. Inside, monks seemed to be waiting. They held me lengthwise and put me onto a wooden table like those on which I'd seen corpses. I tried to push away the nearest monk but managed only a weak extension and retraction of a goonda limb. The monk folded it back gently.

They removed the prosthesis. Was that what they wanted? The goonda arms? Someone fiddled with the clasp, and I meant to protest but could not. Tension released as the vest opened, and there was a great pushing and tugging as they extracted my arms from the control sleeves. I felt raw as a lobster pulled from its shell. I was lifted again as the device was spirited away.

When they rolled me onto my stomach, I glimpsed Yamuna wearing a saffron filter over her mouth and nose. Another monk worked with his back to me, something clinking near his hands. Jars and more jars crowded a small counter, along with unknown medical equipment. Tubes and more tubes.

More clinking.

A baboon had been allowed into the cart, and it sat on a shelf, regarding the proceedings below with unnerving calm. Get that filthy monkey out of here, I wanted to shout. It was sitting like a human, legs dangling, looking back and forth as people spoke. I groaned.

Pala entered my field of vision. 'This might be unpleasant,' he said pleasantly.

'What . . .'

'Don't talk. Your suffering will soon be over.'

What were they going to do to me? I groaned again, thinking of the long incisions I had seen on the corpses.

The other monk turned, revealing an instrument with a needle connected to a tube and with rings looped over his fingers. The tube was full of transparent liquid.

'This is called a syringe,' said Pala.

Someone swabbed my back.

'Please don't squirm,' he said. 'This is delicate business.'

I squirmed as much as I could. I felt the cold tip of the needle against my skin, between my shoulder blades. Yamuna watched without sympathy.

Someone said, 'You can practically see them through his skin.'

'Be careful of his spine,' Pala warned. 'Slowly now . . .'

The baboon was watching it all, and I saw its eyes widen.

The needle passed into my flesh, and at last I had a sensation to rival the continual ache in my gut. I would have flailed and pulled myself off the table, but several hands stabilized my body, kept me in place. I heard the minute squeal of the plunger and felt the irrigation of tissue in my back. The needle remained in place, centimeters of thin steel. I felt its withdrawal, too. Someone taped the entry point.

The pool of water in my eyes bleared Pala as he leaned forward.

'Not too bad?'

I blinked.

'Only five more.'

At some point after that, the scene faded, the baboon deteriorating as blackness cloaked me from sights, sounds, the feeling of the syringe inserted and withdrawn from my flesh. I remembered the corpses with their cleaved backs. *What are you doing to me?* The only clue came during the transition to sleep, as I stared at a minion of the Baboon Warrior but for the first time in years did not dream of him.

*

I woke, unsure how much time had passed. The interior of the cart swirled for a moment. Only Yamuna in her copper gown remained; she appeared to be meditating.

'Have we changed course?' I asked.

Her eyes opened. 'I don't think so.'

'We're following the Baboon Warrior? Heading for Akot?'

'Not that I know of. Why?'

I sat up, feeling woozy, disconnected. It had been years since I was sleepy like this. Thick, dulled at the edges.

'The pain is gone,' said Yamuna.

I rubbed my stomach.

'You look unsteady.'

'I don't feel myself.'

'You haven't been yourself for years.'

'What . . .?'

She was quiet. 'You don't feel wracked by pain, do you?'

'No.'

'Even though you're not presently pursuing the Baboon Warrior.'

'What have you done?'

'Helped you.'

'Did I ask for help?'

'You were unable to ask.'

'You poisoned me.'

'We injected a tincture.'

'A tincture? Of what?'

'Do you still want to kill the Baboon Warrior?'

'Of course.' But I reflected for a moment. 'I think I do . . .'

I swung my legs to the ground and tried walking. Yamuna came to assist. It was true the pain had subsided. Or was it merely submerged beneath my foggy senses? I couldn't feel much, not even the floor beneath my feet, and walking was a problem. I swayed and knocked some canisters across the countertop, and there was a scrabbling in a cabinet before a monkey burst out, and I too was surprised, teetering backward so that Yamuna had to catch me.

My nerves were responding to too many stimuli. I smelled the poultices that were preserving bodies another wagon away, and found the aroma intolerable. I attempted to close down my ability to smell, but the odor lingered; I could escape it only by leaving.

'Where are you going?' said Yamuna.

She gonged as she hurried after me. I swung down the steps like a man unaccustomed to his wooden legs. The heat of Interior Space Number 43 weighed on me. I tried to steady myself against a wagon, reaching with a goonda limb, only to remember that they had been taken from me and I was reduced to my own original pair. I slumped, and horses whinnied. And *smelled* – of oats and droppings and animal musk. I was clumsy and oversensitive . . . like the boy who almost got married, I thought in horror. Time had been pushed back. I had been wakened from a very long sleep, a sleep on that beach. I shielded my eyes from the great light of the Jagannath's hearth.

'Where are you going?' she said.

'To speak to Vasant.'

'You should rest – '

'No!'

'Rakesh, listen to reason.'

'Reason!' I didn't want to think like a Pragmatic. Reason was weak currency. I took a narrow path through the wagons, so that Yamuna, in her big metal maternity gown, was forced to go by a much longer route. This way, I could lose her. She was making bell noises behind me when I left Interior Space Number 43.

But in my altered condition, I found the Jagannath's spaces much more difficult to negotiate than before. I kept reclimbing the same black wooden chute into a terminal ovoid surrounded by crackling white globes. I was frustrated, and frightened. I didn't want to be inside a god. The sacrilege of it suddenly oppressed me, whereas before, everything had seemed necessary, right. Now I could feel the Jagannath's wrath in the tone of its repeated messages, instructions, *Go below, slog through muck, pick out shards, help with gruel, pick out rocks, go lower,* and that complicated getting anywhere, those insistent commands.

I slowed, stopped. I was back in the same ovoid. I held my head, focusing. I tried to remember my arrow blazing through the sky, but it had lost its potency. The arrow was gone, and the sky was black as the lacquered surface before me. I resorted to the impossible cube, tracing it on the floor to compensate for my weakened concentration. I was drawing and redrawing when Yamuna caught up.

'Rakesh,' she said.

'Quiet.'

'This was for your own good.'

'What do you know about my good?'

'Remember Nainpur, Rakesh? Where you saw your bride?'

'I never had a bride.'

'She was supposed to be your bride. But you saw her and were totally indifferent. That cannot be considered normal.'

'I don't care about normality.'

'Rakesh, your single-mindedness was a sign that your mind had been hijacked. Your life.'

'Maybe I liked it hijacked!'

'We dulled your chakras, Rakesh. They ruled your life, shaped your thoughts and feelings, controlled you.'

'Is that a Pragmatic attempt at consolation?'

Yamuna undid the buckle of her gown and stepped out, unencumbered.

I saw her with new eyes. Before, she'd been inter-changeable with the other monks. Her short hair and controlled expressions were standard aspects of the Pragmatic package. Now she was a woman. Her pregnancy accentuated that fact. Or maybe it was that I had wakened. I saw eyelashes. I saw hands. The green of her eyes, the curve of her neck. I saw the sway of flesh under her robe, and realized that breasts were beneath that fabric. When she knelt before me, I smelled her.

'Did you love that woman, Rakesh?'

I said nothing.

She grabbed my hand, my index finger, the one I was using to draw the impossible cube. Her hand on mine, her skin, the shape of her palm – I found myself concentrating on these things.

'You are not a machine,' she said.

'I don't want a life without meaning.'

'You think you're the first person whose life was shaped by his body?' she said. 'Look.'

I looked.

'Look at me.'

I saw her body. Her belly.

'This child was not conceived in the traditional manner.'

'I don't . . .'

'You are familiar with the concept of virgin birth? Doubtless you know Hindu stories where a woman gives birth to a child without male participation. There was a tale of the Buddha, too, being born from his mother's side, of his own will. We investigated the stories. We know the mind is capable of much, and we suspected that the mothers somehow initiated these pregnancies themselves, through some deep act of willpower, some hidden mechanism of the mind. *I* investigated the possibility, Rakesh.'

She placed my hand against her belly. It was hot. Alive. 'I made myself pregnant,' she said. 'That's how I know it's a girl. In my mind I conceived a daughter.'

'Magic . . .?'

'Clear thought. Mind over body; we suspected this was one of the powers locked in our heads. Because I am not distracted by chakras, I could use deep meditation to find that power. I became a mother on my own, alone.' She hurried to the next statement, refocusing on me. 'And now your chakras won't intervene, Rakesh. You will act with your mind, and with your body. You'll make choices that belong entirely to you.'

I withdrew my hand and looked at it. The heat of her child subsided in my palm.

'What will I do without my dharma?'

'Live,' she said.

I shuddered.

The Jagannath rumbled, and I shrank. Where was it going? What would it do? And what were we doing in here, if I no longer felt the imperative of dharma?

'Yamuna,' I said. 'Help me get outside.'

She stood and walked back into her gown. When she had clamped it shut, she offered a hand, and I put both of mine over hers, relishing the contact, something to think about while the Jagannath bombarded my vulnerable mind. *Down below! Down below*! It seemed to take a long time for us to find our way among the black wooden bowels, and I was weak in the knees with thoughts of what horrible possibilities lay waiting behind abstract walls. A group of eight laborers passed, Azis among them, the top of his gown off and his torso dark with grime. His musculature had developed since his absorption into the god's labor supply.

We emerged outside, along a walkway. I straightened, fortified by fresh air and sky. The orders in my head tapered off.

The Jagannath rolled across a green field that I registered as the tops of trees, leaving in its wake the straight line it had cut, to the vanishing point. So Vasant had continued his pursuit. Ahead, I could see the peacock airship circling a set of huge towers staggered against the sky, and I knew the name of the city we approached, the setting for so many apocryphal stories and the one place no Kama Sutran felt threatened.

Here we came.

KHAJURAHO

'RAKESH! YOU'RE UP and about already?'

Pala looked genuinely surprised to see me, and I resisted the urge to bark at him and demand an explanation. With the injections, I had lost my nerve. He stood in Interior Space Number 43 surrounded by a dozen or so monks outfitted with arrows, bows, and packs, on horseback.

'I'm coming,' I said.

'You are?'

'He won't listen to reason,' said Yamuna. 'I'm sure he's too weak for any expedition.'

'Then perhaps you should accompany our Hindu friend, and see no harm comes to him.'

The gate opened, and the Pragmatics trotted out. I mustered courage to follow.

The Jagannath was halted, reluctantly, at the perimeter of Khajuraho. The city was a cluster of stone skyscrapers on a rectangular base, and each individual tower repeated a shape that rose higher the closer its position to the central structure, the sikhara. The towers were curvilinear, rounded at their summits, and each capped by a fat discus of stonework. When the Jagannath had approached, details in the walls of Khajuraho had become plain: statues as big as the people who must have inspired them. Some of the lower strata depicted war scenes and tales from the pantheon, but the higher the eye climbed, the more plainly erotic was the subject matter. It was said Khajuraho was walled by ten thousand unions of man, woman, and animal. The city looked like a vision of sex realized in stone – a vision that left nothing to the imagination. With the Jagannath approaching fast, the peacock airship had taken evasive action, flying into the city via a portal shaped like the yoni. The god rolled up to the wall while the 'tail feathers' of the craft streaked through the hole, and the god reached inside, grabbing for them. It withdrew, empty-handed. Yamuna and I watched from the walkway, ready to retreat into the god as soon as the destruction began, fists flying at the towers of Khajuraho. But only one arm moved, rising, blocking that hole with a wide spread of fingers so the airship could not exit Khajuraho by the same route it had entered. The god remained in this stance, huffing, its tendencies restrained for the time being. Soon, a small figure hurried outside, and I saw it was Vasant, carrying his handmade device.

'Pala will want to see Khajuraho, too,' Yamuna said. 'If only to learn who raided our fortress.'

Vasant's purpose, I knew, was vengeance. And I knew I should accompany him, help him survive in a strange place. But an iciness had entered my arms, my legs, my stomach; faced with a hundred stories of Kama Sutran sex, I felt intimidated, nervous. I tried once again to remember my flaming arrow, but it was extinguished. I wanted to flee and return to Varanasi, home, where memories of childhood would help me forget these profane phallic towers rising against the sky. But Vasant deserved more than a trembling youth who stayed at a safe distance.

So we left, riding down from the chariot. Outside, the sight of Khajuraho stunned me anew. We rode along its base and craned our necks to view the capped tops. I sat behind Yamuna, who had removed her copper gown to mount the horse. It was not easy finding places to hold her.

We split into two groups and trotted along the outskirts. The entrances were guarded, and the guards watched us warily. The Pragmatics elected to stay clear of them and avoid confrontation, to my shameful relief.

We rounded the east corner and saw a long ramp built on bamboo scaffolding; it terminated about twenty meters above ground, at the top of an incomplete tower. Near the base, sandstone blocks waited to be hauled into the construction. There were no workers present, and nobody standing watch. Pala and the other Pragmatics rode in a circle.

'Doesn't look safe,' I said.

'If the ramp can support those blocks,' said Pala, 'surely it can bear our weight.'

The Pragmatics leaned forward as they brought their horses around, and whispered into their horses' ears as they directed them onto the ramp. I could have used some soothing words myself.

We rode single file up the long ascent, and I held Yamuna tighter, sliding my hands around her belly. She did not seem fazed as the ground dropped away on either side. I could hear joints of the scaffolding creak, see the ramp twist and sag with the weight of the

animals. Individual planks gave way and fluttered down
soundlessly. At one point, struck by vertigo, I closed
my eyes and rested my head between Yamuna's shoulder
blades. She made no comment.

When I next looked, the ground was distant, a long,
screaming plummet down, and being on horseback
made the drop seem even worse. But at last the ramp
leveled to the unfinished tower, where I immediately
dismounted.

Facing us was the stone erotica of the towers, men
and women carved into permanent love, their faces
describing a bliss only slightly diminished by rain and
other erosions. Pairs, trios, foursomes. From my limited
perusal of the Kama Sutra, I recognized some of the acts
displayed here, the Congress of the Crow, the Splitting
of the Bamboo. A man coupled with a woman who
held herself upside down by the groins of two more
men, their hands placed on her buttocks and each
other's chest. Lively and unlikely connections followed
the circumference and linked lower levels to higher
ones, providing points of structural support. Khajuraho,
built of intercourse.

The top of the incomplete tower where we stood
provided no access; it was flat. A monk examined the
stones to see if we could force one from position. But
Pala discovered another portal like the one the peacock
had disappeared into, a gaping yoni that opened the
next tower. It was somewhat higher than us, but the end
of a bridge was visible at its lip. The Pragmatics dis-
cussed who among them was the most celibate, and
when the issue was settled, that monk climbed down
to a point where the towers met in a twining of stone
arms. It was strange to watch the monk – before today

I had thought all of them were sexless – pick his way along bosoms and buttocks and open legs, making unavoidably erotic connections with his task. He paused once, and I heard him repeating some mantra to regain his focus. His fellow Pragmatics added a sympathetic chorus.

After he'd crossed over and climbed to the portal, we heard a ratcheting as the trellis bridge extended to our incomplete tower. The Pragmatics rode across. I walked, holding the tail of Yamuna's horse and not looking down.

We entered the city. The rounded corridor had barrel vaulting that swooped down in sandstone flanges. It ended abruptly, placing us in the upper third of a hive of activity. I looked over the balustrade and saw many levels below and above, graded according to the width of the tower, making for a large open center. Surprising turns characterized the interior. I was impressed with the number of stairways corkscrewing from level to level, skipping floors, crossing the open well in the middle, some as tightly curved as a pencil shaving. Decorative flourishes were prolific, motifs of parrots in colorful enamel beneath our feet, peacock heads jutting from the walls, statues of Kama buried in bright flower garlands, stone nymphs supporting balconies in their arms.

There were real nymphs, too.

We had been noticed.

Many people milled about nearby, and I prepared myself for the encounter as a contingent interrupted whatever they were doing to approach us. Both nymph and the male equivalent wore tight-fitting body stockings that flaunted their physiques – beautiful bodies –

topped with eager, pixie-like faces. The confrontation would be different from what I expected, I realized, when some of the nymphs came sliding down handrails.

The Pragmatics took up their bows.

'May I comb your hair?' asked a woman, coming toward me.

'I have none to comb . . .'

'May I shave your head?'

'No . . . Thank you.'

'May I wash your feet? Tend your sores?'

I shook my head, but she persisted.

Similar questions were put to the monks. May I wash your robe? May I oil your saddle? May I feed your horse?

The Pragmatics looked as puzzled as me. The Kama Sutrans did not block our path; rather, they shuffled alongside us, smiling, offering services. They treated us like welcome guests. Or like customers. Some actually cleared the way, moving potted flowers aside so they wouldn't be in our path.

But despite the attention these people paid to us, they were distracted. Pleasantly distracted. They spoke but didn't look at us directly. Their eyes shone, and they smiled, but what were they really thinking? I smelled a scent I recognized from the parlor in Jaipur, something of the body, hot and moist. The Kama Sutrans walked on the balls of their feet as they followed us, a hundred offers on their mouths.

'May I restring your bow? May I sharpen your arrows?'

Pala turned to a handsome young man with skin the color of sesame oil. 'How much do you charge for an arrow sharpening?'

'Charge?'

'What would be the cost? We didn't bring much money.'

The Kama Sutran shook his head. 'No cost.'

Pala raised an eyebrow. 'Well, I can't turn down an offer that good.'

When he handed over his arrow, the man seemed to become even more abstracted, his eyebrows lifting and his face coloring. He rose on the balls of his feet, ran his fingers over the shaft tenderly, then turned and went down a corridor with steps as light as a gazelle's. Pala watched him go.

'May I sharpen your arrow?' came another voice. And another: 'May I sharpen your arrow?' The question swelled around us. A nymph put her hand on my shoulder and said, *Please, may I sharpen your arrow?*

I wished I had one to give her.

May I sharpen your arrow? May I sharpen –

'Can somebody show us to the peacock?' Yamuna said, loud.

Loud enough to quiet them. Until they started answering.

'I can show you the way. This way.' The group splintered, each taking steps in a different direction. 'Come with me, please. This way, madam.'

Pala looked around and said, 'One of them must be right. We'll each take a path and meet at the peacock airship, or back in the Jagannath.'

I followed Yamuna, who had selected the nymph in the white body stocking.

'Can you show us to the peacock?' asked Yamuna.

The woman closed her eyes, flushed, shuddered. 'Oh yes,' she said.

Balloons rose like bubbles from deep within the well of open space, and the Kama Sutrans evidently favored gold, purple, crimson, because these colors repeated in the spherical vehicles rising beside us. Some took passengers from lower floors to upper, some seemed to be delivering supplies, and some, with eyes of papier-mâché mounted atop, carried persons who observed us.

The only other security was a shaggy red creature on the other side of the well. From stories, I recognized it as one of the sardulas, patrons of the Kama Sutran sect. The sardulas looked like red-furred lions, but their faces, surrounded by cowls of red hair, were recognizably human. The sardula trotted to the rail and roared before trotting back. He reappeared above us, and below us, and each time he did the same thing, looked at us, roared, walked away. Letting us know he was nearby, I supposed.

I kept close to Yamuna.

When we came to an intersection, our guide peered in one direction, then in the other. She obviously had no idea where to find the airship. She started, stopped, turned, went the other way. Her breathing changed, grew slower with each wrong turn. But when she corrected herself, her breaths returned to their previous rhythm, then came faster, deeper, a panting not associated with physical exertion but with some ongoing and welcome preoccupation. Her eyes rolled back.

'Do you know where you're going?' Yamuna asked finally.

Without looking at us, the guide nodded.

It was warm in Khajuraho, and fragrant. Kama Sutrans preferred floral scents and musks over incense, and we passed through perfumed zones of varying intent. I tried to turn off my ability to smell, but the Pragmatic injections had not only made me fearful, they had also trapped me in my body. The scents worked on me; the whole place worked on me. Also returning after a long absence was a feeling other than fear: my eyes kept falling on our guide, on the motion of her buttocks as she walked, on curves made obvious by the tight-fitting garment. When I looked away, I found myself watching Yamuna instead, the way she switched from side to side on her horse. Even the horse drew my attention, the movement of its muscles, its haunches . . .

'They don't seem upset here about the state of the government,' I said, to say something.

'I don't think many things upset them,' Yamuna replied, her voice fading, too.

With some coaxing the horse picked its way down a long staircase. The sardula poked its head over the railing and glared at us.

'You're doing good work,' I said to it, my voice quavering.

But the red face didn't change its disapproving expression. The sardula snorted and left.

We descended to the bottom of the well and passed into a wide corridor that led to another tower and a similar, larger space. In this corridor we passed through a tangle of shadows where sunlight pierced erotic sculpture, drenching us in shadows of interlaced arms and legs. In the next tower, we crossed yet another tile mosaic of the god Kama. The woman's respiration was deep and short. She bit her lower lip; her breaths whistled. The smell of her was strong – a hot-bath smell, a steam-bath smell. She raised a hand. Following her finger, we saw the peacock sail through one opening and toward another, its head lowered, its body narrowed.

'There.'

A few seconds of blue glory, and it was gone. The woman gave a small cry of pleasure and fell back, resting against a wall, content.

'Do you wish me to show you the peacock again?' she asked.

'We wouldn't want you to overexert yourself,' Yamuna replied, and nudged the horse onward.

'They're mostly like that,' I said.

'What?'

I nodded to the people passing with tools or papers or food. 'That look.'

'A happy place.'

Balloons continually lifting off, gold, purple, and crimson. Animals in abundance, songbirds and cats and dogs, all well fed and satisfied. But it was something more than happiness that ruled here. We walked past a crowd watching a horse mount a donkey, watching with the deepest interest and pleasure. They paid no attention to us.

The sole image of the Baboon Warrior I saw in Khajuraho was a fresco of him mounting the Rajasthani princess during the ceremony where he was supposed to receive a medal – an episode not usually dwelled upon by his admirers. In the fresco, a crowd of Royals gazed upon this ravishing with unlikely approval. I stared at the Kama Sutran interpretation of his monkey face – and felt nothing. Felt neutral. I was immune. We waded into a flock of peacocks who paused as one, lifting the false eyes of their tail feathers.

'Come,' said Yamuna.

We proceeded down a big hall and saw a shimmering blue ahead.

'There,' she said. 'There it is, waiting for us.'

It was in fact moving very slowly.

'And Vasant?'

'I can't see him.'

Between us and the airship was a circular room, its floor a spread of blankets and pillows.

'What do you think they use this room for?' asked Yamuna.

'It could hold a lot of people.'

Her horse took a few steps inside, but the flooring sank beneath its weight, and the animal would go no farther. No amount of nudging or whispers could change its mind. I tried pulling the horse by the bridle, to no avail. Yamuna dismounted, and we left the horse at the entrance.

We, too, were confounded by the soft surface, which seemed hostile to walking, particularly for Yamuna with her altered center of gravity. We tried walking stooped over, using our hands for support. Finally, we walked on all fours. The sheets smelled laundered, and I found them inviting, although I was not tired. Yamuna was ahead of me, and I watched her instead of the peacock airship.

Halfway across, she stopped and placed her head on the soft surface.

'Tired?' I asked.

'Sex is the currency.'

'Excuse me?'

'They have no use for rupees or gold in Khajuraho.

When they do a service for a person, the person's body rewards them.'

'How could that work?'

'It's a self-contained city. They have the means to provide the services and products of daily life. All they need is a method of making sure that those things are distributed through the population. Pleasure is the incentive.'

Kama Sutran economics.

'A society based on sex,' I said, staring at her.

'You get nowhere in Khajuraho without sex.'

I kept staring at her.

We did not move, and Yamuna seemed to be considering her last comment. 'I should ask Pala about this,' she said. 'The one subject we Pragmatics don't study is sex. I wonder why?'

'You've never . . .?'

'No. The closest was, well, the pregnancy. Pala helped me in that process. With meditations. That was the closest . . .'

'Not even comparable,' I said.

I could see the head of the peacock airship; it must have turned around just now. We should get going, I thought. But I didn't move.

'What would you compare it to?'

'Remember,' I said, 'that my marriage never occurred.'

'So you have no experience with the subject either.'

'In Jaipur, I bit a Kama Sutran's shoulder. It did more for her than for me.'

'So you don't know.'

'It's like riding a horse,' I suggested.

'What?'

'When we were riding your horse.'

I stretched forward and slipped a finger in her shoe. I felt her sole, the warmth of her foot.

'The horse.'

I pulled off the shoe.

'What about it?'

'You in front,' I said. 'And I . . .'

I pressed against her backside.

'You held me tight,' she said, and placed one of my hands under her belly, the other above. I felt a breast.

We moved as if an animal were involved.

'Faster.'

'Hold tighter,' she said. 'We're riding faster.' I put my hand under her robe and spread my fingers against her hot belly, and my other hand went down her collar so I could cup that breast. Yamuna blossomed from her robe, and I looked at her swollen stomach and extended nipples and pulled open my pants to free the beam of my sex. Our collision wasn't smooth, but it vitalized, and rewarded, as we found the stinging intersection where our bodies meant much to each other. Yamuna cried out, and I felt as if the contents of my body would rush in their entirety through this pipeline. I wanted them to. I wanted to feel myself drain and rise again as a level of liquid inside her. We coupled, and as we did, I caught glimpses of the room around us, glimpses heated by our circumstance, the corridors, our horse frolicking with the sardula, the two of them leaping together, leaping one over the other. In the opposite direction, the peacock airship hovered and spun, its tail-feather balloons lifted so it was circumscribed by bright-painted eyes, and I didn't care who was watching or who was aboard, not as we finished,

Yamuna and I, not even as we lay curled together in a soft cavity of pillows, my mouth pressed to her fingers.

I felt freed from the constraints of time: nothing remained to limit me, not my dharma, not time, not any element of India or the cosmos. The room blued. Our skin, our features deepened in hue. Silk pulled above us to make a low blue ceiling,. and I considered standing to trace my hand over its passing surface.

The peacock airship sailed over us, and I saw Vasant clinging to an outer cabin. Briefly his eyes locked on mine, wide.

Interesting.

But still I couldn't bring myself to rise, not until Pala and the others galloped into view.

DOWN WITH THE
GLORY OF KAMA

⊷═◉═⊶

VASANT TOLD ME later how he found himself in that position, clinging to the side of the airship. His experience began after he left the Jagannath. Unlike us, he walked to the front gates of Khajuraho, where guards stood waiting. To Vasant they looked less like sentinels and more like teenagers loitering outside a girls' school. His appearance made them brighten, however, and the brawniest of the bunch blocked his way.

'Residents only.'

'Why is there a stupid grin on your face?'

'I'm just happy to be working.'

'Is that so?' Vasant pointed at the god, steam issuing from vents along the chariot. 'Did you miss something?'

'No, sir. The Jagannath. We are terrified.'

'It will level this city if you don't let me inside.'

'Sorry, I can't. It would be a dereliction of my duty.' And the young man sighed dreamily.

'You would jeopardize your home to protect the peacock airship?'

The guard's eyes widened. 'You threaten the airship? Is that why the Jagannath has come here? But who would ground the most extravagant aircraft of India?'

'Its designer.'

'You're from Delhi?' The guard glanced back to the others and said something Vasant didn't understand; they were employing that Kama Sutran code language. They seemed to reach an agreement.

'You didn't enter this way,' the guard said to Vasant finally, stepping aside to let him pass.

Vasant shook his head and entered Khajuraho, walking down an avenue of phallic arches to the sikhara and its great column of space. His eyes turned upward, following rings of successive levels, and he glimpsed the peacock as it drifted through a passage – his airship, in lewd new format. Assemblage came to him, showing in depth the abuses of his design, the alterations, the gantry of neck built onto the stern, the floating tail feathers. After the craft passed from view, details lingered, a ghost of blueprints, his years of toil smeared across a Kama Sutran firmament. He was so transfixed that he didn't notice the crowd forming around him.

'Can I help you?'

About a dozen Kama Sutrans.

'What? What do you want?'

'I thought I might show you to a room,' said a man, smiling. 'Or carry your . . . object.'

Vasant turned to conceal his weapon.

'May I clean your shoes?' the man went on. 'Launder your suit?'

'I want nothing from you. Keep back!'

But they followed in a loose group, and to Vasant's dismay others joined. They minced from many direc-

tions, and those who didn't traipse along stopped what
they were doing to stare at him. A finger on their lips,
one eyebrow raised. What was wrong with these
people? Vasant would have preferred brutish guards
over these knowing gazes and delicately orbiting steps.
He walked faster, hurrying in the direction he'd seen
the airship, and although he outpaced the initial group,
interest followed him, keeping him surrounded by
pleasant looks and queries as to what service might be
gladly provided him.

Gaudy red and purple substructures in the shape of
pyramids or cubes increased his disorientation; banners
draped from ceiling to floor with lingam and yoni
embroidered down their lengths. Some walls dwindled
to sheer fabric scrims that wafted to reveal deeper parts
of the sikhara, long golden tunnels with uncertain
shimmering ends. Water inside the building? A silver
lake, with silver boats and children splashing the shore?

Through another aperture he witnessed a man and
woman coupling, a bored child riding the woman's
back as she rose and fell against her lover. Degenerates!
And plenty of them. Teenagers groping. The mock
intercourse of children, in full view of adults – with
adult supervision, even! It was as if these people rubbed
their groins when a simple hello would suffice. Vasant
tried to keep his head up, watching for the peacock,
pretending not to notice what he was walking through.
He thought of Rama persevering among the demons
of Lanka.

'May I help you? Do you need help finding
someone?'

'Keep your distance!'

He ignored the implications in their eyes, their pronounced breathing, and raised an authoritative finger if anyone got too close. No Kama Sutran would touch him. After struggling to elude them, he realized he'd lost his way in the complex.

'Your mechanism is gilded in feathers.'

He stopped. The voice was queer: tuned rather than breathed.

'Your mechanism is gilded in feathers,' it repeated, then gave a sigh of exasperation.

Vasant stood before an oval room, like an egg balanced on end, wide steps leading to its entrance.

'Your mechanism is gilded in feathers.'

Did the comment refer to his airship? It sounded as if someone was making a joke of his situation. Whatever the case, he found it annoying, and decided to see who the speaker was, and perhaps also get a better view of the lay of the sikhara from the top of the steps.

Inside the oval structure, two men faced a wall of parrots. The parrots perched in flares of blue and green around the curvature. The taller man wore a silky vermilion robe to rival any plumage; he stood with arms crossed, glaring at a particularly large, cockeyed parrot on a golden stand.

'Your masculinity,' the man said, 'gives me great pleasure.'

The parrot blinked, turned its head. 'Your mechanism is gilded in feathers,' it said with a whistle.

'He won't listen to me!' the man exclaimed.

The other stepped closer, smiling, wringing his hands. 'You must understand, sir, the parrot's point of view. Why is he so fixated on this mechanism? Address the issue. It is none of his concern, the gilding of mechanisms. Make him understand, with your voice, with your conviction, that he should abandon the topic forever!'

The other birds fluffed and preened. The big blue parrot stepped side to side, apparently anxious to resume the dialogue.

The garishly dressed individual turned to the bird with hands on hips. He raised a finger and insisted: 'Your masculinity gives me great pleasure.'

'Your masculinity,' said the bird, pausing, eyeing him, 'is gilded in feathers.'

The others squawked and made tuneful commentary, though it was nonsense. Feathers tossed as they pumped their wings and called. The only bird that remained calm was a white shaft of feathers Vasant had mistaken for a decoration attached to the smaller man's head. It hopped to his shoulders, anchoring itself with its beak. It was unmoved by the ruckus.

'Stranger in the house,' it said. 'Stranger in the house.'

The men looked toward the door, surprised to see Vasant.

'This is a private lesson,' the smaller man said. 'You will please wait outside until we are finished.'

'No,' the other cut in, his face lighting up. 'I've had enough for today.'

As he departed, the parrot said, 'Your masculinity is gilded in feathers.' The man winced, but smiled for Vasant. His face – it was almost familiar, as if the Engineer had seen it once underwater, or maybe in a dream.

'Do you own a parrot?' asked the vaguely familiar man, indicating they should walk down the steps together. 'Wondrous creature. I'll never feel complete until I've mastered their gift. The art of teaching parrots to speak confounds me!'

'Hardly a vital skill.'

'No Kama Sutran would say such a thing.'

Vasant sneered at the thought he might be mistaken for a Kama Sutran.

'May I ask what you're doing in Khajuraho?' asked the man.

'I intend to board the peacock airship. Can you show me to it? Otherwise I have no interest in your company.'

'Show you to it? Certainly.' He pointed upward with a grin.

Vasant waved him off.

'Sorry to tease,' said the other. 'But you see, that airship rarely lands, so going up *is* the only way to reach it. It seldom needs to visit the ground – an aspect of its brilliant design.'

Vasant took the comment as suspicious. Deliberate flattery. He said, 'You know me?'

'We can talk at length, as we travel.'

The man gestured to his craft, a crescent of ormolu encrusted on the underside of a lavender balloon. Its tiny door was open; within, velvet seats awaited. Vasant hesitated, but the Kama Sutran said, 'Aerial conveyance is the only way.'

They entered the cabin, Vasant sitting carefully with his construction, directly across from the Kama Sutran. As soon as the door shut, landing gear extricated itself from mooring hitches, and the craft lifted.

'My apologies,' the man said. 'We have met before. I'll give you a hint.' He placed a leg on either side of the Engineer. 'My testes: do they fall off with each full moon? Or do I raise them like an anchor? Perhaps I have neither male nor female parts but some unique apparatus? These are questions I leave with people.'

'I've given you no thought since we met.'

'Then you do remember me?'

'You're called Symantaka.'

The Kama Sutran pressed his palms together. 'I was between phases when we met in Delhi.'

'Remove your legs.'

'Sorry.' He took his feet down. 'I forget how frankness about the body upsets you.'

'It appalls me. You people are too candid.'

'Why do you say that?'

'Look out the window. Look around you. Rampant indulgence . . .'

'You're the one who's come from Delhi to destroy an aircraft. That is self-indulgence! You might do your soul a favor by taking a more procreative view of life.'

'Procreative!' Vasant snorted. 'Is that how you Kama Sutrans see yourselves?'

'It's a fair description. We oppose violence.'

'A lie.'

'It's true. We can't bear even to defend ourselves properly. Tell me, did you encounter any resistance getting inside?'

'You convert people at every opportunity. I've seen scruffy villages of a hundred people or less, and found you gave them filmees, and who knows what else.'

'Oh, we *convert* people, yes. For their good and ours. We have to perpetuate ourselves, after all! You conservative Hindus in your rages of chastity would imprison us, execute us, drive us into the ocean, if we didn't make inroads among you. The only way we can survive is to take advantage of the fact that even the most sanctimonious Brahmin remains a sexual being. Convert, yes, but coerce, never.'

'What about my abduction?' Vasant said. 'That was violent.'

'I don't know what you're talking about.'

'In the Palace. You abducted me. Your people. They came in the shape of an elephant.'

Symantaka shook his head. 'We don't kidnap or assassinate or perform nonconsensual rape. Those things are abhorrent to us. You blame us wrongly.'

It wasn't worth arguing. Music leaked into the compartment, and Vasant saw they'd risen level with the peacock. Symantaka shifted in his seat, rolling his hips. A gilded lever was snugged between his legs, but most control over the craft he effected through the gimbaled seat, moving his hips so as to position the balloon over the much larger craft.

'What's that music?' Vasant asked.

The peacock had contracted its fuselage laterally, making a narrow blue ellipse with the head thrust forward and the decorative wings tight to the sides, but these dragged against the walls nonetheless, knocking people down, breaking ornamental moldings and showering the pedestrians below with plaster and other materials. 'You'll see,' Symantaka sighed. His craft bobbed above the blue expanse of the airship, moving slowly relative to it as he gyrated his hips in the attempt to dock on one of the platforms. At last, with a pelvic thrust, he set down, and Vasant heard the coupling of landing gear with hitches.

'Thanks for the ride,' Vasant said, but was halted, his door locked.

The Kama Sutran smiled. 'Shall we finish?'

Vasant turned, stared, felt blood rushing into his face.

'Kama made me this way,' said Symantaka. 'Glorious Kama, as a gift for my exquisite love, granted me my desire to know life as a woman, and life as a man. Each month I assume the point of view of the opposite sex, and then the opposite of that, and for a time something between the two.'

'I'm profoundly uninterested.'

'I tell you only to explain the gift I'm about to give you! The gift of *seeing from the other side.* India would be much more peaceable if people could take other points of view. You, Vasant. I want you to see from the Kama Sutran position. For a brief period, at least.'

Vasant tried the door again, with his shoulder.

'All I ask,' said Symantaka, untying his garment, 'is fifteen minutes.' He opened a cabinet, and Vasant immediately recognized the device that folded down.

'You may feel awkward at first, but in the end, well, *in the end* you'll feel wonderful.'

Those words made the sculpture – a nymph fondling herself – twist along its pole. The figure was very near the tip, and Vasant sensed energy increasing in the confines of the compartment, a charge, a current. A teasing, a flirting with strangers, such impulses circulated unseen around him. Symantaka's face revealed a strange beauty suddenly, the submerged femininity, the odd lips . . .

'We should be procreative,' said the Kama Sutran, 'rather than destructive.'

The Engineer shook himself. 'Put it away!'

'Afterward,' Symantaka said in a low voice, making the sculpture turn, turn. 'You won't even remember there is a peacock airship, I promise. Assume our point of view for fifteen minutes, and afterward, if you still wish to raid your ship, I won't stop you. Maybe I'll help.'

'No. Absolutely not.'

'Just relax, allow yourself some liberation . . .'

Symantaka slid a hand down his garment, widening a triangle of flesh.

Vasant raised his device: the jagged construction. His secret trips to Interior Space Number 12 gave it a look reminiscent of the god, black and abstract, no handholds, just asymmetrical machinery clustered about a brick of dung so highly refined, it was almost white.

'What is that dreadful piece of luggage?'

'I helped design weaponry during the Soma War,' Vasant said. 'Imagine a capacitor that stores destructive potential, and you understand what I hold in my hands.'

'Now you're telling me a tale.'

'I brought it for the airship. But it will easily obliterate this carriage.'

Symantaka's shoulders fell.

'I'd rather end this life,' said Vasant, 'than see it from your point of view.'

'But can't you hear yourself? Can't you see what you're doing? Faced with pleasure, you respond with rage! Why not respond with pleasure? Just once!'

'Open the door.'

'Why do you dismiss the value of pleasure?'

'Open it!'

Symantaka sighed. He pushed the nymph capacitor back into its cabinet and twisted in his chair. The door clicked. The Engineer kicked it wide and jumped out, holding his construction like a totem to ward off a particularly evil eye.

Symantaka leaned from the craft. 'You're afraid of your own body.'

'Don't talk to me.'

The craft lifted, the Kama Sutran still visible through the open frame of the doorway. 'You're afraid of sex,' he said.

Vasant walked, not looking up until the little lavender vessel passed and changed its vector, then he shuddered, thinking how close he'd come to intimacy with Symantaka. He concentrated on his new situation.

The airship continued bouncing along the upper levels of Khajuraho, knocking slowly from side to side and creating damage on both. Vasant walked the spongy surface of the primary gas envelope, crossing from one platform to the next. Although the airship appeared to be a single unit, it was in fact composed of several light chassis arranged around irregular balloons, but the cabins were not accessible from the outer shell, where he was located.

He walked to the stern, where the tail-feather balloons were gathered. The airship was descending, pivoting, moving down another wide tunnel between towers. Collisions made walking difficult, shudders rippling across the supple fabric of the envelope, and Vasant stayed close to the upper keel. He hated to imagine himself sliding off and landing with a splat on some tilework image of Kama.

Where the fuselage tapered, he slid down and landed on the main wing, where seven propellers pushed the craft forward. He lifted a panel and found a service ladder into the housing, where blades blurred.

Inside, stepping away from them, he heard the music, a sitar and flute and tabla drums playing seductive raga over burbles of sound he recognized as human voices, laughter, giddy laughter. Beneath the smell of dung-brick fuel was the stink of bhang.

He walked deeper into the craft without turning on any lamps. The strangeness of being here was that these walls had begun as a sketch of his. He knew where he was, exactly, remembering the visions that had been the seeds of all this. It was like coming home. Almost. He regretted what he was going to do.

He emerged from a narrow service corridor to the main engine room and stopped abruptly. Ahead sat a figure, its eyes glowing. Vasant recognized the smell before his eyes fully focused and he almost lost control of his bladder. The creature rose on four legs, gaining a shape overlaid with stripes.

The tiger of Ranthambhore walked toward him unsteadily.

As it emerged from shadow, Vasant saw that a mask cupped its nostrils. Connected tubes fed into chambers of a bhang burner nearby, which the tiger pulled over. It stopped and swayed. A growl issued from deep within, and the great cat took a few more steps, knocking a post. It steadied itself and looked at Vasant with determination. The look in its eyes said, Enough.

It tried walking again. Vasant backstepped, turned, ran, heard the tiger collide with another beam. Glancing back, he saw it shake its head. The sound of his footsteps recaptured its attention. It came faster.

Vasant knew this place, knew where to turn even as clawed feet padded after him. He hoped to increase the tiger's bhang-induced confusion by taking a circuitous route and reaching the engine room from another side.

Nothing behind him. He pulled a service cart to block the way, should the animal find him again.

In the engine room, he worked quickly. Everything was exactly where he expected it. The richness of dung filled the room. He removed a panel from the thrumming wall and leaned into the warm space with his device. He could see only a suggestion of the stacks below but knew that thousands of refined dung bricks were stored here. It would have been simple to plant the device somewhere outside, on the shell of the envelope, but such a rent in the aircraft's fabric could be easily mended. If he wanted to ground the aircraft permanently, he needed to strike at the core.

'Hey!'

Vasant froze.

A figure had appeared at the entrance. 'You can't come back here!'

The Engineer didn't move.

'The Prince keeps his tiger here. You like to get mauled?'

Vasant without sudden motions set down his bomb and triggered the timer. 'I've been searching up and down for a toilet,' he snapped, stepping away. 'Is it too much to ask that a craft this big provide more than one facility for men?'

'Well, you won't find – oh, Kama spare us!'

The tiger leaped over the cart, and Vasant joined the other man in a backward scramble. The man kept running, but when Vasant got past the entrance, he grabbed loop handles hanging overhead and pulled down a paneled door as the tiger pounced. Impact knocked the door out of shape. Vasant turned the lock and looked over his shoulder, to where lights were brighter and sitars sounded like a plea of fingernails across flesh.

Little time remained. He couldn't go back the way he'd come.

No choice.

He walked toward the merriment, or pretense of merriment – he wasn't sure what to think when he saw the gaggle of Kama Sutran women, dressed in garments that revealed most of what anyone would want to see. They stopped, but seemed glad of his arrival. Arms slid over him as he entered the room; hands ran along his shoulders and around his waist. It made walking difficult. The women didn't seem to care who he was or if he belonged, they were just happy to have a male body to add to the mix. He passed a knot of nudes twined across a couch, and the sexual act seemed to be moving out from there, drawing more bodies into its ongoing stitching of mouth to crotch and hand to ass. The compartment overhead, which he'd designed for unruly children, had been taken over by musicians, who squatted inside, working their instruments with cramped intensity. Smoke curled through the crowd, weedy ropes of bhang linking arms and legs, making him as light-headed as the tiger. But he pressed forward, fought embraces he was invited into, fingers slithering across his body.

'I'm not here for this,' he said. 'I don't want any of this.' They tossed back their heads, and he wasn't sure they understood, or maybe they did and thought him laughably prudish, it was too funny that anyone should not want *this*. A woman held still on all fours while someone poured honey down her back, the liquid slowly flowing down the channel of her spine, pooling above her buttocks, meeting the face of a man who lapped happily at the same speed.

'Smoke and flame, smoke and fire,' Vasant said through his teeth. As he pressed past the exposed flesh and braying laughter, he pictured the timer he had assembled with tweezers and a tiny screwdriver. The delicate handiwork of the escapement was now counting down seconds as notches of steel.

Not many seconds left.

He plied forward, and the press of bodies ended at last.

He dove into the room he wanted, a viewing chamber built along the side of the peacock, which he'd designed for Royals whom he imagined flying over India. He'd meant for them to enjoy the splendors of the land. The room was for quality people, high-caste people with refined sensibilities. It was empty. Several large windows made possible views that would never, ever be enjoyed. He charged one such a window, striking it with his shoulder. At a second attempt the glass popped from its frame and fell – the sound of it breaking much closer than expected.

He leaned out. The airship flew remarkably close to the ground floor. He would definitely survive a jump. Easily survive. The airship continued slowly moving as the seconds passed. He climbed through the opening and hung from its rim.

As he hung, gathering the nerve to let go, his luck improved further. The airship passed over a big round room that seemed to be – what? Covered with pillows? It looked like an immense bed, and he could only attribute this to the licentiousness of Khajuraho's builders. But what better landing could he have asked for?

He delayed only because of the sight that came into view, a sight more unexpected even than a room of pillows: if he let go now, he would drop onto a pair of naked lovers.

Rakesh?!

Yes, it *was* Rakesh down there, lying with one of the Pragmatics! Shiva spare him, was everyone possessed? Sex with a monk! In his confusion, Vasant held on too long.

A hard hand clamped his wrist.

He was hauled up.

'No! What are you – ?'

Vasant kicked the wall of the cabin, but it was no use resisting the figure reeling him in. Flung back inside, he landed on the floor, in a sprawl. He looked up at slender legs and a sextet of mahogany arms arranged around a dark, slender torso. The face was considerate and mean.

'Don't be embarrassed,' said a voice behind the goonda. 'It happened to me once.'

A second goonda stood behind the first, cradling in his arms someone wearing a silver codpiece.

The hedonist.

'I almost fell out, too,' said Prince Hapi. 'I got so high, on the roof. Another time out a window, trying to net a butterfly. Opium, poppies. I guess that makes twice I almost fell out . . .'

Vasant could have counted the Prince's ribs. His limbs hung limp, and his head rolled back so that he stared at the ceiling. He was dirty, his legs streaked with dirt or feces.

'Let me go!' Vasant roared. 'You've as good as killed me!'

'That voice . . .' Hapi tried unsuccessfully to lift his head. 'Where do I know that voice?'

Levels of Khajuraho sank past the windows. The airship was rising.

'Land this craft! Now!'

'You have too foul a temper to be any friend of mine. Goonda, throw him out!' This sent the Prince into a fit of giggling.

'Laugh,' said Vasant. 'But the party is finished.'

'We are acquainted, aren't we?'

Vasant pushed past the goonda that had yanked him aboard. The explosion was imminent, and every window showed that their distance from the ground was increasing.

He did not want his life to end in Khajuraho: what consequence would dying here have for his next incarnation? He wanted to live, so he could wash his soul clean of this place and the things he'd seen here. But there was so little time.

And so much flesh.

He remembered Symantaka's accusation.

Vasant wasn't afraid of sex. He wasn't afraid of anything. Yet his hand trembled when he pushed the door open into the next room.

In the lounge they greeted his return with laughter, apparently glad to have him in their fold again. More bonds had formed. He joined the group, moving past those who lay on the divan simply watching and those who were spilling drinks on the periphery, past the women whose clothes were undone toward those who stood completely nude, with men completely nude, and he forged ahead, wedging himself between connections of pressed flesh, until it was worse than his last day in Delhi when he lay dog-piled, and he could taste skin, smell sweat, feel hair against his neck, and hear moist bodily interactions. He wasn't afraid of sex, but he prayed to Shiva as he pushed himself to the center of the knot, feeling the heaves of assorted chests and haunches and an off-kilter rhythm that jerked him in surprising directions, and something warm and pliable was put into his palm as the music pulsed like energy transferred through water, and he could no longer identify the many body parts pressed against his own. He closed his eyes and shut his mouth, trying to block it out, knowing all would soon change. The timer, the device built of Jagannath scrap and rich dung . . .

And it worked.

He was deafened, shaken. He felt a great lurch and pivot and sound filtered back in screams, the snap of flames, and an overwhelming whoosh. The crush of bodies became desperate, some slouching like damp sacks of grain and others struggling. Bodies bounced once, hard, as the airship crashed. Breathing was difficult, the bhang superseded by a less forgiving smoke, dark and bitter.

Vasant pushed at the bodies.

People were burning. He saw them tossing back and forth in flame. Corpses lay scorched and nudes ran blackened. There was blood, and ruined struts thrust in tumultuous disarray. Someone was impaled, staring in horror at the point of entry. Vasant struggled forward. The party was indeed over. Nymphs panicked around him. Terrified, they separated from dead partners, clambered over them, stepped on others trying to escape.

The engineer of this disaster moved forward, planning to make a discreet exit through one of the ragged seams in the wall.

A shape loomed before him, a goonda, its arms charred and peppered with glass, its face blasted into a half snarl. The six arms spasmed as it stepped toward Vasant, reaching with a jerking wooden hand. He retreated, met a post. The goonda bridged the gap and lifted its jittery hand to Vasant's shoulders, neck, the five other arms twitching as the goonda tried to close a grip on the Engineer's throat.

Then hoofbeats, truncated whistles.

Vasant knew that sound. The goonda's head jerked with a *whump whump*, sprouting feathered bolts. The goonda staggered sideways and released Vasant as more arrows found their marks, and Pragmatics bulldozed through the smoke with their quivers and bows, announcing themselves with well-placed shots, surging inside on a madness of horses forced to gallop into flames.

THE BURNING OF
NYMPHS

THE BURNING OF nymphs was an unnerving sight. Unlike the monks, I didn't venture into the blazing hulk of the airship, preferring to stand well back and watch it burn like some long building dropped from the sky, portions of its former glory resisting the flames even as the blue skin parted in curling margins to reveal the distressed geometry of the frame. Broken rooms for dancing, hand-painted wallpaper. I could see the symbol for prosperity and a painting of Ganesha, both mutating with heat. But what struck me most were persons Vasant later said were nymphs: naked women emerging black from calamity like creatures born of a furnace. I could see teeth: their lips had been blasted away. I could see muscles flayed by fire, I could see anatomy. Vasant told me he heard them crying, but when I saw them push out, they made no sound, opening and shutting their mouths silently, a litter of charred nubile humanoids.

From many directions Kama Sutrans came running, firefighters in garish pink outfits and civilians who happened to be in the tower. They came with axes and chopped through the airship, grunting contentedly with each swing. When bodies were pulled from the wreck, I could hear the rescuers breathe sighs of ecstasy. Someone retreated, holding his red throbbing hand, yet he looked as excited as a child holding a bubble. 'Oh, oh yes,' I heard him murmur, his eyes narrowed to slits as he circled the crowd with his sensation. Overhead, balloons got into position, lowering persons in fat suits of fireproofed fabric, who looked like flower heads as they entered the blaze. They were reeled up with sublime expressions, holding the bodies of the rescued. More citizens came running, summoned by cries of pain and cries of pleasure, coming with faces that said that more than their curiosity had been aroused. Sections of crowd who couldn't get close enough to participate raised their hands to feel the heat, and hum.

Victims were handled like delicate treasure, transferred to gurneys with big wooden wheels and flower bedding, then carted off to whatever medical facilities Khajuraho offered. The attendants sighed as they pressed bandages to wounds, and the gurneys zigzagged, graphing the distraction of the people pushing them.

The flames spread, the crowd not failing its task but rather physically sharing it – and the pleasure of performing it – among a growing number. Soon the whole population seemed to surround the blaze with hands in the air or heads tossed back, their gratification now louder than the snap and popping bursts of burning wood. Someone who didn't know better might have looked on this scene and thought the Kama Sutrans worshiped a god with the head of a peacock and a body of fire. The climax came with a gush, a long suspended hose releasing great gouts of pink water.

Nervously I watched the sardulas, three of whom had come to assist. One of the shaggy beasts clamped his mouth on a strut and dragged back a difficult section of the wreck, opening it and revealing Vasant. The Engineer emerged, the jacket of his suit folded over one arm. When he saw the crowd of Kama Sutrans raising their hands to the water that came down and flicking it into the flames, he paused, coughed, proceeded. His face looked changed from when I'd last seen him. He threaded the crowd with rare civility, and when he saw me, he coughed again and made his way over.

'You're all right?' I asked.

He gave me a peculiar look. Me, then Yamuna.

'You got what you wanted,' I said.

'They brought it on themselves. The city is to blame.' But he didn't sound sure. Another frank stare was leveled at me and the pregnant monk.

Our attention turned to others appearing from the ruin. Horses first, single file, then the dismounted Pragmatics, who carried by the head and feet a sizzling goonda. I could see he was dead, because something hard and round had caved in his skull. But in his wooden arms he held a second figure, a survivor. This smaller person's face and body were streaked with char where the arms hadn't shielded him, and when the Pragmatics set down the corpse, the man struggled within its cage of limbs, looking like a captured animal.

'Wha . . . what have you done to me?'

'There was an accident,' Pala explained. 'Your airship crashed.'

'Airship?'

'The vessel you used to attack our fortress.'

'Who . . . are you?'

'My name is Pala. I'm a Pragmatic of Ran-thambhore.'

Hapi pushed at the limbs of the dead goonda. 'Why am I in prison?' he said. 'You have no right to put me in prison . . . Summon the Sovereign . . .'

Pala turned. 'The crash seems to have rattled his brain.'

A hospital gurney rolled up, with a pair of smiling women at the helm. 'May we take away your injured?' one asked. 'May we tend his wounds?'

'We'd like to speak with him when he's regained his senses,' Pala said. 'We'll come along.'

'Whatever gives you pleasure,' said the woman. She allowed herself a groan then attempted to lift the goonda onto the cart. The Pragmatics helped, dropping the statuesque corpse in the bed of flowers, which sent up a cloud of petals. Its head and feet hung over the ends. Hapi squirmed within the arms.

We put the disaster and its contradictory moans behind us, following the cart up a long, winding ramp to the Healing Grounds, a garden organized by high hedges. Sandstone ended as we crossed to earth and grassy slopes. It was like a meadow built into the tower. Beds were situated throughout, some in nooks between bushes, others gathered in groups of ten or more, under young pine saplings. Some of the patients lay with an arm hanging to the ground, a hand dipped in orchids or wild cucumber.

The cart stopped in a ward of crash victims. An attendant pried open the goonda's mouth and popped a green pill inside. The corpse's arms unfolded. Nurses took Prince Hapi from either side and lifted him to a bed, pressing something into his mouth, too, and his anxiety faded. He allowed the attendants to remove his silver garment and swab his limbs.

Some nurses were diverting their patients with a hand slipped under their sheets, and I was about to comment, when Yamuna said, 'Don't try to tell me this sect of Hindus is stranger than any other.'

I wondered what Vasant thought, but he was staring at a group of fresh victims who entered in a huddle, blackened by their wounds into a common unit and apparently blinded. Beneath floral scents I smelled burnt flesh.

Waiting for Prince Hapi's wounds to be cleaned, the Pragmatics wandered through the ward, and I thought that like Pala they were sampling the pleasures of the garden, pausing and pulling over blossoms to inhale their aroma, champac flowers and amaranth, marigold and black mustard. I stayed close to Yamuna, still wary of the sardula. But that wasn't the only reason I wanted to be close to her. I felt pulled. Having seen her nude, I looked at her in her robe with new appreciation. My attention didn't seem to bother her; when we were close, she deliberately pressed against me, or reminded me of her body with a finger on my forearm.

The Pragmatic tour of the ward was a ruse. The monks wanted to approach patients. They seemed to have a question for everyone in India. Toward the rear, where the wall opened to sky and great ramps of light, Pala spoke to a man who had an oddly neutral expression.

The patient was perhaps forty or fifty. His face was not particularly wrinkled, but it looked old: slack and lacking affect, like that of a victim of a brain seizure. His lips moved, puckering like a fish's mouth.

'I am not really a patient, though that is how I started,' he said slowly. 'Now I do jobs here, cleaning sheets, pulling weeds, gardening. The hospital is my home.'

It took effort for him to blink, and his lids were slow to reopen.

'As a Kama Sutran, your condition must be especially difficult,' observed Pala. 'Beauty being so highly valued here.'

The man looked to the floor and said nothing for a moment. Then, 'A dead face is not attractive.'

'Would you mind telling my associates how this condition came on you?'

The man said, 'Karma.'

'For what?' Yamuna asked.

'It happened many years ago, when Khajuraho was not well established. My family was starving. It was horrible, what I did, but how awful it is to see your wife getting deathly thin, to send your children begging. We were Vaisyas. Not meant to beg. But my youngest son died, and it appeared my daughter would soon follow if we did not beg. Then a train struck a cow. Everyone went to the tracks to look at the corpse, to weep and say prayers. We thought Khajuraho must be doomed. But some of us lingered, looking at the dead animal lying in the sun. Mine was not the only family faced with starvation.' He fell silent.

Yamuna said, 'You ate the flesh of a cow?'

He nodded, shutting those slow eyes. 'The next morning, my face was as you see it today. A mask. My punishment.'

'And have you tried to make amends?'

'Every day I pray to Shiva, Brahma, Vishnu. I've made pilgrimages to holy rivers. But there are some pollutions that will not wash away.'

'What if we said you needn't suffer? That your face might be restored?'

'You joke with a man who has no humor.'

'Will you let us try?'

His face remained a mask. But when Yamuna suggested he remove his shirt and roll onto his stomach, he complied. She sat beside him on the bed, studying his back while Pala left for the Jagannath.

Pala returned with the instrument I remembered from my own experience at their hands, and I watched with sympathy as they inserted the needle in his back and injected the fluid.

'He won't need as much of the tincture as you did,' Yamuna told me.

'What are you doing?' said the man.

'Don't worry.'

'I feel . . . tingling.'

They inserted and withdrew the syringe six times while he fingered his lips, his cheeks. When he sat up again, his face still lacked emotion, but there were new twitches. In his eyes, new light. Hope.

'I recommend,' said Pala, 'that you devote this day to your god of healing. Tomorrow morning, you should begin reacquainting yourself with your face.'

The man got off the bed unsteadily, knelt before Yamuna and Pala, thanking them profusely, kissing their feet. Then he rushed off, touching his face. I asked Yamuna why a god of healing should play any role in the gardener's recovery, if the Pragmatics believed the chakras were to blame for his condition. She replied that although the chakras were the key, faith played a role in any recovery, and the Pragmatics found it more expedient to work with such convictions than fight them. Pala did another tour of the ward and returned with a plucked orchid. 'I think we've given the Royal enough time.'

Vasant joined us as we approached the bed.

Prince Hapi seemed more aware now, because at the sight of Vasant a flash of surprise entered his face. He looked from side to side but, seeing no escape, leaned back and glowered like a man confident he belongs to the most privileged caste of life. Vasant allowed the Pragmatics to precede him.

'No need to be frightened,' said Pala. 'We wish you no further harm.'

'I want to talk to someone from the Palace.'

'You're in Khajuraho.'

'I know where I am!'

'We're not aware of any persons from Delhi here. Except for Vasant.'

Prince Hapi scowled at the Engineer.

'Do you remember me?' said Pala. 'Do we look familiar?'

'Judging by your outfit, I'd guess you're some Buddhist dog.'

'A Pragmatic, actually. From Ranthambhore.'

'Oh, Ranthambhore.' His eyes lit. 'I've been to Ranthambhore.'

'In the comfort of the airship.'

'Yes, I remember that visit.'

'Why did you come?'

'I won't answer to some faithless dog. Leave me. Away! You pollute the air I breathe.'

Pala leaned back, as if to consider this comment. 'I think I understand you,' he said. 'Having devoted your life to pleasure, you run from the slightest pain.'

At this point the Prince sat up and yelped; one of the monks had slipped a hand under the sheet and was doing something to his foot. Nurses looked over, but Pala smiled to indicate there was no problem. With one finger, he closed the Prince's jaw. A tear ran from the Prince's eye.

Pala said, 'We don't like suffering, either.'

'You know secrets . . .' Prince Hapi gasped.

'Yes?'

'That was all I wanted . . .'

'What interest are our secrets to you?'

'Please . . . I won't resist further!'

Pala made an almost imperceptible gesture to the other monk, and the hand withdrew. Prince Hapi slumped, and Pala puffed his pillow and helped the young Royal sit up. 'You were saying?'

'I wanted control.'

'What sort of control?'

'Over my body. I wanted my health returned. Strength, vitality, day-long erections. Life without need of sleep. All your tricks.'

'Someone told you we could provide these things?'

'Yes.'

'Why not simply ask us what we might do for you?'

'Why should I ask? You're less than untouchables; whatever you possess is at my command.'

'And the Palace equipped you for your visit.'

'The Palace? You mean Kavita?' He sneered. 'I do what I please.'

'But you came with goondas. And the airship.'

'She was repaying a debt.'

I could almost feel Vasant's patience giving, collapsing like a bridge made of sugar. He pushed forward, and Prince Hapi said to him:

'Is it your turn now?'

'You ruined her!' Vasant snapped. 'Made misery in all India. For decadence! Bodily gratification! The promise of an erection!'

The Prince shrugged.

'You have no excuse?'

'I gave Kavita what she wanted. More than you could.'

'Arrogant little bastard!'

Prince Hapi nodded. 'And you're a blind bureaucrat with a stick up his rear. Aren't you here to beat me? While I'm drugged and in a hospital bed? While you're surrounded by your faithless friends? I'm ready, Vasant. Do your worst!'

The Engineer glanced at me and the Pragmatics. 'That's not what I came for,' he said. 'I'm above all this.'

Pala seemed satisfied, and planted the orchid behind the Prince's ear before we left. The Prince yanked out the blossom and threw it at our departure. 'India has no room for you,' he said. 'There's no mountain tall enough to hide you faithless dogs!'

COLD FIRE

VASANT KEPT FINDING opportunities to glare at me.

Before returning to the Jagannath, the Pragmatics wanted branches, and so we meandered back from Khajuraho, saffron robes disrupting the gloom of a scraggly forest. I traipsed behind Yamuna, carrying her branches. I couldn't gather them myself, because the monks used some esoteric criteria to make selections, stepping over a hundred branches before choosing one. Vasant stopped to scowl at me. I ignored it, but he appeared closer next time, disapproval plain on his face.

'I've been thinking about betrayals,' he said.

'Oh?'

'I betrayed the Sovereign. The First Wife betrayed him.'

'Does that matter to me?'

'Betrayals,' he said. 'People surrendering to urges.'

Yamuna picked up another stick. I refused to indulge the Engineer with a reply.

'You seem . . . meek,' he said.

'Meek?'

'Collecting sticks. Following her around. Did you

become a puppy somewhere inside those walls? Do you need someone to pet you, toss you treats?'

I cleared my throat.

'There has been betrayal here,' he said. 'Am I right?'

'Vasant, I – '

'Shouldn't you be demanding that we return to the Jagannath? Shouldn't these monks be following *you*? Why aren't we back inside the god?'

'My focus . . .'

'Has been misdirected,' he said, with a glance at Yamuna. 'I know. I saw.' He stepped closer, putting a hand on my arm. 'You had a lapse. You caved in – I've described in depth how it happened to me: it does happen to good Hindus. But don't continue this lapse. Don't surrender!'

I watched Yamuna perform the simple act of weighing a stick in her hands. 'It's not simply a lapse of reason,' I said.

'What do you mean? What else could it be?'

I couldn't say it. Yamuna did as much. 'We can help you too, Vasant.'

He glared at her, back at me. 'Help me? I don't understand.'

'They wanted me to try living without dharma,' I explained.

'Without . . .?'

I nodded.

'This isn't possible. Is this really Rakesh speaking?'

'You see, there is a tincture – '

'Rakesh, whom nobody could dissuade from his holy duty? Rakesh has abandoned his dharma?'

I looked to Yamuna for support.

'Shiva help me!' the Engineer cried. 'I accompanied

you here because you convinced me. It took time, but you did convince me. And now you're *without* your dharma? What about the Baboon Warrior? What about your responsibility as a Hindu? What about all that?!'

'I don't know anymore . . .'

'You must have told hundreds of people your intention to kill him. Do you think that hasn't filtered back to him? You threatened his admirers. Destroyed some of them in Nainpur! Do you think he doesn't know? Now that you are *without your dharma*, what will you do when he comes for you, Rakesh? Will you hide?'

'I'm not sure . . .'

'Rakesh, weren't you and I brought together for a purpose?'

I tried to say something to mitigate his outrage, but I felt cowed, dim, unable to argue effectively. When I looked for my previous confidence, I found numbness, a disconnection between me and what before had seemed so certain. I shrugged.

Vasant put it simply. 'Are you a good Hindu,' he asked, 'or not?'

Yamuna came over with another branch, and I added it to my load.

Vasant's face creased with anger. 'What am I doing here?' he exclaimed. 'Why am I here?'

I was going to speak, but he raised a hand. He turned, and long strides carried him through the forest, away. I heard him muttering disbelief as trees blocked my view of his receding figure.

'It's just because I'm a Pragmatic,' she said. 'He'll get used to the idea of us.'

I wasn't so sure.

I wasn't eager to return to the Jagannath, either,

partly because I dreaded its mental manipulations. As for the Baboon, I felt no desire to kill him, or find him, even discuss him. The idea that he might continue to expect me was new and unsettling; I no longer wanted his attention, nor knew what to do if it brought him to me. Maybe I could avoid such a meeting by staying away from the Jagannath . . .

If I kept within arm's reach of Yamuna, all would be right. That's how I felt, at least. I followed so closely, I bumped against her a few times.

A stranger appeared with his own bundle of sticks. He wasn't a Pragmatic, and he didn't glow like a Kama Sutran, but he did appear enthusiastic about something. Looking at my branches, he said, 'Bring them to the pile.'

He was gone before I could ask what he meant. Yamuna took a few steps after him, curious, and I knew we would have to solve this mystery before anything else was accomplished. I was feeling so cowardly that I welcomed any delay.

We passed a few more people stalking the woods, and nearby we found a dusty village, ramshackle huts whose inhabitants wore clothing pale and frayed. Was a kind of game being played? Young and old participated, moving doggedly in and out of the forest. I followed Yamuna to the perimeter and realized that the man must have assumed I was collecting branches for the large heap in the center of town. There was junk in the pile too, and a central pole stood prominently, strung loosely with rope. A few villagers paced; an old woman wept. The focus was an agitated young man wearing what I took to be his best outfit, and everyone, including him, turned sharply at sounds from the woods. When the old woman saw Yamuna, her wailing became louder.

The man frowned and marched over.

'What's going on here?' Yamuna asked.

'No concern of yours! You get away! Away!'

Yamuna made a dismissive gesture and retreated. But she paused when she was out of his sight. Someone whistled, and she whistled back. We walked again, not concerned with branches now; instead, Yamuna checked behind bushes and large deadfalls.

'What are you looking for?' I asked.

'That man's wife.'

'How do you know his wife is missing?'

'Because she wasn't tied to the pole.'

I didn't understand.

'He accused her of infidelity,' Yamuna said.

'Oh.' I wasn't sure how she knew this, but it did fit the scene. The village had been preparing for a fire.

'If you find this woman, what will you do?' I said. 'Help her run?'

'Some Hindu men find it convenient to dispose of their wives by questioning their chastity,' Yamuna said sharply. 'If they have an argument, infidelity. If her face no longer pleases him, infidelity. If he's taken a lover and his wife makes a fuss, infidelity.'

'But if the woman is virtuous, Agni will protect her from the flames.'

'Do you know anyone whom a god has rescued from such a situation? Not stories, not secondhand information. Do you know anyone whom Agni has saved from a husband's accusations?'

I looked back toward the village.

'Yes, I would help her run,' said Yamuna.

I could see orange robes spaced through the forest. The other Pragmatics must have reached the same conclusion: with whistles their search expanded. The more I listened to Pragmatic opinions, the more susceptible I became to them.

Still loaded with dry branches, I helped look for the adulteress.

The search ended at a small defiant hill. Yamuna ascended, using weeds for support, climbing to a fissure in the rock to see if the woman was squeezed inside. I saw the fire first. I said nothing, perhaps hoping that Yamuna would not see it and that I wouldn't have to feel culpable. I had turned, looking back toward the village, where smoke rose. A curling wisp, but undeniably the marker of a fire.

I heard Yamuna stop suddenly; I couldn't look at her.

Sounds issued from the village, but we were too far to discern what was shouted. Or shrieked. I watched the trees nearby flare with color.

No sign of Agni, no intervention. Maybe the woman had indeed been unfaithful. The thought, however, was not reassuring.

Below, the monks continued searching, unaware of what we could see, but the hollowness I felt was something they must have known very well. Their energy, their pursuit of answers, no doubt their whole lives stemmed from what I presently experienced: the emptiness of a terrible moment with not even a hue of religion to redeem it. What a cold place India was for the monks. No wonder they threw themselves into studies.

And for me?

A cord of smoke reached for the heavens, but fell far short.

The only god in sight was the Jagannath, still standing near Khajuraho, exhibiting no concern for the death of an anonymous wife.

'We should be going,' Yamuna said.

I stood at the ramp, staring into the trees. Yamuna went up into the god, and fifteen minutes later Pala came out.

'Maybe he's lost,' I said.

'Lost?' The monk smiled sadly. 'With a signpost like the Jagannath?'

Not lost, then.

'More likely,' said Pala, 'Vasant has decided not to come back.'

'Why wouldn't he?'

'Of course, he barely tolerated us Pragmatics. And he achieved what he wanted in Khajuraho – with a vengeance! What reason does he have to continue traveling with the Jagannath? None.'

Irritability was another sensation newly restored in me, and sharper than I remembered it. I couldn't refute what Pala said, so I lashed out:

'What would *you* know about loyalty?'

He looked surprised. 'Loyalty?'

'What would Azis say about your loyalty, if he could?'

Pala opened his mouth to respond, stopped. 'I didn't mean to . . . Rakesh? Is something else bothering you?'

I wouldn't tell him; I'd shown the monks too many weaknesses since being injected. I refused to add fear of the future to that list. I was afraid to get back into the Jagannath, but I would not let Pala know. I walked up the ramp, stormed up it. At least Yamuna was inside, I told myself. But my stomach dropped when I crossed onto the chariot, because the moment I did so, the god's engines fired and the wheels shifted against the earth.

As if it had been waiting for a vital piece of cargo.

EIGHT PERFECT
SHOTS

◆━◎━◆

A HUMAN PYRAMID marched forward.

Prior to seeing this arrangement, I'd wondered how the tubes running along the ceiling of Interior Space Number 16 were accessed. Here came the towering answer: a row of five laborers made a bottom row, four more stood on their shoulders, three on theirs, two, then a single man at the apex, the ceiling within his reach. When he finished, the bottom row stepped back, transporting him to the next job. In this configuration, the laborers seemed even less human; those supporting the topmost member stared blankly as he worked, and none registered my presence, as far as I could tell. Or the presence of the monks, who stood facing them in a line.

Pala gave me a brief look before he returned attention to the pyramid that he and his brothers blocked. 'Azis,' he called. 'We've come to take you back.'

I could pick out Azis only by following Pala's gaze to the middle of the pyramid, where, yes, Azis served as a central support, his expression as neutral as a staircase.

'Azis!'

A hammer was passed up the ranks. No response from Azis.

The Pragmatics launched into a word game about one day passing into the next: *The first day of the second month of the third year comes one day after the last day of the first month* – and so forth, an evolving mental puzzle that, like the Jagannath's commands, insinuated itself into my thoughts. But it did not affect the pyramid. A fluttering eyelid on one woman's face was perhaps related. Azis did not blink.

Pala walked around the pyramid. It turned. He made a gesture, and three monks climbed shoulders to form a unit level with their former comrade.

'What would your mother think,' Pala said, 'if we let you become one more anonymous custodian to this unkind god?'

The uppermost monk uncapped a vial of ammonia; but, even held under Azis's nose, it produced no visible reaction. Another monk climbed his three brothers and attempted to cross from them to the pyramid. The plan was for him to replace Azis in the structure, but as soon as he stepped over, a grubby hand clamped on his foot. He tugged, but his foot remained fixed. The other monks grabbed him and hauled back, their effort unavailing, the foot locked in that soot-stained grip. More arms extended from the pyramid, grabbing the man at several points. The pyramid marched backward, plucking him away. His face showed surprise but no fear as he was turned upside down and lifted. The other Pragmatics rushed after the laborers and the apprehended brother.

The laborers didn't simply release him but hurled him, as if throwing a spear, and if not for an immediate response his head would have been damaged against the floor. Instead he was caught in friendly arms and promptly set on his feet.

The monks formed a circle around the pyramid and linked arms so it couldn't break through. So fenced, the unit turned and turned, a wall of grimy bodies rotating in a ring of saffron robes. Dalvara, one of the monks who often worked in the head-compartment, tossed a rope through the formation, on Azis's left side. It was caught and thrown back through the gap on his right. As Dalvara tied a noose, the pyramid began its evacuation.

That top laborer opened a portal in the ceiling and held fast while outer members climbed. The pyramid dissolved upward, without urgency, as if this was how they always left a room. The noose cinched around Azis's waist as he stood in a column of five, his hands gripping the feet above him. The Pragmatics quickly arranged themselves along the rope, gripping tight, but Azis was climbing, hauling himself up the last two laborers who hung in place, then through the portal.

In the following tug-of-war, the Pragmatics seemed pitted against more than fifteen laborers: nothing could be seen or heard past the rectangular aperture through which they'd disappeared, but resistance was tremendous, as if from the god itself. The Pragmatics strained, slipping on the floor, losing any gains they made to jerks of strength from the other end. Briefly, the front monk was lifted up, and I had a vision of the whole string of Pragmatics being sucked up that hole, never to be seen again.

Then they found a rhythm. *Oy-hah, oy-hah, oy-hah*. On the second beats they took a step, took a step, took a step, marching back. A thump overhead, and something gave, the monks surging back as Azis crashed down, landing in a pile.

Pala walked over. 'Not dead,' he pronounced.

Azis lifted his head, tried to stand. When this failed, he moved on hands and knees toward the exit, apparently eager to leave this space and return to work. The monks blocked his path, and he pushed against their legs, trying to squeeze between. Dalvara tied his ankles, and Azis attempted to pull himself away on his hands. The hands too were bound. Then he was hauled upright, looking like a convict in leg irons, and escorted from Interior Space Number 16, his former comrades making a second knot of bodies around him. I tried to catch Pala's eye as the huddle moved past me, but he was too involved – or else deliberately avoiding me.

I had come looking for Pala, having resolved to confront him.

The day before, some determined blundering had brought me to the head-compartment, where Dalvara and two other pilots sat amid the controls. They didn't give me more than a glance. Nothing outside, through the eyes, looked familiar. I rubbed my temples as the Jagannath ordered me to plumb some dark bowel of its waste system. I ignored the order. I concentrated, to say exactly what I wanted.

'Where are we going?'

The pilots looked at one another.

'Where are we going?' said the woman pilot. 'You weren't told?'

'I wasn't told.'

'Ranthambhore.'

'Back to your fortress?'

'Yes.'

'When was this decided?'

They paused. 'You should talk to Pala.'

'Why are you taking the Jagannath to Ranthambhore?'

'Really,' said Dalvara, 'Pala will tell you what you
need to know.'

What I needed to know? What did that mean? I
wanted to shout, *Tell me yourself!* I wanted to see them
cringe at my anger. But I only clenched my fists.

They returned their attention to the controls.

'Very well,' I said, hating my weakness. 'I'll do that.'

I left, steeling myself to face Pala. But now here I
was, unable to follow through, as they filed past me.
I stood in the vacant space, shamefully relieved that the
capture of Azis had postponed the encounter.

At least with Vasant gone, nobody would comment
on my timidity. The injections had left me meek. It
had taken me a full day to ask where we were going,
and I might never muster the courage to ask Pala why
I hadn't been consulted. I stood and watched a pair of
baboons in the corner wrestling over a piece of colored
fabric. Walking closer, I saw it was one of the tapestries
torn down in Nainpur, part of the Baboon Warrior
still visible.

There was only one reason I remained aboard the
god. Only one thing I cared about.

I found Yamuna in Interior Space Number 10 sitting
before a document, back in her copper garment. Her
mouth bent into a smile as I walked toward her, pulling
off my shirt. She opened the door of her gown, and I
squeezed inside, where it was hot and cramped beyond
reason. Yamuna shut the door after me, and I wedged

myself between her legs and the metal shell: no finer place in all India. Here my head was protected from the Jagannath's directives, and I almost believed it was Yamuna herself and not the metal providing shelter.

'I want us to go,' I said.

'What do you mean?'

'You and I. Alone, somewhere.'

'Leave the Jagannath?' She pulled her hand into the gown to stroke my scalp.

'Our hair will grow long,' I said. 'We'll give each other something to run our fingers through.'

'Are you suggesting I leave the Pragmatics?'

I supposed I was.

'Because it's not possible.'

Her hands paused for a moment, moved to my neck. *Why not?*

I didn't ask. I didn't dare, I didn't want to hear the answer. I gave myself to the feeling of her, singling out each place where our flesh met.

We'd made love every time I entered her gown. Sex was regimented by the copper garment, but I had learned to apply very small movements, twisting around her back, through her legs, under her buttocks. Perhaps some branch of Kama Sutran teaching covered the tiniest strokes of love, but for an amateur it was a challenge of yogic proportions. The day before, she'd pulled an arm into the gown and placed her hand over my mouth. As I pressed into her, I realized she was talking to somebody who'd come into the space – talking as if nothing were happening. Did she keep a straight face? Did she run through some Pragmatic koan to maintain composure? I had kept going, my fingertips hard against the wall as we continued in a couple. I felt their conversation as only the faintest tremor in the copper.

'What appeal does it have?' I asked her now.

'What?'

'Pragmatism.'

'Oh,' she said, and her hands stopped moving.

'Who are you?' I asked.

'What do you mean?'

'I know so little about you. How did this begin for you?'

'The beginning . . .' she said. 'I came to Ranthambhore as a child, with my father. He took me from our family after he finished helping to carve the fortress out of the peak. He was one of the originals.'

'When did he die?'

'I'm not sure he has died.'

'He left the sect, then?'

'I can't think of any reason he would have left.'

'But . . .?'

'I've forgotten who he is.'

My brow creased. 'You'll need to explain.'

'My father was a deeply committed Pragmatic who wanted me to be the perfect adept: to feel no special attachment to any one group member, including him. So I learned to forget his identity.'

'You've forgotten who he is?'

'Yes.'

'He could be one of the older monks?'

'It's possible; of the originals, seven survive.'

'Firdaus?'

'Maybe. I don't know.'

'Don't you look at their faces – don't you search their faces for a resemblance to yours?'

'If I do, and if I've ever seen a resemblance, I've forgotten it. Even if you guessed who he is, even if I wrote it down as a child and saw the truth in my handwriting, I would forget immediately. His identity is something I've trained myself to be unable to retain.'

I was silent inside the darkness of the gown, her words still humming in copper.

'This is a prized skill,' she said. 'The ability to erase certain memories.'

'But what was the rationale? Why forget your father?'

'A current in Pragmatic thought holds that there is no advantage to customizing relationships to the many people in our lives: it is more effective to see people as nodes of larger groups, without individual differentiation.'

The thought wheeled in my head: *Everyone is the same to you. No one has more value than another.*

'But I met you,' she continued, 'and discovered I was not a perfect student.' She touched my face, as if memorizing it for some future occasion when we would meet in darkness. I touched her navel, her knee, the bumps around her left nipple. Sex grew out of our touches, a passion more intense for its miniaturization, and for the things we had abandoned to find ourselves here, together. Afterward, Yamuna dropped down into the gown too, and we lay in a single mass filling the cone, lay there for an hour or more saying nothing, my fingers on her breast.

'The light,' Yamuna said.

'What about it?'

'It just got brighter.'

We heard a rumble, distant footfalls. We lay, wondering.

Another rumble.

'I don't want to find him,' I said.

'The Baboon?'

'It's gone, that urge. I don't want to encounter him. I'm afraid.'

She said nothing.

'All I want is to be somewhere with you, where we won't be noticed.'

'Where he can't find you?'

'Yes.'

She traced a finger through the short new hair on my head as we listened to further rumbles. Then, on some cue I couldn't detect, she rose and put herself back in the sleeves and collar of her gown. Footsteps. Someone else was in the space.

Pala's voice: 'Have you seen Rakesh?'

'No.'

'Are you sure?'

'Why do you want him?'

'Something is happening.'

'With the Jagannath.'

'The pilots have lost control. As with the cranes, but not quite.'

'Now you want Rakesh's opinion?'

'Before, it didn't matter.'

'You should have included him in all your decisions.'

'I have no time for this, Yamuna.'

'So leave.'

'If you see him . . .' Pala stopped, and I wondered if he knew I was here, listening. 'I didn't include him in decisions that had no bearing on him. This was reasonable. Maybe he will come to appreciate reason more, with our ongoing help. But if he wants to make a difference right now, he must come see me.'

His footsteps diminished. Yamuna straightened her legs and lifted the gown off me.

'Do you know what's happening?' she asked.

'No.'

After we gave Pala time to get ahead, we moved through the Jagannath ourselves. The change was obvious. The lights were brighter, and the engines worked at a pitch that made my feet vibrate, turbines rolling noisily inside their tall black cladding. The Pragmatics hurried about, and in the head of the god their difficulties were plain. Dalvara jerked to and fro as he attempted to steady a lever. The other pilots were similarly abused by the controls, which moved without manipulation, batting them, as if the spirit of the god had taken possession of the instruments. I saw that a new, long lever had risen from a slot in the floor that before we routinely stepped over: the new instrument was slick with dark grease, and it seemed to be showing itself now only to defy the monks more.

'What does the Jagannath want?' Pala said to me.

'How should I know?'

'I assumed there was a Hindu explanation.'

I took the telescope from one of the monks and looked out the window. The sun was smeared into twilight, but I could see no cranes or other demons that would have captured the Jagannath's imagination. 'Maybe it just doesn't want to go to Ranthambhore.'

Pala frowned at this. He seemed to take the situation as a personal insult. He wanted, I supposed, to quantify the god, to contain it in a system, believing that if the monks composed enough good mantras to describe its components, then they would understand its whole – and control it. But this was clearly not the case, and I heard an uncommon note of frustration in his voice as he issued orders.

'Send someone outside,' I suggested.

'What for?'

'To see where the Jagannath wants to go.'

'You?'

My heart shriveled. But despite my apprehension, Yamuna and I soon found ourselves on horseback. We rode down the ramp onto quaking ground. The sun had set, and the valley was exaggerated with shadow. We pulled away from the god, rode at a steady pace.

'Are we still in Madhya Pradesh?' I shouted.

'I've lost track.'

The ride improved as we distanced ourselves from the Jagannath, when we could at last hear the clop of hooves beneath us. We predicted the god's course and urged the horses faster, getting ahead. Looking back, I saw the expression on its face and was reminded of when Vasant and I dangled before it in midair in Sholapur. There was a hunger in those old wooden features.

Soon after, I heard voices, and my heart again contracted with fear. I recognized the rhythm even if I couldn't distinguish syllables. *Sim wi ta sicc'm, ep fel sim.* Everything became obvious when we crested the hill and saw where the god was summoned.

Later we would learn it was Gwalior. A metropolis. In the twilight we saw lights spread for miles. The Pragmatic scouts had not anticipated this place. Our horses slowed as if they too understood. Yamuna looked physically struck. Tens of thousands of lives lay before us. Doomed lives, now. Already strains of panic rose from the city, questions, cries, as the population felt the tremblings of the earth.

'I think I'm going to be ill,' said Yamuna.

'Maybe Pala and the others can divert the god.'

She leaned forward so her head rested against the horse's mane.

'Should we warn them?' I asked, feeling queasy too. 'Is there time?'

In Sholapur my confidence in my dharma had given me immunity; I had been present but unconnected to the calamity. I was not unconnected now. We would see people die by the thousands because our path had taken the god too close to this city.

'We can't blame ourselves,' I said weakly. 'You Pragmatics still don't understand the will of the Jagannath. You must accept its nature.'

Yamuna raised a hand, then her head. She straightened in her saddle. 'Do you hear that?' She brought her horse around.

The chant. Squinting, I could make out fire on a nearby slope and perhaps half a dozen shapes interplaying with flames. Yes, I heard the voices. Yamuna's horse took a few steps in that direction. Her bearing had changed.

'Yamuna,' I said, 'there are only two of us.'

She stared at that hillside. 'What you don't realize about Pragmatics,' she said, 'is that we believe we can make a difference.'

She kicked her horse, and after a moment's hesitation I stopped restraining mine. Could I have convinced her not to go? The woman who made herself pregnant by sheer willpower? The woman who forgot her father with self-discipline? Her horse charged down the hill where we'd gazed on Gwalior, crossed a goat trail, and rode up toward a ridge where eight Brahmin priests of the Jagannath sect were bathed in the glow of a bonfire. *Sim wi ta sicc'm, ep fel sim.* By firelight I could see implements of ritual strung from their dhotis, sandal-wood paste smeared over their bare chests, rapt devotion in their faces, a servility to lord and master no less intense than what we'd witnessed in those who labored inside the god.

They saw us coming, and one of them lifted a chain with a flaming weight. He swung it in an orbit around him.

'Stop!' Yamuna was shouting. 'Stop what you're doing! You can't!'

Sim wi ta sicc'm, ep fel sim. Their voices grew louder, drowning out her protest.

'Don't you realize – '

I suppose the Brahmin swinging the chain thought he'd scare our horses away with fire, but Pragmatic steeds knew far worse, and Yamuna's did not falter. It stumbled when the chain wrapped around its forelegs, knelt, and was brought down.

'Yamuna!'

I pulled to a halt. She had fallen clear of the tumble, and I thought of the child. She put one hand on her belly and waved to show she was all right.

But her horse whinnied awfully. It couldn't get up, its front legs tangled in chain and fire. The Brahmin took out a knife and stepped closer, not breaking his mantra even as he threatened us. All eight of the Jagan-nath's faithful regarded us, fanning out as they continued to call for the god.

'Get up,' I told Yamuna, my hand outstretched. 'Get on my horse, or we'll die here too.' For if the Pragmatics were unable to stall the god, there was no reason to think it would make distinctions once it reached this hill. There were further rasps of steel as the Brahmins drew more knives.

Yamuna took my hand, and I pulled her up behind me. The first Brahmin advanced, but my horse reared, kicking, and he stood back from its hooves. We rode around him, bursting through the others as they made cursory slashes at our legs. *Sim wi ta sicc'm, ep fel sim.*

'This isn't good enough,' Yamuna complained. 'Turn back!'

I did not.

The Jagannath was coming fast, almost smiling, arms spread wide.

Inside, after our hurried explanation, the Pragmatics attempted to call the mantra themselves, but it made no difference to the defiant movement of the controls or to our course: the god had heard the summons of the Brahmins first. Archers swung out of the eyes and climbed to the shoulders of the god, but as it traveled up the slopes, it rocked and shook and roared, so the arrows went wide of their mark and none of the Brahmins were hit.

'Hundreds of thousands of people,' Yamuna said to Pala.

'Yes, I heard the first time.'

'What do you intend to do?'

He raised a weak hand. 'Obviously,' he said, 'we have reached the limit of our control.'

Yamuna turned and left, furious. Pala slouched in one of the seats. This was more than he had anticipated.

The eyes of the god narrowed before us, and Pala lifted his gaze. 'I can't watch,' he said. But he did.

The first lights of the city came into view. The fire on the hill was closer too, and the horse lying tangled nearby. The Brahmins were silhouettes against the bonfire, arms raised in celebration of our arrival. Their voices seemed to possess the Jagannath. *Sim wi ta sicc'm, ep fel sim.* The rhythm moved the controls, as if the god was articulating the mantra the only way it could. It climbed the hill.

'I can't watch,' Pala repeated.

But we all watched.

And then, something strange.

The bonfire guttered, disappeared, as if the flames had been sucked away. By wind? But it happened too fast for wind, and not even a glow of coals remained afterward. The scene blinked out, and returned, lit by stars. Many stars pierced the sky, a multitude, and they all seemed to be coming out *now*. Maybe I would focus on them after we crested the hill, and search for patterns rather than watch the Jagannath roll over Gwalior and take in hundreds of new laborers.

The next unexpected thing was a gunshot. I heard it through the noise of the Jagannath, which seemed to reduce a notch. What was happening?

'Rakesh!'

One of the archers was calling me, from outside.

'Isn't that your veteran?'

My flesh tingled. I leaned out the eye, looking for him. The seven silhouettes on the slope were all Brahmins.

'There!'

And I did see someone else on the hill, aiming at the next Brahmin, who turned on him but only got a few steps before being shot. The mantra faltered as the six remaining Brahmins faced this figure, who wheeled about with his rifle, and *bang, bang, bang,* their number was less than half what it had been moments ago.

The Jagannath slowed. It drifted up the slope on fading voices. The mantra ceased altogether. The remaining Brahmins were fleeing. They ran in different directions, arms whipping, terrified. Behind them walked the calm one. He lifted his rifle, and with another perfect shot, another Brahmin stumbled, dropped. Another perfect death. The last ran like a child, as if in fear of more than death. The veteran lowered his rifle, perhaps to appreciate the attempt to escape.

'It is he,' said Dalvara. 'That crazy old man.'

Yes, I thought. He looked like a veteran.

But was more.

He threw his rifle like a spear, and I lost sight of it; the last Brahmin twisted in mid stride, fell forward, but did not drop all the way, propped by the gun sticking through his chest. The entity who had followed me all the way from Sholapur walked up the hill, his silhouette drawn against the stars, getting taller as he walked. And taller.

I dropped to my knees.

'Rakesh?' said Pala. 'Rakesh, what's the problem – ?'

I pressed my palms together. 'He has been following me,' I whispered. 'All this time.'

'You mean the veteran,' said Pala. 'The veteran has been following you.'

I shook my head.

'Who, then?'

Surrounded by the monks, I found that I could not speak a name so holy.

Interior Space Number 22 was tub-shaped and big enough to accommodate all the Pragmatics. They squatted in this impromptu auditorium, crowded along the sides and across the end. I had never counted their number, but there were many, maybe three hundred men and women. In staggered rows, they faced the same direction, each holding a bow.

I sat in the very back, alone. Their meditation excluded me. The Jagannath was not moving, and it was so quiet, I could hear their breathing, the synchronized rise and fall.

Then, a clanking.

Their eyes opened.

Behind the opposite wall was a sound of big bolts sliding free. A panel opened, and further panels rolled aside, creating a tunnel through the hull of the god all the way to the night sky, outside, where I could see a smattering of stars, and a silhouette blotting them. It grew bigger, and I heard his footsteps getting louder, each making me cringe as he came forward.

Something like a smile tweaked his face when he entered space 22, and I supposed it was the sight of those Pragmatics, weapons in hand. He didn't deign the monks a direct glance.

Shiva was perhaps three meters tall, smeared head to foot with ash and soil. I could see how he had appeared before, as a veteran, and how this guise had melted to reveal the more famous form of a statuesque ghoul.

There was a disruption of the ashes across his torso, the corded movement of a snake wending over his chest. His belt was also a snake, and then a belt again, alternating between the two, and movement also animated his hair, something weaving through the gaps between matted locks. A garland of skulls hung around his neck, and I saw Shiva had brought along his trident and the club Khatwanga. Both, thankfully, were hooked to his belt for the moment.

'I wish to speak to the one who betrays all gods.'

His voice was terrible: several voices stopping and starting, a sentence emerging from a drone.

'I wish him to come forward, the one who betrays all gods.'

Nobody replied. I sank more.

Shiva gestured. 'I wish him to show himself, the one who is a great disappointment.'

A monk whose name I didn't know leaped to his feet. 'Why can't you leave him alone? He's done nothing to you!'

Shiva at first did not seem to hear this outburst, surveying the scene with distressing calm. A rope of flesh dropped from his torso, a snake powdered with ash, and it slithered toward the monk, writing and rewriting itself across the floor. Arrows sang from around the room, sticking upright in the snake but doing nothing to slow its progress. The monk tried to escape, but the serpent promptly wound around his ankles, his waist, and it bound his limbs to his body as he fell. Those standing nearby wrestled with the snake, throttled it, struck it with bare hands. The bound brother gasped; his face lost color, turned blue. He was suffocating.

'All right!' I said. 'All right!' I managed to stand. 'I'm here.'

Shiva turned to look at me. 'Do you know who these people are?' he said.

'Please release him. I beg you!'

The gasping stopped, and although the snake remained wrapped in place, it must have released its pressure, because we could hear the monk sucking in breaths.

'Yes,' Shiva said to me. 'You come.'

I moved through the assembly, my legs as weak as cooked rice.

'Come, disappointment.'

I could see his wicked beneficence and blue throat. His face was severe in a way paintings and sculptures failed to capture, the eyes a part of it, boring into me. His third eye was puckered shut in the wrinkle of his brow. His hair hung matted, immobile as bone.

'I want a closer look at disappointment,' he said, waving me nearer.

The Pragmatics watched as if I were walking to my execution. Shiva didn't stop beckoning me closer until I stood within arm's reach. I saw the skull-tipped weight of Khatwanga swinging on his belt.

Shiva placed a hand on my head. He ran both big hands over my head, almost lovingly, but too hard. Each stroke pulled my face out of shape. He turned me around to face the monks. Their grips tightened on their bows, and the bows moved one notch closer to fully drawn.

'Do you know who these people are?' Shiva asked.

'Comrades . . . friends . . .'

'They poisoned you.'

I tried to shake my head, but Shiva forced me to nod.

'Your head with untrue thoughts. Your body with impure fluids.'

'They only wanted me to see India – from another – viewpoint.' Difficult to speak, with him pulling my face. 'Their viewpoint . . .'

'You remember the injection?'

'Yes . . .'

'Do you know what these people did?!' His voice rippled the walls. 'Deceivers, liars, heretics.'

The monks didn't blink. I wrenched myself free, leaving skin on Shiva's fingertips, and turned, resisting the urge to bolt. 'Why have you followed me? Lord Shiva, please, I don't understand. Why are you here?'

He glowered. In multiple voices: 'We gave you one simple task.'

'My dharma . . .'

'The Baboon Warrior.'

'But – '

'You let these people distract you. Poison you. We know what happened; we have been watching.'

'But why don't you do it yourself? That's what I don't understand. Why not kill him yourself?'

'The Baboon Warrior cannot be killed by me.'

'Why?'

Shiva looked from side to side, smiling, grimacing, smiling, grimacing. His face phased through expressions without transition. I saw frustration, contempt. No doubt the mere act of speaking to a mortal irritated him. The room started to smell of smoke and cordite, although nothing burned. Shiva answered, 'The

Baboon Warrior cannot be killed by any god. Have you not yet learned the history of the Baboon Warrior?'

I shook my head.

Snakes circulated across his body. He raised an arm and pointed at the audience, and I looked, wondering what he indicated.

Firdaus stood blinking. The old man glanced around, surprised to find himself the center of attention.

'Me?' he said.

Firdaus took a small step forward. He looked around and cleared his throat.

'The secret history of the Baboon Warrior?' he said. 'I think I know what you mean. His origin? Of course I've heard many explanations – pure fabrications mostly, regional variations of obviously untrue tales – but of those, one concerned a Hindu god named Hanuman. Is that the story you wish to hear?'

Shiva said nothing.

'Well, let's assume so. Hanuman is ancient even by the standards of the gods. I don't know what became of him, but it's possible he died of old age. He is associated with the Baboon Warrior because he, too, was part monkey. Hanuman, growing very old, wished to see his legacy carried forward, and so he attempted to father a child by ravishing mortal women who appealed to his monkey sensibility. He was successful in only one attempt. The child born to him, a son, was beautiful. All human, and exquisite, the boy had a grandeur envied by many of your pantheon. Hanuman brought him to Mount Meru, causing a sensation: humans were not allowed in the heavens, and a boy so beautiful was bound to draw attention. Such was the uproar that it disrupted you, Shiva, from a meditation that had lasted more than three hundred and sixty-five days. Which was, ahem, the occasion of the boy's death.'

No comment from Shiva.

'It is said you opened your third eye and with its burning glare turned his face to cinder. Your intention was to make him less handsome, but you lost control of yourself. The son was killed.

'Hanuman was inconsolable. He threatened, he wailed. His mourning could be heard throughout India. And finally Vishnu came, hoping to soothe the monkey god. What could he do to make amends? "Restore my son's life," Hanuman told him. And Vishnu consented to do so. But the body required a new head, and so Vishnu instructed Hanuman to find a replacement. The senile old god went to his monkeys and selected the second most beautiful creature he'd ever known: an exceptionally rare beast called a baboon. Vishnu removed the head of this creature and placed it on the body of the son. Vishnu also granted Hanuman's request that his son never again endure persecution by gods. So the boy was granted a power: no god could harm him. Not even, ah, you.'

Firdaus coughed and stepped back into place.

Shiva said: 'Hanuman did not understand that this monkey was deranged.' He lowered his arm. 'Hanuman and Vishnu made a monster who cannot be killed by gods. But they left it vulnerable to humans. The monster protects itself from mortals by presenting himself as their warrior hero.'

Shiva was quiet. So too the Pragmatics. Somewhere the Jagannath groaned.

'But Shiva,' I asked, with all the humility I knew, 'why me?'

'QUESTIONS ARE NOT A PRIVILEGE OF FAITH.'

His bellow pushed me back two steps.

In the rear of Interior Space Number 22, there was movement. The monks looked surprised, were shoved aside, and they glanced down as something moved through them. The suit of goonda arms emerged, walking like a mechanized crab, pushing its way with two of the limbs and scuttling toward me on the other four. It clasped my legs, clambered up my body. Its grip was inexorable; breathing became almost impossible.

'I,' said Shiva, 'am the destroyer of all things.'

He looked at me.

'All but one.'

'The Baboon Warrior . . .' I gasped.

'*He* was yours. You failed.'

The grip tightened.

'You, disappointment, are my compensation.'

'Leave him be!' Pala shouted.

Shiva whirled. The monk lifted his bow.

'YOU ARE NEXT!'

All the monks lifted their bows, with the groan of a few hundred bowstrings.

The club Khatwanga opened and closed its small mouth as it swung on Shiva's belt. I was terrified by the sight of Shiva's hand, open and eager to take that infamous weapon off its hook. Pangs of music rose, and a drumbeat, coming from nowhere or perhaps from Shiva, and I grew cold. The Pragmatics fanned out, ignorant of what the music meant, pointing their few hundred arrows at the god of destruction.

'You don't frighten us,' said Pala.

'Stop!' I gasped.

'We're not afraid of you.'

'You can't threaten Shiva!'

'Ask him why he wants the Baboon Warrior dead,' Pala said. 'Why does the Baboon Warrior frighten you, Shiva?'

'THIS I WILL ENJOY.'

He took a stance; formalized a move: the opening step of his dance.

'Stop it! Stop!'

'He's powerless against the Baboon,' Pala continued. 'He's afraid!'

Shiva stepped methodically with the music, approaching the monk. He took Khatwanga in hand.

'I'll do it!' I shouted. 'I'll do it!'

The god paused.

'I'll do it.'

The goonda arms relaxed enough for me to speak.

'Don't give in,' Pala said to me. 'We aren't afraid of Shiva. There are hundreds of us, only one of him.'

I shook my head. That math was not favorable.

'I'll do it,' I told the god. 'Please, let me.'

His head tilted. The music subsided.

'If you agree not to harm any Pragmatics,' I added.

'YOU ARE NOT TO BARGAIN.'

'It is no bargain, no offer,' I said. 'It's the only way possible.'

His head swiveled back in their direction.

Pala looked tempted to let his arrow fly.

Shiva grinned at the small monk. 'I will dance on your corpse,' he said, 'another night.'

He retreated a step. Another.

The goonda arms let go of me. On the floor, they reconfigured, the sleeves turning up. For me.

I'd known for some time what I had to do. Now I knew why.

'Don't do it,' someone said.

Firdaus. Pala. But most of all, Yamuna. There was ˜ only one way to save their lives.

'He's afraid of the Baboon Warrior,' Pala insisted. 'Don't indulge him.'

I looked at Yamuna, then inserted my arms in the goonda prosthesis. The suit came on me like an embrace; the vest closed with the finality of a prison door swinging shut.

Shiva's expression was happy and mad. The monks were still poised to shoot him, but they must have known it would have been useless. I was back in the multiple arms, suited for what must be done.

STRINGING
THE BOW

─═●═─

VASANT HAD CHOSEN a route that bypassed major centers of population; he wanted to be discreet, as well as avoid the lawlessness he'd suffered in Jaipur and other cities. But making his way along rough village roads, he was surprised to find he was not the sole pedestrian. An increasing number of people walked in the same direction as he — young men all. He could see them spaced to the horizon. He asked the nearest what was happening, where they all were going, but the oaf looked him up and down and sneered.

'You don't have a chance!'

'Excuse me?'

'Look at those arms! You're wasting everybody's time!'

'I don't know what you're talking about.'

The oaf shook his head with derision. 'Why don't you go back home? You have not the slightest hope!'

Vasant stopped to let the oaf distance himself.

Wasting his time?

Something must have been happening in the capital, he thought. Which was good; whatever event drew these young men to Delhi would provide him greater anonymity. In Delhi, he had a bank account. He wanted only to withdraw his savings and leave with nobody from the Palace aware of his visit.

He gave a silent prayer of thanks to Ganesha for this good fortune and continued following the many farm boys and other lugs. He didn't again give thought to what might be drawing them to the city until a bell rang behind him.

A bicycle made its unsteady way up the road, swerving. A boy was pedaling, and an even younger boy made it unstable, sitting on a wooden container built onto the frame.

'Care for a cup of strength tonic, sir?'

'Keep going.'

'Only three rupees, sir, for big strength.'

They rode around him, and Vasant saw stacked cups and a jug of something in the box, which the younger boy was apparently in charge of dispensing.

'Very old recipe from a great wrestling clan. Only three rupees.'

Vasant shooed them and concentrated on the road.

'I've sold tonic to many of your competitors,' the boy persisted. 'I wouldn't want them to have an advantage over you.'

'Competitors?'

'They've made excellent business.'

'What would they need strength tonic for?'

The boy looked surprised. 'For the bow!'

'What bow?'

'You don't know?' He seemed to find this amusing.

'Get to the point or go away,' said the Engineer. 'What is happening in Delhi?'

'The First Widow has announced she will remarry.

Whoever can string the Harmony Bow wins partner-
ship with her.'

Vasant stopped abruptly. 'All these people — ?'

'So far no one has been powerful enough to bend
the bow, but who knows? Perhaps you're meant to rule
India. Sir? Are you all right?'

He shook himself. The notion was absurd. Would
Kavita really marry a dimwit farm boy simply because
he could string a weapon? Even these dullards must
have known that caste prevented them from holding
power. It was a sham, then . . . but for what purpose?

'Three rupees is a small investment,' the boy said,
circling, 'if it buys you all the riches of India.'

Vasant looked at the long line before him, which
seemed now a question mark pointing at the capital.
He considered the boy's awful bike and slap-together
container. 'I won't pay for your drink,' he said, 'which
appears to be nothing more than rainwater collected in
the family bedpan. But you might earn ten rupees.'

The boy's face lit up.

'Give me a ride to this bow. I want to see it.'

The expression of interest changed to doubt as the
boy appraised his rear tire and brother. 'It's a long way.
I don't think I'm strong enough to haul both you and
Sanjay.'

'Naturally I wouldn't pay ten rupees to share a seat
with your brother.'

Soon Vasant found himself traveling more quickly,
the boy laboring at the pedals and his brother struggling
to keep up behind them. Vasant took pity on the
younger boy and so paid him a rupee to carry his
jacket. This was no palace rickshaw, but his feet were
glad for respite, and with every sullen young man the

bicycle passed, he felt another twinge of curiosity. What was really happening in the capital?

Scenery changed; the road improved and gained more urban flavor; horse-drawn tongas, dung-driven vehicles, and seasoned cyclists combined to make challenging cross-circuits of traffic. The boy entrepreneur panted, toiling at the pedals, swerving to avoid collisions. Night fell, and they still hadn't reached the district where the great weapon was located, but the boy put his foot on the ground, braking.

'Why are you stopping?'

'Sanjay and I,' the boy panted, 'are supposed to be home by dark.'

'I can't pay you if you don't fulfill your part of the bargain.'

'I'm too tired! My legs!'

Sanjay caught up and started to wail.

'Okay, okay! Take me to that grassy area, and we'll split the difference.'

After receiving payment, the boy turned the bicycle around and teetered off. 'Maybe you should have a cup of strength tonic before you go,' Vasant suggested.

He settled in a place where he was screened by trees but could still watch the road. He disliked sleeping outdoors but could not afford a hotel, and this was an improvement over the night before, the topography and denser housing resembling more and more the Delhi he knew.

Listening to the boy's breathing and the squeak of the pedals had almost put Vasant to sleep earlier, and he fast surrendered now. In sleep, he saw muscle-bound lugs on a conveyor belt to Delhi, transported into the arms of the svastika of the Palace. He tossed and struggled against the hard ground, but when this image subsided, his sleep was long and full. He might have slept into the next afternoon if not for the music.

Music from the heavens.

He got to his feet and wiped his eyes. Traffic had stopped in the street, people craning their necks. Ethereal strains descended from above, with something soft and pink.

Now what?

He held out his hand, and collected flower petals. They were falling in abundance, dappling the ground, and they kept coming, fluttering, turning through the air like the notes that accompanied their descent. Gandharvas could produce music in the sky, but he suspected this was something other.

High above floated a hand. At first he mistook it for the hand of a god, but when he used assemblage he could see it was actually balloon crafts joined together artfully and covered with a skin of papier-mâché. He could see, inside, where bellows pumped out the flower petals, and presumably the musicians were also sitting inside.

Everyone had stopped, staring, commenting on the beauty of this vision. Vasant walked through the fluttering pink. Not far off lay the boy who'd given him a ride, asleep with his bike between his legs and feet still on the pedals. Pink drifts accumulated over him. The lid of the wooden container creaked, and Sanjay poked out his head.

'What's happening?' the brother asked.

Vasant brushed blossoms off his sleeves and said, 'Someone must have strung the bow.'

★

A handsome young woman danced in the street, and as Vasant got nearer, he thought, *She is going to kiss me.* And she did, but he braced himself and didn't take it as an affront, blaming her behavior on the delirium of the day.

Crowds danced, statues of gods were taken into the street, garlands were tied around the necks of cows. Most people celebrated too heartily to talk. The few phrases he heard were optimistic. *The bow has been strung! The bow has been strung! Turmoil will end, at last!*

Vasant went to see. With the news of the stringing, some young men had turned around, but most, like him, continued, wanting a look at the thing that had drawn so many people from all the castes and states of India.

The bow was of a size worthy of its fame, maybe two meters long from tip to tip, thick as two fists at the middle. Stringing it would have challenged a god, and strung, it looked explosive, the curvature suggesting great violence even as the weapon rested on a stand. A pair of royal guards flanked it, preventing anyone from touching it now. Stories of recent attempts circulated: a few strongmen had actually managed to bend the bow before being flung back. The crowd remained swollen with dreams of marrying the Widow and becoming leader of India. Conveniently, and not coincidentally, a tent had been pitched nearby, where disappointed adolescents of the Kshatriya caste could enlist in the army, and so serve the Widow in some respect rather than return home embarrassed. For others, the excitement had less to do with the stringing of the bow than who strung it.

Who else?

Vasant thought of Rakesh as images of the Baboon Warrior unfurled from windows, appeared painted across faces, and gamboled through the street in gaudy costume.

The Baboon Warrior: the next Sovereign.

The implications so startled Vasant that he abandoned plans for discretion. He went, instead, to the Palace. He entered the grounds surreptitiously, made his way to the royal forest, and was surprised by baboons, who thrashed about, eating flower heads or chasing one another through rituals of dominance and submission. He couldn't remember seeing baboons in Delhi before. Monkeys like the macaque had always been around, but baboons? Uncommon. Now, however, their breed seemed to have displaced the smaller ones around the Palace, and Vasant spied a doglike male sitting on a tree limb with a dead macaque in its mouth. The baboon gave him a bored look.

Part of the river had been diverted into palace grounds so the Royals could enjoy its holy waters without enduring slippery ghats or crowds of variable caste. The river bent sharply into retreat near the northern arm, and Vasant positioned himself nearby, waiting for most of the afternoon.

She came with retinue, and he watched her being undressed. Several attendants stood holding her garments as she entered the water, and Vasant thought he recognized the sari as it was unwrapped from her body. The First Widow saw him before her servants did; she dropped until her shoulders were under the waterline, and then her attendants cried out, shrilling for goondas. He must have been a sight emerging from the trees, darkened by soil, darkened by sun, his suit torn. The women didn't recognize him – or maybe they did.

'Goondas! Goondas, hurry!'

'Quiet!' the First Widow ordered.

Vasant approached without decorum.

'Why are you here?' she demanded. 'Were you hoping your position was still open?'

'Curiosity won over good judgment.'

'What is that supposed to mean?'

'I want to talk to you, Kavita. Without Sudra ears around.'

The Widow seemed to appraise him, then rose from the water stepping backward, her modesty protected by girls positioning towels and rewrapping the sari. 'I will speak with Vasant alone,' she said.

The younger servants obeyed, but one of the crones took token steps and lingered at a tree.

'Give us some privacy, hag!' Vasant shouted.

The old woman pursed her lips but complied.

'I see your personality has survived intact,' said the Widow.

'As a matter of fact I am very much changed.'

'I assumed you were dead.'

'This must be a happy surprise.'

'How did you get inside?'

'Palace security is no challenge to someone who served as Chief Engineer for ten years.'

'I suppose *how* is not the issue.'

'I came to congratulate you, of course. On your wedding.'

She shrank.

'To the Baboon Warrior, no less.'

'You're here to mock me.'

'No, no. You're a shrewd woman, and someone should be telling you so. What about the bow? Was that your idea, too?'

'It was a means of capturing public attention.'

'You realize you're betrothed to a half-animal?'

'My choices,' she said, 'have been limited.'

'You suffer from too much choice, I think.'

'He's not as wild as he sometimes appears. I've been surprised to find him so . . . rational.'

'And this is what you want for a husband? A rational monkey?'

'It's what the people want. You can hear them singing from inside the Palace. Listen. Love songs! The anthem! How long has it been since you've heard people spontaneously singing the anthem?'

'But what drove you to – '

'They never accepted my rule. A widow is not respected; the public wants a man in power. Even my advisers! And the only man totally respected is the Baboon Warrior. With me in control of India, people hated themselves. With him, they will feel proud. Can you understand now what I mean by limited choices? It's crushing, you know, to be the source of national discontent.'

'A burden you wouldn't have known if the Sovereign hadn't died so, ah, mysteriously.'

She cast her gaze downward.

'You won't answer that?'

'There were circumstances . . .'

'You admit to his murder?'

'There were circumstances!'

'What circumstances could justify such – '

'Did you not notice how much time he spent in Rajasthan, Vasant? Did that never strike you as curious?'

He considered this. Yes, the Sovereign had been in Rajasthan more often than not, in his final year.

'Did you never wonder why?'

'A lover?'

She nodded.

'Even so . . .'

'He promised to marry her. My spies informed me of the plans. He promised her my title. I couldn't sit back and accept the fate those two arranged for me. I refused to find myself on a pyre so he could make room for another woman. I couldn't accept that. Do you understand?'

'A lover,' Vasant said. 'That disappoints me. But it doesn't forgive your relationship with Kama Sutrans.'

'After I decided to do it,' she said, 'I realized I would need to secure the loyalty of key officials. I'd heard how Kama Sutrans organize their society, and I asked Hapi about it. He introduced me to one of them – a man or woman, I'm not sure – and this person told me how I might forge political allegiances the Kama Sutran way.'

'So you arranged for me to come to your chamber.'

'You seemed a natural choice, to try it.'

'How flattering. And a day later, Kama Sutrans kidnapped me. Left me to die in the air!'

The Widow shook her head.

'No?'

'I ordered your removal.'

He said nothing.

'As soon as our act was finished, I felt great remorse. I had manipulated you. I was sick about it, and I confided with my counsels – ' She glanced at one of the crones standing in the distance. 'Your removal was put into effect.'

'Then it wasn't you.'

'I could have stopped it. I was consulted.'

'And you didn't.'

'They wanted you dead! I insisted you should only be expelled. Doesn't that make a difference? Can you forgive me? Because, Vasant, if there's some way I might redeem myself . . .'

She touched his forearm.

He removed her hand, with only a moment's hesitation. 'I'm a holier person,' he said.

'Than what?'

'This time away from Delhi has been revealing to me. I've seen hedonism, decadence, lack of chastity, lack of self-restraint. You demonstrate for me that caste is no defense against moral lapses.'

'But I want what is best for India! Can't you understand? Only someone with the stature of the Baboon Warrior can return stability. That's the only reason I agreed to wed him.'

Vasant stopped. 'He approached you . . .?'

'Yes.'

He considered this. 'I'm not sure the Baboon will bring stability,' he said.

'Of course he will! He's loved like a god. Can't you hear that singing? That is for him.'

'He is not loved like a god by everyone.' Vasant scratched his head, uncertain how much he should tell her.

But Kavita spoke first: 'You mean the one named Rakesh?'

SMOOTH

I STOOD IN Interior Space Number 15 trying to hold two goonda arms perfectly straight while I extended and retracted each of the remaining four. The exercise was not going well. I heard someone come inside and poked myself in the eye. It wasn't Yamuna – I knew the sound of her footsteps. Pala, then.

'How many people will we kill in Delhi?' he asked.

I shrugged, and three arms ratcheted backward with the gesture.

'Because the Jagannath will meet resistance.'

'What happens will happen. I can prevent little.'

'Rakesh, please reconsider.'

'What difference does it make to you? Why do you care what I do?'

'Let me answer that by showing you something,' he said. 'Come.'

My limbs often batted the walls or complicated my passage through doorways as I followed him; Pala didn't notice my problem, or pretended not to. We entered space 43, and I saw that the inexhaustible industry of his brothers and sisters had transformed the wagons into a sub-building custom-fitted to the space, using

canvas tarps for a roof. Inside the low, barnlike structure, a percentage of monks continued to hammer,
while others sat reviving the lost art of bookbinding.
On a cot lay the monk who had spoken in my defense
against Shiva, the snake around his legs having turned
to stone. He looked comfortable enough. Others stood
at the far end of the structure, and the crowd rippled,
allowing us closer.

I saw Azis. 'He's not bound,' I said.

'We've made progress.'

Someone had gone to the trouble of scrubbing his
skin to bring back his natural coloring, and he looked
much as I remembered him from the march to Bundi.
He looked like a Kashmiri again. But he continued to
stare blankly, and the lack of affect was total. One
eyebrow raised higher than the other, as if glued that
way, and his eyes focused on nothing, certainly not the
press of monks scrutinizing him. They watched his
finger, which was wiggling.

'What is he doing?'

His fingertip was blackened, periodically dipped in
ink by the monk sitting next to him. Another pulled a
piece of paper beneath this finger, and Azis drew
recognizable characters. Letters, digits. 11HF5352\
\101111. . . . Pala handed me a sheaf of such markings.

'He wrote all this?'

'We tried to reach him through mantra,' said Pala.
'But he wouldn't participate. We tried to pull him into
our koans. Nothing. We have talked to him for hours,
we have questioned him, we have pleaded, but he is
yet to utter a word. This morning, however, someone
noticed his finger moving. It seemed more than muscle
spasm, and with ink, you see what it produces.'

'Gibberish.'

'A code.'

'Code? For what?'

'It's too complicated for us to break,' the monk conceded, 'but we've seen enough codes in our lifetime to recognize it as such.'

I flipped through the pages of marks.

'Rakesh, these things that run your life. You call them gods, but they're machines.'

'Divine machines, some.'

'No. Just machines.'

I started to protest, but Pala forged ahead.

'Azis remains under the influence of the Jagannath. His natural language has been displaced by the language of the god. When he tries to communicate, he reveals its language. Its code.'

'I don't see what that proves.'

'You're aware of the carpet weavers in the north who, for generations, recited codes to guide their hands? Nowadays, those northerners prefer mechanical looms, with the codes represented in notched wheels. This has allowed the weavers to work beyond the limits of their minds, and create patterns of much greater intricacy. The wheels substitute for the mental process.'

'You think the Jagannath is nothing but a mechanical loom? A machine following codes?'

'In essence.'

'Shiva too? He looks like no machine I've ever seen.'

'He and other gods don't fit our conception of a machine. They are more complicated than you or I can fathom. But, Rakesh, this is where our investigations have led. We hoped to uncover evidence by taking the Jagannath to Ranthambhore. That plan was dashed, but now Azis is showing us what we suspected. He is showing us that the Jagannath has no real language, no thoughts of its own.'

'Who devised these codes?' I felt myself getting angry. 'Who could build divine machines?!'

'We don't know.'

'It surprises me you should take so seriously the nonsense from one shaky finger.'

'To you it is nonsense,' Pala replied. 'To us it is evidence. Of men.'

'*What* men?'

He lifted his hands. 'There are always questions, Rakesh. We answer one, and it leads to a different question.'

'Answers lead to questions! You bring me down here to put forward your outrageous theory, then all you can say is that answers – '

I stopped abruptly.

'Is something the matter?'

'I just realized it,' I said, incredulous.

'What?'

'You want the Baboon Warrior for yourself.'

This silenced Pala for a moment. 'You're getting ahead of me.'

'You *do*.'

'Before, we thought that your desire to kill the Baboon Warrior was a private delusion, shaped by your chakras. Last night we saw that your gods do want him dead. Shiva wants him dead. Why?'

I could see where he was going, and felt myself getting frustrated.

'Who else might know, but the Baboon?' Pala said. 'Who else might answer our questions?'

I said firmly, 'Pala, there is no dialogue with the Baboon Warrior.'

'We must seek one.'

'He is dead, or he is alive. And last night you heard my decision.'

'But Rakesh, we must ask him –'

I raised three hands. 'You must accept the fact that some questions go unanswered.'

He started to say something, stopped.

The room, I noticed, was quieter. A few monks peered at Pala, and he deliberately tapped the sheets of markings into a pile. Azis continued drawing symbols, ignorant of the surrounding controversy.

'Well,' said Pala. 'We'll arrive in Delhi soon.'

'That's right.'

'Nothing remains to be said.'

No disagreement there. But inside, there was great disagreement, a divide that yawned open between our goals.

The monks returned to work.

Later, I tried not to think of the disappointment I would cause them. They had defended me against Shiva; they wanted to be my allies. A shame that I would have to extinguish their hopes for enlightenment from the Baboon Warrior. But I wanted a life of my own, and his death was the only way to that life.

My goonda arms flinched and twitched as I moved through the Jagannath. Before I could disappoint the monks, I needed to address a problem that I had realized soon after Shiva left but that I had not mentioned to anyone. Seeking privacy, glad to escape Pala's theories, I took my razor and bowl to Interior Space Number

12 – the Factory – reacquainting myself with its layout by what I could hear and feel.

The lack of lights didn't hinder the laborers, who worked comfortably in darkness. I brushed against one as he moved between machines, carrying a load. What were they doing? I lit a lamp and saw slats of fresh lumber sliding out of the machinery. Several stacks had been prepared, high as the ceiling. The wood was a fabrication, a product of debris the Jagannath had absorbed, and close examination revealed foreign matter locked into the grain: flecks of metal, earthenware, bone. The Jagannath was made of things it had consumed. I considered this in relation to Pala's hypothesis but could see no connection. I took my bowl and razor between two stacks and sat against the wall.

With one of six hands, I held the razor. Lifted it, quivering. With another hand I tried to cup some water but instead knocked over the bowl. I rubbed a third hand in the puddle and swabbed my scalp. I brought the blade before me and stared at it, the light wobbling unsteadily on its edge.

I passed the razor over my head. It was not long before I felt a seam of skin open, a very straight wound.

I looked at the blade. Bloody. Blood ran from the cut, through my short hair, and a single drop expanded until it rolled down my forehead and around the orbit of my eye. I sat like this, bleeding, tapping the razor against the floor.

Out of the gloom appeared her copper gown.

'Oh,' Yamuna said. 'Are you killing yourself?'

'Not deliberately.'

She sat beside me and pressed her thumb against the cut.

'Trying to shave.'

'You're doing a bad job.'

'I can't afford the hair. It's a distraction.'

'So why shave with a goonda hand? Use your own.'

'Because I need practice with them. I don't have the control I had before.' Her brow furrowed, and as she turned the bowl upright, I told her, 'You must remove the tincture.'

'What do you mean?'

'It's the only answer. You can inject me again afterward, but for now I need my control back. My instincts. I'm frightened, Yamuna. I was never frightened before. My hands shake, my arms. I need my instincts returned if I'm going to have any chance against him. Please.'

'Oh, Rakesh.'

'What?'

'The effects of the tincture wear off eventually. But we have no way to reverse them immediately. No antidote.'

I should have guessed.

'Don't plunge into Delhi like this,' she said. 'Wait. Wait until your chakras recover, wait for those instincts to come back to you.'

'Shiva said the Baboon must be stopped in Delhi.'

Yamuna looked at me, her eyes intense. 'Why did you agree to this?'

'Because I want my life. It won't be mine until this is accomplished.'

She was quiet for a while. 'Pala has become interested in the Baboon, too,' she said.

'I know.'

'The Baboon is all he talks about today. The Baboon, and your gods, and a connection.'

'Well, I can't indulge his curiosity.'

Yamuna looked suddenly distressed.

'What is wrong?'

'Rakesh,' she said. 'Was Shiva right?'

'About what?'

'Our injection – did we poison you? You're going to face the Baboon Warrior himself. Stripped of your . . . instincts.'

'That's a secondary concern.'

'What could be more important?'

I touched her face. The gauntlet allowed little sensation.

'Me?'

'I need help,' I said. 'But you're . . . a Pragmatic.'

She looked down, placed her hand on my cheek. Pulled me forward, so my head was near her bosom. She took the blade from my hand, wiped it clean on my pant leg.

'Someday we'll run our fingers through each other's hair,' she said. 'Our long hair.'

Then she shaved my head, careful of the gash.

Unwanted Guests
to the Wedding

➤═◉═◄

Delhi.

The Jagannath rumbled toward the Palace, wattle structures crumpling below like some child's model made of cardboard boxes. I heard the pilots discussing the approach, plotting the most efficient route. Was it easier to plow through stone temples or brick warehouses? Which avenues provided the most room to maneuver? Square kilometers of cityscape stood before the god, but none of it, ultimately, would pose a problem. I stood looking over the shoulder of one of the pilots as life streamed away, people dispersing below, fleeing in threads of spreading panic.

The pilots stopped talking and glanced up at me.

'Time to leave,' I told them.

'Leave what?' said the female monk.

'The head.'

'Why?'

'It's time for you to go.'

She turned. 'I don't recall Pala saying anything. You'd better talk to Pala.'

With one goonda hand I grabbed her neck and lifted her from the seat.

'Rakesh! What — ?!'

I tossed her back. The other two rose from their chairs, and I grabbed both by the throat.

'Rakesh! What's possessed you?!'

I pushed them toward their sister. 'Out.'

'But we were taking you where you wanted to go! What is the problem?'

I pointed at the door.

'Rakesh, we can do whatever — '

I lifted two hands and placed fingers against my ears: I wouldn't listen. Unable to think of anything else, the monks retreated through the portal.

'Shut it behind you,' I said. 'Tell the others to stay away.' And I sat.

With their departure, the Jagannath had slowed, drifted off course.

Structures of Delhi were sized according to caste. The next neighborhood was taller than this one, home to Sudras, and the next taller still, for Vaisyas. In tiered squares the city rose to the center, where the Palace formed its grand svastika, four bent arms reiterated in the surrounding streets. The only exception to the pattern was the river, whose course I could infer by the trench curving through neighborhoods north of the Palace. The Jagannath was south, and would take a long time getting there if allowed to indulge too much in its personality. It had pulled into a ramshackle marketplace, obliterating the densely packed stalls like cubes of sugar under its wheels.

I put one of my hands on the nearest lever.

The Pragmatics had painted text directly on the controls, outlining groups of buttons that worked together and connecting others that related. It was a complicated diagram and, as experience had shown, was fallible. I extended my legs until I felt pedals, recalling what Vasant had demonstrated. I reached out a second hand and grabbed another polished hardwood stalk. More than enough instruments to occupy three pilots, but I had the arms of three.

I pulled the Jagannath from the market. It resisted at first, reluctant to be weaned of the flimsy buildings, strewing bolts of cloth and the unhinged remains of a storefront as it turned.

The god sometimes paused, sometimes roared to release an overload of heat, but with my adjustments it rolled up the avenue. People scattered, struggling to get out of the way, shutting themselves into homes and businesses, or simply running to keep ahead of the great wheels of our chariot. Sometimes the god could not resist pursuit. A tiny figure darted into an apartment building, and the Jagannath surged after him, shouldering the front wall, driving a fist through the demolished result, and digging in the rubble for the impure person who dared try to escape.

I felt that figure. I felt it in my hand. Through my six goonda limbs I received feedback when the god struck debris. I felt the Jagannath's arm pulling free of rubble, then felt the compromise between my body and the body of the god as it retracted, proceeded.

The avenue deepened. On both sides the architecture rose, above the chariot, above the hips. The god rolled chest-deep into Delhi. Behind us was a long path of rubble and crushed roadway, incidental fires. Our mark on the capital.

'What do you think you're doing?' Pala stood in the

doorway. 'You chased away my brothers and sister like thieves? What is the meaning of this?'

'My apologies,' I said, 'but I'm trying to be pragmatic.'

He didn't smile.

I said, 'I can no longer risk your involvement.'

'But we got you here.'

'You helped.'

'Now you push us aside? Simple as that?'

I exhaled. Pala might never understand. 'This is the only way to get my life back,' I said.

'You don't trust us.'

'Pala – '

'Have you considered that the Baboon Warrior's life might be more valuable than yours?'

I didn't reply to that.

'I didn't think so,' he said. 'But, of course, you want more than *your* life, don't you? There's a second life you want for yourself. Isn't that the truth of your desperation?'

After a moment's pause he continued:

'Have you asked Yamuna which she would rather have? You, or the Baboon's life spared?'

'Get out, Pala.'

'Rakesh, you must at least consider our – '

'Out!'

'You can eject me, too, but there are more of us, many more, and no matter how many arms you have at your disposal, I'm sure we could delay – wha – ?!'

I turned as far as my configuration allowed. One of the laborers had pushed past him, and another. And another. Pala stared, wide-eyed. My flesh crawled as six filed in and formed a line between him and me. They had their grease-smeared backs to me, but I knew they were staring ahead without expression, as the monk in the doorway fumed.

'What is this?'

'It looks like a barricade,' I said.

Pala frowned at me through the gaps. 'Okay, Rakesh. You've made your decision. You no longer want our help. We have different objectives. *Understood*. But let me leave you with a question. Where is the army? The air force? Why haven't you encountered any resistance from the Royals?'

And he left in a whirl of saffron.

I turned, looked outside.

Resistance?

Opposite I could see part of the svastika, the squared end of one of its arms. We were close, and Pala's comment was correct – we'd encountered less resistance here than Sholapur had managed to throw together. Where was the army? Where were the crowds appropriate to the capital?

The laborers seemed to guarantee there would be no further disturbance from the monks, so I could focus on the Jagannath's advance. Our approach lifted from the ground something pink and swirling. I had seen the color scattered over the roads and wondered what it was, and as it swirled into a flux before me, I saw it was flower petals, millions of them. Streamers, hung along balconies and across the street, broke on the torso of the god, one after another, collecting until the Jagannath was garlanded.

Decoration increased toward the Palace. Blossoms on the road, trees festooned. The Jagannath roared, and in a hundred windows faces looked out, frightened.

They knew we were here.

The Palace had built-in defenses, cannons nosing into place along the southern roofline. Soldiers rode them, aiming and sending eruptions of iron. The cannons were chemical, huge, having a bore big enough for a man to stand upright in. The blows rocked the god but did nothing to stop it. I steered closer. The Jagannath mowed down a line of decorated trees as I lifted a hand and bashed the cannons, knocking off operators. The god raked its fingers across the svastika, dug into windows, pulled off a long strip of facade and exposed Delhicrats scrambling back from the crumbling margin.

The Baboon Warrior would come out. For the sake of his reputation he would face us, he would defend the Palace. If not, I would dismantle it building by building, until he was uncovered. We motored along, continuing to strip away walls, more officials tumbling down with the debris.

When we turned the corner, I saw, farther north, a head above the skyline.

A second god?

I could see no more of its body, but, judging by the head, it was only slightly smaller than the Jagannath.

My belly tensed. The lack of people in the streets, the decorations, another god . . .

I tracked its progress. The head was moving north, without delay. It must be traveling on the river.

The Jagannath accelerated. We passed the royal forest, moved alongside the western arm of the svastika, and more cannons blasted, pounding our hull. The Jagannath shuddered, but its preoccupation mirrored mine; it received the blows like stings as it made for that other deity. We cruised, pulling past the svastika, flower petals fluttering in abundance as we proceeded to the river.

I rolled down an available street, through a section of luxury housing that featured statuary intricately carved and gilded, gaudy with trimmings. Suddenly I faced a crush of people, boxed by the constraints of the avenue – a thousand dots of color looking back in horror, mashing themselves against the limits of the street. I heard their panic, and hated how it swelled as the Jagannath bulldozed forward, toward the river.

The road narrowed; the crowd became an unwilling barricade as people found themselves corralled in the terminus. I lifted the hands of the god to roofs on either side, hauling the god up and forward. We burst through a riverside hotel, breaking through the middle, cleaving a cross section of rooms and plumbing and crumbling plaster. The energy of the Jagannath spread into me, the satisfaction of forcing my own path through a city. We tore through the hotel and lurched to the river.

On the water was the boat I'd mistaken for a god.

Boat or aircraft. Here was the resistance.

Military units had given themselves to this construction. Where was the air force? In the torso and arms of the figure. The navy? In its tail, joined in a superstructure of wood and draped in sheets painted with scales. My earlier mistake was understandable: this huge figure had been deliberately made to resemble the god Matsya. Half man, half fish. Ships and aircraft provided the body, papier-mâché provided the skin over them, and wooden artifice formed the remaining features. It had four slender arms, and I saw that these functioned,

moving with the actions of balloon craft and rope
systems webbed into the body, where all was controlled.
As the arms moved, my eyes fell to that long coiled tail
floating behind the torso. The tail was a ring of river
vessels, their adjacent decks used as a platform upon
which white and pink pavilions had been constructed,
looking temporary and decorative.

I wanted to declare to the thousands of Hindus who
stood on ghats along the river watching this thing float
past them that it was a lie, an illusion, and certainly not
a god – no god would bless the celebrity who rode on
board, or anyone who honored him.

The Jagannath could not tolerate such deception.
When I stamped my foot, it roared disapproval, the
sound of the swath of Delhi that had been fed into its
engines. Up and down both banks, people turned to
look, having seen the god burst forth, having felt the
concussion of its voice.

I drove the god forward, not caring when I felt ghats
buckle below. How the Jagannath would fare in water,
I had no idea. But I felt its eagerness to reach this false
Matsya and no hesitation as steps split beneath us.
People toppled after us as the Jagannath plunged
forward and the waves rushed up, the river accepting
us by becoming larger and angrier itself, sweeping along
bottom steps in great gushes, carrying spectators with it.

The Jagannath proceeded.

Movement was sluggish, wheels rolling over river
bottom. Water rose to its belly, and higher. Tones
changed within. The Jagannath had sunk to the level
of Matsya, and from my vantage the adversary looked
eager. Through its paper skin I could see muscles of
warcraft; I could see the interplay of balloons with

ropes, sinuous gestures effected by the hundreds of soldiers who manned the interior.

We moved between the disconnected terminals of a bridge, approaching the Matsya construction. It had seen us. That is, its operators had seen us. As we got closer, I spotted some of them in its crown, men pointing at the Jagannath and running among the gold spires, down stairs that wound around its neck. They worked to adjust ropes and pulleys throughout its right arm, and Matsya lifted a hand, palm up. A gesture of fearlessness. All four arms repositioned, opening as if to embrace us, to welcome us.

I reached out with the Jagannath, still feeling its arms as my own, and grabbed Matsya's shoulders. My first instinct was to push the craft underwater, but the balloons in its torso and ships in its tail made it too buoyant. I grabbed its throat. Papier-mâché crumpled instantly in the Jagannath's grip, but the head remained aloft, connected by rigging and rope ladders. It bobbed, the operators on the head so close that I could hear them shout, see them drop down these tendons or climb back up. I swatted them, sometimes deliberately, sometimes inadvertently, and watched them bounce against the torso of the Matsya construction before splashing in the water.

I sunk the Jagannath's fingers into the torso, raking through paper, and the tears widened to release balloons. Through all this, the false Matsya gave no counterblows. It simply pressed its hands to the Jagannath, and when necessary withdrew them and waited for an opportunity to reapply them. I shook them off, but monitoring all four hands was difficult, and the enemy operators were quick to reposition them. I saw this as no particular threat – perhaps because the painted head bounced on its tethers before me with an expression of permanent benevolence. Perhaps I was lulled into thinking that the figure was not fighting back.

Through the rumble, I heard pounding. I didn't associate this with Matsya's hands until I happened to pull back and the huge construction jerked after me.

Within its arms people moved, running to the hands, which were nailed to our hull. I rolled back, and Matsya followed at arm's length. I bashed the arms, trying to break them off, but like the neck they were strung with rope and cable, flesh-colored papier-mâché falling away to reveal rigging, harnessed balloon craft, and people moving on these bridges, crossing from Matsya to the Jagannath.

I worked fast to sever them, but wherever a bridge remained intact, soldiers kept streaming aboard. Finally, Matsya was made armless, its head smiling atop a rope tether and badly damaged torso. Parts of arms floated in the air, and the four hands, broken off, remained affixed to the Jagannath.

Below, new murmurs. Sounds I hadn't previously heard in the Jagannath. Shouts of protest, hurried foot-steps, a howl of pain. More knocking noises. Here in the head, the laborers who'd served as my barricade twitched and shuddered.

With one arm of the Jagannath I grabbed Matsya by a rent in its chest, then bent the torso sideways until I could see the bulk of its tail and the platform fashioned above. A pavilion, archways, ephemeral buildings. Streamers and petals. A flower-covered canopy. My heart sank.

It was a wedding.

That was how the Baboon Warrior was establishing himself in Delhi. By a marriage to royalty.

'Rakesh!'

'I said nobody was to come into the head.'

'But I have an important message.'

The voice was familiar: Firdaus. I couldn't see him because of the barricade of laborers.

'He is allowed,' I said.

They didn't seem to hear, but a moment later, they squatted. The old man was sopping, his robe plastered to his body.

'Why are you so wet?'

'Why do you think?'

'Ah.'

'Rakesh, the Jagannath has been boarded. Goondas.'

'The god will subdue them.'

Firdaus shook his head.

'Why not?'

'Come see.'

I looked again out the eyes of the god, staring down at the setting for the ceremony. I wanted to stay linked to the controls, to pull apart Matsya, to tear away the canopy and throttle the Baboon.

'The Jagannath will be stopped,' said Firdaus, 'if the goondas get their way.'

'You're trying to distract me from my goal.'

'No. The opposite.'

'Why would you do anything else?'

'Because, unlike Pala, I want you to succeed.'

'You do?'

He seemed to weigh further words but then shook

his head. 'No time for talk. Rakesh, you must come now.'

I took one more look at the collision of the two colossi and the pavilion beyond. Reluctantly, I disengaged. The laborers replaced me at the controls. They separated where they were squatting and re-formed at the helm. The Jagannath continued to function with their input, but with different character. Instead of trying to break apart the false Matsya, the Jagannath leaned against it, torso to torso, bending it backward. But Firdaus was pulling me along. 'Come!'

We descended through chambers of the god, shouts of surprise and fury resounding around us and pierced by the whine of Pragmatic arrows. Firdaus hung back as I moved into Interior Space Number 22. Light fell through a corridor, illuminating a melee. Three palace goondas had got in here. Two were occupied by laborers who had run into the flurry of long wooden arms. The laborers made mediocre fighters but, as we'd seen, were tenacious and indifferent to pain. They piled around the goondas, accepting blows of carved hands.

But how could the goondas function? Why didn't the Jagannath overwhelm them mentally? When I looked more closely, through the storm of limbs and up the impossibly slender torsos, I saw that their heads were protected.

Helmets of copper. The implications held me.

'Rakesh!'

I ducked in time for a Pragmatic to loose an arrow. The goonda rushing me caught it in a flash. I turned with six arms operating. The goonda lunged on a calculation of steps, but I was not afraid, not even as we met in a great percussion of wood, our false limbs hitting with staccato fury. I forced myself to stay calm in this duel; I waited for an avenue to what remained human. When his throat became available, I struck hard, so hard that he staggered and fell back against the wall. A monk sent arrows into his chest, but I called off this attack and leaped on the figure, yanked off his copper helmet.

Within moments his face slackened. He dragged himself away on his collection of limbs, and I stepped off. Obedient to the god, he pulled himself into a ventilation shaft.

'Are they all wearing helmets?'

'Every one I've seen,' said the monk.

'There are more?'

'We tried to hold them off, but they were too many.'

I looked around space 22. 'Where's Pala?' I asked.

But he took up his bow against another goonda. I asked Firdaus the same question.

'He left earlier. A group went.'

'Where did they go?'

'Where else?'

Of course. Where else.

'The goondas are wearing copper helmets,' I said. 'Vasant must have helped prepare this defense. Which means they probably know the layout of the Jagannath.'

'It's worse than that. When they boarded, some were carrying devices.'

'Bombs?'

'He knew the inner workings better than anyone. The overall structure.'

'So what do we do?'

'You've known what you must do for some time.'

I stared at him.

'There is no time to explain myself,' Firdaus went on quickly, waving off my curiosity. 'You must do your duty.'

'How do I get to him?'

'This way.'

We descended farther. The invasion made strange dynamics. Laborers rushed past us along catwalks. They broke from tasks to join others running toward a goonda wreaking havoc, but thrown off from one of these invaders, they immediately returned to some mundane chore. When another skirmish blocked our progress, I intervened, pulling off the helmet of the goonda and so making him vulnerable to the god's directives. He turned from me and raised multiple limbs against a fellow thug. We skirted around this rapping of wooden blows. Other goondas moved surreptitiously, scurrying through passages, suspicious objects cradled in their arms. There were too many of them, too many things happening at once, and Firdaus kept pulling me along.

We got down to Interior Space Number 38. Water covered the floor. Firdaus stuck his hand into the water, opening a hatch.

'You can swim down to 43 and leave by the chariot gate.'

'You're not coming?'

'Look at me. I'm old. But I'll try to –'

An explosion interrupted.

'A bomb,' he said when the shuddering ceased, and he looked up at the ceiling. 'Only the first, I'm sure. Go. You must be quick, or Pala and the others will beat you to the Baboon.'

'Firdaus.'

'What?'

'Why are you doing this? Pragmatics work together. Why are you helping me?'

He shook his head. 'There's no time,' he said. 'Let us just say that some things run deeper than Pragmatism.' He clapped my shoulder. 'Go.'

I knelt in the water, felt for the portal.

'Take a deep breath,' he said. 'It will be a long swim.'

I inhaled deeply, feeling my ribs against the goonda vest. Then I plunged down into the sloped corridor I'd walked many times to enter or exit Interior Space Number 43. Swimming was different. The weight of my goonda limbs surprised me underwater, and it was difficult to concert their action so each provided a meaningful stroke. I could no longer see, since the globes were extinguished, and I bumped against the ceiling several times. How would I find my way out of space 43? It was a long chamber, I would be starved for oxygen by the time I reached the end and fumbled for the gate.

But there was light after all. A quirky glow coming from the hearth. Behind glass, fire continued to burn, somehow sheltered from the deluge, and its flickering provided an otherworldly view of what I had accomplished. Horses floated. I swam around one still tethered by its harness like some grotesque balloon. Other bodies floated: laborers, mostly, but a few wearing saffron, suspended around the low structure they'd built. I recognized the monk who had spoken against Shiva; with the stone snake weighing down his legs, he seemed to stand on the floor, his face desperate. Space 43 must have flooded quickly . . .

And Yamuna, where was she?

But there was no time to wonder; she could protect herself. I swam past other swimmers, laborers working underwater, taking turns to swim away to some air supply.

My lungs burned as I opened the gate and swam up. Gasping for air, I surfaced near the collision of the Jagannath and Matsya.

Fragments of papier-mâché and wood bobbed on the surface. I heard another explosion, and looked up to see smoke issuing from the Jagannath, from its elbow. Before the smoke cleared, laborers appeared in the rupture with wooden slats and tools.

I swam to the tail of Matsya and climbed a sheet of painted scales. The flotilla was a long oval of closely gathered ships, the biggest vessels in the outermost ring. I stood at the edge, looking into the platform. Central was the wedding pavilion, although other structures were clustered nearby. Moving across the shifting segments of floor were royal guests, who looked nervous and upset as they circulated among elephants in ceremonial robes and goondas painted gold for the occasion. There was fear, the longing to escape, because the Jagannath continued to press down on the torso of Matsya, and an effort was under way to evacuate members of royalty in ships cut loose from the flotilla.

Other guests appeared too drunk or too happy to worry about the smashed-together colossi hanging over them, even when another explosion sent smoking planks tripping through the sky and dropping into the river with a sizzle. Soldiers struggled to keep the torso of Matsya upright as it groaned and buckled and let loose beams under the Jagannath's increasing pressure.

I walked through decorations. More flower petals,

more streamers, more pastel paper creations. I crossed from one ship to the next, until I could see into the pavilion.

The Baboon Warrior stood beside the First Widow. Royal family members and crones huddled around them, and a Brahmin priest, who glanced up nervously at the Jagannath and hurried through wedding verses. The First Widow held an offering for the sacred fire. I crouched and let my gaze fall on the Baboon.

He was built differently from what I expected. His body, although human, had simian proportions: short legs, long arms. I had imagined him as he was usually depicted, with a heroic body of obvious and classical strength, topped by a fierce animal head. Instead he was short, with awkward posture. There were marks on his chest I decided must be scars. He stooped so far forward, I thought that any moment he would rest on his knuckles, and I remembered Firdaus's telling me how stories changed with their passage from speaker to speaker. The Baboon Warrior – a flawed creature – watched the proceedings with eyes that showed neither satisfaction nor concern.

'Get up,' someone said behind me.

I turned.

Another baboon.

But I knew it for a costume. She stood several feet away and aimed at me a bow so big, it had been mounted to a cart, winches drawing the string.

I rose. 'What will happen to his concubines?' I asked.

'What?'

'After he's married, he can have no concubines. The First Widow would never allow it.'

Shanti pulled off her mask.

'Strange,' I said, 'that we should find ourselves at a wedding.'

'You shouldn't have come here, Rakesh.'

'Will concubines like you be disposed of, I wonder?'

'That's not for me to decide.'

'You don't care?'

'I've never had much say.'

'You mean in your caste? In your life? What?'

'All of it.'

'I've come to wonder,' I said, 'about outside forces and how much they dictate our lives.' I tried to smile, but it came out wrong on my face, and she returned a strange look.

She indicated her large weapon. 'Don't make me do this,' she said. 'Turn around, drop back into the river.'

'You can't hurt me.'

'Of course I can!'

'Try.'

'Rakesh!'

'It might be a blessing.'

She hit the trigger, and my arms reacted. They came around and grabbed the oversized shaft, taking hold in several places, arresting its motion so the tip was stopped inches from my chest. I looked at Shanti and made another attempt at a smile before I snapped the big arrow over my knee and tossed the pieces at her. As I turned and walked away, I wondered if she'd be foolish enough to jump me from behind. But she did worse.

'He's here!' she shouted. 'He's here!'

The ceremony below stopped; heads turned, faces looked at me. I walked toward the crowd. They'd known I was coming. They'd been expecting me, hoping to ward me off. I raised a finger to point at the Baboon Warrior as I crossed the next ship in the flotilla. He stepped in front of his bride.

Behind me, another explosion. I glanced back, and the Jagannath's forearm became separated at the elbow, falling, landing hard on the platform, where it continued to function, connected by long lines of cable. There was ruin in the tower of Matsya, too: it pitched under the Jagannath's weight, soldiers falling from every spire and platform. Beams split, a few key levels collapsed in the middle, and I heard crowds gasp as the big torso toppled, the Jagannath coming down on top of it, slowly. In the shadow thrown across the ceremony, there was a scramble. I lost sight of the pavilion when the two figures landed, and I swayed with the impact. Waves splashed high, and the whole flotilla rocked with the enormous collapse.

When the motion subsided, goondas rose from their poses, painted bodies gleaming as they lifted sets of arms, six, ten, thirty: forests of limbs. They rose like mechanical flowers blossoming, their advances beautiful and disturbing. Ever loyal to royalty, they stepped toward me. Around the fallen hulks of the Jagannath and Matsya I could see Royals hurrying, withdrawing under the protection of guards, but the collapse had ruptured the flotilla and made dangerous gaps. Goondas walked through the aftermath with stylized steps, coming at me in diagonals, moving their arms in related sequences.

'You shouldn't have come here,' I heard Shanti say.

Goondas swarmed. They seemed to emerge from everywhere, as if they had been hiding beneath the platform, like cargo. They pulled themselves up, or rose without using the great number of arms available to them.

I ran into their crowd.

I fought them as they fought me, our wooden limbs meeting in syncopated flurries, and while I parried their blows, I waited for weaknesses, for what was human in them to show. But they were so many – all I could see were goondas, more goondas, their saturnine faces, their arms raised, jostling for position, waiting for a turn to strike me, batting one another in their eagerness.

How long could I keep this up? They could delay me forever, and eventually my arms would surrender to their persistence.

But then, a change.

The goondas became distracted. The pressure against me relaxed somewhat, and their effort split down the middle; I was receiving help. I could hear a repeated smashing and a clatter I realized was the sound of artificial limbs hitting the floor. When I fought some space for myself, I saw that Shiva had arrived.

Shiva, swinging Khatwanga.

He had come to my assistance. Dancing, and his dance anticipated these soldiers as they started to break away and flee. He brought Khatwanga down on one and struck another in the backswing. It must have occurred to the goondas that they were acting against the will of Shiva: I felt their willpower dissolving. I pushed one aside as Shiva stepped backward, his head turning a full 180 degrees to show me his delirious face. Khatwanga was still sucking blood from one victim's wound as Shiva peeled it away to smash another, so hard that boards broke under the goonda's feet. Shiva circled me, pulling back his club. He looked tempted to incorporate me into his dance. Instead he said one word:

Go.

I went.

Everything around me seemed to be arms. Broken limbs on the floor; goondas running from Shiva, their arms dangling; overhead, part of Matsya's arm floating; and ahead lay an arm of the Jagannath.

Sabotage had blown it off at the shoulder. It lay across the platform, enormous, fingers turned up. I moved around its disconnected end, walked along the fallen torso. The neck of the god, too, ended in a ragged fringe, through which I could see inside to familiar passageways, a smoky space. The head of the god had landed nearby, inverted, eyes closed.

I kept walking. The last guests milled in panic yet knew enough to give me berth. If anyone got too close, I pushed him aside. Most knew better.

The left arm of the Jagannath was also broken. But in the breaches stood laborers, holding hands, linking arms, filling the gaps where cables had snapped. Some tugged at cables. With this assistance, the arm continued to function. It shifted against the platform, over the pavilion. At the far end, it lifted a hand. Fingers curled tight.

Holding one figure.

The Baboon.

He struggled. His thrashing was enough to rock the giant arm, but he could not break free of its black wooden fingers. I remembered what Shiva had said. No god could harm the Baboon Warrior. But it could hold him still. It could hold him for me.

A crowd had gathered around.

The First Widow of India tugged unceremoniously at the Jagannath's arm. A few other Royals and what I took to be advisers stood about, some weeping, some praying, some turning to me. The saffron robes of Pragmatics were splashed throughout, the monks damp from their swim here.

Again I raised one of my hands to point at the Baboon.

Pala wove through the crowd. 'Rakesh!'

'I recommend that you stay back.'

He did not. 'Rakesh, just listen to me – '

I pushed the monk aside.

The Baboon stopped thrashing.

'Rakesh Tiwari.'

Strange to hear him speak, and say my name. I stopped where he could see me.

'They convinced you to kill me,' he said, forcing his animal lips to form the words. His face twitched with the effort. 'They told you it was your holy duty.'

He looked small in the hand of the Jagannath. Puny.

'Leave him!' the First Widow cried. 'Who do you think you are?! I can have you executed!' She came at me slapping; I pushed her away.

I climbed the Jagannath's forearm and could see more Pragmatics on the other side. Yamuna stood among them, staring up at me like everyone else. Their eyes followed me as I walked along the forearm and over the wrist. Pala moved, keeping pace with me on the opposite side. 'Just listen to what he says, Rakesh – just hear him out!'

The Baboon Warrior craned his neck to watch me come.

I stepped along the hand until I was close, and knelt.
He looked up at me.

'Talk,' I said.

'What do you want to know?'

'Who are you?'

'Nobody.'

'That tells me little.'

'I am a tool.'

'A machine?'

'Not as you would understand. I was built into the
baboon species. Programmed into it. The species produces me, when necessary.'

'Necessary?'

'When humans no longer comprehend their
machines.'

'I don't understand.'

'These things that influence India, your life, your
culture: what you call gods. They were built long ago
to improve your lives, in harmony with your faith.
They evolved. Over time, the thought of them as
machines eroded – along with the knowledge to build,
maintain, decommission them. They became integral,
accepted. Because they are self-maintaining, an
increasing human ignorance posed no difficulty; in fact,
it guided the roles they developed for themselves. They
allowed Indians to forget that Indians had built them.'

'I asked who *you* are.'

'I was built into the baboon species to check the
machines of Hinduism once every hundred years. They
are unable to harm me; this is programmed into them,
at their core. Ancient engineers saw the possibility of
the god simulations becoming too influential, and so
introduced a new monkey breed that contained me. A

safeguard. I would arise periodically, even if all other knowledge deteriorated. Even if the people of India no longer realized they were surrounded by machines. And if in my evaluation the god simulations had become too dominant, my task would be to decommission them.'

He stared at me.

'Our present situation,' he continued, 'should suggest their reaction.'

My head was spinning. I wasn't sure how much I understood of what he said. I asked: 'Why didn't you reveal yourself from the beginning? If this is true, why didn't you announce your purpose all those years ago in Mangalore?'

'Previous manifestations of the Baboon Safeguard failed,' he said. 'They were destroyed by righteous Hindus like yourself, whom the simulations convinced I was a menace. Or by persons whose faith could not allow such a message. Your culture has been modified to support the existence of these things that present themselves as gods. I evaluated this situation in a new way; my best chance of success was to work within the established culture: to become mythic. Only a mythic figure could succeed in doing what I must do.'

'Killing the gods.'

'Decommissioning. Yes.'

I looked back and saw Shiva sitting atop goondas. Those who had not fallen in gestures of humility lay stacked beneath him. He sat, watching us. On the ghats, another god. Judging by his stature and blue radiance, it was Vishnu who had appeared on the steps, and loving worshipers surrounded him with praise and prostration. On the opposite shore, Brahma. Swaths of color representing thousands of Hindus positioned to be near him, to touch him, their song rising to his four faces. I could not say that I comprehended what the Baboon told me. But I knew that if he was allowed to succeed — whether or not his claims were true — it would make a terrible rent in the fabric of India.

My chakras pulsed.

Being so close had reawakened them. I wanted to accomplish my duty. I ached to do it. If I didn't kill him now, I would never kill him, I would never get him out of my life. This wouldn't stop: I would remain forever obsessed.

And if I didn't kill him, there was something else I would forfeit.

Looking to my left, I saw her. Like all the other Pragmatics, like the Royals and the First Widow, like Shiva, Brahma, and Vishnu, she was watching to see what I would do.

Yamuna.

I squatted.

With all six arms I grabbed the top finger of the Jagannath, which was pressed so firmly against the Baboon Warrior that his breaths whistled. I grabbed the phalange, and with the energy surging through me pried it backward, splintering, cracking, the god's digit snapping. It took great effort.

The Baboon's upper body was free. His arms were free. Yet he didn't lash out at me, didn't even move.

I grabbed his upper body and pulled him out, lifting him from the god's grasp.

I could feel the energy coursing through my body; it would be so easy to let it flow through my goonda limbs and crush his chest, throttle him, push my thumbs into his eyes.

I set him on his feet.

'I don't know what you mean for India,' I said. 'But I must let India make its own decisions.'

The Baboon Warrior looked at me with strange eyes. He put a hand on my shoulder.

The crowd murmured. I heard Pala exhale with relief.

Expression changed on the Baboon's face. His lips pulled back, making an imperfect, animal smile.

'You made the right – '

Cut off by a truncated whine, a *thwap*. He jerked in my arms, his eyes widened, and his hand clutched me too tight.

FLIGHT

THE FIRST WIDOW shrilled. Crones and Royals shouted in horror as the Baboon Warrior – the Safeguard, as he called himself – leaned away from me, his fingers no longer clutching me as he slowly pitched backward, fell. He landed near Pala, who stood frozen with shock. A flurry of activity ensued, people converging to the place where the hero lay fallen.

His face stared up at me. Looking surprised.

I had imagined his death so many times. Never like this.

The crowd struggled to touch him. Purplish blood spread into his mane. I surveyed the faces, so many faces.

Who had done it?

I was stunned, perplexed, and – something else.

It was gone.

The tincture had anesthetized me to my dharma before, but now, only now, the pressure dissipated completely. There was nothing left of it. My nerves, my soul – all was lightened, expelled of compulsion, liberated.

That was how I knew the Baboon was dead.

I jumped down, landing in the crush of people

trying to get close to him, to touch him. Monks, Royals, others, they all wanted to hold him, prop his head, lift his body, stand him on his feet. For many reasons, they wanted the truth to be something other than the arrow jutting from his ear, something other than the dark blood running from deep within.

He was dead. Slain.

And people now began to look around the platform, at one another. I could hear their frantic voices. Who had done this? Who? The first theories and rumors. I shoved my way through. It was difficult to get past the harried guests and monks politely, so I pushed. I parted and pried. They continued swarming.

Who did this to him? Who did this?

Heads turned from the arm of the Jagannath to the shaft buried in the Baboon's head, as people tried to guess the trajectory of the missile and where it would lead back. They narrowed their eyes at me, despite what logic must have told them. I was the only one who *couldn't* have shot the arrow. But I wouldn't pause for accusatory stares or dumb suspicion. Nothing could stop me.

She stood near the back of the crowd, but I didn't dare say her name aloud. Mine was also withheld, unspoken but flashing in her eyes, and we both worked our way out of the knot of people, stepping well clear of their speculation before we came together. She touched my cheek. Beautiful Yamuna.

Her face changed to worry.

We had been noticed. Someone stepped up behind me and said, 'You come with me.'

Vasant looked so prim in his new suit, I almost didn't recognize him. His face was firm with authority, the self-assurance of a man at last returned to his source of power. Delhi was his city. And it appeared to have welcomed him back.

'Come,' he repeated, 'or there will be trouble.'

'What do you want with us?'

'This way,' he insisted.

I didn't want to draw more attention. He led us through the throng, one hand on Yamuna's arm, steering us to a vessel tied to the outermost ring of the flotilla. It sat low in the water, and after brief hesitation we climbed down a rope ladder, to below the deck. Someone stood at the wheel, waiting, and the engine had already been fired by another man wearing the garb of a palace menial. Vasant barked for the hatch to be shut and for the pilot to take us downriver. As the boat pulled away, he looked out a window, watching the platform recede. Yamuna and I stood in the middle of the room, unsure what to do.

'Did they compensate you well?' I asked.

'Excuse me?'

'The goondas wore copper helmets when they raided the Jagannath. How much did the Royals pay for your assistance?'

'No payment was involved.'

'I don't believe you.'

'Don't take that tone with me, Rakesh. You're speaking to a palace official.'

'Ah,' I said. 'The return of your position was your compensation.'

He frowned. 'I was introduced to the Baboon Warrior shortly after returning to Delhi. I heard him explain himself, as you have now heard. I was convinced, yes, that you shouldn't be allowed to succeed in your goal. For what little good my assistance did him.'

'Where are you taking us?' Yamuna demanded. 'We've done nothing wrong.'

'Nothing wrong, hm?' Vasant looked at her. 'And you think you're my prisoners?'

'What else?'

'I'm helping you escape from Shiva.'

'But Shiva,' I said, 'got what he wanted . . .'

'Yes. But if the Baboon's story is true, Shiva can't allow those who heard it to live.'

'So you are . . . rescuing us?'

Vasant exhaled and put his hands on his hips. 'How many times do I need to say so?'

I felt myself smiling. 'Excuse us,' I said. 'We're not so quick.'

'If Shiva poses no threat, the crowd soon would have. It was only a few pitchforks short of a mob. Someone will determine who shot that arrow. And it will be evident that the aim required was more than an ordinary Hindu could have managed.'

He eyed Yamuna significantly.

Yes. Formidable accuracy. Delivered with the characteristic whine of a Pragmatic arrow. Did Yamuna even know? I wondered. Nothing in her face suggested she did.

'Vasant, help me with this,' I said.

With some fiddling he and I managed to unclasp the vest of the goonda and shuck off the prosthesis. The Engineer dragged it away, taking it to some rear compartment for storage. And with my own two arms I took Yamuna's shoulders.

'What is it?' she said.

I let her fill my senses. The Baboon was dead. I wasn't sure what his murder meant for India, but it made everything possible for her and me. As I studied her eyes, green as hills of tea, I decided she didn't know who shot the arrow.

She couldn't know.

Because if she knew *who*, she would have had to ask herself *why*?

I hadn't been sure myself who did it, not when I stood on the Jagannath's arm watching the Baboon fall away from me. He was gone before I understood what happened. Who wanted him dead other than me and the gods? It didn't occur to me until Vasant led us away and I saw the killer follow us. We climbed down the ladder into the awaiting boat, and there, watching us go, stood Firdaus.

Old Firdaus. Watching Yamuna go.

In his face I saw the answer.

She had forgotten her father. I had assumed the same held true in the opposite direction: that, in order to be a complete Pragmatic, the father had forgotten his daughter. But maybe he didn't have enough mental discipline, or maybe he had changed his mind. As he told me inside the Jagannath, some things ran deeper than Pragmatism. For Firdaus, having a daughter was such a thing. He watched as Yamuna left the flotilla, and it seemed, before she climbed down into the boat, he had almost called to her.

He regretted, I suppose, the life he'd made for her. Yanked from her family. Pregnant without sex, without a partner. Her father nearby but forever absent. Now, an old man, he wanted to give her the one thing he could – me – and the only way to do so was by ensuring the death of the Baboon Warrior.

He almost called to Yamuna as we left.

But what could he say?

No time to explain his identity, or his reasons. Even if he'd shouted, *I am your father*, she was bound to forget.

So in silence he watched us go.

I would tell Yamuna the things he meant to say. Tonight, I'd tell her.

She would forget, and I'd tell her again tomorrow, and the day after, and the day after, however long it took, when words had to substitute for memories.